"This engrossing debut . . . evokes memorable protagonists, vivid landscapes, and high suspense, not only in the gut-wrenching action but also in the relationships between her characters." —*Publishers Weekly*

"An impeccably researched novel with a sure feel for the arid landscapes of New Mexico." —*Kirkus Reviews*

"I thought I was pretty well informed about the Civil War. But *Glorieta Pass* is a surprise from beginning to end. Not only is the history startling, the story is told by some of the most engaging characters I've encountered in a long time. I especially liked O'Brien—but I found the women equally interesting." —Thomas Fleming, author of *The Wages of Fame*

"A well-done, very readable historical novel." —*Booklist*

"Nagle develops each character with sympathy tempered by a sharp eye for human foibles. Indeed, these are real people with familiar moral quandaries. Nagle endows them with emotional complexity and unpredictability. Studiously authentic . . . Nagle succeeds . . . in emotional resonance and truly magnetic storytelling." —*Albuquerque Journal*

"Nagle tells a profoundly affecting tale. *Glorieta Pass* reflects the thorough research of the author including the use of actual diaries and other historical documents to bring authenticity as well as excitement to this excellent military novel." —*Abilene Reporter-News*

By P. G. Nagle

Glorieta Pass

The Guns of Valverde

Available from Forge Books

GLORIETA
PASS

P. G. Nagle

A TOM DOHERTY ASSOCIATES BOOK
NEW YORK

This is a work of fiction. All the characters and events portrayed in this book are either products of the author's imagination or are used fictitiously.

GLORIETA PASS

Copyright © 1999 by P. G. Nagle

Map by Chris Krohn
Edited by James Frenkel

A Forge Book
Published by Tom Doherty Associates, LLC
175 Fifth Avenue
New York, NY 10010

www.tor.com

Forge® is a registered trademark of Tom Doherty Associates, LLC.

ISBN: 0-812-54049-2
Library of Congress Catalog Card Number: 98-23447

First edition: May 1999
First mass market edition: May 2000

Printed in the United States of America

0 9 8 7 6 5 4 3 2 1

For my father,
who believed in me

By geographical position, by similarity of institutions, by commercial interests, and by future destinies New Mexico pertains to the Confederacy.

—Henry Hopkins Sibley, 1861

Acknowledgments

A great many people lent their advice, support and expertise to the creation of this book. Among them are Wm. Charles Bennet, Jr., Gene Bostwick, Pat McCraw Brown, Ken and Marilyn Dusenberry, Robin Fetters, Sally Gwylan, Steven J. Jennings, Bruce and Marsha Krohn, Chris Krohn, Joe and Nancy Leeming, Robert B. McCoy, Maria del Carmen L. Martin, James L. Moore, Jim Ed Morgans, Avery Nagle, Mary Rosenblum, Melinda Snodgrass, Chuck Swanberg, Beau Tappan, Sage Walker, Vic Watson, Cory Weintraub, Walter Jon Williams, Natasha Williamson, and Ward Yarbrough. Thanks also to the Museum of New Mexico, the Palace of the Governors, the New Mexico State Archives, the University of New Mexico Library Center for Southwest Research, the Colorado Historical Society, Fort Bliss Historical Museum, Fort Union National Monument, Pecos National Monument, the Bureau of Land Management (Fort Craig), The Rio Grande Press, and many others, especially the editors and authors of works covering the New Mexico Campaign, whose interest has kept alive the details of this eventful episode in New Mexico's history.

UTAH TERRITORY

Colorado River

NEW MEXICO
TERRITORY

*and the Santa Fé Trail,
1861 - 1862.*

0   50   100   150
SCALE IN MILES.

CALIFORNIA

MÉXICO

⌘ Fort Yuma

⌘ Fort Breckinridge

• Tucson

⌘ Fort Buchanan

Golfo de
California

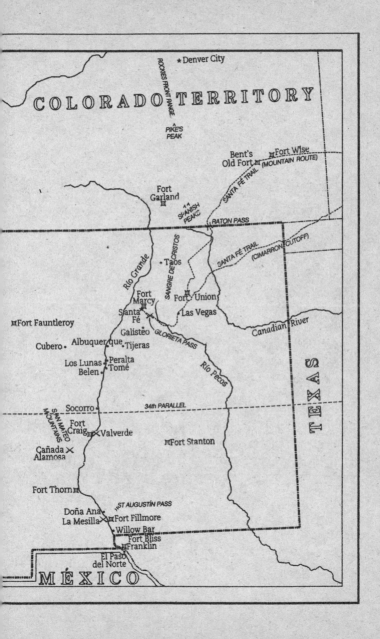

1

---◆-◆-◆---

*There seems to be no reason to apprehend any immediate
disorder in this Territory.*

—W. W. Loring, Brevet Colonel, U.S. Army,
Commanding Department of New Mexico

Silence fell in the rickety shanty of Dooney's tavern as
O'Brien prepared for the duel. He himself saw no point in
such drama—if you didn't agree with a fellow, best to settle it quick with your fists—but at the grand age of twenty-
nine he was older than most of the lads, and they'd turned
to him as referee. He ought to be flattered, he guessed. All
the miners in Avery had crowded the tavern to watch.
O'Brien ignored them, spoke quietly with the seconds to
be sure they had done as he'd told them, and kept an eye on
the nervous principals.

They were miners, too: Denning, a Georgian, and Peters
from New Jersey. Best of friends, they had been, until news
of the great conflict to the east had at last found its way
into Colorado. "Hurrah for the North" and "Hurrah for the
South" had been the first volleys. Others had joined the
dispute, till the clear mountain air rang with bullets and
violent words. Now these two fine young lads, grave determination in their eyes, faced each other across a rough
table to settle on behalf of the infant town of Avery the
question of Who Was Right.

The other tables, all three, were pushed back to the
walls, with the crates and the stumps that were seats. Men
stood atop them the better to see, blocking the light of the
greasy candles set where the wallboards met at odd angles
and adding their looming shadows to the already ghoulish

atmosphere. The doctor—an infamous grumbler—arrived at long last. O'Brien greeted him with a nod and stepped forward.

"Shaunessy, Morris," he said, summoning two men with heavy six-shooters to stand by the table, "if either man fires before I count three, you're to shoot him down." He took out a handkerchief—provided by Mr. Dooney himself—and gave a corner of it to each combatant to hold in his left hand. In the right each held a Colt navy pistol carefully prepared by the seconds. The distance between the men, marked by table and handkerchief, was no more than four feet. It seemed a short distance indeed, but O'Brien had gotten the seconds to agree to it.

"Make ready," he said, and the men brought up their pistols, leveling them nearly breast to breast. O'Brien felt an odd pride in them as their eyes met and held, for each must have sensed his own death in the cold tunnel aimed at his heart.

"One," O'Brien said, as every man in the room held his breath. "Two. Three."

The guns roared together, a great flash, and the duelists fell shrouded in smoke. The tavern exploded with noise. Men jumped down from their perches, whooping and cursing. O'Brien pulled the table aside while the doctor on his knees sought the pulse of the victims.

"He's alive," the doctor cried, his hand on Peters's wrist. He moved to Denning. "They're both alive!"

The miners exclaimed at the miracle. O'Brien, leaning against the table, smiled as the doctor tore open the Georgian's shirt to search for his wound. He found none, no mark on either man save for a red spot on his chest. The duelists got to their feet, looked at each other in wonder, then turned their eyes to O'Brien.

"There, now," he said, folding his long arms. "It's settled the way it began, with nothing but a lot of hot air."

The spectators burst into laughter, and the faces of the late contenders dawned with the understanding that they'd been betrayed. The New Jerseyan grabbed his second by the collar. "P-powder," he said between gasps of laughter. "Red said t'use powder only!"

"Ah, leave him alone, Peters," O'Brien said. "Didn't you agree to fight by my rules?"

"O'Brien, you bastard," Denning said, but a grin of relief broke across his face.

"I'd be a bastard indeed if I let you make Mary a widow over such nonsense," O'Brien said.

Denning laughed, blushing, and shook hands with Peters. Both men claimed they'd been knocked down by the force of the powder rather than by fear. The company, having had their fill of conflict for the moment, heartily agreed and as one turned to Dooney demanding liquor.

O'Brien helped the mortified doctor to his feet, saying, "Don't be embarrassed. You'll still have your fee."

The doctor glowered as he picked up his coat and bag. "My gun has bullets in it," he said, heading for the door.

O'Brien dismissed him with a shrug and made his way up to the wooden plank where the taverner served the drinks. Behind it, hidden by a curtain made of flour sacks, was the hole—someone's old false start of a mine—where Dooney concocted his liquors.

"Clever work, Red," Dooney said, pouring homemade whiskey into a glass. "This one's on me."

"Sweet Jesus bless you, Dooney," said O'Brien. He picked up the glass and, accepting congratulations and back-slappings, retired to a stump in a corner of the tavern.

He was tired. The duel had been only a moment's escape from the hard truths of life. He sat with his back to the wall and nursed his liquor with the careful avarice of one trapped in toil and poverty. Another long day in the mine had brought nothing; the vein that had promised an end to his struggles had faded like a will-o'-the-wisp of a summer's dawn. It was almost as hopeless as Ireland.

New York had been better. There'd been money enough for his efforts, though the work had been low. But a dock-hand, bricklayer, teamster, or carrier—none of them could hope to rise in the world as he wished to do. New York thought the Irish scarcely better than Negroes. The way O'Brien saw it, if he must work like a slave it might as well be all for his own benefit, so when the siren call of gold had reached the city from Colorado, he had answered. Gold had promised an end forever to poverty. Gold had charmed him to come west and sink all he had into a claim in the high, blue-white mountains.

And now here he was, starving at the feet of those beautiful mountains. Gold he had found, but in dribs and drabs rather than floods, and what he had mined the first summer had been drained away by a long, harsh winter. Now, in May, snow still lay on the ground in dirty heaps and the air in his mine was bitter cold. With the last of his savings spent on candles and shot, a shadow of despair had begun to creep over him.

"Evening, Red. That was a mighty fine trick."

O'Brien looked up at a fur-trimmed buckskin coat and the grinning, tanned face above it. "Joseph Hall, if it isn't the Devil," he said. "And here I was thinking you'd gone back to Mobile."

"Not a step past St. Louis," Hall replied. "Buy you a drink?"

"Now I'm sure you're not the Devil," O'Brien answered, matching his grin. "You're a bloody saint, that's what you are."

Hall laughed, upended a crate for a table, and tossed down his saddlebag on it. "Stay there, I've got something to show you."

O'Brien watched him saunter through the crowd to the bar. On a fine day the previous summer he had nearly shot Hall in the woods, mistaking him for a deer. The command of foul language Hall had shown on that occasion was enough to earn even the roughest Irishman's respect, and thereafter they'd killed many a buck and not a few bottles of whiskey together. Then in autumn Hall had decided to become a trade merchant, and disappeared eastward with a crew of ruffians and a wagon train loaded with buffalo hides. O'Brien had not thought he'd see him again.

Returning from the bar with two glasses, Hall handed one to O'Brien and pulled a stump up to the table. He set down his own glass, pulled a newspaper from his coat, and spread it out on the crate. O'Brien ignored it, his attention reserved for the whiskey, which by its golden color was the genuine spirit, not the drug-based concoction the taverner usually served. Hall must have fetched it back from Missouri for Dooney. O'Brien sipped, and savored the mellow fire on his tongue.

"Have a look at this," Hall said, pointing to the newspaper. O'Brien glanced at the meaningless print, anger flaring, and raised flat eyes to stare at Hall.

"Oh," Hall said. "Sorry, I forgot."

O'Brien filled his mouth with whiskey and let it burn all down his throat. Easy for Hall to forget what he'd taken for granted all his life. Never mind, never mind.

"It's about President Lincoln," said Hall. "He's called for seventy-five thousand volunteers. I think we ought to sign up."

"Soldiering's worse than mining," O'Brien said.

"Three squares a day and a new Enfield rifle?"

"It's no better than slavery."

"Well, you're wrong there," Hall replied, "but I'll make allowances for your lack of firsthand knowledge. What matters, Red me lad, is that a soldier can rise from the ranks."

"In a blue moon," O'Brien said. "My father was a soldier, and he died a private after twenty years."

Hall sat back and gazed at him. O'Brien ignored him and took another slow, savoring sip of whiskey.

"I am disappointed in you, Red," Hall said. "I thought you had a sense of adventure."

"Adventure, is it?" O'Brien set his glass on the table and held it to the uneven surface with one hand. "Am I to leave my mine for the first bloody claim jumper who wants it? Am I to walk five hundred miles to Leavenworth, with Indians trying to shoot me and scalp me, and all for the honor of being killed in somebody else's argument?"

"It's not just somebody's argument, it's a rebellion!" Hall said. "Red, this country's going to war, do you know what that means?"

"Means a lot of poor beggars'll get poorer."

"It means some men are bound for glory! Men who can lead others, who can run a good fight and win it, they'll rise like the blazing sun. Doesn't matter where they started, do you see?"

O'Brien looked hard at him, trying to decide if he mocked. Hall liked his jokes, and he knew of O'Brien's dreams.

"You could be one of them, Red," Hall said. "You could be a colonel, a general even. Then all those fine gentlemen would be bowing to you."

"Generals don't rise from the ranks," O'Brien said, "and how am I fit to become one? I don't know about armies, or tactics—"

"You can learn those things." Hall's eyes were aglow. "And they're not as important as courage. That's what counts in a war, and you've got it, my boy!"

O'Brien heard the echo of a siren's call. He wanted to believe Hall, believe he could rise in this way, above the past, above the contempt of his betters, far above ever having to grub in the dirt for a living. He saw a ghost of himself, mounted on a mighty war-horse, metal glinting on his shoulders and in his hand, the roar of the battle in his ears.

"'Tis a pretty dream," O'Brien said slowly, "but that's all it is. I'm not throwing away what I have to go chase it."

Hall was silent, staring at O'Brien with eyes gone cold all of a sudden. Then he reached for his whiskey and downed it in one pull.

"Suit yourself," he said, setting down the glass with a graceful flick of his wrist. O'Brien could almost see the lace cuff, the cavalier's sword, the plumed hat that would so suit Hall's brow. It was at such moments that he felt the great difference between them. Hall was a gentleman by virtue of lifelong training, and O'Brien admired and envied him for it.

Hall got up, took his saddlebag, and walked away without another word. It was like him, the sudden withdrawal. He'd be back, perhaps, cheerful as ever, but heaven knew when. O'Brien looked down at the newspaper Hall had left behind, touched it with his fingertips. Had he been too suspicious? Had good fortune been offered, and he passed it by? The tavern door banged and O'Brien frowned at the words beneath his hand, resenting them as he resented all good things that he'd hoped for and never received.

The mail coach had come to a river, and Laura clenched her teeth in anticipation of what was to come. She had lost count of the rivers and streams they had crossed, though she'd managed to keep track of the days—twenty-three since they'd started down the Santa Fé Trail from Independence—as if the knowledge would help her should she have to find her way back to civilization.

"Water's high," her uncle said, leaning across his neighbor to peer out of the window. "Don't worry, my dear. The river bottom is solid rock here. No fear of getting stuck again."

Laura nodded, unable to speak. A dull ache filled her head. She had, in the past few days, begun to wonder if she would die and if that would be easier than enduring the rest of the journey.

The elegant wooden mantel clock in her lap clanked softly as the coach started down the riverbank. Laura held it close, lifting it to soften the impact of the bumps. Sometimes she felt as if preserving her father's clock was the only reason for her continued existence. It was all she had left of him, save for a small daguerrotype framed in silver.

She found old nursery songs running through her mind, tunes she hadn't thought of since her mother had died so many years ago. Father had comforted her then. Now she had no one to turn to, except the uncle whom she had never met until he had greeted her train in St. Louis. She glanced at him, still craning to see out of the window. Wallace Howland was a man of few graces. He did not, as

Laura had hoped he might, resemble her departed father, having neither the fineness of form nor the refinement of mind that had characterized his elder brother. Laura did not wish to appear ungrateful, so she strove to conceal her disappointment.

The coach tilted forward to enter the water, and Laura pressed her heels against the floor to keep from sliding off the bench. The front wheels hit bottom, and with a splash they were into the river and starting across. Shouts and another splash drifted back over the noise of the coach and the water; the second coach, full of mail and provisions, had followed them into the river. The guards on the roof over Laura's head whooped as they neared the bank, and the driver snapped his whip at the mules. The coach bumped, tipped back, leaned crazily toward the water for a heart-stopping moment, then groaned and lurched its way up the bank, to rumble at last to a stop.

Laura closed her eyes and let out her breath in a sigh. The shouting began anew, and she didn't need to hear the words to know what the argument was about. The sergeant in charge of the military escort wanted to halt again to let the animals graze and rest, and the coachmen wanted to press on to the next stage stop. They were making poor time, but the mules were tired; the same teams had pulled the coaches and the military escort's wagon all the way from Fort Larned. In the end, a halt was called.

As the door was pulled open, Laura blinked at the bright sun—so much more intense than in Boston—and drew her black veil over her face. The other passengers—all men— got out first, leaving Laura her choice of privacy in the coach or a walk in the sunshine. No words were spoken; by now it was all habit. In three weeks the travelers had exhausted their small talk and now merely tolerated each other as they tolerated the hardships of travel.

Laura shaded her eyes with a hand and peered out of the window. The line of blue mountains in the west seemed no nearer. The plains were beginning to be broken up by long, flat rock outcrops, rising slowly westward. The land still seemed empty, with not a green thing to be seen save the few shrubs and trees that clung to the river banks. Laura leaned in the corner of the bench seat and tried to sleep. She had learned to snatch what moments of rest she could get, but they were few. Even when the coach stopped for the night, even when a mattress on a dirt floor in a stage station had been offered (though it was some time since she'd had that luxury), her weary mind would not let her rest, taunting her with the past, haunting her with specters of the future.

Laura sat up. Impossible to sleep; she gave up and left the coach to walk the cramps out of her legs. Her traveling hoops were too narrow for her black dress, and the hem was laden with dust from brushing along the ground. The veil kept out only some of the dust and sun, but it did shield her from the prying eyes of the soldiers in the escort. They had climbed out of their wagon and stood stretching, eight pairs of eyes following her, though the men kept a respectful distance. She glanced at their faces—hard faces—worn and weathered though not old. They were not like any of the soldiers she had known back in Boston. She had been to the State Encampment and seen dozens of eager recruits all in shining new uniforms, and had wished she were a man so she could join them. They were no more like these weary, dusty soldiers than were the old heroes of the Mexican War—friends of her father—who had enlivened their parlor with tales of heroics. These soldiers did not look like heroes. They only looked tired.

The thought of home caused Laura's throat to tighten, and she blinked several times to keep back sudden tears. She pushed away memories of the funeral, months ago now, though it seemed only yesterday. She had been left to settle her father's affairs; not so difficult, as she had kept house for him since Mother's death, but hard to bear in her grief. She had dealt with the letters, the agents, the sale of his meager belongings, the removal of her own few things from Church Street to a modest hotel, and the growing fear of being reduced to labor for her own survival. Then hope had arrived, in the form of a letter from her Uncle Wallace Howland in Santa Fé, the last of her immediate family, offering to take her in. She had written her grateful acceptance, said her good-byes, and undertaken the long journey by train, steamboat, and now stagecoach. During that journey a war had begun, but Laura had no grief to spare for her tortured country. She had come to realize how much she had depended on her father, not only as a provider, but as a friend. Now, surrounded by strangers in a foreign country, Laura paced along the riverbank hugging her father's clock tight to her chest, fearing that if she ceased to move she would crumble altogether.

Her uncle approached and fell into step beside her. "Are you tired, my poor child?" he asked. "May I take that clock for you?"

"No, thank you," Laura answered. "It isn't heavy."

"You're a good girl," her uncle said, to which Laura could think of no reply. He was, after all, a stranger, to all intents and purposes. Laura reminded herself that he had offered her a home, and had gone to great trouble and expense to meet her at Independence and accompany her on the last portion of the journey to Santa Fé. The thought of that city was her brightest hope. It would not be like Boston, she knew, but it was a city, with shops and hotels and people. She must be grateful.

"Cheer up, my dear," he said. "We shall reach Fort Union tomorrow, most likely."

Laura nodded, and made an effort to smile.

"Have I mentioned to you my young friend who is there? Lieutenant Owens? A delightful young fellow," her uncle went on without waiting for an answer. "Quite the gentleman. I have told him of you, and he is most anxious to meet you."

"I shall be happy to make his acquaintance," Laura managed to say. Her uncle had mentioned Lieutenant Owens at least once every day since they'd left Independence, and she had begun, simply and irrationally, to hate the man.

She began to hum the tune that was foremost in her mind, a lullaby her mother had sung when she was small.

Hushabye, don't you cry—

"Care for a little refresher?"

Laura stopped, staring in astonishment at the flask her uncle proffered. It was uncapped and she could smell the bitter whiskey. It made her feel ill.

"No, thank you," she replied, and continued walking.

"All right, then," Uncle Wallace called after her. "You can always change your mind."

When you awake, you shall have cake—

"Board up," the driver called, words Laura had come to dread. She turned to face the ordeal once more.

The coach will be shadier, she told herself, looking for the best of the situation. As she walked toward it, the armed guard to whom the driver referred as "shotgun" began hitching up the team. The mules seemed hard, lean, as drained of life by this wasteland as Laura felt.

—and all the pretty little horses.

Hoofbeats penetrated Jamie's awareness, making him lose track of the sums he was doing. He looked up, knowing what he would see through the window over Mr. Webber's desk. Coming up the Camino Real was a company of cavalry.

Jamie glanced at his employer, who was helping two ladies choose some calico, and quietly got up from the desk. He walked to the doorway of the general store to stand and watch the horsemen riding proudly up the street from the Military Plaza. They were lancers, each carrying a long spear with a small red pennant beneath its blade to drink the blood of the enemy. Each pennant bore a single white star, matching the Lone Star on the guidon carried by one of the horsemen. The lancers sat proud and erect in their saddles. They were Germans from town—he recognized some as customers—and they had uniforms, probably made by German wives and sisters determined to send their men to war properly dressed. Across the corner in

Main Plaza a brass band had begun to play. He could hear the strains of "Dixie" from the doorway.

"Excuse me, young man," a voice behind him said, and Jamie hastily moved out of the way. The two ladies stepped past him with their bundle, barely glancing at the martial display. Such sights had become common in San Antonio this spring.

Mr. Webber came and leaned against the door frame, running a hand through his graying hair. "Think you might go for a soldier, Jamie?"

Jamie felt himself blushing. "I wouldn't want to leave you in a bind, sir."

A small smile crept onto Mr. Webber's face. "Well, do as you think right," he said.

Jamie watched the horses go by, picking out the ones he knew. Ranch horses, farm horses, cart horses. Brushed to within an inch of their lives and glowing under the hot sun, looking finer than they ever had.

"You rode with Kearny, didn't you, sir?" Jamie asked.

"I did indeed," Mr. Webber replied.

"Was it glorious?"

Mr. Webber gazed at him, a smile twisting up one corner of his mouth. "To a young soldier everything is glorious," he said, and walked away to put up the bolts of cloth left out on the table.

Jamie stayed by the door and watched the lancers out of sight, imagining himself among them, dressed in crisp gray with a spear in his hand and Poppa's big gelding, Old Ben, under his saddle. Old Ben was needed on the ranch, though, and Jamie was small for his age. Likely he wouldn't be accepted for the cavalry. Likely he'd stay here, being better suited for clerking than soldiering. He was nineteen years old, he'd worked in the store since he was sixteen, and it seemed sometimes like he'd be here until he was gray as Mr. Webber. He sighed and was about to turn back to the desk when he spotted a familiar wagon rolling up the street.

"Captain Martin!" he called, grinning, and stepped out onto the boardwalk waving his arms.

The driver of the wagon, wearing a dusty frock coat and a wide-brimmed cavalry hat, pulled up his team in front of the store. "Hey, young Russell. Came to check on those blankets and beans."

"Yes, sir!" Jamie said. "They just arrived this morning."

"Good. Let's fill up the wagon and I'll send for the rest."

Captain Martin jumped down and tossed his hat onto the seat. His teeth showed white against his sun-cured skin. Martin was an assistant quartermaster—an A.Q.M.—for the army and was constantly prowling San Antonio for supplies. Jamie liked his easy smile and offhanded kindness, and did his best to find everything the captain requested. Now he hurried to help Martin load the wagon with sacks of dried beans and bundled wool blankets.

"Have you ordered those tin plates yet?" Martin asked.

"Yes, sir! They should be here in a month," Jamie answered.

"Then I'm afraid I'll have to trouble you to write again. I need a hundred more than I told you."

"No trouble, sir. I ordered five hundred, just in case."

"Son," Martin said with a grin, "you've got the soul of a quartermaster."

Jamie grinned back. "Come on in, I'll write up the bill."

They went inside, grateful for the cool dimness of the store. Not yet June, it was already sweltering in southern Texas. As Jamie neatly wrote out the captain's bill, Mrs. Webber came out of the back with a tray full of glasses and a pitcher.

"Good afternoon, Captain," she said. "Would you care for a glass of lemonade?"

"Don't mind if I do," Martin answered. "Thank you, ma'am."

Mr. Webber joined them, shaking hands with Martin. "How are the volunteers shaping up?" he asked.

"Helter-skelter," Martin said. "Companies forming and disbanding and forming again. Then they disappear for Richmond."

"In a hurry to get their share of glory." Mr. Webber smiled.

"Well, they're young."

Jamie sipped his lemonade and listened hungrily to every scrap of gossip Martin let fall about the troops headed east. When the captain rumbled away again in his wagon, Jamie went back to the desk to finish his tallies and daydreams. At six o'clock he tidied the papers and gave the store a quick sweep while Mr. Webber was locking up, then slipped out the back door.

Cocoa whickered at him from the corral behind Cutter Blacksmiths next door. "Hey, girl," he said, stroking her soft, dark-brown nose. She came up to the fence and reached over to nuzzle his neck, and he laughed at the tickle of her whiskers. She might not be a war-horse, but she was his—the only living creature who was all his own—and he'd loved her since he helped her stand up to reach for her first meal.

Jamie's stomach growled. A hundred suppers were cooking in the town, their scents making his mouth water as he hurried to saddle the mare. He hauled himself onto her back, tightened the strings of his straw hat to keep off the sun, and rode down Soledad to the corner, turning west toward home.

As he passed the Military Plaza he searched it for signs of more new companies, but saw only the usual food vendors setting up for the evening. He clicked his tongue, urging Cocoa to trot a little faster past the savory smells of chili stew and fresh bread. Before long they were out of town, and Cocoa nickered, asking for a gallop. Jamie gave her her head and they flew over the hills, past fields glittering with water from a spiderweb network of acequias that fed the young crops. Every year more farms sprang up along the Overland Trail west of town, bringing San Antonio a little closer to Russell's Ranch.

The sun was starting to sink as Jamie turned down the lane to the broad, white ranch house, nestled under live oaks in the hollow of two hills. He unsaddled Cocoa and turned her loose in the corral, gave her some water and hay, then headed for the house. From inside he heard Poppa's voice raised in anger, and a cold feeling settled in his stomach as he ran up the three steps and pulled open the door.

Poppa stood by the fireplace, his hands clenching and unclenching at his sides, a sure sign that he was truly angered. Nearby Momma sat in the rocking chair, weeping while sister Emmaline bent over her, murmuring words of comfort. Daniel, the eldest, stood nearby hugging baby brother Gabe who was just twelve. Everybody's eyes were on Matthew, the center of all the fuss, standing in the middle of the room in a brand-new Confederate uniform.

2

---◆---

My Dear Loring: We are at last under the glorious banner of the Confederate States of America.

—H. H. Sibley

"I don't care," Matt said. "I already swore in with the Tom Green Rifles, so I can't back out, and that's that!"

"Just joined, and that's that!" Poppa scoffed. "Didn't think about your mother! Didn't think about brother Dan, who's been wanting for weeks to join the army. Dan's too well behaved to go against his parents' wishes, but I suppose that means nothing to you—"

"Fine, I don't belong in this family! That's what you're saying, isn't it? Well, I'm leaving, so all that's fine!"

Matthew stormed toward the door while Momma wept with new anguish, but he came up short when he saw Jamie blocking the way. Jamie stood stubbornly between his older brother and the door. Dan came up beside Matt, speaking words of calm sense in his quiet, steady voice.

"You don't want to leave like this, Matt. Please." Dan took his brother's arm and brought him back to the family room. "Poppa, I don't mind if he goes. I just thought I'd like to see a little of the world, but I can do that any time. This may be Matt's only chance to shoot a Yankee."

Poppa sneered. "A fine ambition for a young man. Think it's all a game, don't you?"

Matt clenched his jaw. "I'm going to Richmond," he said, "to defend our state in our family's name."

Poppa's face softened, and suddenly Jamie saw the fear that had been hidden behind his anger. Everyone sensed the change; Momma's whimpers subsided, and Gabe clung to Emmaline's hand.

"Very well, I can't stop you," Poppa said, his shoulders sagging. "I suppose you want me to provide you with a mount."

"He can have Buffalo," Dan offered.

"Buffalo's your horse," Poppa said gruffly.

"I can get another."

"No." Poppa turned to Matt and shrugged, which was his usual way of apologizing. "Take Old Ben," he said.

Matt's eyes widened, and Jamie bit his lip in sudden envy.

"Poppa—" Matt began.

"Go on, before I change my mind."

Matt flushed red with gratitude. He went over to kneel by the rocking chair and took Momma's hands in his. "Don't cry," he said. "I'll be in camp up at Austin for a while. Promise I'll write every day."

Momma caught his face in her hands. "My boy, my boy" was all she could say. Matt reached up to hug her, kissed her cheek, then got up and kissed his sister. He tweaked Gabe's ear and told him to behave, then turned to face his father.

"Thank you, Poppa," he said.

"Go on, then," said Poppa, offering his hand. Matt shook it gravely, and Dan's, too, then turned toward the door. He nodded as Jamie stepped aside.

"Keep safe, Professor," he said, giving Jamie a slap on the back and a wink, and was out the door and down the steps, gone.

Everyone stood silent for a minute.

"Supper's getting cold," Emmaline said, breaking the spell. "Let me help you, Momma."

"Oh, yes," Momma said in a worried voice, and got up out of her chair, coming back to life with the need to get things done. They all crowded around the table as if to escape what had happened, but Matt's empty chair was a reminder. Momma refused to let Daniel move it, and kept glancing over at it all through supper. No one had much appetite although everyone pronounced the meal first rate. Finally they got up, each to seek solace in his or her own little evening task. Jamie, feeling ready to burst, fairly ran out to the corral where he caught Cocoa and Buffalo and brought them in for the night. He gave them each a share of oats, brushed Cocoa till she gleamed in the lamplight, then went back out for the other two ranch horses, Smokey and Pip. He met Dan leading them in and took charge of Smokey, the gray. By silent consent the brothers tended the horses, then went back to the tack room together and sat on sacks of grain. Dan took down a bridle that didn't need polishing and set to work on it. Jamie watched him until he could stand it no longer.

"How could you do that?" he said. "How could you let him go, when all you ever wanted was to be a soldier?"

"Easier to let him go than make him stay," Dan replied.

"But—"

"Think a minute, James. Now Poppa has to admit it's right for us to fight."

Jamie stared at his brother in wonder. Daniel wasn't a storm of emotions like Matt, but when he moved it was with inexorable determination. He would get his way, Jamie realized. He would go to war. It was simply a matter of time, and Dan didn't think time of much account.

"Matty's Poppa's favorite," Dan remarked. "Poppa never could tell him no. Now he can't rightly say no to you and me."

"Somebody's got to mind the ranch," Jamie said.

"Gabe's been lending a hand for a while. I'll stay till he's learned the ropes. Emma can help some, too. She'd do it." Dan glanced up at him. "How about you, Professor? Gonna sign up? I know you want to."

Jamie tried to swallow the lump in his throat. "Doubt I'd make much of a soldier," he said.

"There's all kinds of soldiers."

Jamie thought of how his mother would react to losing a second and then a third son to the army. Not likely she'd stand for it. "Wonder where Matty got the uniform," he said glumly.

"I made it," Emmaline said from the doorway. Jamie and Dan both looked up.

"Oh, you did?" Daniel said.

"Yes. Mind if I join you?" She sat next to Jamie and leaned forward so as not to bump her head on the saddle tree above. Emma was tall for a girl, taller than Jamie and almost as tall as Dan. She had Matt's coloring—darker brown than the rest of the family —and a little of his wildness, too. "I worked on it some every night, after bedtime," she said.

"You knew Matt was joining the Rifles?" said Jamie.

Emma nodded. "He could never pass up an adventure. And you, Dan, I know you want to join the army because you believe in the cause. What I can't figure out is why Jamie wants to go." She turned her gaze on Jamie, who looked down at the straw-scattered floor.

"Guess I just want to show I'm good for more than counting sacks of beans," he said. It sounded inadequate to his own ears, but Emmaline nodded.

"You could go, you know," she said. "Poppa's used to you being gone all week. Won't make that much difference."

"If Dan can't go I won't," Jamie replied. His throat tightened on the words, but he meant them. Dan had given up a lot through the years for the sake of his younger siblings.

"Funny how you want what you can't have sometimes," Emma said. "You both want to go away, and I want to stay."

Daniel hung the bridle back on its hook. "Momma still wants you to go to Aunt May?"

Emmaline nodded. "She says I won't ever be a lady unless I get some polish. Like I was a candlestick or something. But I don't want to go to Houston!" Her dark eyes flashed as she looked up.

"Maybe it won't be so bad if you just go for a little while," Jamie suggested.

"Momma'd find ways to keep me there. You know how she is. She just doesn't understand how much I love this ranch."

"Maybe she thinks you'll find a husband in Houston, like Susan did," Daniel suggested.

"Maybe I don't want a husband," retorted Emmaline.

Jamie's eyebrows rose. "You want to be an old maid?"

"I want to stay *here*. Either that, or marry a soldier and follow the drum."

"You, too?" Jamie laughed. "Why don't we just enlist the whole family?"

Emmaline laughed. "Gabe can be the drummer boy."

"And Poppa can be the general," Jamie said.

"Nope. Momma," Dan said. "She always gets the final say."

Emmaline wailed, and they all laughed until their sides ached, then hugged each other.

"Things'll work out," Dan said, standing up. "Don't worry, Professor. You'll get your chance."

Jamie smiled a grim little smile to himself as he followed Dan and Emma back to the house. He didn't know how long the war would last, but he did know that he would rather become a skeleton behind the counter of Mr. Webber's store than prevent Daniel from getting his grays.

"Come on, Mac," Owens said in his soft, lazy voice. "They'll make you a captain."

Lieutenant Lacey McIntyre watched the men loading Captain Sibley's wagons with supplies from the depot: rations, ordnance, crates of new rifles marked REPACKED FORT UNION DEPOT, 1861, all of it destined for Texas and the Confederacy.

"Doesn't look like there'd be any room for me," he said with a halfhearted laugh.

Owens shrugged and stroked the ends of his sandy mustache with a glove hand. "El Paso's a long road away," he said. "We've got to have supplies for the journey."

"Ordnance?" McIntyre asked wryly.

"Apaches, Mac," Owens replied. "We must be able to defend ourselves."

"You've already got more than we took on last winter's campaign."

"You're trying to change the subject," Wheeler said, leaning his shoulders against a wagon crammed with supplies. "Are you coming with us, or aren't you?"

"My father'd disown me if I resigned," McIntyre said. "He's a big one for oaths and all."

"But you swore that oath in Tennessee," Owens said. "Doesn't that mean you should defend Tennessee? Isn't that what your daddy would want?"

McIntyre sighed. Owens was good at making things sound reasonable. He'd led McIntyre into a number of scrapes that way, but this was more serious. This was a war, which was nothing McIntyre wanted any part of, but it looked like the only choice he would have was which side to fight on.

"Here comes the stage," Wheeler remarked. "Last chance for a letter from the U.S. Mail." McIntyre looked at the cloud of dust up the valley and fell in with the others as they ambled to meet the coach. Wheeler had declared himself; he was going south with Sibley and Owens and the rest. Rumor had it only Major Canby's influence had kept his old friend Sibley from marching off the enlisted men as well. McIntyre could count on one hand the officers who were staying: Captain Shoemaker, Lieutenant DuBois, Lieutenant McRae. Himself?

He wanted to do the honorable thing, but he wasn't quite sure what it was. Duty, honor, country. Tennessee had sceded. He had sworn an oath to serve the United States. Which had the stronger claim?

"Alec!" Owens said. McIntyre glanced up to see Alec McRae coming out of the headquarters building. The rifleman looked grim as he stepped off the wooden porch and around yet another wagon, this one being loaded with Sibley's office accoutrements. McRae nodded as they met, his bad eye squinting a bit against the midday sun.

"Major Canby has called a staff meeting," he said. "All

officers are to report to the commander's office in half an hour."

Owens's eyebrows went up. "Major Canby is not the commander of this post," he said.

"He is for now," McRae answered. "Sibley's turned in his resignation."

Something cold moved in McIntyre's stomach. He glanced at Owens, who was smiling, eyes hooded, at McRae.

"How about you, Alec?" Owens said softly. "You coming with us? You're a Carolina boy."

McRae gave him a stony look. "My duty is to the Union," he said. His dark eyes fell on McIntyre, who fidgeted. Alec had no doubts, it seemed, though he knew McRae's family had urged him to resign. Why was it so easy for Alec, and so hard for himself? He didn't want to lose McRae's respect. The gruff rifleman had been a friend to him—to Owens, as well—when they'd first arrived in the Territory a year before. He'd initiated them into the delights of the fandango and coached them on surviving the harsh climate and the natives' tempers, and had even managed to teach McIntyre a little Spanish.

"Half an hour," McRae said after a moment, and turned away before McIntyre could say anything. McIntyre watched him stride off toward the depot.

"Half an hour," Owens echoed. "Think you can make up your mind by then?"

McIntyre frowned. Owens had been in his class at West Point, and they'd campaigned together over the winter. McRae was older, serious-minded but often surprisingly witty and never averse to adventure. How could he possibly choose?

A chorus of exclamation distracted him. Looking up, he saw a pretty girl in black stepping down from the stagecoach with a box of some sort in her arms. Wisps of pale hair blew about her eyebrows, which were darker and strongly drawn. McIntyre was struck by the sadness in her eyes in the instant before she drew her veil over her face.

"Now that's the prettiest thing I've seen in months," Wheeler said, grinning.

"Boys," Owens said softly as a large, round fellow came out of the coach, "I do believe we are about to have a treat."

"Lieutenant Owens!" the round man cried. He caught the girl's arm and propelled her toward them. McIntyre found himself standing straighter. He couldn't remember the last time a white lady had come to the post.

"Lieutenant Owens," the man repeated, out of breath as he came up to them. "This is my niece, Miss Howland."

Owens bowed with a flourish. "Very pleased to meet you, ma'am," he said.

The young lady dipped a curtsey, and McIntyre saw it was a clock, not a box, that she was holding. A wooden clock, shaped like a pointed arch.

"Allow me to introduce my friends," Lieutenant Owens said. "This is Lieutenant Joseph Wheeler, Lieutenant Lacey McIntyre. Miss Howland, and Mr. Wallace Howland."

"Yes, yes," Howland said. "Now, Owens, I thought the three of us could—"

"I'm afraid my plans have changed, sir," Owens interrupted. "I'll be leaving shortly."

"Leaving?" Howland blinked several times and peered at Sibley's wagon. "When will you be back?"

"That depends on Mr. Lincoln, I suppose," Owens answered in a lazy drawl. He turned to the young lady. "Sorry to disappoint you, ma'am."

"I'm not at all disappointed," she replied. Her voice was clear and musical, and held a note of challenge. New England, McIntyre thought. It reminded him of his days at the Military Academy. He caught himself squinting to see through her veil, and looked sidelong at Owens. The Georgian was grinning and seemed about to say something more, but a crash from nearby prevented him.

All eyes turned toward the back of the wagon, where Sibley's Negro house boy stood frozen over a shattered crate of champagne. Green glass fragments frothed with the wine that was fast soaking into the dust. The wagon's driver swore, grabbed his whip from the box, and started toward the hapless slave.

"No!"

The force of the cry startled McIntyre; it was followed by a rustle of black skirts. The driver came to a surprised halt, staring at Miss Howland, who had darted between him and the boy.

"He didn't mean to drop it," she said in a passionate voice, wholly different from her cool tone a moment before. She held out one black-gloved hand before her to stave off the whip.

"Miss Howland," Owens said, stepping toward her, "come away from that." His smile had vanished, and his tone was that of an officer to his men.

"I will not allow this man to be brutalized," Miss Howland said, standing her ground.

Wheeler chuckled. McIntyre shot a glare at him to shut him up. For himself, he thought this righteous young lady was magnificent.

"It is not your concern, ma'am," Owens said, "and you might be hurt. That glass could cut right through your boot."

"I will step away if you will promise this man won't be beaten," Miss Howland replied, gesturing to black Jimmy, who was as astonished as the rest of them.

"You know how much that champagne cost?" the driver shouted.

"Beating him will not bring it back!" she answered.

"Well, Bill," said an amused voice from the steps, "you've got to admit that's true."

McIntyre looked up at Captain Sibley, who stood on the porch admiring Miss Howland with a twinkling eye. He still wore the Federal uniform that set off his auburn side whiskers so well. His mustache drooped around the corners of a smile as he stepped down to the ground. "I don't believe I've had the pleasure," he said, approaching Miss Howland.

"Miss Howland," Owens said, "allow me to introduce

you to Captain Henry Sibley." He caught McIntyre's eye
and gave a little shrug of resignation.

"Delighted to make your acquaintance, Miss Howland,"
Sibley said with a bow even grander than Owens's. "Are
you related to George Howland? Mounted Rifles?"

"I don't believe so," Miss Howland said. "I was not
aware of such a person."

"Well, in any case, welcome to New Mexico," Sibley
said. "How may I be of service to you?"

"You may tell that man to put away his whip," Miss
Howland answered, her voice resuming its prior dignity.

Sibley's eyes flicked to the driver, and his smile
widened. "You heard the lady, Bill. Go on about your business. You, too, Jim."

The slave, as if released from a magic spell, hurried into
the building while the driver returned to the wagon box,
muttering to himself. Sibley stooped and extracted an
unbroken bottle from the mess at his feet, wiped it off with
his pocket handkerchief, and offered it to Miss Howland.

"I hope you will accept this in place of the hospitality I
would like to offer you," he said. "Unfortunately, I'm on
the point of departure."

"Thank you, sir," Miss Howland replied, a trace of frost
in her voice, "but I would not further depreciate your
stores."

"Very generous of you, Captain," said the uncle, stepping in to take the bottle. "Wallace Howland," he added,
shaking Sibley's hand. "Dined with you in Las Vegas last
fall."

"I remember," Sibley said. "You bought the faro bank
and held it till three in the morning."

Howland laughed, a deep booming sound.

"This your daughter?" Sibley asked.

"My niece," Howland said. "My dear brother's only
child, rest his soul."

Sibley's brows rose. "My heartfelt condolences,
ma'am."

"Thank you," Miss Howland murmured, so softly McIntyre barely heard it. Footsteps sounded on the porch, and he glanced up to see Major Canby had come out of the commander's office.

"She has come to live with me in Santa Fé," Howland said. "Perhaps we will see you there, Captain Sibley?"

"It's *Major* Sibley now," Canby said, joining them, his clean-shaven face a stark contrast to Sibley's flamboyance.

"Until Washington gets my letter," Sibley said. "I appreciate the gesture, though. It'll get me a colonelcy in the Confederate army."

"Much good may it do you," Canby said quietly.

Sibley laughed. "You sound jealous, Richard. You can still join us, you know. The star of the South is rising," he said, his voice suddenly vibrant.

All fell still. McIntyre glanced at Miss Howland, wondering what thoughts her veil concealed. Looking back at Canby, he saw the major's eyes narrow as he silently shook his head.

"Well, I'm sorry, then," Sibley said, offering Canby his hand. "I shall miss the good times we had."

"So will I," Canby said quietly.

"Give Louisa my best regards."

Canby nodded, and Sibley slapped his shoulder before turning back to the Howlands. "Pleasure meeting you, ma'am. Mr. Howland." Touching his hat, he stepped past them to the front of the wagon. "Finish up, Bill, and let's get moving."

Sibley strode toward the depot with Wheeler on his heels. Owens started after them, then paused.

"Coming, Mac?"

McIntyre glanced at Miss Howland, and at Canby behind her. "No," he said on impulse.

Owens stared hard at him for a second, then turned and walked away without a word. McIntyre blinked, frowning at the sun that had suddenly started to hurt his eyes. He turned his back on it, and found Major Canby's cool gaze on him.

"Miss Howland, this is Major Canby," he said to cover his discomfort. "And Mr. Howland."

"How do you do?" Canby said. "I must beg you to excuse me, I have a great deal to do. I'll see you at the staff meeting, Lieutenant?"

"Yes, sir," McIntyre replied. He'd decided, it seemed. Didn't make him feel any better.

Canby gave a short, approving nod and returned to headquarters, passing Jimmy in the door. The slave carried a second crate of wine, which he carefully placed in the wagon under the sharp eyes of the driver. Shouts from the teamsters by the depot heralded the departure of the wagon train. McIntyre glanced back at the long line of wagons, trying to spot Owens.

"Mr. McIntyre?"

The sound of his name in that New England voice sent a chill down his back. Turning, he saw Miss Howland beside him, close enough he could almost see her eyes through the veil. He was suddenly glad he had chosen to stay.

"Is that man indeed a slave?" she asked.

"Yes," McIntyre said, watching Jimmy climb into the wagon among all the furniture. "He belongs to Captain Sibley."

"I had thought the Territories were free of slavery," Miss Howland stated.

"It's kind of up in the air," McIntyre said.

The driver's whip cracked, making Miss Howland jump, and the wagon rumbled forward to join the train.

"Come, my dear," her uncle said. "The post sutler will sell us some refreshment."

McIntyre watched Miss Howland walk away with her uncle. The wagon train was moving, blocking their path to the sutler's, and they stopped to watch it pass.

"So you stayed." McRae's voice came from behind him.

McIntyre turned to see McRae coming up to join him and gave him the best smile he could muster. Together they watched the train's departure. McIntyre spotted Owens riding in the foremost wagon with Wheeler and a handful of others. Sibley was among them, he saw, and as their wagon passed the headquarters building, Sibley stood up and turned to them.

"Boys," he called, "if you only knew it, I am the worst enemy you have!"

McIntyre glanced at McRae, whose mouth curled in a grimacing smile. "You're your own worst enemy, Henry," McRae said softly. He turned and headed up the steps to the commander's office.

McIntyre stayed to watch the train a little longer, though the dust raised by the wagon wheels was beginning to block it from view. Still, he thought he saw a gloved hand raised in farewell. He waved back, then hurried into headquarters, hoping Canby would give them too much to do so he wouldn't have time to think.

3

Colonel Loring, of the Regiment of Mounted Riflemen, in anticipation of the acceptance of his resignation, left this place today, after placing me in the general charge of the affairs of the department.

—Major Ed. R. S. Canby

"Look, my dear, that's an old Indian city."

"Pecos," said Mr. Krohn, a fellow passenger.

"Like the river?" Laura leaned forward to peer out of the window and glimpsed a heap of crumbling mud walls and the remains of a Spanish church. The sun was behind it, sinking toward the stair-step mountains and hurting her tired eyes. The trail had left the river and begun to rise as it turned north and skirted the mountains beyond which lay Santa Fé. Now that they were close to the journey's end, Laura was able to take more interest in the country they passed through.

"Just a mile or two to the next stop," her uncle said. "The supper is worth waiting for, I assure you."

Laura sat back, making an effort to smile. Her uncle's assurances, she had learned, were generally exaggerated. As they had stopped at a ranch not an hour before, she made up her mind not to expect less than ten miles in the next leg, which would bring them within a day's travel of Santa Fé. Rubbing her thumb along the peak of the clock in her lap, she stared out of the window at the cedar-dotted hills. Though her middle seat had a poor view, it was better than staring at her fellow passengers.

Her mind returned to Fort Union, as it often had in the last few days. Her uncle had expressed his disappointment in her behavior there; she had failed to captivate Lieutenant Owens, and she had interfered with Captain Sibley's "property" in a most unseemly fashion. Laura had swallowed her indignation, but could not bring herself to apologize for a simple act of humanity. It troubled her to find herself in a country where slavery was tolerated, and it troubled her deeply to know that her uncle acquiesced in that tolerance.

A cool breeze reclaimed her attention. The trail had swung west again, passing between rising hills. Pine trees began to appear, dwarfing the cedars and casting long shadows in the slanting sunshine. The stage slowed, mules laboring uphill as they entered a little canyon. Ridges of rough, lichened rock closed in on both sides. The sun was hidden by the cliffs, and the air in this valley was much cooler. Laura shivered at the sudden drop in temperature. She was beginning to wish for her shawl when the trail rounded an outcrop and sunlight spilled through the window once more, dappled by a sea of fluttering green leaves.

"Oh!" Laura cried involuntarily. The valley had opened into a little bowl, surrounded by pine-covered hills and filled with rustling cottonwoods. The trail bisected the grove, and in the middle a ranch house appeared, its mud walls glowing golden in the late sunshine, a rocky ridge overlooking it to the north with a blue, domed mountain beyond. It was the loveliest place Laura had yet seen in New Mexico, and her spirits rose as the stage slowed to a halt before the house.

"Here we are," Uncle Wallace said. "Not so bad, was it?"

"No," Laura replied, and this time her smile was heartfelt. As she stepped down from the coach she inhaled cool air tinged with the smells of woodsmoke and forest earth. Rock walls marked a large corral west of the ranch house. A covered portal shaded the whole front of the house, which had three doors facing onto the trail. From one of these emerged a tall, lanky man in rancher's clothes, waving long arms in welcome and saying "Bonjour, bonjour! Welcome to Glorieta!"

"Glorieta?" Laura said. "What a pretty name."

The Frenchman's face crinkled in a smile. "And you are a pretty lady, madame. May I carry that for you?"

Laura sensed kindness, as though this gentleman drew great joy as well as a living from serving his guests. His hair and mustache were black, just beginning to be peppered with gray, and his eyes had a merry twinkle. She liked him, she decided, and allowed him to relieve her of her clock.

"Thank you, Monsieur—?"

"Alexandre Vallé," he said, bowing with a flourish. "But I am also called 'Pigeon.' "

"Thank you, Monsieur Vallé." Laura gazed around the valley again, drinking in its beauty. It was a peaceful place. The wind in the cottonwoods reminded her of the ocean, and instead of making her homesick, it made her feel at home.

Uncle Wallace trudged up with his portmanteau and Laura's traveling case. "Hallo, Pigeon," he said. "When's the next fandango?"

"You just missed one." The Frenchman grinned. "For three days we were dancing."

"You'd outdance the devil himself," her uncle said. "I see you met my niece."

"Ah!" Vallé exclaimed, turning to Laura. "So this is Miss Howland? You did not tell me she is so beautiful! She will break all the hearts, my friend!"

Laura gave a cough of surprised laughter and tried to frown at Vallé, but he was smiling and she found herself smiling back. She had not been teased since her father died, she realized. She glanced down at her dusty half-boots, suddenly lonely.

"Supper?" Uncle Wallace asked.

"It will be ready in half an hour," Vallé said. "Meanwhile, I will show mademoiselle her room, yes?" He waved them to the center door, through which the other passengers had already gone.

The house was Mexican in style, like every other ranch

they had stopped at since Fort Union: thick walls made of the mud bricks called adobes, dirt floor covered with black and white checkered rugs, and wool mattresses rolled against the walls. Two rough tables and several chairs formed the rest of the furniture. One of the curious little beehive fireplaces common to the country was tucked into a corner, and a larger conventional hearth crackled with bright fire over which a pot of something savory was simmering. A diminutive Mexican woman with a long, glossy black braid down her back looked up from stirring the pot as they entered, and smiled when her eyes fell on Laura. Very bright, those eyes, giving her an elfish look.

"Carmen," Vallé called to her, and paused to exchange a few words in Spanish. The stage passengers were setting their bags on the mattresses, claiming their beds for the night. Uncle Wallace hurried to secure one while Vallé led Laura to a door in the lefthand wall.

The second room was as large as the first, though it had but one table and one corner fireplace. Luxurious accommodations for a solitary female. "Shall I light the fire, mademoiselle?" Vallé asked as he set Laura's clock in a little niche in the wall.

"Yes, thank you," she answered. Vallé knelt by the beehive fireplace, and Laura went to the front wall, where a door and a window faced the trail. There was glass in the window—attesting to Monsieur Vallé's prosperity—and the curtain tacked over it was clean, if a little faded. As Laura looked out, the mail coaches rumbled past on their way into the corral for the night.

Uncle Wallace came in with her traveling case, which he set near the fire. "Well, now," he said. "Quite cozy, aren't we?"

"Yes," Laura said. "This is a beautiful valley."

"Knew you'd get to liking New Mexico. It grows on you."

Laura glanced at Vallé and refrained from expressing her opinion of New Mexico in general: hot, dry, dusty, filled with starving Mexicans and American adventurers. Instead she opened her case and took out her black shawl. "I think I'll walk while there's still light," she said.

"Bien," Vallé said, dusting off his knees as he rose from the fireplace. "When you hear the bell, supper will be served."

Laura went out into the crisp evening, crossed the dusty ruts of the Santa Fé Trail, and found a stone well to the south of it, with a stand of young corn nearby. Beyond the well was a small pond, fed by a stream that trickled down the valley from the west. Spring had lingered in the shelter of the mountains, and purple and white wildflowers flourished at the water's edge. A *plink* of water told her of fish, and she glanced up in time to see circles widening on the pond's surface.

This place I could live in, she thought as she strolled into the woods that were something like the green she had known at home. She had always loved the outdoors, both wild forests and civilized gardens. She and her father had taken long, frequent walks, looking for herbs to make into medicines, discussing philosophy and politics, pondering how to improve his career as a lecturer on health and homeopathy, making grandiose plans that had never been put into motion and now never would be.

Laura's throat tightened, and she came to a halt in the middle of a little copse of trees, pulling her shawl closer around herself. She had tried so hard to help her father's success. They had struggled. They had made sacrifices, stood by their beliefs, and then he'd been drowned in a fishing accident—of all useless ways to die—just when he'd seemed on the verge of success. Why? she asked silently, as she'd done a thousand times in her prayers. God had a reason for everything he did, but this she had not yet been able to understand, and she was tired, so tired, of the weariness of grieving. She tilted back her head and closed her eyes, inhaling the smell of forest earth, hoping still for an answer.

"La glorieta," a soft voice said. Laura started and looked up to see Monsieur Vallé at the edge of the glade.

"Forgive me," he said. "I did not mean to frighten you."

"You followed me?" Laura accused, anger replacing the momentary fear. Her heart was still racing from surprise.

"I am sorry," Vallé said. "When I saw you go into the woods, I came to be sure you were safe. Many people travel on this road, mademoiselle," he said, gesturing toward the Trail.

"Oh," Laura said. "I see. It's kind of you to be concerned."

"Also, it is almost time for supper," the Frenchman added. "Shall I walk back with you, or do you wish to be alone?"

"Let's go back," Laura said with a glance at the hills behind which the sun had dipped. Twilight was falling in the forest, and she fell into step with Vallé, who kept a respectful distance as they walked up the gentle slope to the trail. "What did you say?" she asked. "Glorieta?"

"Yes," Vallé said. "That is what you were like, standing in the middle of those trees. Like a glorieta. The Spanish give that name to any place where something special is surrounded by trees. A fountain, a shrine, a statue—"

"Are you saying I looked like a statue?" Laura asked in mock indignation.

"It was not how you looked," he said. "To me it is the feeling that makes a glorieta. There is a special feeling . . . eh, bah. I am talking nonsense. Please pay no attention."

Laura looked at his sun-weathered face, wanting him to continue. Shyness prevented her from asking; she did not know him and didn't wish to be rudely inquisitive. Yet she had the feeling that what he had been about to say was important.

The clear sound of a bell broke the silence. They reached the house as Carmen was hanging a lantern from the portal's roof. The coachmen started coming in from the corral, and with a last glance at the whispering cottonwoods, Laura followed her hosts in to supper.

"It's grown," O'Brien said as he and Hall rode into Denver City. A jumble of tents and shacks clustered the town's outskirts on both sides of the South Platte and eastward along Cherry Creek.

"Yes, there's always another fool trying to find his fortune out West," said Hall.

O'Brien shot Hall a look, then glanced back at the cold Rocky Mountains, the wind rolling down from their rugged peaks out to the eastern plains. He was not such a fool as to let Joseph Hall annoy him. Hall was still in a prickly mood, though he'd come back to Avery much sooner than O'Brien had expected.

"So, what do you think of him?" Hall asked.

"This bag of bones?" O'Brien said, patting the thin withers of the horse Hall had loaned him. It was the first horse he'd had a leg over since New York, and the worst excuse for a horse he'd seen since leaving Ireland. He hadn't mentioned it to Hall, because Hall could turn such things against one, but in fact he'd grown up around horses in Racecourse, and loved them, and hated to see them broken down like this poor old nag. He shook his head and said, "I think he has maybe a year or two left in him."

"Well, he's in better shape than when I bought him. Let you have him for fifty dollars."

O'Brien laughed.

"I could get twice that," Hall said.

"And you paid half as much, I'll be bound," O'Brien answered. "No, save your breath. I've got no fifty dollars to give you. Dooney only gave me ten for a week's diggings, and I need every penny for clothes. I've a hole in one boot that's as big as a dollar."

"Well," Hall said, "I just happen to know where you could get that fifty dollars, and more besides. Did you hear our new governor's planning to call for volunteers?"

"That again. Aye, I heard."

"Hear he's going to make any man a captain who brings in twenty-five men?"

O'Brien had not heard that. "I see," he said slowly as they headed down Larimer Street. "And when am I to congratulate you, Captain Hall?"

Hall laughed. "Oh, not me. I'm too lazy to be a leader of men. A captain's got to be able to knock heads together— I'd just want to shoot 'em and be done with it. I was thinking of you, my friend."

"Me?" O'Brien laughed. "A captain in the army?"

"Why not?"

"Because they don't want my sort for officers, even if I had the money. They want the fine gentlemen for that."

"You weren't listening, Red. You don't buy a commission here the way they do in Europe. All you need is twenty-five men, and you can get them in Avery."

"You've got it all planned, have you?"

"Yep," Hall said, smiling as he leaned back in his saddle. "It should be a cavalry company, I reckon. Twenty-five brave fellows, galloping into Denver. What do you think?"

A shadowy army of warriors appeared to O'Brien, descendants of King Brian Boru, bright swords aglitter and proud horses snorting. It pulled at his heart, that vision, and whispered of honors to be won. He drew in a deep breath, and just as he did so the nag stumbled—a bad omen.

"I think," he said after he'd steadied the horse, "that you're hoping to sell me your breakdowns for this fairy-tale company. Best look elsewhere."

"Now, Red—"

"Joe Hall!" The voice came from down the street. O'Brien glanced up.

"Hey!" Hall shouted, breaking into a grin. He waved to the man who had hailed him—a tall fellow with a wide, friendly face and mutton-chop whiskers—and kicked his horse into a trot. O'Brien followed, reining in beside Hall, who had dismounted and was pumping the tall fellow's hand.

"Good to see you, Logan," Hall said.

"Likewise," Logan replied. "Come have a drink—I'm meeting Hambleton at the Criterion."

"How'd you get him to go in there?" Hall asked. "I thought he didn't care for Southerners."

Logan grinned. "No, but he knows Charley Harrison's got the best whiskey in town."

O'Brien slid from his saddle, and Hall glanced his way. "Sam Logan, I'd like you to meet my very good friend Red O'Brien. He's got a claim up in Avery."

"Oh?" Logan said, shaking hands. "And how's mining in Avery?"

"Cold and dry as a witch's teat," O'Brien answered.

Logan laughed and said, "Come on along, then. You can warm up with a glass of whiskey."

"I'll catch up," O'Brien said, nodding toward Wallingford & Murphy's Mercantile nearby. "Need to buy a few things."

"Don't be long," Hall said, throwing an arm around Logan's shoulders. As they went on down the street, O'Brien tied his borrowed nag to the rail outside the merchant's and went in.

"Good morning, Mr. Murphy," he said, taking a gray woolen shirt from a stack near the door.

"Morning," Murphy answered from behind the counter. He seemed preoccupied in unwrapping some cloth. O'Brien chose two pairs of trousers, some socks, and long underwear, and carried his purchases up to the counter, where Murphy added them up.

"Six dollars and thirty cents."

"How much for the boots?" O'Brien asked, pointing to a shelf behind the counter.

"Seven dollars a pair."

"Could I pay you on credit?"

Murphy shook his head. "Sorry. Cash only."

"Then where can I find a good cobbler?"

"Independence," Murphy said with a laugh.

Annoyed, O'Brien paid for the clothes and went down the street to the shop of a saddler, who agreed to add some leather to his boot soles for fifty cents. O'Brien left the boots and the horse with the saddler and walked barefoot back toward the Criterion. Before he had reached it a shouting arose up ahead. He passed by the saloon to see what was the matter.

A crowd was collecting outside Wallingford & Murphy's. On its roof was a flag he'd not seen before—one wide, white stripe between two red ones, with a circle of stars on the blue corner. Murphy stood before his door exchanging hard words with the crowd. O'Brien moved closer and caught the words "damned secessionist."

"That again," he muttered.

"You got something to say about it?"

O'Brien looked up to find a great buffalo of a fellow glaring at him. "Not a thing," he said. "What flag is it, then?"

"It's a damned Confederate flag, that's what!"

"They call it the Stars and Bars," Hall's voice drawled from behind them. O'Brien turned. Logan was there, too, frowning at the shopkeeper's new flag. "Take it easy, Hambleton," Hall added. "O'Brien's all right."

The crowd was getting bigger, and the shouting louder. A man pushed at Murphy and he yelled back in anger.

"Someone's going to get hurt," Logan said, and began to push forward. Hall and Hambleton went with him, and O'Brien followed, mindful of heels near his feet. Logan reached the store and climbed up on the rail out front. This distracted the mob, which paused in haranguing the merchant to watch Logan scramble up onto the roof. In two steps he was at the flagpole and hauling down the banner. A cheer went up, and Logan jumped back to the ground with the bundle of cloth in his hands.

"Keep it to yourself, Murphy," Logan said, handing it to its owner. "Your neighbors don't like this flag."

"I have a right to display whatever flag I wish on my own property," the merchant fumed.

"Colorado is a Union Territory!" someone from the crowd shouted, and a roar of agreement went up.

Hambleton stooped to pick up a rock, which he aimed at the store's expensive glass window. O'Brien jostled his arm, and the rock struck the wooden wall instead. Hambleton turned on him, eyes blazing with fury.

"I wouldn't," O'Brien said, his thumb stroking the hilt of the sharp hunting knife that a flick had brought into his hand. Hambleton glanced at the blade, and then back at O'Brien's face. O'Brien knew the look; a fighter thinking, wondering how strong his opponent might be and if flesh could be quicker than blade.

"Try it then," O'Brien said softly, shifting his grip on the knife. Someone screamed, and the crowd melted away, leaving Hambleton and O'Brien facing each other across two yards of dirt.

Logan hurried up to put a hand on the buffalo's shoulder. "Enough, Josiah," he said. "It's over."

Hambleton, nostrils flaring, stared hard at O'Brien, then strode to the merchant and pulled the flag out of his hands. To the crowd's great delight, he threw it in the dust at Murphy's feet and ground his heel into it. "No one flies that rag over this city!" he shouted, and the crowd cheered.

Logan came between his friend and Murphy, and began coaxing Hambleton away. The buffalo tossed one malevolent glance at O'Brien, who watched him away down the street, then looked at the merchant. "Best get inside," he said with a jerk of his head.

Murphy, still angry, picked up his flag and went back into his shop. Left with nothing to look at, the watchers began to disperse. O'Brien put away his knife.

"That was good of you, Red," Hall said slowly. "You a friend of the Confederate cause?"

"Just a decent citizen trying to keep the peace," O'Brien answered. Privately, he thought he was more a damned fool who reacted without thinking. This quarrel was none of his business.

"You deserve a reward, then," Hall said. "Come on, I'll buy you a drink."

O'Brien glanced at the Criterion, famous for two things: good whiskey, and the rowdy Southerners who made it their haunt. "No, I'm not in the mood anymore," he said. "You go on."

Hall frowned at him, looking puzzled. "Murphy's no friend of yours, is he?"

"No." O'Brien looked at the empty flagpole atop the store. No, he wasn't a friend of secession, but he'd seen enough hopes trampled down in the dust to last him a lifetime. "A flag doesn't belong in the dirt," he said with a shrug.

A corner of Hall's mouth turned up. "Why, Red!" he said softly. "I do believe you have the makings of a patriot!"

West of the mountains at last, the Santa Fé Trail turned northward and began a gentle descent. Laura leaned forward eagerly, trying for a glimpse of the city, but the country was hilly and still rural, scattered with adobe houses and patches of corn and beans. The houses grew closer together, and at last the coach splashed through a stream running along a stone gutter and rattled to a stop at the top of a hill.

"Exchange Hotel," the shotgun shouted, and began hauling luggage off the roof of the coach. Laura stepped down to the corner of a large, dirt square, sparsely shaded by young cottonwoods and inhabited by burros, a few Mexicans, and several sleeping dogs.

"Welcome to Santa Fé," her uncle said proudly.

Laura's arms tightened around her clock as she gazed in dismay at the flat-roofed adobe buildings surrounding the square. Nearly all had long, covered portals. Some seemed to be private residences, others housed merchants and wine shops, but none looked remotely like the shops she had expected. There were no graceful houses, no green parks. Except for the flag hanging limply from a pole in the square's center, it was a Mexican village, like every other they'd seen, if perhaps a bit larger.

"This is the Plaza," said her uncle. "Over there's the old Spanish governor's palace. It's the military headquarters now."

"Palace?" Laura repeated, unable to see any structure that came close to deserving the name.

"There," her uncle said, pointing to the building that ran the length of the plaza on its north side. To her it looked more like a stable. A number of soldiers lounged near a doorway, where two mules and a horse stood tied to some of the wooden pillars of the portal. A pair of dogs began to wrestle in the dirt, growling good-naturedly. The entire image presented by the plaza of Santa Fé was that of a dusty, packed-earth barnyard.

"Come, my dear," said Uncle Wallace as the mail rumbled away toward the post office on the square's west side. "You'd like to settle in, I expect." Laura turned to see him poised in a wide, double doorway set at an angle into a building on the plaza's southeast corner, marked FONDA by one sign and EXCHANGE HOTEL by another. Beyond, at the end of the street to the east, stood a large Spanish church with the blue mountains rising behind it.

"We're staying here?" she asked.

"Of course," her uncle said. "It's the best place in town."

"I—assumed you had a house," said Laura.

"House? Lord, no! D'you know what it would cost to build a proper house out here? Come along, now."

Chastened, Laura followed him into the hotel's office, which besides a desk boasted a real Turkey carpet on the floor and two cushioned chairs. An open doorway beyond led into a cantina; she could see the dark wood of a long bar.

"Mr. Howland!" A man in a white shirt, vest, and dusty trousers looked up from the desk. "Good to see you back!"

"Thank you, Phillips. Where's Parker?"

"Around somewhere. Want your usual room?"

"If it's free, yes, and one for my niece."

"Yes, indeed!" The clerk's gaze made Laura uncomfortable. She looked away, only to find a couple of men in the doorway of the cantina staring at her, as well. She drew down her veil.

"Number four," the clerk said, handing keys to her uncle. "It's on the placita." Laura thought she saw him wink.

"This way, m'dear," Uncle Wallace said, starting toward a closed door. "Fetch in her trunk, will you, Phillips?"

"I surely will," the clerk drawled in a lazy tone, going through the double doors to the street. Laura sighed as she followed her uncle. So far, Santa Fé was a great disappointment.

"Damned fool thing," her uncle muttered, fiddling with the door latch. "Ah, there we are."

The door swung open, and Laura was surprised to see that it led outside again, into a garden entirely surrounded by the hotel. Portals were set back on all sides, shading doors. The center, a rectangle perhaps ten feet by sixty, was filled with rosebushes just starting to bloom, raising a heady scent in the afternoon sunshine. Beneath them hid pansies, oregano, and marjoram, and along the ground grew tendrils of thyme covered with tiny purple blooms. Mockingbirds sang from wicker cages, and vines climbed the great tree-trunk pillars of the porch roof.

"A glorieta," Laura whispered, enchanted.

Uncle Wallace led her down the portal to the centermost door on the western side, which he unlocked and held open for her. As she peered into the dim apartment Laura saw a small fireplace, an actual bed, pegs for clothes, and a rough-hewn table and chair. A rug of the black and white wool rug that Monsieur Vallé had called jerga covered part of the floor. How humble I've grown, Laura thought, smiling. Back east she would have been insulted at being offered such a room— even her father's scant means could command decent lodgings—but compared to the accommodations she'd had along most of the Santa Fé Trail, it was palatial.

"That opens on the street," her uncle said, pointing to a second door opposite the first. "Keep it locked. If you need anything ask Phillips, or come and find me. I'm in number eight, back of the cantina."

"Thank you, Uncle." Laura set her clock down on the table.

"I've got a few things to see to," Uncle Wallace said,

patting his pockets. "I'll come back in an hour and we'll have some supper. Oh, here's your key," he added. He pressed it into her hand and withdrew, leaving the door open behind him.

Laura sighed, untied the strings of her bonnet, and hung it on one of the pegs. She drew out her small gold watch, which she had taken to wearing on a long chain inside her dress to protect it from the dust. Monsieur Vallé had given her the correct time that morning. She set the mantel clock, then pulled out its weight, which had been wrapped in cloth and tucked into the case, and carefully rehung it. Winding the clock with the key, which she kept on her watch chain, she smiled as it began its gentle ticking. It was almost the half hour. Laura lay on her side on the bed, watching the minute hand slowly move toward the six, waiting for the musical chime.

"Where d'you want it, miss?"

Laura started, and got hastily to her feet. The desk clerk stood in the door with her trunk, wearing a grin.

"By the wall, please," she said, regaining her composure. The clerk carried the trunk in and placed it near the foot of the bed. "Could someone bring me water and a basin?" Laura asked.

He straightened up and gave her a long, appreciative look, and the grin widened. "Sure thing, missy," he said on his way out. "If you need help with your bath, let me know." He slipped out before Laura could reprove him, and she threw the door shut with a snap.

This is not a civilized country, she thought in the resulting darkness. She pulled back the window curtain to let in some light, then unlocked her trunk and took out a candle and matches. With candlelight dispelling much of the gloom, she covered the window again and sat on the bed to remove her dusty half-boots. The place might not be civilized, but she would remain so. Her feet rejoiced at the freedom of slippers, and she knew that with a fresh gown draped over a proper hoop, she would feel more herself.

A soft knock heralded the arrival of a Mexican maid

with her wash basin. "Thank you," Laura said, letting her in. "Set it on the table, please."

The girl looked apprehensive. "No entiendo."

"Here," Laura said, touching the table.

"Ah, sí." The girl brightened. She set down the basin and a towel, bobbed her head, and turned to leave.

"Thank you, thank you very much," Laura said, smiling and nodding as she closed the door. "I suppose I should learn Spanish," she added to herself. She went to the table, removed her gloves, and splashed the cool water on her face. Spanish didn't interest her, but it appeared she would need to know it if she remained in Santa Fé.

The clock chimed once. Laura straightened, wondering for the first time just how long she would be there. She picked up the towel and dried her face, then undressed and began sponging her weary body. Surely this dusty village in what was, to all purposes, a foreign country would not be her permanent home. The idea that her uncle intended to stay in this dingy hotel astonished and worried her. She had meant to keep house for him, as she had done for her father, and thereby earn her support, but it appeared that was not to be.

How, she wondered as she dressed, did her uncle pay for his accommodations? She had assumed he had some profession, but he had not described his business to her, and while he seemed to have money enough, she felt precarious all at once. An ache came into her heart, an intense longing for green Massachusetts. Suddenly she couldn't bear the dark, tiny room. Snatching up her gloves and bonnet, she hurried out into the garden.

Her hoops kept her from going out on the narrow path among the roses, but it was just as well, for the sun was intensely bright after the dimness of her room. She strolled along the portal instead, gazing out at the flowers. Their scent soothed her, and the warmth of the sun-baked walls made her drowsy. She found herself at the end of the portal, facing a pair of doors that stood open to a dining room.

"May I help you?" a man inside said, noticing her. He came to the doors, smiling. He wore a neat coat and waistcoat, and had dark hair, thinning a little, and bushy side whiskers.

"No, thank you," Laura said. "I'm just exploring. Forgive me for disturbing you."

"Not at all," the gentleman replied. "If I can be—"

"Parker!" her uncle called, coming up beside Laura. "Been looking all over for you!"

"Mr. Howland! Welcome back."

"This is Mr. Parker, my dear," Uncle Wallace informed her. "He owns the hotel. My niece, Miss Howland."

"How do you do?" Mr. Parker's smile widened. "I trust you've been given everything you need?"

As Laura began to reply a great ringing of bells commenced from nearby. Mr. Parker beckoned her and her uncle into the dining room, and shut the doors against the din.

"It's the parroquia," he said, gesturing eastward.

"The Spanish church down the street?" Laura asked.

"Yes. There are others, too, which you'll hear if you walk about the town at all. Would you care for some dinner? I was just about to sit down, and I'd be honored if you would join me."

"Delighted," Uncle Wallace said. He and Laura followed Mr. Parker to a table near the kitchen, where they were served a lavish dinner of roast beef and potatoes, peas, scalloped onions, rice with tomatoes, and fresh bread. There was also a dish of pork in bright red sauce, called cárne adobada, just the smell of which made Laura's eyes water. She declined to taste it, but the rest of the meal was delicious, and she ate hungrily while listening to her uncle catch up on gossip. He seemed mostly to be inquiring which of his numerous acquaintance were presently in town. He must be reasonably prosperous, she decided, to know so many people.

The cook brought out individual dishes of caramelized custard for dessert, and Mr. Parker poured the coffee. "You will find very pleasant society in Santa Fé, Miss Howland," he said. "There are a number of Americans in town, and some of the better Spanish families are quite cultivated. There are also some good people with the military, though they're all at odd's ends just now. I heard Captain Sibley resigned."

"Yes," Laura said. "We saw him leaving Fort Union."

"Did you? He laid out that depot, you know. Knows every box of biscuits in it."

"He appeared to be taking a number of them along," said Laura dryly.

Mr. Parker shook his head. "It's a bad business. Most of the West Pointers are going south. Captain Ewell, Captain Wilcox, Major Longstreet. And I understand Colonel Loring's resigned."

Uncle Wallace's brows went up. "I thought Loring was the departmental commander," he said.

"He is. Was. He's packing up to head for El Paso right now. Wanted to take the Fort Marcy troops with him, but Canby's blocked it."

Laura raised her head. "Major Canby?" she asked.

"Yes. You know him?"

"I met him at Fort Union."

"He's about the only loyal officer in New Mexico," Mr. Parker said. He glanced at Laura and seemed to decide the topic was too grim for her tender ears, for he smiled and changed the subject. "Do you enjoy dancing, Miss Howland?"

"Yes," Laura said, laying down her spoon, "though I have not been dancing of late."

"Oh, of course not. Forgive me. I was just going to mention that we have little bailes here occasionally. This room has the best floor in town, you see," he added with pride, gesturing toward the long expanse of wood.

Laura smiled. "I'm sure it makes an excellent ballroom."

"They have concerts, too," Uncle Wallace said. "There's a bang-up band at Fort Marcy Post."

"I shall look forward to hearing them," Laura said, rising

from her chair. "Thank you for the excellent dinner, Mr. Parker. Will you pardon me if I retire early?"

"That's right, you rest up," her uncle said. "Tomorrow I'll come round and show you the town."

The gentlemen rose, and Laura left them to seek the quiet of her room. The dinner had done much to restore her spirits, and as she went out into the garden she sighed. It would be impossible, of course, for this place to compare with home, but it was not so very unpleasant, after all. Mr. Parker was certainly a gentleman, and he had said there were other good people in Santa Fé. If she could find intelligent company, who perhaps even shared her views, she thought she would do very well.

She glanced past the garden at the opposite portal, where sunlight was beginning to slant in beneath the roof. No guest rooms on that side—only a door into the kitchen and another, standing open now, which appeared to lead into the cantina. A form moved inside, and the hotel clerk came out to lounge in the doorway. Laura quickened her step, feeling the clerk's gaze on her as she hurried to her room and locked the door.

4

To Hon. Caleb B. Smith, Secretary of the Interior, Dear Sir:
I have the honor to acknowledge the receipt of your favor of
the 11th instant, calling the attention of this Department to
the condition of New Mexico and the danger of invasion
from Texas. I take pleasure in saying in reply that the atten-
tion of this Department has been duly given to that subject,
and that measures have been or will be taken commensu-
rate with its importance.

—Simon Cameron, Secretary of War

McIntyre shivered, wishing he'd brought his overcoat. It
was windy on top of Fort Marcy Hill, the sky all gray
clouds, more like winter than mid-June. Perhaps the farmers would get the rain they'd been praying for.

"Give over, Cummings," he said to his friend, who was
shedding his own jacket. "It's too cold for this, and
besides, he's not worth the trouble."

Cummings's face was stubborn as he handed his coat to
McIntyre. "He has offered me an intolerable insult. Would
you have stood for it?"

"I'd have done my best to deck him at Consuelo's, not
challenged him to a duel!" McIntyre said.

"You can't duel, you're in the army," Cummings
retorted.

"You don't have to remind me! I'm not even supposed to
be here. I ought to arrest the lot of you!"

"Arrest us, then." Cummings strode across the wispy
grass toward three men who had just arrived on horseback.

"Damn it, Cummings!" McIntyre said, throwing the coat
over his own shoulders and following his righteous princi-

pal. He glanced back to where their horses were tied to a piñon near the crumbling adobe walls of Fort Marcy. The grand old maid of forts looked gloomy under the dull sky, a silent monument to the power of threat, its virgin battlements unmanned.

McIntyre hurried to get between Cummings and the others, doing his proper duty as a second. Phillips and his friend stood by their horses, talking. The third man was Dr. Connelly, who actually lived nearly a hundred miles away in Peralta but kept a store in Santa Fé and had had the bad luck to be present at the disturbance the night before at Doña Consuelo's. McIntyre gave him a nod and received a weary look in return.

"I'm too old for these shenanigans," Connelly sighed, but though his silvered hair might be considered proof of this, McIntyre knew the old fellow had plenty of energy in him.

McIntyre turned to Cummings. "Maybe Phillips will apologize," he said. "Let me talk to Snodgrass."

"No," Cummings answered. "There's nothing to discuss."

McIntyre sighed. "All right," he said, and together he and Connelly went out to meet Mr. Snodgrass for the inspection of the weapons: matched navy revolvers provided by Connelly, who was to serve as both referee and doctor.

"Beast of a morning," Snodgrass grumbled, slapping at his arms. "Let's get it over with."

Together McIntyre and Snodgrass inspected the pistols and loaded each with a single charge. Phillips, being the party challenged, was offered first choice of weapon. He seemed as unconcerned as if they were merely out to shoot rabbits instead of each other. McIntyre and Snodgrass placed their principals back to back, then retired while Connelly counted out fifteen paces. The men turned and aimed, but only Cummings's pistol fired. Phillips swore, and McIntyre hastened to Cummings.

"There," he said. "Honor satisfied, and no one the worse for it. Come on, let's get breakfast."

Cummings started toward Phillips instead, and McIntyre had to run a few steps to get between them. Connelly, who had gone with Snodgrass to look at the gun, raised his head and called out "Broke the cap." McIntyre kept a nervous eye on his principal as the five men came together.

"Heard your ball go by, Joe," Phillips said, looking up with a taunting grin. "Guess it's your lucky day."

"Will you take back what you said?" Cummings asked to which both seconds protested. Phillips spoke over them.

"Sure, I'll take it back. You're not a nigger-lover."

"Sir, that word is unacceptable," Cummings said, his frown deepening.

"Come on, Joseph." McIntyre took Cummings by the arm. "You might as well argue with a windmill. He's only trying to see how far he can goad you."

"I am sorry that I missed my aim," Cummings said, fury underrunning his voice.

"God'll rid the world of him when He's ready," McIntyre said.

"Maybe God'll rid the world of you, army mule," Phillips said. McIntyre looked him hard in the eye but said nothing. He hadn't steered Cummings through this mess only to be caught up himself. He led his friend away to their horses, trying to shake off the ugly morning.

Halfway down the hill into Santa Fé, Connelly caught up with them and reined in his horse. "That was blessedly easy," he said. "May I join you for breakfast?"

"Absolutely," McIntyre said. "Consuelo's?"

"That's where Phillips is headed."

"The Exchange, then."

"Phillips works there!" Cummings protested.

"Joe, he won't be in the building," McIntyre exasperated. "I'm not breaking fast at the post, thank you!"

"The Exchange it is," Connelly said. "Champagne and oysters, my boys. Parker just got a new shipment."

McIntyre grinned. "He didn't happen to get it from Connelly & Company, did he?"

Connelly only smiled as they headed down the hill into town.

Laura peered out of the lobby doors at the blue-green mountains, then glanced down the street toward her uncle's room. He had promised to escort her to look at the Loretto Convent and its chapel that afternoon, but apparently his business had detained him. Not caring to go through the cantina to reach his room, she had waited half an hour in the lobby, but her patience was wearing thin.

Well, it was getting late for excursions, anyway, Laura thought. She would content herself with taking a turn around the plaza and do a little shopping, perhaps. She sought out Lupe, the maid who saw to her room, and bribed her with a penny to accompany her.

Outside the air was warm and stiflingly dry. Laura made her way across the busy street with Lupe straggling behind, and strolled along the plaza's south side under the portals, gazing at shop displays. The sun was westering, making her squint as she walked toward it, though it wouldn't set for some time.

In the plaza, three burros stood loaded with firewood piled so high they seemed buried, while their master lounged beneath the cottonwoods smoking a homemade cigarrillo. All the natives smoked them, even the women. Laura had been fascinated to watch them rolling the tobacco in little squares cut from dried corn husks. Many of the Americans staying at the Exchange had also acquired the unattractive habit, but at least Mr. Parker restricted them to smoking in the cantina and in their own rooms.

On the whole, Laura couldn't complain. Since their arrival her uncle had of necessity been away quite a bit, catching up on his business, but she had found it easy to sleep through the long afternoons, making up for the rest she had lost on the journey. She was beginning to feel, if not at home, at least more at ease.

"Miss Howland?"

Surprised to hear her name, Laura turned to see a young man in military uniform staring intently at her. His face was familiar: blue eyes under a high, tanned brow, framed by dark-brown hair. With him was a lady of perhaps forty, with delicate bones and large, deep-set eyes that looked sad despite her smile.

Laura recovered her composure enough to give the gentleman a slight bow. Fort Union, that was where she had met him. "Good afternoon, Mr.—"

"McIntyre," he supplied. "Is your uncle with you?"

"No," Laura said, raising an eyebrow.

"Oh, excuse me," he said hastily. "Miss Howland, may I present you to Mrs. Canby?"

"How do you do?" the lady said in a soft, rich voice.

"How do you do, ma'am?" said Laura, curtseying. "I had the pleasure of meeting Major Canby at Fort Union."

Mrs. Canby smiled. "I take it you are new in Santa Fé?"

"Yes, I came in on the last mail with my uncle."

Mrs. Canby smiled warmly. "Then you must come to tea. May I send you a card? To the Exchange, I presume?"

"Thank you, yes," Laura said gratefully. "That's very kind of you!"

"We are always happy to welcome another lady," Mrs. Canby said. "They are a rare commodity in New Mexico. Now, if you will excuse me, I have some business to conduct. Were you on your way to the post office?"

"No, I was just taking a turn around the plaza," Laura said, glancing at Lupe.

"Why don't you go with her, Lacey?" Mrs. Canby told her companion. "Do you mind, Miss Howland? He can tell you all the history." With a smile, Mrs. Canby went into the post office, leaving Laura facing the lieutenant.

"May I escort you?" he asked, with a bow.

"If you wouldn't find it dull."

"Not at all," he said. "Have you seen the governor's palace?"

"Not up close."

"It's got quite a history," Mr. McIntyre said as they

began to stroll toward the long building on the north side of the plaza. "Been besieged, burned, built over—"

Laura stopped, staring in amazement at the roof of the palace, which now that she was closer she saw was covered with a profusion of wildflowers in full bloom, swaying slightly in the breeze. Mr. McIntyre followed her gaze and laughed. "Happens every year," he said. "There are five feet of earth on the roof. It's to soak up the rain, you see, only when there's a real deluge it leaks."

"How distressing," Laura said, continuing along the front of the building. "The governor must find it very uncomfortable."

"Oh, it's not the governor's house anymore, not since Mexican days. It's used for offices and meetings and such. And our headquarters. In fact, we're just cleaning up the mess Colonel Loring left."

Laura stole a glance at his face, remembering Captain Sibley's departure from Fort Union. Lieutenant McIntyre had been one of the few officers who had declined Sibley's invitation to join the Confederate army, a choice of which she approved.

"It is a pleasure to find an acquaintance in Santa Fé," she said. "I had not expected to see anyone here from Fort Union."

"Major Canby offered me a place on his staff," he said. "He's commanding the northern part of the department now." They had reached the eastern end of the palace, and Mr. McIntyre paused. "I'm happier here, I must admit," he said. "It gets lonely out on the plains." The smile that accompanied these words was warm enough to make Laura look away.

"What are those mountains called?" she asked, indicating the range that looked over the town from the east and north.

Mr. McIntyre followed her gaze. "Sangre de Cristo. It means 'Blood of Christ.' "

"Charming," Laura said with a laugh.

"It's because they turn red at sunset. The Spanish are very romantic, you know."

They are not the only ones, Laura found herself thinking. It was pleasant to be admired, even if only because one was a rare commodity. She turned south toward the hotel and passed a doorway standing open into a wine shop within which were a number of Mexicans making merry, along with a couple of soldiers. All were evidently quite drunk. Laura continued to the Exchange with a brisker step.

"Thank you, Mr. McIntyre," she said as they reached the hotel's door. "I shall release you now, as I see Mrs. Canby is finished with her business." She nodded toward the post office, where Mrs. Canby stood talking to a Mexican lady and gentleman in American dress.

"Happy to be of service, Miss Howland," the lieutenant said, bowing. "At any time," he added. Laura favored him with a brief smile before stepping into the hotel.

"Thank you, Lupe," she said, turning to the maid and handing her the promised coin. "Gracias."

The girl smiled, bobbed a curtsey, and vanished into the cantina. Laura passed through the office to the placita and strolled down the portal, gazing at the roses. Stopping by her door, she turned and glanced up at the mountains. Yes, they were just beginning to turn pink. Laura's lips curved in a soft smile. Santa Fé, she decided, was improving.

As he entered the adjutant's office, McIntyre was obliged to dodge a green apple that flew past his head and smacked against the adobe wall.

"Traitor!" accused his attacker, a lanky lieutenant leaning back in a chair with his feet up on the adjutant's desk.

"Me?" McIntyre asked indignantly. "What have I done to you, Nico?"

"Been flirting with the new gal," Lieutenant Nicodemus said. He bit into another apple and made a face, then threw it after the first. "Saw you walking her round the plaza."

"She needed an escort," McIntyre protested, privately delighted. He came forward to pick through the shallow basket of apples on the desk. They were all small, hard, and green.

"Mrs. Canby told him to, I expect," said Anderson from the desk. His uniform immaculate—unmarred by any hint of dust, unlike those of his companions. He was going through a jumbled stack of papers, methodically sorting them into piles. "Nico, would you light the lamp? It's getting dark in here."

"I'll get it," McIntyre offered, and rummaged a cluttered bookshelf for a matchbox.

"I think that was Anderson's polite way of asking me to get my boots off his desk," said Nicodemus, smoothing the ends of his dark, recently grown mustache. "Didn't work, Allen."

"Didn't think it would," Anderson said stoically.

McIntyre lit the oil lamp suspended from the ceiling and flopped into a chair. "Where's himself?" he asked.

"Meeting with the governor," Nicodemus replied. "Told us to wait here. He'll probably have us running errands all night."

"Or riding off in all directions tomorrow," Anderson added. "Is she pretty?"

"Very," McIntyre said with a grin. "Actually, I met her at Fort Union. She remembered me," he added smugly.

"Traitor," Nicodemus remarked again. The sound of a brisk tread out in the corridor caused him to remove his feet from the desk in a hurry, and all three came to attention as Major Canby strode into the room.

"Good evening, gentlemen," he said. "In my office, please."

They followed him into the next room, a large sala that had been Colonel Loring's office until he had turned the reins over to Canby. Officially Loring was "going to inspect the southern forts," but he had taken his entire staff with him, including Lieutenant-Colonel Crittenden, and everyone knew he was bound for Richmond like Sibley and the rest. Canby was now, effectively if not officially, in command of the whole department.

McIntyre lit the oil-lamp chandelier, revealing latent signs of the jumbled mess in which Loring had left the commander's office. Most of the shelves and drawers had been set to rights, though piles of papers still sat here and there waiting to be sorted and refiled. Anderson and the others had been working for a week to restore it to order, and the job still wasn't done.

"Sit down, gentlemen," the major said, seating himself at his desk. He reached into his coat and pulled out a cigar, which he placed unlit in his mouth. From another pocket he drew two letters, one of which he handed to Anderson. "These both arrived today. I took the liberty of opening them, as Colonel Loring was not present to attend to them. That one's from Sibley."

McIntyre read over Anderson's shoulder. " 'My Dear Loring: We are at last under the glorious banner of the Confederate States of America—' "

Anderson made a sound of disgust and handed the letter to McIntyre, who scanned it. " 'Four companies of Texans to garrison Fort Bliss'?" He glanced at Canby, who merely gestured to the note. McIntyre hastily read the rest, which dealt mostly with the supplies available near Fort Bliss and advice for Loring's departure: advice that had arrived too late to benefit Loring but that offered considerable insight to his successor.

" 'Movements are in contemplation from this direction which I am not at liberty to disclose.' It doesn't sound good, sir," McIntyre said, passing the letter to Nicodemus.

"Nor does this," Canby said, gesturing with the second letter. "I won't trouble you to read it. It's from army headquarters, ordering Loring to have me march all the infantry in the department to Leavenworth."

McIntyre's jaw dropped. *"All?"*

"All. Allen, you'll draft a response for me, please. We'll say they'll be delayed until we can arrange transport." He handed the order to Anderson, who glanced through it.

"How can the department be run without infantry?" Nicodemus asked. "The Rifles can't do it alone—"

"New Mexico has been authorized to raise two regiments of volunteers," Canby said. *"If* we can scrape up that many. The governor has promised to do what he can, but we'll have to try to build them around the militia."

Canby's lieutenants were silent. The militia consisted of poorly armed Mexicans—farmers and ranchers, mostly—many of whom were scarcely aware they were American citizens. Canby had dealt with some of them on the winter Navajo campaign, in which McIntyre had taken part. They knew the land and the Indians' ways better than the Americans, and hadn't hesitated to rub Canby's nose in that fact, hanging a Navajo captive the major had wanted to interrogate. It did not bode well for future cooperation.

"You'll be carrying messages tomorrow," Canby continued. "D'Amours will go to St. Vrain and Carson in Taos. Lacey to Chaves; Nico, you'll go south and talk to Stapleton, see what he can scrape up around Socorro."

"I'd never go south," Nicodemus muttered.

"What's that?" Canby asked softly, his clear eyes intent on the lieutenant's face.

"Nothing, sir."

"We'll consolidate our forces and hope we can stall their departure until the volunteers can take over for them," Canby continued. He rose and strode to a map of the Territory that hung on the wall. On it were marked all the military outposts in New Mexico, a number of them penciled in Anderson's neat hand. "We'll withdraw from Forts Breckenridge and Buchanan—"

"What about Tucson?" said Nicodemus. "The Apaches—"

"Tucson will have to fend for itself, I'm afraid. We'll concentrate troops at Fort Fillmore, Fort Union, and Albuquerque. Allen, make a note to draft a letter to Governor Gilpin in Colorado. See if he can garrison Fort Garland. That'll help."

"Yes, sir," Anderson said, writing in his pocket notebook, "and congratulations on your brevet to lieutenant-colonel, sir."

McIntyre raised an inquiring eyebrow, and Anderson tapped the order from Washington.

"Thank you," Canby said briefly, his attention still on the

map. "Fort Fillmore will keep an eye on Bliss. We'll have to strengthen Union as well—I've had word there may be a force concentrating in the north of Texas. That information is not to leave the room, gentlemen," Canby added.

McIntyre nodded, as did the others. The major wasn't the jolliest of commanders but he was honest and fair, and his staff, though new in his service, admired him. McIntyre guessed he would rather die than harm Canby, and was sure the others felt the same.

"That's all for now," the major said. "Rest up. You have long rides ahead." With the cigar still clenched in his teeth, he returned to his desk, frowning over the papers there. His young staff officers retreated quietly and spent a few minutes tidying the outer chamber, which meant chasing down the apples that had rolled all around the floor and taking them out to the horses.

"I'm starved," Nicodemus said as they finished. "Anderson, you ready for supper?"

"Go on without me," Anderson said, turning back toward the palace. "Got to draft those letters."

"Slave of duty," Nicodemus remarked.

McIntyre gave a halfhearted smile as he followed Nicodemus up the street to the post. Duty, a slippery word. He wondered where Owens was; halfway to Richmond, he supposed. He hoped the war back east would end quickly so things could be normal again.

On Saturdays Jamie stayed home and helped with the ranch work, which since Matt had gone meant catching up everything that hadn't been done during the week. The massive demand for more beeves to feed the volunteer recruits put pressure on the Russells to get more of the herd market-ready, but Jamie knew better than to complain. The ranch was having a good year, and Poppa was carefully setting money aside for the uncertain future, some in war bonds, some in gold. Poppa never put complete trust in any one person or thing.

Today they were branding calves, a hideous and

exhausting chore made more frustrating by Gabe's inexperience. Poppa rounded up the calves while the boys did the branding, switching jobs so that Gabe could learn how to hold the bawling calf without getting kicked, brand it quick for a clean mark, and castrate the bulls not chosen for breeding. As a result of the teaching, the branding took about twice as long as it should have and involved more than the usual number of bruises from stray kicks. By the time the three boys set the last calf free they were hot, filthy, and sullen, with the stench of burned flesh clinging in their nostrils.

"You boys get cleaned up for supper," Poppa said, getting down from Smokey's back. He looked tired, Jamie thought as he watched his father turn out the horse and go into the house.

"Come on," Dan said, drawing up a full bucket from the well.

They doused the coals, washed off their gear, and put everything away. Jamie turned to fetch Cocoa in from the corral, but Emmaline was there ahead of him, leading Buffalo and Cocoa toward the barn. He caught Pip and followed her.

"Don't you come near me, James Russell!" Emma called over her shoulder. "I'll feed, you go clean up."

Jamie put Pip in his stall and went back to the well where his brothers were taking turns dumping water over each other. He joined them until his arms were aching from drawing up the bucket and they were all three soaking wet and laughing. Jamie scrubbed at Gabe's head with a cake of soap, and his own, then held Gabe and shrieked while Daniel poured cold water over them both.

"What's that?" Daniel asked, pausing with the empty bucket in his hands.

Jamie looked up to where a dark line had appeared to the east on the Overland Trail. "Wagon train?"

"No." Daniel shook his head, frowning.

They watched while the line resolved into a column of mounted soldiers, the Lone Star flag hanging limp from the color-bearer's staff. Daniel looked at Jamie, and in silent accord they scrambled into the clean clothes Emma had lain over the rails for them, then ran down to the trail where it passed near the house, with Gabe scrabbling behind and calling to them to wait up.

"Soldiers don't march this road," Daniel said, panting as they stopped in the shade of an oak tree on top of a hill.

Jamie nodded, leaning against the trunk. Soldiers went to training camps up at Austin until they were ready to head east to Richmond, like the camp Matthew had gone to. These men were riding west, on the trail that ran through wilderness to Mexico and California.

The soldiers were armed with rifles and revolvers. Behind them came a train of supply wagons pulled by mules. Officers rode up and down the line shouting orders to keep together. The column had maybe three hundred men in all.

"Where you headed?" Jamie called out.

Two of the men riding by exchanged a glance, then one grinned and yelled back, "Out to the plains, to shoot buffalo. Why don't you come along?"

"Wish I could!" Jamie shouted.

"You ain't mean enough, boy!" the other called. "Colonel Baylor'd eat you for breakfast!" The men near him laughed, and Jamie felt his cheeks start to burn.

"Come on," Daniel said, turning away. "We're late for supper. C'mon, Gabe."

"Aww, I just got here!"

Jamie followed, listening to Gabe's wheedling and Dan's quiet sense, and wishing he was mean enough to eat Colonel Baylor instead of being eaten. When they got to the house Emmaline was waiting on the porch with her hands on her hips. "Hurry up!" she said. "Supper's on the table, and Momma's got a surprise!"

Jamie and his brothers hurried inside and took their places at the table where Momma and Poppa waited. There was a soft light in Momma's eyes and a smile on her lips as she said grace. Jamie glanced at Emmaline but didn't catch her eye, so when Momma picked up her fork he dug in. Hungry from the hard work of branding, he made quick business of two helpings of chicken and dumplings, and argued with Gabe over the last drumstick.

It wasn't until the dishes had been cleared and Emmaline had brought out a cherry cobbler that Momma revealed her surprise. She cast a beaming look around the table at her family, then pulled a thick letter out of her pocket. "It's from Matthew," she announced, unfolding it. Jamie glanced at Emmaline, who smiled. It was good that Matt had written, for though he'd started out true to his promise they hadn't had a letter from him in some time.

"'Dear Momma and Poppa and All,'" Momma read. "'I am well and happy and hope you are the same—'"

The letter began like the others all had, with tents and drill and the new friends he'd made in his company. Then Matt went on (Momma's voice caught a little) to announce the Tom Green Rifles' departure for Richmond with three other companies, starting on the train to Houston and Beaumont, taking a steamer from there to Niblett's Bluff, then marching through the endless swamps of Louisiana. Finding it impossible to post a letter every day, Matt had settled for writing some each night so that the letter was like a journal of his march, and he'd mailed the pages from New Orleans before boarding the train that would take him all the way to Richmond. The letter ended with a recommendation for Daniel to hurry up and join, or he'd miss all the fun when the army got to Washington.

Jamie could picture Matt's march, following long, muddy roads, one small cog in the great military machine gathering power in the northeast. He found himself cutting his cobbler into tiny bits with his spoon, and pushed the dish away.

"There were soldiers on our road today," Daniel said. "Did you see them, Poppa?"

"No," pouring himself some coffee.

"They were going west," Gabe said, not to be left out. "To shoot buffalo, they said."

"Probably 'cause they can't buy enough beef," Poppa

said in a tone that meant he'd heard enough of the subject.

"I'll go brush down the horses," Jamie said, unable to sit still any longer. He got up, gave Momma a hasty kiss, and escaped into the warm blue evening. He ran down to the trail just for the sake of running, and stood on the same rise to squint westward into the fading light, but there was nothing left to see of the westbound column. He walked back to the barn, lighted the lamp, and grabbed a brush. As he entered her stall, Cocoa looked around and nickered at him. He put a halter on her and led her out into the main part of the barn, where there was just a faint hope of a breeze to cool them down.

"Good girl," he murmured, stroking her neck. She bent her head around to bump his ear and whuffed at him. Laughing, he started to brush her sweat-caked back.

"Should've brushed you right away. Sorry, girl," he said. Cocoa sighed and shifted her weight while Jamie scrubbed at the stiff, dry fur where the saddle had been. Jamie sighed, too. Cocoa always made him feel better. Maybe it was just that it was soothing to touch her warm fur, her soft muzzle. Maybe it was because she never asked him hard questions. He asked enough of them himself.

"There you are," Emmaline said from the doorway. She grabbed a halter and opened Buffalo's stall. "Thought I'd give you a hand."

Jamie went to the tack room for a curry comb to work out the caked parts of Cocoa's coat. Emmaline came in after him and picked up another set of brushes.

"Matty wrote a good letter, didn't he?" she said. "Momma was so pleased."

Jamie nodded, not really in the mood to talk. He followed her out and watched her start to brush Buffalo down.

"You'll get hair on your dress," he said, turning away to work the curry comb over Cocoa's back.

"I don't care," Emma replied. Something in her voice made Jamie look up. She kept brushing for a minute, then glanced up, eyes bright with tears. "Momma got a letter from Aunt May, too."

"Oh, Em." Jamie dropped the comb and went to hug his sister, who sniffed angrily and rubbed at her eyes.

"She wants me to go to Houston in the fall."

Jamie hugged her tight. He wanted to tell her she didn't have to go, but it would just be a lie.

"I wish I could go join the army," Emma said.

"They won't take you," Jamie said, thinking of the soldiers that had ridden west. "You're too mean."

Emma gave an indignant cry and pushed him away, then laughed. "You're just jealous, James Russell!"

"You're so right." Jamie grinned as he retrieved her brush and handed it to her. "Maybe Aunt May'd take Buffalo instead," he said, playing with the gelding's ears. "Want to go to Houston, boy?"

"He doesn't need to. He's already got better manners than me."

"But he can't cook worth beans," Jamie said, and laughter chased off the last of Emma's tears.

5

I question very much whether a sufficient force for the defense of the Territory can be raised within its limits.

—Ed. R. S. Canby

McIntyre urged his horse up the yellow grass slopes in the direction of Hacienda de Ojuelos. It had taken him three days to reach Tomé, and Ojuelos was over a dozen miles farther. He glanced back toward the river and the round mound of Cerro de Tomé, topped with ten-foot crosses where the villagers liked to leave offerings. The sun was already descending, glinting gold on the river's surface. McIntyre took off his hat to wipe his brow; the dark wool of his uniform was hot.

Passing a large flock of sheep tended by peons, he climbed up to a level plateau from which he could see a distant clump of trees. He spurred his horse to a trot and made for the spot of green at the feet of the Manzano Mountains. Soon it resolved into a cottonwood grove shading a large hacienda built of adobe and stone. There were loopholes in the walls, McIntyre noticed. Manuel Chaves took no chances with his family's safety in a country Apaches had been ravaging for decades.

McIntyre reined in under the trees, dismounted, and allowed his horse to drink from a small acequia that trickled past the thirsty roots on its way to feed a walled garden. A Mexican paused in repairing a wagon to gaze up at him. The man wore a sarape and dusty cotton breeches with seams that hung open below the knee.

"I have a message for Señor Chaves," McIntyre said,

pulling Canby's dispatch out of his coat. "Uh—mensaje de—"

"Here, señor," Chaves called, coming out of the house. "It is Lieutenant McIntyre, yes? You were on the campaign last winter."

"You have a good memory, Colonel."

Chaves smiled and came forward to shake hands. He was shorter than McIntyre, little more than five and a half feet, but McIntyre knew there was a will of steel beneath the benign, handsome face. Chestnut hair framed high cheeks and gray eyes that missed very little. Chaves's ancestors had come to New Mexico with Oñate, and he himself had won considerable respect as a lieutenant-colonel of militia in the Navajo campaigns. He had a quiet dignity much like Canby's, though McIntyre had seen it flare into sudden anger. El Leoncito, the Mexicans called him.

"What brings you to Ojuelos?" said Chaves.

For answer McIntyre handed him the dispatch. "From Colonel Canby," he said.

"Colonel?" Chaves's eyebrows went up as he opened the letter. "Your war is bringing you promotions."

"And you, too," McIntyre said. "Command of Fort Fauntleroy."

Chaves smiled slightly and folded the page. "Colonel Loring was here before you, señor," he said in a mild tone. "He offered to make me a full colonel in the Confederate army."

Hell, McIntyre thought. Dismayed, he stared at the acequia. At this rate, the Confederates would build an unbeatable force. For an instant he saw the place he could have had, at the head of a company perhaps.

"I was sorry to disappoint Señor Loring," Chaves continued, "but having sworn allegiance to the United States, I am bound to give my services to her flag."

McIntyre raised his head to look at Chaves, relieved. "You'll take it? It's fairly remote—"

"Oh, I know the place well. I came close to dying near

there, many years ago. Are there American soldiers at the fort?"

"They're being recalled," McIntyre said. "But the governor's been authorized to form two regiments of volunteers. If you can raise enough Mexicans—"

"We are not Mexicans, señor," Chaves said quietly. "We have not been Mexicans for fifteen years."

Silenced, McIntyre glanced at the dust beneath his boots. El Leoncito was not a man one ought to offend. When he looked up again, Chaves wore a hint of a smile.

"Stay the night," he said. "I'll give you a letter for Colonel Canby."

"Thank you, sir."

Chaves called one of his peons to see to McIntyre's horse and led him into the hacienda. It was spacious inside, with plastered walls in soft hues and good wool rugs on the floor. Lamps had already been lit. Chaves introduced McIntyre to several men—all cousins, it seemed—who were helping with the ranch, and to his two young sons, who addressed him in halting English. Señora Chaves and her shy daughter served the evening meal on a simple table pushed up against a wall; half the family sat on the banco built into the wall and the rest in chairs. The meal consisted of beans, tortillas, and a savory mutton stew pungent with the summer's first crop of chile verde. The spice burned, but the meat was tasty and McIntyre was very hungry, so he ate while his eyes watered, and tried to understand the rapid chatter of the Mexicans. Natives, he amended mentally. Natives of New Mexico. New Mexicans, Mexicans, Spanish. He wondered what they called themselves. He doubted it was Americans, despite their citizenship.

The men glanced at him now and then, and he knew he was under discussion. He watched them, listening for any derogatory phrases and resolving to improve his Spanish. Chaves addressed several remarks to him in English, to which he replied politely.

When the meal was over, McIntyre went outside to check on his horse. Dusk was falling. Somewhere in the hills a coyote started its skirling cry, sending a shiver up his spine. Strange country, he thought for the thousandth time since he'd come to New Mexico. Harsh and beautiful and savage and peaceful. Never the same two days running. He turned back to the ranch house, tired, and suddenly longing for the more familiar hills of Tennessee.

"Battle" had been whispered for days now. It was on the lips of every gossip in San Antonio. Jamie listened to the words but they were empty. No battle had occurred, though news had been expected hourly for days, even weeks. The army was massing in northern Virginia, and Federal troops were gathering to oppose them. There would be a battle, no doubt; a big one. The only question was when.

Matt was there, in Virginia, a thought that made Jamie clench his teeth as he stocked the shelves at Webber's. Matthew had sent another letter from Richmond when he arrived, mostly about the train cars and how the girls had given them presents and kisses at every stop. Nothing more had come and Momma's anxiety grew while her temper shortened. Emmaline bore the brunt of her ill humor. Jamie was impressed at his sister's store of patience. He had to figure she preferred even Momma's sharp tongue to being packed off to Houston.

Jamie finished stacking tins of baking soda and got to his feet. It was almost sunset, still viciously hot. He stretched the cricks out of his back and gazed around the empty store.

"Shall I close up, Mr. Webber?" he asked.

"I'll do it," his employer said from his desk. "Go on home, Jamie. I'll see you tomorrow."

Jamie hung up his apron, fetched his hat, and headed out the back door. Cocoa greeted him with a whinny, and he saddled her up and rode down to the post office as he did every other Monday to check for a letter from Matt. A crowd was gathering on the plaza. Jamie heard "battle" again, but this had a different sound to it. He spurred Cocoa to a trot and dismounted as he reached the crowd.

"Mr. Cutter!" he called, spotting the blacksmith. "What is it?"

"There's been a battle!" Cutter said. "The mayor just got an express! We won, Jamie! We won!"

Jamie laughed and clapped him on the back. "Where was it?"

"Virginia. Manassas. Five thousand casualties."

"Five *thousand?*" Jamie whispered. His heart started to thump in his chest. A gunshot nearby made him wince, and Cocoa sidled.

"Yeeaa-hoy!" a man nearby shouted, and others took up the cry. More guns were fired into the air. Someone started singing "Dixie," and more voices joined the song.

Jamie led Cocoa out of the crowd and mounted up, riding hard for home. Sensing his mood, she willingly raced down the trail, and was almost winded by the time they reached the ranch. Daniel and Gabe were just going in for supper, but Daniel turned back when he saw Jamie galloping up. He ran over to help unsaddle the mare.

"What is it?" he asked.

"A battle," Jamie said. "Gabe, bring her a bucket of water," he called, slapping Cocoa's rump as he turned her into the corral.

"Where?" Dan demanded, hefting the saddle onto a rail.

"Virginia. Come inside so I can tell everyone at once."

The rest of the family were already at the table when the three boys burst in. Jamie paused to catch his breath, and saw a shadow of fear cross Momma's face.

"There was a battle in Virginia," he said. "We won."

"Oh!" Emmaline cried, her eyes lighting up. Poppa was on his feet, demanding details Jamie couldn't give. Gabe was yapping like an excited pup, and Momma reached out a hand toward Jamie, asking, "Matthew?"

"Don't know, Momma. We won't hear for a while. The news just came in."

"He's fine, Momma," Emmaline said firmly. "Matty's just fine."

The family could talk of nothing else over dinner and

made Jamie repeat everything he'd heard over and over. Momma turned a little pale when she heard about the casualties, but Daniel quickly pointed out how little it was compared to the size of the army and that most of them were likely to be Yankees, since they had lost the fight.

"Did you check at the post office?" Momma asked.

"I'll do it first thing tomorrow," Jamie promised. "If there's a letter I'll bring it straight home. Mr. Webber won't mind."

Momma smiled and patted Jamie's wrist, then went off to help Emmaline with the dishes while the menfolk sat in the family room. Quiet fell, and Jamie watched Poppa rock back and forth in his chair pretending to read yesterday's newspaper. Dan was also watching. Finally he spoke.

"Likely they'll call for more volunteers," he said quietly. "Think I'll join up this time."

Poppa continued rocking for a minute. Then he lowered the paper to look at Daniel.

"Gabe's doing fine now," Dan went on. "He can cut as good as me—"

"What about your mother?" Poppa said. "You see how she is about Matt."

"I know," Dan said. "She'll be all right. It's important now, don't you see, Poppa? Now it's a war in earnest."

Poppa held Daniel's gaze for a minute. Jamie had expected him to blow up, but he didn't. He just sat there looking tired and a little old.

"All right, Dan. Look out for Matthew if you can."

"I will, Poppa."

Poppa raised the paper again, signaling the end of the conversation. Jamie met Daniel's eyes, which were blazing in triumph. It was Dan's kind of victory, silent and sweeping. With one accord the boys rose and went out to tend the horses.

"Sorry, Professor," Daniel said, taking charge of Buffalo. "But I'm a better fighter. And a better shot—"

"I know," Jamie said, swallowing the lump in his throat. "You'll be a better soldier, I know."

"Your time will come. This won't be a short war."

A chill tightened the muscles of Jamie's shoulders. War was a word that had never much impressed him. In school it meant famous generals and dates to be memorized, not something your brothers got involved in.

Daniel was speaking, planning aloud when and where he would go. He would take Buffalo, of course, and the pistol he'd bought with his own money. The army would supply a rifle, or he'd buy one if need be. As he listened, Jamie realized that Dan had already left some time ago in his heart. He had thought it all out, merely waiting for the best moment to inform Poppa of his intentions. And he'd chosen the moment well, Jamie thought. Dan would make a good general.

The next morning Daniel packed his saddlebags with all the treats Momma pressed on him and rode into town with Jamie on his way to Austin, where volunteer companies were forming. There wasn't much they hadn't already said, so they rode in silence most of the way. Dan waited while Jamie checked at the post office, but there was no letter from Matt. At Webber's an army horse was tied at the rail out front—Captain Martin's big gray. Jealous at the reminder, Jamie swallowed and looked away, offering a hand to Daniel. "Good luck, soldier," he said.

Dan smiled and shook hands. "Good luck, Professor." Then he turned, clicked to Buffalo, and headed up the street at a trot. Jamie dismounted and led Cocoa to Cutter's corral out back. As he hurried up the back steps of the store he sighed, a dozen small duties crowding in his mind. Grateful for the distraction, he hung up his coat and hat, donned his apron, and went out to the counter. Martin was standing by the stove drinking coffee with Mr. Webber.

"Good morning, Mr. Webber. Captain Martin," Jamie said, putting on a friendly smile that he didn't really feel.

"Morning, Russell," the captain said. "Have you heard the news?"

"About the battle? Yes, I heard last night." Jamie took out an inventory list and began counting spools of thread.

He heard Martin's boots striking hollow on the floor as the captain approached.

"We're raising three new regiments," Martin said. "I've been made quartermaster for one of them."

"Oh. Congratulations," said Jamie, not wanting to think about it. He lost count of the thread and started over. "Did you come to put in an order?" he said.

"I'd like to give you an order. A number of orders, in fact."

Jamie looked up and saw Martin break into a grin.

"I've been authorized to commission an assistant," the captain said. "I'd like it to be you, Jamie."

A spool slipped from Jamie's fingers and clattered away on the shelf. "Me?"

Martin nodded. "You've got all the skills it takes. It's not very glorious work, mind, but a lieutenant makes good pay."

Jamie caught his breath. *"Lieutenant?"*

Martin's grin broadened. "I need someone I don't have to train. I'm still A.Q.M. for the department, besides gearing up my regiment. I'm swamped, Jamie. Will you come?"

Jamie glanced at Mr. Webber who had stayed by the stove. Now the merchant came forward, a smile curling his lips. "It's all right," he said. "I can manage."

"Thank you, sir!" Jamie said, a swell of excitement going through him. It was dampened a moment later by the thought of what Poppa would say. He turned to Martin. "I don't know if I can. My father might not allow it."

"Let's go discuss it with him, shall we?" Martin said. "You don't mind, Mr. Webber?"

"Not at all." He offered Jamie a hand. "Best of luck, son."

Jamie thanked him again, shaking hands, then hurried out to the corral to saddle Cocoa. His heart was going like thunder, and he couldn't help glancing up the road toward Austin as he and Martin mounted up. *Lieutenant,* he kept thinking over and over. Lieutenant, without ever marching a step. Dan would be shocked. Matt would be livid.

Jamie found himself grinning, and glanced up at the captain.

"My older brother just left to join," he said. "Poppa won't like letting me go, too."

"I'll just have to convince him how vital you are," Martin said. "A good quartermaster's worth his weight in gold. It's not something just anyone can do well. Takes a thinking man."

Jamie's mind was in a whirl. He had a hundred questions but he saved them, not wanting to raise his hopes too high. Poppa could say no. Would say no, almost certainly at first. Jamie hoped Captain Martin's easy charm would have an effect.

"You know it won't be like regular soldiering," Martin warned. "We'll be away from the regiment a lot. Had you thought about joining before?"

Jamie nodded.

"Anxious to carry a rifle?"

"Just to be in the army," Jamie said with a shrug.

Martin laughed. "You'll do, then."

As they rode into the yard Gabe was saddling Smokey and Pip. He gaped up at Martin, then hollered "Poppa!"

Jamie jumped down and led Cocoa and Martin's gray to the rail. Poppa came out of the barn, and when he saw Martin his brows drew together.

"Poppa," Jamie said, "this is Captain Martin. He's the quartermaster I told you about." Quartermaster, echoed Jamie's brain. Lieutenant quartermaster.

"How do you do, Mr. Russell," Martin said. "Pleasure to meet you."

Poppa shook hands, glancing from Martin to Jamie. "My son Gabriel," he said, putting a hand on Gabe's shoulder.

"Howdy, Gabriel," said Martin, shaking hands with him too.

"Go on inside, Gabe," Poppa said. "Tell Momma we've got company." He watched Gabe run to the house, then turned back to Martin. "What can I do for you, Captain?"

"I won't waste your time, sir," Martin said. "I want to recruit Jamie as my assistant. He'll be a first lieutenant, second in command of my detail."

Poppa glanced at Jamie, then out over the corral. "I've given two sons to the army already," he said.

"I understand, sir, but it won't be like losing him. We're stationed at department headquarters in San Antonio, gearing up the new regiments."

Jamie held his breath. Poppa was looking at Martin with the glare in his eyes like he got from reading about the government in the paper. "I can't spare him," he said gruffly.

The door of the house banged open. Momma was on the porch, coming toward them with small, quick steps. "Is there a letter?" she asked, then faltered as she saw Captain Martin. "Matthew?" she said, her voice breaking.

"No, Momma," Jamie said. "Nothing yet."

"Oh." Momma's eyes wandered down, then up to the captain's.

"Momma, this is Captain Martin. You remember I spoke about him—"

"Oh, yes. How do you do, Captain?"

"Ma'am," Martin said, touching his hat.

"We'd better go inside," Poppa said, heading for the house.

Emmaline had seen them coming and brought out a plate of fresh corn cakes. "There's coffee brewing," she said, leading the way to the living room.

"Emmaline, this is Captain Martin," said Jamie. "He's the assistant quartermaster for the Department of Texas."

"Well, my!" Emmaline said, dropping him a curtsey.

"How do, Miss Russell," Martin said as he removed his hat.

Emmaline looked up at Martin as if something about him surprised her, then she said, "How do you do?" and scurried off toward the kitchen. Everyone else sat down, Momma and Poppa in their chairs, Jamie and Martin on the sofa. Gabe plopped himself down on the floor by

Momma's chair, reaching up for a piece of corn cake. Momma picked up her knitting.

"Captain Martin wants to make Jamie a quartermaster," Poppa said.

Momma's hands froze for a second, then the needles clicked on. "Oh?" she said. "Thank you, Emmaline. Put it on the table."

Emmaline set down the heavy tray and proceeded to hand out cups of coffee while Momma's needles danced. As she gave Jamie a cup her eyes gleamed fire at him; she seemed as excited as he was. She passed around the corn cakes, then fetched her own cup while Captain Martin made room for her on the sofa.

"Yes, ma'am," the captain was saying. "It wouldn't be much different from the job he has now. We'll be supplying the 4th Texas Mounted Rifles—that's my regiment—as well as helping gear up the other new regiments. Jamie would have to stay in town, but he could come home Sundays. Officer's privilege."

"Officer?" Momma asked.

"Lieutenant," Jamie blurted, unable to keep silent any longer. "I'd be a lieutenant, Momma!"

"Oh, my," Momma said faintly.

"Jamie's ideal for the Q.M. department," Martin went on. "He's intelligent and organized, just what I need in an assistant. So many of the boys that join up would rather carry a rifle, but I know Jamie'd do his job well." The captain sipped his coffee, seemingly unaware of the powerful effect his words were having on Momma. Jamie stole a glance at Emmaline, whose face was pink.

Momma's needles had stopped moving. "James," she said, "you've been wanting to join the army, haven't you?"

"Yes, Momma," Jamie said in a tight voice.

"Well, perhaps . . . Earl?"

"Need him on the ranch," Poppa said. "Sorry, Jamie, but it takes three to mind the herd."

"Then I'll help," Emmaline stated simply.

Jamie sucked in a breath and stared at his sister who, following the captain's example, took a sip from her cup as if what she'd just said hadn't been outrageous.

"Hush, Emma," Poppa said. "This is no time for jokes."

"I'm not joking. I can ride better than Gabe—"

"You cannot!" Gabe protested.

"Can, too. And I can cut cattle—Matty taught me how."

"Emmaline Russell!" Momma cried, aghast.

"And I'd much rather help on the ranch than go visiting," Emmaline continued. "I said so a month ago, didn't I, Jamie?"

Jamie nodded, struggling to keep from breaking out into a gigantic grin.

Poppa stood up. "Now hold on—"

"It's not fair to let Matty and Dan go and make Jamie stay home." Emmaline put down her cup and stared right back at him. "I want to stay. Let him go." There was a light in her eyes the whole family knew well; she got it from her Poppa, and with her as with him it meant trouble if you crossed her. Now she lifted her chin at Poppa, silently daring him. Poppa stared back for a second, then laughed out loud.

"Why, you saucy little cat," he said. "Wait till Aunt May hears you'd rather punch cattle than visit her!"

Emmaline blushed, but she got up and went to him, putting her arms around his shoulders. "I want to do it, Poppa. I love the ranch. And I can do the work, I know I can. Please?"

Jamie stared in amazement at his sister sweetly begging her father to make her a cowhand. A surge of affection for her threatened to choke him and he hastily swallowed some coffee. She would win, he realized. She was every bit as sure to win as Dan had been. He glanced up at Captain Martin, who was watching Emmaline in amused wonder. Poppa had lost all his gloom, smiling down in delight at his audacious daughter.

"No, it is not all settled," Poppa told her, trying to frown. "We'll discuss it later. I'm sure Captain Martin has better things to do than listen to a family squabble."

"You remind me of my duty, Mr. Russell," the captain said, standing up to take his leave. "Ma'am," he said, bowing to Momma. Then he turned to Emmaline and bowed even deeper. "Thank you very much for the coffee, Miss Russell." Emma ducked her head and dropped him a prim curtsey. Martin took a step toward her, smiling. "If your brothers have as much courage as you do, the army's got some fine soldiers in it."

Emmaline glanced up at him. "Thank you, Captain. Pleasure to meet you," she said in a voice so soft it surprised Jamie.

Martin turned to Poppa as Jamie stood up. "I hate to rush you, sir," he said, "but I'm pretty hard pressed. Do you think you could decide in the next day or two?"

"I think we've decided already," Poppa said with a glance at Momma. He put an arm around Emmaline and squeezed her shoulders. "You can go, Jamie. With our blessing."

A shimmer ran down Jamie's nerves. Momma came forward to hug him, murmuring in his ear. He nodded though he hadn't heard a word, and held her tightly, then shook Poppa's hand and gave Emmaline a hug that made her yelp. Captain Martin agreed to wait while Jamie packed a few things. Gabe came and stood in the doorway of their room, and Jamie looked up, then walked over to his younger brother.

"Just you and Poppa now, tiger," he said. "Hold the fort."

"I will," Gabe said. "I don't want to go get shot at. Besides, now I'll have a room to myself."

"That's true." Jamie grinned.

"And I can ride better than Emma," added Gabe.

"Course you can. She just said that."

"You're coming home, right, Jamie?"

Jamie took Gabe by the shoulders. "Every Sunday," he said. "Promise." He hugged Gabe, grabbed his satchel, and went back to the living room.

"Good to meet you all," Martin said. "Hope to see you again."

Jamie took his leave, making promises over his shoulder to Momma as he and Martin went back to their horses. Poppa and Gabe came out to get Pip and Smokey, who stamped with impatience at being tied so long when they'd expected to be out riding herd. Jamie glanced back and saw Momma and Emmaline standing on the porch waving good-bye. He waved back, and exchanged a grin with Martin as they rode down to the trail.

"Quite a sister you have," the captain said.

"Best in the world," Jamie replied, laughing with delight as they turned east and rode back to town.

6

The dependence exclusively of this industrial population upon supplies imported from the States over a line of communication of 800 miles, liable to be cut off by Indians as well as other hostile attacks, makes a complete home organization peremptory for self-defense.

—William Gilpin, Governor of Colorado Territory

O'Brien carried three brace of rabbits into Avery, smiling as he splashed through the stream that ran down the middle of the town. In midsummer it was as pretty a place as could be. Tall pines swayed in the breeze, their feet buried in drifts of flowers, boughs casting green and gold shadows that softened the starkness of miners' huts and tents.

The footpath that led to Dooney's ran between two large boulders called the Trolls by the locals. After the duel, Dooney had hung a U.S. flag from a rod of birch outside his door to forestall further quarrels. O'Brien flicked the banner aside as he ducked his head to enter the tavern, and found Dooney on his knees fixing a table that had broken the night before beneath the combined weight of six miners and four pints of whiskey.

"*Arragh*, Dooney," O'Brien said. "Where's your lady?"

"At home."

"These are for her." O'Brien handed him a pair of rabbits.

A month before, Dooney had gone to Denver City for whiskey and brought back a wife. She was young, not so pretty, but had a sweet voice when she sang songs in the strange tongue of her motherland. The miners showered her with presents and crowded the tavern every night; O'Brien had spent many an hour listening to her, hearing an echo of his mother's voice singing her children to sleep by the fire.

"She'll want me to thank you," said Dooney, getting to his feet and accepting the coneys.

"I'll drink her health, then." O'Brien grinned, and laid down a nugget on the counter.

"Oho! That's a nice little morsel," Dooney exclaimed. He went behind the bar and brought out his scales. "Start of a vein?"

"Could be. Too soon to tell." O'Brien watched him measure the gold and count out twenty-two dollars in coin—a fair price—which O'Brien tied up in his leather pouch, all but one dollar.

"Whiskey," he said. "Irish, not Colorado."

Dooney poured him a glass and gave him fifty cents change, then put away scales and gold and went back to hammering at his table. A scuffle of boots in the doorway was not enough to distract O'Brien from savoring his liquor.

"Alastar! See, I told you."

O'Brien turned to see Shaunessy, Duncan, and Morris all in a row. "You've had a strike!" Shaunessy cried.

"No, just a pebble," O'Brien answered.

"It's a big pebble if you're drinking Dooney's best," Morris said, sauntering forward and pulling a deck of cards from his satchel. "Would you be interested in a game of bluff?"

"What, this minute? For shame, you should all be at your work."

"We've been digging like moles all the morning," Shaunessy said, his eyes following the glass to O'Brien's lips. "Two hands only."

"All right, then," O'Brien agreed, hanging his rabbits from a nail on the wall and setting his rifle in the corner. "But be warned, it's a lucky day for me." He sat down and riffled Morris's cards. Bluff poker was a game O'Brien loved, maybe because he could do it as well as any other man, or better. He started off by cutting the ace of spades.

"There, you see? Best get ready to give up your goods," he said, starting the deal.

Two hands weren't enough. It became two rounds, then half an hour, then till supper. For supper they gave Dooney two more of O'Brien's rabbits and a dollar from the pot to have his lady roast them, and kept playing. The tavern began to fill up with miners, from Avery and from other towns nearby, who'd come to hear the Dutch Songbird, as they called Mrs. Dooney. She would not be appearing till later, Dooney told them, and they bought whiskey to pass the time.

Early in the evening Hall came in and was welcomed into the game. He slapped a handful of silver onto the table and made himself comfortable on an empty whiskey barrel. O'Brien handed him the deck to cut, then began the deal.

"Did Hambleton speak to you, Joseph?" Shaunessy asked.

"Nope," Hall replied. "What's he got to say?"

"He's raising a company, that's what."

O'Brien glanced up from dealing, just before Hall's eyes flicked away from him.

"That so?" Hall said.

"Haven't you seen the bills he's got up everywhere?" Duncan asked. "All over Empire City, and Nevada—"

"Are you thinking of joining him?" said Hall.

"Aye," Shaunessy said, sorting his cards. "There's good money in it, all for marching up and down to please old Gilpin's pride."

"There'll be more to it than that, I expect," Hall stated.

"Hambleton says there won't," Morris answered. "Says Governor Gilpin offered the States a regiment and they turned him down."

"Now, how would Hambleton know a thing like that?" Hall asked.

"The governor told me himself," said a voice from the doorway. O'Brien looked up to see the black-haired giant that had trod on the Rebel flag in Denver City. Hambleton came forward. "Mind if I join your game?"

"It'll have to be the next hand," O'Brien said, watching him. "This one's dealt."

"Pull up a seat, Josiah," Hall said casually. "I don't believe I've seen you in Avery before."

"Come to hear the Songbird." Hambleton dragged a log-stool up to the table and watched the hand played out. O'Brien won it and pulled in his best pot of the day. Shaunessy dealt the next hand and Morris opened the bet at five cents.

"How did you come to be on speaking terms with the governor?" Hall asked.

"I applied for a commission," Hambleton said. "He promised I'll have it as soon as I bring my company to Denver City. Raise twenty cents."

"Too rich for me," Hall said, folding his cards. "When do you suppose that will be?"

O'Brien put twenty cents into the pot and watched Hambleton's face.

"Well, I've nearly filled it up," the giant said. "Won't be more than a few days. I could fit you in if you like."

Shaunessy and Duncan had folded; Morris took three cards, Hambleton none. O'Brien asked for one.

"Got room for us, too?" said Duncan.

"Expect so."

"And we get horses?"

"That's right," Hambleton said. "Raise thirty."

"Horses?" O'Brien asked.

"Gilpin's promised a horse for each recruit," Morris said. "Your thirty and ten more."

"I hadn't heard about that," Hall said.

"It's not all the companies," Hambleton told him. "Just mine. Cook brought in his men mounted, and the governor wants another cavalry company."

"Where will he get them?" said O'Brien, matching the bet.

Hambleton glanced up. "Eh?"

"Where is he getting the mounts? There aren't twenty-five horses to be had in Denver City. Hall here's got the most horses around, and he's been gathering them for weeks."

"Does he? Maybe Gilpin's thinking of buying them," Hambleton replied.

"He hasn't approached me about it," Hall said, reaching out a lazy hand to pick up the coins in front of him and let them chink back to the table.

O'Brien noticed a tiny crease in Hambleton's forehead. "Your bet," he said.

Hambleton turned black eyes on him and said, "Raise a dollar." He scattered a handful of silver into the pot.

Morris dropped his cards facedown on the table. O'Brien stayed motionless, holding Hambleton's black gaze and waiting for instinct to guide him. Behind Hambleton the last sunlight sifted through the door; he saw a flash of black and white and a woodpecker started to thump on a tree outside. Buried treasure, O'Brien thought. "I'll call," he said, putting out his dollar.

Hambleton laid down two pair. O'Brien broke into a smile as he showed his straight.

"You drew to that? You've the devil's own luck, Alastar," Shaunessy exclaimed.

"Didn't I tell you so?" O'Brien raked in the pot.

"I knew he was bluffing," Duncan said, which earned him a glare from Hambleton.

"When do your men get their horses?" O'Brien asked, and the glare was turned on him.

"After they're mustered in." Hambleton said.

"So they're not free, then," O'Brien said.

"What's that?" Morris asked. "Not free?"

"If they're issued after muster, likely the cost'll come out of the soldier's pay," O'Brien stated.

"No, it won't," Hambleton said irritably.

"No? What's a horse cost in soldier's wages, Hall?"

"With saddle and all? Nearly a year's worth, I reckon."

"So the governor's giving a year's worth of wages free to your company, and yours alone?" O'Brien asked Hambleton.

The table was silent. Morris gathered up the cards and began to shuffle them. O'Brien sat at ease in his chair, watching every small movement. Duncan, Shaunessy, and Morris seemed unhappy, and Hambleton looked to be at a slow boil.

"I think the men who've joined you on the promise of a horse are bound to be disappointed," O'Brien said softly.

"Are you calling me a liar?" Hambleton turned on him, bumping the table so that the coins all chittered.

"I'm thinking," O'Brien said with deliberate calm, "that maybe you misremembered what the good governor told you."

Hambleton stood up swiftly and O'Brien had to stop himself grabbing for his rifle. The big man backed away, glanced around the table, and seemed to conclude not to take any volunteers just then. With a last glare at O'Brien, Hambleton turned and strode out of the tavern. Morris let out an audible sigh.

"As you say, Red," Hall said, bringing his revolver out from beneath the table and uncocking it, "it's your lucky day."

"The devil's own luck." Shaunessy shook his head. "He'd have throttled me for saying that."

"Red here is the devil's godson," Hall said. "Didn't he tell you?"

"Deal the cards," O'Brien said, annoyed.

"The devil's godson? How'd he earn that blessing?" Morris asked.

Hall leaned forward with a sly grin. "Born on Halloween." The others laughed, and O'Brien cursed himself for ever telling anything to Hall.

"What, did something frighten his mother?" Duncan asked.

"Aye," Shaunessy cried. "*He* did!"

"All right, you whoreson bastards," O'Brien said. "If you want to keep laughing you'll have to keep losing. Ante up."

The deal went round the table again as Dooney lighted

the candles. O'Brien won a pot, then lost heavily in three hands running and began to bet more conservatively. Threes were a sign, he believed, not just from the Holy Trinity. He was always watchful of signs; his mother had thought him sensitive to portents because of the dark powers flying on the night of his birth.

"Well, that's it," Hall said after Shaunessy won a hand. "I'm done for, you have my last dime."

"Poor Hall," O'Brien said. "Best go sell your horses to Governor Gilpin."

Hall leaned back in his chair and lit up a cheroot. "Rather sell them to you—"

"Oh, not again."

"—and your company." Hall blew a stream of smoke toward the ceiling.

Shaunessy turned blue eyes on O'Brien. "You forming a company, Red?"

O'Brien glared at Hall, who grinned. "It's a golden opportunity," Hall said. "Captain's uniform, all the ladies in Denver sighing over you—"

"All three of them, aye," O'Brien said. "Lady Squints, Lady Spots, and Lady Wall-eye."

"—and the pay, of course," Hall continued. "How many of those nuggets do you find each month?"

"I'd join you," Morris said. O'Brien glanced at him, surprised, and Morris shrugged. "Rather serve under you than Hambleton any day."

"Same here," Duncan agreed, and Shaunessy nodded. O'Brien stared at the three of them, wondering what he'd ever done to earn such a tribute. Caught off guard, he couldn't form even a thank you.

"Now about the horses," Hall said, leaning an elbow on the table. "I'll give your boys a good price on them—say, seventy-five dollars—and take twenty up front and the rest in credit against pay—"

"You'll have to put that away, Joe," Dooney said, coming up to the table. "Gerta's about to sing, and she can't abide smoke."

"Oh, certainly, certainly." Hall pinched out the coal of his cigar and carefully put the rest back in his pocket. He winked at O'Brien and turned his attention to the corner by the bar where the Songbird always made her stand. Tonight there was a fiddle player with her: McGuire, who made more from the pennies tossed to him at Dooney's and other taverns along Clear Creek than he ever had from his mine. Mrs. Dooney stood up beside him in a high-necked green dress with a little frill of lace at her throat, and began to sing in her sweet, clear voice.

At the first notes all other voices fell silent save for the mournful violin. The words she sang were meaningless, but it didn't matter a bit; they spoke to each man there in tones of home and loved ones, of fair days and glad nights and God's favoring grace. Her next song started with a smile, a playful tune that drew answering smiles from her audience. Then, with a nervous glance at the fiddler, she began to sing "The Star-Spangled Banner." Her English wasn't good—O'Brien had never heard a word of it out of her before—but the voice was so fair it didn't matter. When she sang the highest notes—"land of the free"—he felt as if his heart was being pulled right out of him. What a country it was that could bring such feelings out of a jaded Irish peasant through the instrument of a Dutch girl's voice. As she let go the last note and drew a breath, a cheer began that was taken up by every man in the tavern. Silver and copper—even gold—showered on the Songbird, and she laughed as she caught at the coins.

O'Brien let his breath out in a long sigh. 'Twas a good thing *he'd* not gone to Denver and found the Songbird, for he hadn't the money to keep her, but he just might have been mad enough to try. "You're a lucky man, Dooney," he called to the taverner, getting up and putting his money in his pocket. He took rifle in hand and slung his last two rabbits over his shoulder, heading toward the door as the next song began. He didn't want to lose the mood and he needed to think.

Pausing by the tavern door, he looked up through pine

branches to the sky powdered with stars. This wild country was as much home as he had now. He felt free here and didn't want to let go of that freedom, but some silent voice whispered to him to take Hall's advice and join the army. Was it his father's ghost, trying to make his son follow after him? Or mere vanity, thinking a captain's rank would transform him into a gentleman? No helpful sign came to guide him, so he shook his head and started up the path. He'd work the mine while fair weather held. If he made no more progress, perhaps he'd join up in the fall.

As he passed between the Trolls a movement made him jump. Owl, he thought as something dark fluttered above his head. Then he was struck a sharp blow from behind and knocked sprawling, grazing a hand on the rock as he went down. His attacker was on him at once, trying for a hold on his neck. The boulders on either side prevented him from rolling away. O'Brien kicked and squirmed and by good luck got within biting range of a hand. A cry of enraged pain followed, and the hold slackened enough for O'Brien to buck the fellow off and turn round before the attack was renewed. The hulk looming over him looked more bear than man, but he needed no sight to tell him who it was. Hambleton's voice came in a vicious growl to ears already ringing from the pressure at his throat.

"This is for crossing me," he said, slowly choking O'Brien's breath out of him. O'Brien jabbed both fists into Hambleton's gut, then put his hands through the bigger man's arms and struck outward, knocking them sideways with enough force to break free. He thrashed out blindly, gulping painful, croaking breaths and trying to conquer the animal terror that kept him from thinking.

A blow landed on his skull and others on his ribs, but he fought on, found the fellow's face with a hand and clung to it, grinding his thumb into one eye. An outraged howl, and Hambleton was off him. O'Brien scrambled to his feet and was slammed sideways into one of the Trolls, tasting blood as he bit his own cheek. He tried to kick but there wasn't room; wound up walking up the opposite rock with Hambleton trying to knock his head against the one behind him. A glimpse of stars with a black shape blotting them. He got his hands on Hambleton's ears and twisted. The bastard howled but wouldn't let go, and picked up O'Brien bodily, thumping him onto the rock. His shoulders took the worst of it but his head hit also and a flash of lightning seemed to strike behind his eyes. In desperation he kicked off from the opposite boulder and landed both knees in the center of Hambleton's back, which brought the giant forward off his balance. Squirming sideways, his arms tangled with Hambleton's, O'Brien got one foot on the ground and with the other on the boulder he pushed off again to throw Hambleton against the other Troll. A sickening thud; the vise-grip on his throat slackened and O'Brien pulled free, coughing and spitting out blood as he backed away. It was only then that he heard the cheering.

Dark shapes were moving beyond the Trolls. He could see them against the gleam of light from Dooney's door down the path. Hambleton peeled himself off the boulder and swayed. O'Brien advanced, swinging a fist into his jaw once, twice, backing him away from the Trolls and dodging the big arms that moved slower now. A third punch sent Hambleton over backward into the crowd that had come out from the bar. They applauded as O'Brien stepped toward his foe and tripped on something, his musket, he thought. Reaching for it, his hands found a staff of smooth wood, which he lifted. Cloth drooped at one end; Dooney's flag. That was the fluttering he'd seen. Holding it in both hands, he stood over Hambleton.

"Flags don't belong in the dirt," he said, panting.

"Finish him off, Red!" someone shouted.

O'Brien set the end of the staff in Hambleton's gut. "Listen close, now," he said. "I don't care where you do your recruiting, so long as you don't do it here. Take your carcass to some other tavern, and don't show it in Avery again." With a push of the flagpole for emphasis, O'Brien backed away.

Hambleton rose. O'Brien stepped aside to let him pass,

watchful of another attack. Hambleton muttered a curse as he limped away up the path.

O'Brien located his musket a few feet away, along with his battered coneys. He handed the flag to Hall, who had come up to clap him on the back.

"Sorry I couldn't see that," Hall said. "Must've been a pretty fight."

O'Brien grunted as he stooped to pick up his gun. "Wish you'd had the pleasure of fighting it, then," he said. "He half twisted my head off. I need a drink."

"Yours for the asking, Red," Hall replied, leading the way back to the tavern.

Inside, the men crowded O'Brien with praise and back-thumpings on fresh bruises, making him wince. The Song-bird had wisely retired while her audience was distracted by the fight. In the corner, McGuire was scraping out some aimless tune on his fiddle. Hall bought O'Brien a glass of whiskey. The first swig of it made him cough and stung his abused mouth and throat, but he finished it and another was in his hand before he drew breath to ask.

"Hey, Red, now you've *got* to form a company," Morris said. "Think of the look on old Ham-hand's face when you ride into Denver at the head of your own cavalry!"

"The Fighting Irish," Shaunessy said.

"Avery Guards!" McCraw yelled.

"Bear-Killers," another shouted, and a dozen voices took up the argument.

"More like a lot of mud-grubbing trolls," O'Brien said, but no one attended.

Morris pulled on his hat and folded up one side of it, held the fold up with an exaggerated salute, bowed in O'Brien's direction, and began marching around the room. Duncan fell into step behind him, and soon there was a file of men weaving their way among the tables. McGuire started to play "Yankee Doodle," and those not marching clapped their hands in time.

O'Brien looked at Hall who stood grinning, still leaning

on Dooney's flag. Without a word Hall held out the banner to him.

"Take it, Red!" Duncan shouted, and the whole tavern took up the cry.

O'Brien worked his jaw, running his tongue along where he'd bitten the side of his mouth. He hadn't asked for this, but fate seemed to have her own ideas. It wasn't just Hall; Hall hadn't brought Hambleton to Avery or made him jump O'Brien. Something higher was moving them all. God's tools, they were, and if he was to be moved he might as well do it as something more than a pawn. He took hold of the flagstaff, and the cheer that went up made him grin in spite of himself.

"Congratulations, Captain O'Brien," Hall said, holding out a hand.

O'Brien shook it. "Congratulate yourself," he said, grinning wider. "You're my first recruit."

Hall's brows went up. "I'm a man of business, sir. I have affairs to attend to—"

"Tend to 'em then, and settle them up, for I won't do it without you." O'Brien kept hold of his hand, and a slow smile spread on Hall's face.

"All right, but you'd better make me your lieutenant," he said.

"Done." O'Brien let go his hand and looked round the tavern. "The first five who give their names to Mr. Hall get a glass of the barley-bree," he said. "The next five get beer." He stepped back, sipping at his own glass, and watched the men rush toward Hall. *His* men, he realized.

"Christ help us all," he muttered, laughing at himself.

"I can't stay long," Uncle Wallace said as they crossed the baking-hot plaza. "Got a few matters to attend to."

"But I told you of Mrs. Canby's invitation three days ago," Laura protested. "Surely you could have arranged—"

"Don't worry, my dear," he replied. "I'll come in and do the pretty for the ladies first."

Laura kept her disappointment to herself. Her uncle's business affairs were taking up more and more of his time, and she was tired of sitting in her room, reading the month-old St. Louis papers that were the freshest news in town. She was determined not to mope, however, and looked forward to meeting new friends at Mrs. Canby's tea.

The Canbys lived northeast of the plaza on Palace Avenue, in one of a row of adobe houses interconnected by thick mud walls pierced at intervals by heavy gates. Uncle Wallace stopped at one of these into which a smaller door was set, and knocked. A servant admitted them to a breezeway large enough, were the gate open, for a wagon to pass through. Beyond was a placita something like the one at the Exchange. Laura glimpsed chickens and a splash of green before the manservant led them through a door in the side of the breezeway. The room they entered was much cooler than the outdoors—one of the advantages of adobe construction. The thick mud walls were whitewashed, then covered with calico tacked three-quarters of the way up. Laura had discovered the purpose of this custom when she had accidentally let her skirt touch an uncovered wall at the Exchange and spent an hour brushing whitewash from the taffeta.

The servant brought them to a parlor where a dozen or more ladies and gentlemen, most of the latter in uniform, were chatting comfortably. My new social circle, Laura thought, straightening her shoulders as she saw Mrs. Canby rising from a red velvet chair.

"Miss Howland." Mrs. Canby smiled, coming forward. "And Mr. Howland, welcome! You've both met my husband?"

"A pleasure to see you again, Miss Howland," Colonel Canby said. He seemed less grim than she remembered, but then she had met him only briefly at Fort Union, in the midst of Captain Sibley's departure. She returned his smile. Mrs. Canby introduced her to the other guests, the most formidable of whom was Doña Cabeza de Vaca, a regal Spanish dame wearing a mantilla draped over a large comb. She had a pretty daughter named Doña Isabel, whom Laura immediately liked for her shy smile. Mrs. Canby introduced several American ladies, and officers of both the regular army and the New Mexico Volunteers.

"And you already know Lieutenant McIntyre," she concluded. "Oh, excellent! Gracias, María." Mrs. Canby turned her attention to the tea tray that a Mexican woman had brought in.

Laura smiled at Mr. McIntyre. "I'm glad to see a familiar face," she said.

"You must be bewildered by all these new people," Mr. McIntyre said. "Shall I offer you an escape? There's a not-very-interesting view of the parroquia from the windows."

"No, thank you," Laura said, "but you may offer me a chair."

"Right here," another soldier said, coming up with two chairs in hand. "Too late, Lacey. You'd better find one for yourself." He set a chair for Laura and put his own beside it.

"Thank you, Mr.—Anderson?" Laura said.

"Brava," said the soldier, a glint of humor in his eye. He was all bronze—rather like a statue—his skin made much the same color as his hair by the action of the sun. "Now if you remember my title, you shall win the prize."

"Acting . . . ad—ad—"

"Adjutant," he said, smiling.

"What does it mean?" Laura asked.

"Paper-pusher," Mr. McIntyre said, placing a chair for himself on her right.

"Milk or sugar, Miss Howland?" Mrs. Canby asked. "I'm afraid there's no lemon."

"Milk, please."

"Are you out of lemons, Mrs. Canby?" Dr. Connelly asked from a chair by the empty hearth. "I'll have some brought up for you from Mexico."

"Thank you," said Mrs. Canby. "I must have all possible comforts if I am to tempt Miss Howland to share the latest news and fashions with us. Mr. Nicodemus, would you hand this cup to her, please?"

"Never fear, Miss Howland," Mr. McIntyre said. "Your defense is at hand."

"Defense?" Laura asked.

"Mrs. Canby is well versed in the techniques of interrogation," he explained. "She'd wring every last drop of gossip from you, if we were not here to protect you."

"Thank you, Lacey, for blackening my character to my guest," Mrs. Canby stated dryly. "Come and get your tea."

Laura smiled and sat back, savoring the fragrant tea and the pleasure of being in good company again. She assumed the attitude she'd developed at gatherings her father had taken her to, which was to listen and watch the little gestures and expressions that told so much more than words. She was sure, for example, that the handsome Captain Sena was courting the shy young lady, though he was speaking to her mother and not to her.

"Mr. Anderson," she said softly, "have I remembered that lady's name correctly? Miss de Vaca?"

"Cabeza de Vaca," said Mr. Anderson. "Or just C de Vaca. It means 'head of the cow.' "

"Gracious," Laura said. "Well, she seems very sweet."

"Too shy," Mr. McIntyre said. "I like a lady with courage."

"But not so much that she can provide her own defense?" Laura asked, arching an eyebrow at him.

"Got you there, Lacey," Mr. Nicodemus said, hovering nearby with his teacup in hand. "I like smart ladies, myself."

Mr. Anderson glanced at Laura with an amused grin. "You're both presuming a lady can have only one shining quality—" then he stopped abruptly, his smile fading.

Laura looked up to see the manservant beckoning to Colonel Canby from the door. Behind him in the hall stood a soldier, dusty with travel. Canby went to him, exchanged a few soft words, then turned to his wife.

"I'm afraid I must ask you and your guests to excuse me," he said. His voice was gentle, but no smile accompanied it. It was Mrs. Canby who smiled.

"Certainly," she said. A look passed between them that

Laura could not interpret, save that it bespoke a trust so deep it touched her with longing. Such was the feeling she and her father had shared. She had not missed it until this moment.

"Allen," Canby said quietly, summoning Mr. Anderson with a nod. Laura sensed the lieutenant's tension as he rose and left the room with Canby, and saw Mr. McIntyre and Mr. Nicodemus exchange a glance in the moment's silence that followed.

Something is wrong, she thought. All at once the air in the room seemed stiflingly warm, making it harder to breathe.

Uncle Wallace heaved a sigh and got to his feet. "I'd better be going myself," he said. "No, my dear, you stay and enjoy yourself."

"Please do stay, Miss Howland," Mrs. Canby said. "I will see that you get home safely." Her eyes, so winsome, seemed to be asking support. Laura resumed her seat in silence as her uncle left the room.

"Mrs. Chapin," Mrs. Canby said, turning to a lady of perhaps twenty-five, with high cheekbones and a somewhat brown complexion, "I understand your husband is now a captain."

"Yes," Mrs. Chapin said. "Though he may not know it yet. Buchanan is so far away, and of course they are marching now." She seemed worried, where before she had been cheerful.

The mood of the party had changed, and despite Mrs. Canby's efforts the guests began drifting away. Doña Cabeza de Vaca took her daughter home, with Captain Sena for escort. Most of the army men found excuses for leaving. Soon only Mrs. Chapin, Mr. McIntyre, and Dr. Connelly were left. At Mrs. Canby's request, Laura described the latest style in ladies' hats, but her account was made dull by the knowledge that her audience was preoccupied.

Dr. Connelly made no pretense of interest but stared at the door, musing. "I heard an odd rumor last night," he said when Laura had finished.

"Of what?" Mrs. Chapin asked, suddenly alert.

"Rumors are so often exaggerated," Mrs. Canby said gently.

"I have a right to know," Mrs. Chapin replied, her tone a challenge. "My husband's company is marching across bad country. What did you hear, Doctor?"

Laura glanced at Mrs. Canby, who was looking sternly at the doctor. He turned from his hostess to Mrs. Chapin.

"The natives are saying Fort Fillmore was taken by Texans," he said. "They say there are a thousand men marching north from Mesilla."

"That cannot be true," Mrs. Canby exclaimed. "We would surely have had news of such a large force—"

"Fillmore is where my husband's command was going," Mrs. Chapin said, her voice breaking on the last word. She sat very erect, gripping her hands in her lap. Laura's heart filled with a sudden ache for her, and impulsively she reached out to lay her hand over Mrs. Chapin's. The lady's eyes met hers: dry, but fearful. Laura's throat tightened on words of empty comfort.

The door flew open, thumping against the calico-covered wall. Laura and Mrs. Chapin both jumped.

"Oh! Beg pardon, ma'am," Lieutenant Nicodemus said from the doorway. "I thought the party was over."

"Come in, Mr. Nicodemus." Mrs. Canby said.

"Thanks, but I can't stay. The colonel sent me for Lacey."

Laura glanced at Mr. McIntyre, who slowly rose. Mrs. Chapin also stood. "Is it true?" she demanded.

Mr. Nicodemus glanced at her warily. Mrs. Chapin strode purposefully toward him. "Is it true that Fort Fillmore has fallen?"

"I really can't say—"

"If it's true we will know soon enough." Mrs. Canby's voice was resigned. "You'd better tell us, Lieutenant, unless my husband has forbidden it."

Eyeing Mrs. Chapin, Mr. Nicodemus said, "Major Lynde abandoned the fort."

"What?!" Mr. McIntyre exclaimed.

"Marched the whole command off in the middle of the night. He was trying to reach Fort Stanton, only they had no water. The Texans caught up with him at St. Augustín Springs, and he surrendered without firing a shot."

Mrs. Chapin made a small sound, quickly choked. No one moved for a moment.

"Thank you," Mrs. Canby said. "You'd better go, Mr. McIntyre."

"Yes." Mr. McIntyre's voice was numb. "My apologies," he added, and the glance he threw Laura as he left was unhappy.

Laura lifted her teacup to her lips. The tea was cold, and she set it back on the saucer with a small click.

"Surrender," Mrs. Canby said quietly, "means your husband is probably alive."

Mrs. Chapin nodded, and sat back down on the sofa. Laura glanced from her to Mrs. Canby, whose eyes were full of unspoken sympathy.

"Please," Laura said, "I don't understand. What Texans are these?"

"Texans have been gathering at the southern border for several weeks," Dr. Connelly told her. "I hadn't heard there were a thousand—"

"Four hundred, last we knew," Mrs. Canby said. "But even if there had been a thousand, Major Lynde should have been able to hold the fort against them."

"Apparently he didn't try," the doctor remarked.

Laura frowned. "But why would they want Fort Fillmore?"

Dr. Connelly looked at her with raised eyebrows. "They want New Mexico, Miss Howland," he said.

Twenty-five mounted men rode south from Denver City to Camp Weld, a mass of tents large and small, some in rows, some scattered along the river. O'Brien ran a hand over his clean jaw as they slowed to a trot. A scraggy beard half the colors of the rainbow might do for a Pike's Peaker, but it wouldn't do for a captain; O'Brien had shaved because gentlemen shaved, and a captain should be a gentleman or at least look like one.

"Quite a jamboree," Hall said cheerily, looking at the tents. He was in a good mood, having sold most of his horses to O'Brien's men. O'Brien had picked the best nag and paid for it out of the sale of his claim, for he didn't like being in debt.

The pounding of hammers came to their ears as they reined in to a walk. Framework for new buildings reached skyward like the bleached ribs of some dead animal on the plains. The camp was bustling with men—some in uniform, most not—hurrying every which way, wagons being unloaded, and the sounds of carpentry and curses. There was no gate or guard to meet them, and O'Brien halted his men at the edge of the camp, searching for someone in authority. He waved at a Mexican who was leading an empty mule-cart back to the road.

"You there," he said, "where's the recruiting officer?"

"No hablo inglés, señor," the man answered.

"Recruiting officer," O'Brien shouted, trying to make himself understood. "Where?"

"¿Dónde está el oficial de refuerzo?" a voice nearby asked.

O'Brien turned in the saddle and beheld an elegant youth, mounted upon a bay gelding—a purebred, he was sure—so beautiful it took his breath away. The animal was not so high in flesh as it might have been, but was otherwise perfect, its coat brushed to gleaming, eyes bright. The bay sidled as if in disdain for O'Brien's humbler-bred horse, and O'Brien looked up at its rider. He was no more than eighteen, somewhat frail in stature but with dark, lively eyes beneath curling black hair. He was clearly a gentleman, dressed impeccably from polished boots to immaculate gloves.

"Ah," the Mexican said, pointing back toward the camp. "En esa carpa bien grande."

"Gracias," said the stranger with a genteel nod, and

turned to O'Brien. "It's in the large tent," he said, his voice a cultured, slightly hoarse tenor.

Chagrined at being given assistance unasked for, O'Brien started toward the tent. The bay gelding snorted.

"You're welcome," the youth said wryly.

O'Brien kicked his horse. "Park Avenue bastard," he muttered.

Hall leaned toward him with a sly grin. "Hope he's not joining up. Can you imagine an army made of those?"

The men dismounted in front of the large tent, and some held the horses while the rest ducked beneath the white canvas door flap. Inside at a rough wooden table sat a uniformed man with neatly trimmed goatee, flying eyebrows, and an uncompromising gaze that he fixed upon O'Brien as he looked up from his paperwork.

"We're here to join the Volunteers," O'Brien said.

"Are you?" the officer said, glancing over the men. Hall handed him a piece of paper, which the officer examined. "You are—Alastar Edmund O'Brien?" he said, looking up at Hall.

"I am," O'Brien answered.

One of the officer's eyebrows twitched. "I see," he said. "I am Captain Tappan." He drew a sheet of paper toward him and scratched at it with his pen. "You have twenty-five men, Mr. O'Brien?"

"Counting myself, yes."

"No, there must be twenty-five in addition to yourself. You'll need one more for your captaincy."

O'Brien looked at Hall, a stab of frustration hitting him. Hall shrugged, and O'Brien turned back to Tappan, but before he could protest a voice from behind his men said, "You can count me if you like."

O'Brien knew as he turned that it was the elegant young gentleman. The youth came forward, beaver hat in hand, his leg turned at a graceful angle as he made a deferential bow. On foot, his head barely reached O'Brien's shoulder.

"I don't have a company yet," he said with an airy smile. "I suppose yours will be as good as any."

"Your name?" demanded Tappan.

"Charles Franklin."

Hall's lip curled as he looked the lad over. "Shouldn't you be at home with your mama, Chas?" he asked lazily.

Franklin's eyes narrowed, then to O'Brien's surprise he grinned. "I'm sure she'd agree with you," he said softly, and turned his back on Hall, tugging gently at his gloves. "Well, Mr. O'Brien? Shall I join your company?"

O'Brien frowned. He didn't like this Franklin. It was unfair that a scrap of a boy should so carelessly flaunt the advantages money had bought him—unfair that O'Brien should have to accept him in order to get his commission. Life, however, was often unfair, as O'Brien had learned at an early age. The thought that young Franklin was likely to feel out of place among the rough men of Avery softened the blow to his pride. A fairy-lad amongst the trolls, he thought, hiding a smile. He nodded, and Tappan resumed writing.

"Very well, Captain O'Brien," he said. "You and your men will be Company I. Sign here."

O'Brien hesitated when offered the pen, and Tappan looked up, sharp brows rising. Reddening, O'Brien took the pen and painfully scrawled his name. It was the only thing he could write, and he felt as if Tappan knew it. As he handed back the page a large, burly man in preacher's clothing entered the tent from behind Tappan's desk.

"Well, well." The newcomer's voice boomed. "A new crop, eh, Tappan? Strong-looking men, too!"

"Strong enough to keep you safe in your pulpit, Reverend," Hall said.

The preacher laughed heartily. "They'll have to be strong for that!" he said while Tappan glared at Hall from the desk. "I'll see you all at evening prayers," he added. "Seven o'clock sharp!" He passed through O'Brien's men on his way to the front of the tent, greeting them with handshakes and smiles.

"Who's the Methodist?" O'Brien asked, gazing after him.

Tappan frowned. "That's Major John Chivington."

"The commander of Camp Weld," Franklin added, brushing a bit of dust from his sleeve.

O'Brien glanced at Hall, who'd gone red. Hall glared at Franklin, then shrugged it off. Captain Tappan took down the men's names, recording them in neat columns along with descriptions of their horses and weapons, then turned the new company over to a corporal who took them to the quartermaster depot to be issued equipment and tents.

"No uniforms yet," the corporal said. "Governor Gilpin's requested some from Leavenworth. Come on, I'll show you where to put your horses."

This turned out to be a corral, as stables would not be built until the barracks and headquarters were done. By the time Company I had carried their gear to the area assigned to them, the sun was setting. The first perquisite of O'Brien's new rank was a tent all to himself. He set to pitching it, driving the stakes easily into the ground until Hall's laughter stopped him.

"What?" O'Brien demanded, hammer in hand.

"You're a captain. You're supposed to have one of the men do that for you," said Hall, grinning.

Piqued, O'Brien said, "You do it, then," and held the hammer's handle toward him.

"Yes, massa," Hall replied, reaching for it.

O'Brien turned the hammer around and threatened Hall with it, then broke into a grin, and the two of them pitched the tent together. As they finished they heard a commotion from the direction of the corral. O'Brien looked up to see Luther Denning—the fellow who'd been in the duel—running toward him full tilt.

"Fight," Denning gasped.

O'Brien dropped his hammer and followed him to the corral, where the dark shapes of horses moved restlessly behind the fence. Before it men were clustering around a loud, red-faced blasphemer hurling every curse in creation at the unconcerned form of Charles Franklin. The smaller man leaned against the fence, one gloved hand caressing the neck of his stunning bay, the other holding a small, wicked knife in plain view of his abuser and any other potential challenger.

"What the hell's going on?" O'Brien said.

"Who the damned hell are you?" Franklin's adversary yelled.

"Captain O'Brien," O'Brien roared back in his face. "Who are you?"

The magic of the word "captain" worked a swift change; the fellow fell silent and backed away. O'Brien felt a rush of giddy delight at his new power, and took a step closer. The fellow was clutching his right arm above the elbow.

"Th-that bastard attacked me, Cap'n," he said.

O'Brien, incredulous, turned to Franklin.

"At the risk of sounding childish," Franklin said with a laugh and a wild look in his eyes, "I'm afraid he attacked me first."

"You cut him?" O'Brien said in disbelief.

"Not badly."

O'Brien turned to the wounded man. "You, what's your name? Speak up, now," he added as the man muttered under his breath.

"His name's Cassady," said a large figure, joining the circle.

"Hambleton!" O'Brien, caught off guard, stared at his former rival.

"That's *Captain* Hambleton," the other said. "Cassady here's in my company."

"Oh? Well, keep him away from my lads," O'Brien said.

"I don't hold with knives," Hambleton said, glowering. All was still, so still O'Brien could hear the wind softly moaning in the riverbed a few yards away. He waited, and at last Hambleton moved. "Come on, Bill," he said. The wounded man followed his captain off into the shadows, and O'Brien exhaled in relief.

"What are the rest of you looking at?" he demanded. "D'you think it's a circus? Go back to your camps! Not you, Franklin," he added, and stared at the lad till the others had left. In the shadows a few feet away he saw, Hall, but ignored him. "I don't hold with knives, either, Charles Franklin," he said. "First night here and there's trouble already—what do you think our saintly major would say to that?"

"I have a right to defend myself, sir," Franklin said, showing white teeth in a grim smile.

"Assuming you were really attacked," Hall drawled.

Franklin's gaze shot to Hall as the latter came forward. "I don't seek out petty fights," he answered.

"Oh, they just come and find you, Chas? Drawn by your beauty, perhaps—"

"Stow it, Hall," O'Brien said. The sound of a bugle made him look up. Soldiers emerged from tents and started toward the open space in the camp's center. A movement from Franklin's direction made him snap his head back in time to see the lad draw a watch from his pocket. It glinted softly in the dimness.

"Seven o'clock," Franklin said. "Evening prayers. They're mandatory, sir. Major Chivington's standing orders."

"How do you know?" Hall demanded.

"I had a chat with the quartermaster this morning," said Franklin, his voice had gone airy again. "Thought I'd find out a little about the camp. If nothing else it ought to be entertaining. He says the major is full of brimstone."

O'Brien studied Franklin, searching for something he suspected was hidden behind the youth's casual smile. "You religious, Franklin?" he demanded.

"I was brought up to be, yes," replied Franklin.

"That's not what he asked," Hall said. "You don't listen too good, do you?"

Franklin's eyes measured Hall for a moment, then returned to O'Brien. "I have faith in God, Captain. Will that do?"

The bugle sounded again. O'Brien looked at Hall, then at Franklin. "Guess we're all Protestants now," he said. "Won't me dear mother be surprised."

Franklin gave a choke of laughter, and O'Brien stifled a

grin. "Go on, then," he said roughly. "We'll be right behind you."

"Yes, Captain," Franklin said. "And thank you, sir," he added. With a last pat for his horse, he strode away. O'Brien reached a hand toward the bay, who nickered and ran off.

Hall stood looking after Franklin. "Chas is going to be a problem," he said. "Glad I wasn't the one to offend him. Has it occurred to you that he could have solved it all with a kidney punch?"

It had occurred to O'Brien. "He's small," he said, rubbing his chin. "Disadvantage in a fight."

Hall gave a mirthless laugh. "What does he want with the army, anyway?"

"Wants to be a little hero." O'Brien shrugged. He started up the hill toward the camp, and Hall fell in beside him.

"He's not the heroic type," Hall replied. "He's some rich man's son, looking for something to do with himself, and thinking how fine he'd look in a pretty uniform. A few days of hard work'll teach him different."

"You're a rich man's son," O'Brien said.

Hall's head snapped up, his eyes suddenly hard, then his face relaxed into a slow smile. "I was once," he said. "Now I'm just a freebooter like the rest of you."

7

To the Assistant Adjutant-General, Washington, D.C.:
Sir: I have the honor to inclose a copy of a report from
Major Lynde, Seventh Infantry, commanding at Fort Fill-
more. This report is in all respects unsatisfactory.

—Ed. R. S. Canby

Laura hastened to keep up with her uncle's long stride as
they crossed the plaza on their way to the Canbys' for dinner. "Have you inquired about seats on the mail?" she asked.

"No," Uncle Wallace said. "Don't be in a panic, Laura.
There's no need for you to go back to Boston."

"But the Territory is being invaded!"

"Bah. Only a handful of rabble. Major Lynde's a great
fool."

"Well, wouldn't it be safer—"

"You are not going back to the States!" He stopped at
the corner and turned to face Laura, looking exasperated.
"It would be extremely inconvenient at this time."

"Inconvenient?"

"Laura," he said, "I have a number of business negotiations in hand—delicate negotiations—that I cannot abandon simply because you are feeling alarmed by these
Texans." He offered her his arm and led her down the
street, saying, "I assure you, your friend Major Canby is
very competent. He will not allow them to cause any more
trouble."

"Colonel Canby," Laura said unhappily.

"Yes, yes. Well, here you are. Enjoy the party." He withdrew his arm and knocked on the Canbys' gate. Laura
stared at him in astonishment.

"But you're coming in, too, are you not?" she said.

"No, I've got business. Give Mrs. Canby my regards."

"Uncle, the invitation was for both of us! Mrs. Canby is expecting you!"

"Got a possible buyer for the mine," her uncle said. "Can't put him off. You have a nice time, now."

The Canbys' manservant opened the door, and Uncle Wallace turned away and strode off up the street before Laura could protest further. She turned to the servant, who averted his eyes and silently beckoned her inside. Feeling her cheeks aflame, Laura stepped gratefully into the shade of the entryway. Juan Carlos led her into the house, and she gave him her bonnet and shawl, biting back angry tears and trying to compose an apology for her uncle's behavior. She pressed her hands to her cheeks, hoping to cool them, before following the servant to the parlor.

"The whole affair's a disgrace," a voice said as she entered. "Lynde should be court-martialed!" The speaker, a tall, sandy-haired officer, had features that were pleasant but just now lit with indignation. "We'd have marched right into their arms if the express from Craig hadn't reached us."

"You came off better than poor Gibbs," the officer beside him said. He had dark hair, a mustache and goatee, and looked rather familiar, though Laura couldn't place him. "After all the trouble he took to evade the Texans, to be surrendered without even being consulted! He must be furious."

Laura, her feelings a good match for the military men's, looked around until she spied Mrs. Canby chatting with Mrs. Chapin by the fireplace, and made her way to her side.

"Miss Howland," Mrs. Canby said. "Is your uncle not with you?"

"No, ma'am." Laura felt the warmth return to her face as she curtseyed. "He sends his regrets."

"No matter," Mrs. Canby said kindly. "I am somewhat overwhelmed with gentlemen as it is. I hope you won't mind all these soldiers."

"Of course not," Laura said, attempting to smile. "I'm delighted to be here."

"Come and meet my husband," Mrs. Chapin said, reaching for Laura's hand. "Yes, he's here! He was not taken after all!"

Captain Chapin, in fact, was the gentleman who had been venting his feelings as Laura arrived. He greeted her cordially and introduced his companion as Captain McRae. McRae's eyes were rather stern, one with a slight flaw from some past injury. Laura noticed he wore a black armband over one sleeve.

"How do you do?" Laura said. "Have we met?"

"Not officially, ma'am," McRae replied. "I was at Fort Union when your party stopped there."

"Oh, yes, I remember."

"Are you any relation to George Howland?" he asked. "Lieutenant in the Rifles?"

"Not that I know," Laura said. "Is he here?"

"He was stationed at Fillmore," Chapin told her. "Transferred up to Fort Craig just a week before the fiasco. You'll see him on his way through town, whenever he finally ships out."

Laura looked at him in surprise. "The army can't still be leaving? Not after the Texans?"

"Can and will," McRae said. "It's only a question of time. We're wanted for the war back East, especially after Bull Run."

"Don't be frightened, Miss Howland," Lieutenant McIntyre said, coming up with another man, also in uniform. "We won't leave until the volunteers are in place to defend the Territory. It'll take awhile, won't it, Colonel Chaves?"

"A while, yes," the handsome man beside him replied. "Our regiment is still being built. It is not easy to find recruits."

The sound of the outer door presaged the entrance of Colonel Canby and Lieutenant Anderson. "Good evening, Miss Howland," said the lieutenant, joining the small circle.

"Good evening." Laura curtseyed.

"Have you learned where the Seventh is?" Captain McRae asked him. "Fort Bliss?"

"No," Lieutenant Anderson said. "They've been paroled. Not enough Texans to guard them; they outnumbered the fellows nearly four to one."

"Disgusting," McRae said, shaking his head.

"Not as disgusting as this fellow Baylor," Chapin said. "Did you hear about his little announcement?"

"Who is Baylor?" Laura asked Lieutenant McIntyre quietly.

"The Texan commander," he said.

"Governor of Arizona, if you please!" Chapin corrected. "Fellow's had the nerve to issue a proclamation claiming the whole southern half of the Territory for the Confederates!"

"What, Fort Craig, too?" McRae asked.

"Everything below the 34th parallel," Anderson answered.

"He's mad! Craig is stuffed full of troops!"

Laura turned to Colonel Canby, who had joined his wife by the empty fireplace. "Can Baylor hold the land he has claimed?" she asked.

"There is no need to be alarmed, Miss Howland," Canby said. "He will not get anywhere near Santa Fé."

"That is not what I asked," Laura said. "If he can hold his claim it will open that Territory to the expansion of slavery."

A silence followed this comment, and Laura realized all the officers were looking at her. She straightened her shoulders. "Can Baylor hold Arizona?"

"I trust not," Canby said slowly, a measure of respect in his eyes. "At the moment he holds only Mesilla. Once we are organized we shall dislodge him."

"I do hope so, Colonel," Laura replied.

"Miss Howland!" Mrs. Chapin exclaimed. "I did not know you were an abolitionist."

Laura glanced at her but detected no criticism. "I am," she said. "My father and I were very active in the movement."

"Well," McRae said slowly, "if you plan to take up the

cudgels in defense of the Negroes, you will find few in the
Territory to defend."

"It is the principle that interests me," Laura said. "Does
not President Lincoln intend that the Territories shall
remain free? Yet I have heard that some Indians keep
Negro slaves—"

"Not in New Mexico," Canby said. "Here they get their
slaves mostly from other tribes."

"And from New Mexican families," Colonel Chaves
remarked.

The pause that followed this made Laura less certain of
her ground. "They should keep no slaves at all," she said.

"I agree, but it has been a custom for many generations,"
Chaves said with polite calm. "Like our custom of peon-
age, to which I expect you would also object."

"We are the newcomers here, Miss Howland," Mrs.
Canby said. "We must go gently if we are to maintain
peace."

Laura looked at her hostess, whose dark eyes shone with
understanding tempered by a hint of caution, and realized
she knew too little of this country to discuss its customs
intelligently. She made no further remarks on the subject,
and soon Mrs. Canby summoned everyone to the dining
room.

Laura was seated between Colonel Chaves and Captain
McRae. The table was lopsided owing to her uncle's
absence; across from her were Lieutenants McIntyre and
Anderson, flanked by the Chapins. Mrs. Canby's dinner
was excellent: venison, quail, and albóndigas, accompanied by fresh greens and hot bread. Laura's mind kept
returning to her uncle's desertion. She wondered why he
had chosen to sell his gold mine, if it was, as she had
believed, his main source of income. Perhaps he had other
resources of which she was unaware. Or perhaps he had
merely used it as an excuse not to attend the dinner.

"Miss Howland?"

Laura started, and found Colonel Chaves looking at her
kindly, offering to fill her wineglass.

"Oh! Thank you, sir. I'm afraid I was daydreaming."

"I understand you have come a long way to Santa Fé."

"Yes." Laura sought for something pleasant to say.

"You are homesick, perhaps?" The colonel's voice was gentle.

"Sometimes, yes," Laura replied, "but I am very happy to have found new friends here."

"You have found excellent friends," Chaves said. "The Canbys are very good people."

Laura found herself slowly relaxing as she listened to his description of Colonel Canby's diplomacy in dealing with the native population during the Navajo campaign of the previous winter. Midway through the meal, Mrs. Canby turned the table's conversation and Laura found herself regarding Captain McRae. She noted the field of his shoulder straps was green, and said, "Please tell me, what branch of service do green trimmings signify?"

"Mounted Rifles," he said. "But we've just been redesignated. We're to become cavalry."

"Which would be yellow?"

"Yes."

"I'm afraid I like the green better," Laura said.

A corner of his mouth turned up in response. "So do we, ma'am. The Rifles' history is—distinctive."

Laura restrained her curiosity about the Rifles' history, suspecting it might not be a fit subject for dinner conversation. "I see you are also in mourning," she said instead.

"Yes," McRae answered. "My mother died in May."

"I am sorry."

"Thank you. She had been ill for some time."

"I lost my father last December," Laura said.

McRae nodded. "It makes one feel a bit useless, somehow."

"Yes." Laura looked down at her cherry pie, and pushed the plate away.

"Are you making Santa Fé your home, Miss Howland, or are you visiting only?"

"I—would like to return east," Laura said.

"That will not be easy just now," McRae said.

"No. I expect I shall be in New Mexico for a little while, until things become more settled. They will, won't they?" How foolish, Laura, she thought. The captain will think you a ninny.

"I promise you, ma'am," McRae said gravely, "we will do our utmost to preserve the Territory."

Mrs. Canby rose from her place, and Laura and Mrs. Chapin joined her in the parlor, leaving the gentlemen to their cigars and brandy. They had not long to wait; soon the men emerged from the dining room in a cloud of blue smoke, carrying their conversation with them.

"I hear you're to form an artillery battery," Captain McRae said to Lieutenant Anderson.

"We'd like to, yes," Anderson replied. "We don't have much available in the department, though. A couple of 24-pounders at the depot, but their carriages are pretty well useless."

"Weren't there some guns at Buchanan?" McRae asked.

Chapin nodded. "They're at Craig. Not in very good shape."

"Well," McRae said, "I'm going down there with Colonel Roberts. I'd be happy to look over what's there for you; I've played about a bit with artillery."

"At West Point?" Anderson asked.

McRae nodded. "Parents wanted me to go into that branch but I thought the Rifles a better opportunity." He looked at Laura as he said this, and smiled. "Besides, red trim wouldn't suit me at all."

"You are mocking me, sir," Laura said, blushing.

"Not at all," he said kindly. "I believe a lady should always be consulted on matters of taste. You're much better at it than we poor brutes."

Laura smiled, but her spirits remained low. She was unable to absorb much of the conversation, which turned increasingly to military affairs. The Chapins took their leave early, and as Mrs. Canby saw them out the remaining gentlemen gathered around a table and spread a map over it, chattering and arguing. Laura found herself staring at the empty hearth until Lieutenant Anderson came to sit beside her.

"Are we boring you to death?" he asked.

"No, indeed," Laura told him. "It is only that I understand so little of what I am hearing. I feel quite a stranger."

"Please don't think we're unable to talk of anything besides soldiering," he said. "Won't you tell me about Boston?"

"You'll have to forgive me," Laura said with a laugh. "I have already told my Boston stories this evening. And in fact," she said as Mrs. Canby returned, "I believe I should go, before I embarrass myself by falling asleep on the sofa." She rose and shook Mrs. Canby's hand. "Thank you for a delightful evening, ma'am. I have enjoyed meeting all of your guests."

"Thank you for coming," Mrs. Canby said. "Allen, would you be kind enough to escort Miss Howland to her hotel?"

"A pleasure," Mr. Anderson bowed.

"Don't be frightened by all this martial talk," Mrs. Canby added. "Mesilla is hundreds of miles away, and Fort Craig is between it and us."

"I am not frightened, ma'am, so long as Colonel Canby is in charge of the Territory's defenses," Laura replied.

Mrs. Canby smiled. "You are very good, Miss Howland. I will call on you tomorrow, if you still wish to come to church?"

"Yes, thank you," said Laura. "Good night."

Outside a crescent moon shone overhead. Early August; the evening was warm, and music and laughter spilled onto the street from the open doorways of cantinas. Laura let her shawl drape from her elbows and strolled along looking up at the stars.

"I understand we have you and your friends to thank for our dinner," she said.

"Hunting's been good this summer," Mr. Anderson replied. "Plenty of game."

"I am glad to know there is something plentiful in this country besides dust."

Anderson laughed, and Laura glanced at his dark form. "I hope that doesn't offend you," she added.

"No. I disliked New Mexico at first, too, but it grows on one. The land is so amazingly lovely. . . . I can't explain it. You need a poet to tell you."

"It is pretty, but I prefer the freedom of civilization."

"Freedom? You can't find more of that anywhere else."

Laura paused halfway across the plaza to peer at his face in the darkness. "For you, perhaps, Mr. Anderson. For me New Mexico is very restrictive."

"You mean because there are fewer social opportunities? But there are other kinds of freedom. There is freedom of thought, and ideas. A frontier is where rules are reshaped, ma'am, for those who have the courage."

Laura frowned slightly, wishing she could see him better. "You are in love with this place, aren't you?" she asked.

For a moment he didn't answer, then: "I'm a soldier. I go where I'm sent."

They were silent the rest of the way to the Exchange. There were certain things, Laura had noticed, that soldiers and their wives did not mention aloud. She was sure these were some of the very things they cared most about, and wondered if perhaps, in the privacy of their quarters, such matters were discussed in hushed tones by Colonel and Mrs. Canby, Captain and Mrs. Chapin, or among Mr. Anderson and his friends. She felt brief envy for those who enjoyed such closeness, then remembered its cost: long separations, waiting, fear, sometimes bad news. To endure such strains would require a considerable investment of faith. She doubted she would ever have the courage to give her heart to a soldier.

"You'll be paid as soon as it's approved," Jamie told the saddler apologetically. "Don't worry—"

"What about my tents?" complained Colonel Green,

commander of the 5th Texas. "My men are still sleeping in the open!"

The 5th wasn't Jamie's regiment. He and Martin were in the 4th Texas, but as Martin was A.Q.M. for General Sibley's brigade, and the quartermaster himself was busy drumming up funds, they wound up ordering all the supplies. To add to the burden, Sibley was raising a third regiment—the 7th Texas—so far only partially filled.

"They're on the way, sir," Jamie told Colonel Green. "It should only be a few more days."

"That's what you said two weeks ago!" Green exclaimed. His fierce eyes glared wider. Tom Green was a hero, famous from San Jacinto days, normally a quiet man but used to having his way, and Jamie could well understand his frustration.

A German merchant elbowed forward. "I have two hundred barrels flour—"

"Hold on a minute." Jamie silenced him with a gesture and turned to the colonel. "We're expecting the tents any day, sir. I'll send word the minute they arrive, I promise." As he spoke he put his hand in the drawer of Martin's desk and pulled out three Cuban cigars, which he slipped to Green in a handshake.

"Very well," Green said. He put the cigars in his coat pocket as he left, and Jamie turned to the waiting German.

"I have two hundred barrels flour in my warehouse two months," the German said, stabbing two fingers into the desk. "If army not pick up and pay, I will selling them!"

Jamie clenched his jaw shut and glanced at the rest of the crowd. It was like this most days, and he and Martin had fallen into sharing the burden by trading off handling the office and overseeing the depot, which was just as chaotic but less tense. Jamie had wanted to learn to drill with the regiment, as well, but he'd only made it out to Camp Sibley once in five weeks.

He dealt with the merchants politely, jotting down notes in a memo book already filled with reminders of the dozens of tasks needing immediate attention. He gave the

German a note to take to the chief of commissary about the
flour, and gave the numerous creditors the best he could
offer, a promise to inquire about their status. He carefully
took down all their names and sighed in silent relief as one
by one they drifted out of the office. The last bill was
shoved under his nose and he wrote the name mechanically
before he realized it was his own. Looking up, he saw
Emmaline grinning wryly at him from under a flat-
brimmed hat.

"Working you to death, I see," she said.

Her hair was tucked up into the hat and she was in the
men's clothes she'd taken to wearing for ranch work, something she and Poppa kept from Momma by tacit agreement.
She kept her work clothes in the barn and changed there,
never setting foot in the house except in her dress. Jamie
was sure Momma knew, but as no one ever mentioned the
subject, a dignified peace reigned inside the ranch house.
This was the first time Jamie had seen his sister dressed this
way in town, and he couldn't help glancing at the door, not
wanting her to be the object of any rudeness.

"Hello, Emma," he said. "Where's Poppa?"

"Taking your beeves to the corral. He sent me to get the
bill signed."

"Captain Martin will have to do it," Jamie said, lying
through his teeth. "I'm not authorized for this amount."

"Where is he?" Emmaline asked carelessly.

"In a staff meeting."

"I'll wait, then."

Jamie hid a grin as he bent over his paperwork, and
covertly watched her stroll to the window. He didn't think
Poppa knew it yet, and Emma hadn't said anything, but
Jamie was sure she and Captain Martin were courting.
He'd invited the captain to dinner one Sunday, and
Momma had taken a liking to him and asked him back several times, until lately Sunday dinner at Russell's Ranch
was a standing invitation that Martin rarely missed. Jamie
had noticed that he and Emma seemed to always wind up
on the porch after dinner watching the stars come out, and

had quietly taken it upon himself to keep Gabe out of their way. He liked Martin, and would like nothing better than to have him in the family.

Emmaline shifted, craning to peer down the street. Jamie guessed she was nervous because Martin had never seen her in her work clothes. It was all Emma to come here in person and dare him to disapprove, though Jamie didn't think he would. Martin liked her spirit.

A step sounded from the hallway. Emma looked up, but it was Poppa who came into the office.

"Good afternoon, Mr. Russell," Jamie said with a grin. "I have your bill right here, it's just waiting for approval."

"There's no hurry." Poppa smiled. "Bring it Sunday. Come on, Emma, time we got back."

Jamie saw Emma hide a pout. "Got a letter from Dan," she said, lingering by the desk. "He's better about writing than Matt."

"That figures." Jamie nodded. "Tell Momma go ahead and read it without me. I don't think I'll get home before Sunday."

A couple of dust-bitten teamsters came in. "Captain Martin?" one asked.

"Not here at the moment. How can I help you?" Jamie said.

"We'll get out of your way," Poppa said, nudging Emma toward the door. She went slowly, then at the door she stepped back, her face brightening as she gave way to Captain Martin.

He was frowning, but this changed to astonishment as he recognized Emmaline. For a second he just stared at her, then he smiled and said, "Well, hello." Emma smiled back as Martin nodded to Poppa. "Mr. Russell. Will you excuse me a minute?"

He moved past them to talk with the teamsters, who were just in from Houston with a shipment including the badly needed tents. Jamie dashed off a note and ran downstairs to get an orderly to take it to Colonel Green. Once outside he was surprised at how late it was—the front of the building was already in shadow. He walked a few steps down Houston to where it crossed St. Mary's Street, stepping into the last of the sun and enjoying the heat on his face. Day's end inspired laziness in the people strolling by, a pleasant contrast from headquarters, which was always frantic. The Vance House bustled night and day. Exciting times, but tiring, too, and Jamie treasured every moment of relaxation.

Two boys a bit younger than Gabe came up to him, wide-eyed. "You a real soldier?" one asked, staring at Jamie's gray shirt.

"Yes," Jamie said.

"How come you don't got a rifle?" the other said.

"I have a pistol. I just don't have it with me."

"You gonna kill Yankees?"

"Someday, I expect," Jamie answered.

The boys looked profoundly impressed. Jamie tousled their hair, then hurried back to the office to find the teamsters gone and Emma fidgeting with her cowhide gloves while Martin and Poppa chatted about nothing much. Things didn't feel right to Jamie. The frown was starting to come back on the captain's face; he was saying yes, the regiments were filling up fast.

"Well," Poppa said when Jamie came in, "we'd best get home. You're coming Sunday?" he asked Martin as they shook hands.

The captain hesitated just a second, then said, "Yes, of course. I'll see you then." He was looking at Emma as he said that, smiling and frowning at the same time.

Jamie walked his father and sister out to their horses and said good-bye. He watched Emmaline's face, but she had a blank mask on and he feared there was trouble brewing. He wished he had the time to go home and talk with her, but there was no way he could leave before Sunday. As she mounted Smokey, Jamie put a hand on her rein and whispered, "You all right?"

Emma shrugged and turned the horse toward the sunset. Jamie watched her and Poppa ride away, then returned to the office where he found Captain Martin sitting at the desk, hands folded on top of the papers and his frown getting deeper.

"What is it?" Jamie asked.

Martin looked up at him and nodded toward the door. Jamie closed it and pulled a chair up to the desk, trying to read the captain's face as he sat down.

"This isn't known yet," Martin said quietly. "There'll be a general order tomorrow. We're marching in a few weeks."

8

Who but a soldier can form any idea of the thoughts and feelings of a soldier on his leaving home for the battlefield?

—Private William Randolph Howell, 5th Texas
Mounted Volunteers

Jamie's mouth made a silent "oh." He had known the regiment would leave San Antonio eventually—had been gently preparing Momma for the inevitable—but it seemed to have come up faster than he'd expected. Evidently the captain felt the same.

"When?" Jamie asked.

"As soon as the brigade's complete," Martin replied. "General Sibley said we'll start for El Paso next month, but I think it'll take a little longer. The 7th is just getting organized." Papers crinkled as he shifted his elbows. "You may have guessed—I've taken a liking to your sister."

Jamie nodded, hiding a smile. "I thought maybe you had."

The frown deepend on the captain's tanned forehcad. "I hoped—"

Jamie waited, realizing the captain's frown was for Emma; he didn't want to leave her. Suddenly he was glad he didn't have a sweetheart. He looked down at his hands, not wanting to embarrass Martin.

"Jamie, you know Emmaline better than I do. Should I talk to her now, or wait?"

His fingernails needed trimming, Jamie noticed. Hadn't had time lately. He rubbed at a broken one, trying to think of what to say.

"I don't want to tie her to anything if it'll cause her

grief," the captain added. "There's no telling how long we'll be gone."

Or if we'll be back, Jamie thought. He sat up, shrugging his shoulders to throw off the sudden chill. Of course they'd be back. They were quartermasters, not line soldiers.

"She's pretty strong-willed," he said. "When she wants something, she usually gets it."

Martin's lips curved into a knowing smile.

"I don't think she'd mind waiting on a promise," Jamie added.

The captain sighed. "Thank you, Jamie."

Their eyes met and Jamie grinned, trying to imagine calling the captain "Stephen." Emma, he knew, would be overjoyed.

"Shall we get back to work?" Jamie said, looking at the heap of papers on the desk.

"No," Martin said, grinning as he stood. "I think we'd better go down to Menger's. I believe I owe you a beer!"

O'Brien paused and set down his hammer to wipe his face. Cool breezes were already rolling down from the Rockies; he looked up at the peaks iced with early snow and couldn't help thinking of Avery, where he might now have been preparing for a long, hungry winter. Instead, he had three meals a day and a roof over his head, compliments of Governor Gilpin. Colorado Territory had no money for military purposes, so Gilpin had taken the initiative and issued drafts on the U.S. Treasury, enabling him to purchase the land for Camp Weld, the supplies to build it, and food and the like for the regiment. Officer's Row was already complete and O'Brien had given up his tent for the private quarters allotted him, but he felt odd there alone, and spent most of his time with his men. As a captain he needn't have helped with the building, but he didn't like sitting idle.

"Water?" Hall said offering him a canteen. O'Brien took a swallow and nearly choked. It was whiskey, and bad whiskey at that.

"Didn't think it was water." Hall laughed as O'Brien coughed. "Just wanted to make sure—I know you've got a good palate."

"Bastard!" O'Brien said when he could get a breath. The men had all stopped work to laugh, and O'Brien grabbed the nearest one by the shirt. "Think it's funny, Ryan?"

"N-no, sir!" Ryan said unsteadily.

O'Brien upended the canteen, letting its contents gush onto the dirt to a chorus of protests. "Mr. Hall wants water," he said, pushing the empty canteen into Ryan's chest. "Fill it and bring it back. The rest of you back to work," he added, picking up his hammer as Ryan hurried toward the river.

"Losing your sense of humor, Red," said Hall, reaching for another board. "You're becoming quite a tyrant."

"You want a roof over your head before the weather turns sharp?" O'Brien asked, pounding a nail into the floorboard with two strokes.

"I plan to be in Officer's Row with you, thank you, soon as we have our election," Hall replied. "We need more wood."

"Franklin's fetching it."

"Shouldn't he be back by now?" Hall stood up and turned to look across the parade grounds. "Hey, there's Gilpin, come to visit his Pet Lambs again."

O'Brien followed Hall's gaze to where the governor stood with Major Chivington. With them was a stranger in a splendid uniform and cape, with polished boots up to his knees. "Who's the dandy?" O'Brien asked. "Never seen him before."

"Me, either," Hall said. "I'd've said it was Chas, but he's over there. Looks like he's having some trouble, too."

O'Brien shifted his gaze and saw Franklin struggling toward them pushing a wheelbarrow piled deep in lumber. With an impatient oath he strode forward to help. Franklin, to no one's surprise, had proved unhandy with hammer and saw and so was left to fetch and carry—backbreaking, menial work—which he did without complaint, if not with the greatest of speed. He had left off his coat but was otherwise still the fashionable sprig, meticulous in neat shirt and waistcoat even while the others stripped down for the hot work.

"You'd have a better grip if you took off those gloves," said O'Brien, taking the barrow's handles from him.

"Would I?" Franklin said lightly. "I fancied I had a better grip with them. Thank you, Captain," he added, panting as he followed O'Brien the last few steps to the skeletal barracks.

"Best let him keep the gloves, Red," Hall said lazily. "Wouldn't want him to dirty his lily-white hands."

O'Brien gave Hall a sharp look. Franklin's eyes flashed, but he turned away and started unloading the lumber. Hall's mouth curled up in a sneer.

The governor's party was approaching, and O'Brien went toward them, though he'd met Governor Gilpin before. Gilpin was an old army colonel and was known to be immensely proud of the regiment he'd created for Colorado; he visited them so often that the Denver paper had dubbed them his Pet Lambs.

"Captain O'Brien," Major Chivington said, "I'd like you to meet Colonel Slough, our commanding officer."

O'Brien stared in astonishment at the dandy next to Chivington. The colonel was almost as large as the major and had a long, full beard and belligerent eyes. The cape draped over his splendid uniform was lined in cavalry yellow, and his new leather belt gleamed as bright as his buckle and buttons.

"This is a captain?" Slough said. "What is he doing in a work detail?" His gaze passed disdainfully over O'Brien's sweat-stained Pike's Peakers.

"Just lending a hand, sir," O'Brien replied.

"Out of uniform, as well. I could bring you up on charges, Captain. Conduct unbecoming an officer."

O'Brien's cheeks burned. "I haven't got a uniform, sir."

"Hasn't had time to order it, I expect," Governor Gilpin said. "You and your men just enlisted, didn't you?"

"Yes, sir," O'Brien said.

"Well, see that you acquire one at once," Slough told him. "I'll not have any shabby officers in my command." He moved on with Chivington, leaving O'Brien stunned.

Gilpin hung back a few paces and smiled, saying, "There's a good tailor on Twelfth Street. Tell him I referred you."

"Thank you, sir." O'Brien said. Slough's sneering had only made him angry, but the governor's kindness made him ashamed of his naked chest and grimy trousers, and he turned back to work.

"So that's our glorious colonel," Hall said, laying a new board in place, "condescending to visit his slaves."

"What the devil made Gilpin choose him?" Shaunessy asked.

"He recruited Company A and helped with some of the others," Franklin said. "And he's donated money, I believe."

"Bought himself a pair of eagles, eh?" Hall said. "Too bad you didn't think of that, Chas."

"He also," Franklin continued as if he hadn't heard, "was expelled from the Ohio state legislature."

"Oho!" Morris said, looking up. "What for?"

Franklin flashed a grin. "Got in a fistfight with another member, right in the house," he said, and the men laughed.

"Know a lot, don't you?" Hall said. "Been spying?"

"Just listening." An odd smile turned up one corner of Franklin's mouth. "One can learn a lot that way."

Hall had no answer and instead slammed a nail into his board. O'Brien watched him scowl, then reached for his own hammer, likewise feeling the need to pound something.

Cottonwoods on the plaza were beginning to turn yellow, and the air had the crispness of fall. The day could not have been more perfect for an excursion, and Laura looked forward to touring the old Pueblo city she had only glimpsed on her way into Santa Fé. As Mrs. Canby's carriage stopped outside the Exchange, Laura stepped to the open doorway, smiling and waving at Lieutenants Anderson, McIntyre, and Nicodemus, who accompanied the carriage on horseback.

"Good morning, Miss Howland," Mrs. Canby called. "Oh, I should have told you to bring a wide-brimmed hat. Shall I have Juan Carlos put up the top?"

"No, it's such a fine morning," Laura said, "I do not think the wind will trouble me."

"It is the sun you must beware of," Mrs. Chapin said, helping Mrs. Canby rearrange the picnic hampers to make room for Laura to sit. "Mountain sun burns quickly. Take my hat, I am brown already."

"No, no," Laura protested as she climbed into the carriage. "We will be going through Glorieta, and it is shady there."

"You'll be burned before we reach the pass," Mrs. Chapin warned.

"Miss Howland?"

Laura looked down to see Lieutenant McIntyre standing beside the carriage holding out a hat of plain straw. "Seligman Brothers," he said, gesturing down the street. "They didn't have a black one, I'm afraid."

"That's very kind of you, Mr. McIntyre," Laura said. "Thank you." His smile made her feel suddenly shy, and she busied herself changing her black bonnet for the more practical straw.

Dr. Connelly arrived on horseback, completing the party. Mr. McIntyre mounted, and the carriage and its military escort started southward at a smart trot. They splashed through the Río de Santa Fé, as Laura had learned the little stream was called, and passed two Mexican—no, native—women, walking together down the street, masked in red paint.

"What have they put on their faces?" she asked.

"Alegría," Mrs. Canby said. "It's the juice of a native plant. They use it to protect their complexions from the sun."

"Sometimes they use flour paste instead," Mrs. Chapin

added. "They wash it off and become Spanish beauties when they are going to a fandango, and then smear it on again when they go home."

"What exactly is a fandango?" Laura asked.

"A dance," Mrs. Canby said, "or a party, of sorts. They can last several days and travel from house to house."

"That sounds a bit wild." Laura said.

"They are more than a bit wild," Mrs. Chapin said, laughing. "I made my husband take me to one once. Never again! You would not think they were a Christian people!"

The day warmed quickly and Laura was regretting her blacks by the time they stopped to break their journey at a place Mrs. Canby called Cañoncito, just west of the entrance to Glorieta Pass. A little creek, overlooked by the modest buildings of a ranch, trickled between steep brown hills. The rancher, Mr. Johnson, kindly allowed them to picnic in the shade of his portal, as there were only scrub cedars and piñon trees on the hills, too small to protect them from the sun. Mrs. Canby and Mrs. Chapin had packed sandwiches, pickles, and two large jars of lemonade for which Laura expressed enlightened appreciation.

"You may thank Dr. Connelly," Mrs. Canby told her. "He brought me a whole barrel of lemons from Mexico."

"Thank you, Doctor," Laura said gravely.

"De nada," he replied just as gravely, though there was a twinkle in his eye.

"I suppose you shall not have time for such trifles, now that you are to be governor," Mrs. Chapin said.

"On the contrary, madam," Connelly said. "It is business as usual. Government would be nothing without commerce."

"Do you see this hill behind us, Miss Howland?" Mr. McIntyre asked. "That is where General Armijo put his cannon to meet Kearny."

Laura turned questioning eyes to him. "I had thought Kearny's conquest was unopposed."

"It was," Mr. Anderson said. "Armijo fled to Chihuahua before Kearny entered the pass. Ask Colonel Chaves about it—he was there."

"May we climb it?" Laura asked, looking up at the hill.

Mrs. Chapin chuckled. "It is steeper than you think."

"Ah, but I am in need of exercise. I have been hiding away too long. Don't you agree, Doctor?"

"Miss Howland, I am more a trader than a physician, and in any case I would not presume to prescribe for a young lady who enjoys such evident good health."

"I shall take that as license, then." Laura got up, brushing crumbs from her skirt. "Who will accompany me?"

Three volunteers answered in chorus. Laura and the lieutenants started up the hill, while Mrs. Canby and Mrs. Chapin remained in the shade with Dr. Connelly. The hill was indeed steep; in the East it would have been called a mountain, but here at the feet of blue peaks it had a humbler status. The earth was dry and powdery, puffing up dust at every step, and Laura resigned herself to the smudging of her skirt hem. Mr. Anderson warned her away from cactuses hiding in little clumps of curly silver grass. The sun beat upon her black dress, and by the time they reached the top she welcomed the cold breeze blowing out of the mountains. Holding her hat onto her head with one hand, she gazed eastward to where the Santa Fé Trail disappeared between tall hills on its way toward Glorieta Pass.

"It is a striking view," she said. "How grand Kearny's army must have looked marching through that gap!"

"It's called Apache Canyon," Mr. Nicodemus said. "Named after Indian raiders. They used to hide in the hills and come down the canyon to attack the wagon trains."

"Dear me," Laura said. "So close to Santa Fé?"

"Apaches are fearless, ferocious," said Nicodemus. "Why, they burned the whole town once, back in Spanish days!"

"That wasn't Apaches, Nico," Mr. Anderson said dryly. "It was the Pueblos."

"Was it? I forget."

Laura smiled. "Have you been in New Mexico long, Mr. Anderson?"

"A little over a year."

"And have you had to fight Apaches?"

"No." He smiled. "The tribes in this area have signed a peace treaty."

"It's Navajo ladrones that are troubling us just now," Mr. McIntyre said. "They keep raiding the tribes we're at peace with, and the farmers and ranchers. It's virtually impossible to prevent them. Canby had my company out after them all winter, while Allen and Nico here were snug and warm in Santa Fé."

"So," Laura said, "the Apaches are at peace, and the Navajos and Pueblos are dangerous—"

"No, no," Mr. Anderson said. "The Pueblos are very much at peace. The rebellion was a long time ago. I've had the honor of meeting some of the leaders at Tesuque and Taos. They're quite intelligent, good people, really."

"I had not realized there were so many tribes," Laura said. "I assumed it was all much simpler, and—well, more organized."

"No, it's all wild," Mr. Nicodemus said in a thrilling voice. "All we can do to keep savages from burning the towns!"

"Let's find Miss Howland some wildflowers, shall we?" Mr. Anderson cast her an apologetic glance as he took Mr. Nicodemus by the arm and led him away.

"Would you like some water?" Mr. McIntyre offered a pocket flask. The gesture reminded her of her uncle, but she shook off the memory and smiled.

"Thank you," Laura said. "It is so very dry here."

"Different from Boston."

Laura took a sip from the flask, then handed it back. "Have you been to Boston, Mr. McIntyre?"

"No."

"I miss the sea." Laura sighed deeply, and the wind seemed to echo her, sighing through the boughs of the piñon trees. "I suppose we ought to start back," she added, glancing around for the other gentlemen.

"Miss Howland . . ."

Laura looked up and found Mr. McIntyre gazing at her with an intensity that made her heart beat a little faster. His silence confirmed her suspicion: He wished to become her suitor. She looked away, pleasure and alarm assailing her together.

When he spoke again, his voice was hoarse with feeling. "I hope—"

"Here you are, Miss Howland," Anderson said, returning through the trees. "Samples of local flora. This is Indian paintbrush, and here's yarrow, and bluebonnet."

"Oh, thank you," Laura said, managing to smile as she accepted the flowers. "Red, white, and blue. How patriotic!"

"Here's some yellow to go with them," Mr. Nicodemus said, handing her a cluster of small five-petaled blooms.

"And these are?"

"Er—little yellow things," he said.

"Thank you," Laura said, laughing. "Thank you both!" She glanced up at Mr. McIntyre, who had walked a few steps away.

"We're being summoned," Mr. Anderson said.

Laura looked down to where Dr. Connelly was waving an arm and pointing toward the sun, which was past noon. They started down the hill, much faster than going up; Laura had to make her steps very small to avoid breaking into a scramble. At the ranch house she stopped to beat the dust out of her skirts while Mr. McIntyre filled an empty pickle jar with water from the creek for her flowers, then got back in the carriage and leaned gratefully against the cushions.

As Apache Canyon closed in on either side, the air was immediately cooler. Laura watched the forest change from dusty scrub cedar to the darker green of tall pines, with cottonwoods here and there and meadows of greener grasses dotted with flowers: speckled white, and great sweeps of purple aster. The trail wound between hills, rising until it crested at the top of the pass, after which they could see Pigeon's Ranch at the bottom of a long slope, surrounded with cottonwoods turned gold by the first frost. They stopped briefly to bespeak supper and rooms for the night, and Laura got out of the carriage and crossed the trail, entering the woods south of the road. Rays of sunshine pierced the canopy of golden leaves, setting them gloriously ablaze. She held her hands out as she walked, catching at falling leaves, enjoying the dry sounds beneath her feet and the rich smell of autumn.

"Glorieta," she said softly. The word had acquired a kind of magic for her—a special meaning. Sanctuary. Peace.

And change. A leaf drifted before her and she caught it, traced its veins with a gloved finger. It was neither quite brittle nor completely supple. It was changing with the coming of autumn, and so was her life.

Her uncle was pressuring her to marry. She had always assumed she would do so, but she did not like being pressed. She had other interests. In Boston she had been very interested in civil rights, including the rights of women. She knew Mrs. Stanton had been able to manage marriage and motherhood along with her noble work and saw no reason why she could not do the same, yet at home it had never seemed urgent; marriage was something that would occur some day in the vague future. Here, in the West, there was pressure to acquire a husband who would be both provider and protector.

And Mr. McIntyre wished to court her.

"Miss Howland!" It was Mrs. Chapin's voice.

"I'm here," Laura called, and hastened back to the road.

"We thought we had lost you," said Dr. Connelly, handing her into the carriage. "The young men were about to organize a search party." Laura glanced at him, noting his wry expression, and concealed a smile.

Soon they were rolling along eastward again. Sunlight flickered over the ladies' faces. Laura toyed with the cottonwood leaf, twirling it by the stem. It was spade-shaped, and spades in a deck of cards represented swords, or the military. That was the trouble, she realized. Her would-be suitor was a soldier, and she was not at all sure she wished to be a soldier's wife. Even Mrs. Canby, the wife of a colonel, had to endure the stress of her husband's absence. Mr. McIntyre would be going east soon, going to war. Was it selfish of her to wish to protect her heart from possible grief?

"There's the ruin," Mrs. Chapin said, pointing south. "Pecos Pueblo."

Laura had scarcely glimpsed the crumbling Indian city on her trip in to Santa Fé. Now she saw that it was much larger than she remembered, built atop a long, low mesa, with the remains of the Spanish church standing guard at its eastern end.

"This was a pueblo?" Laura asked as she stepped down from the carriage.

"Two, actually," Mrs. Canby said, joining her. "There were hundreds of people here once. The last few disappeared about twenty years ago."

"Disappeared?"

"They went to Jemez Pueblo," Dr. Connelly said. "There was only one family left."

"Shall we begin with the church?" Mrs. Canby asked, leading the way up the hill. The Spanish church, built in the shape of a cross, was the only structure left standing and was no more than three hundred years old, according to Dr. Connelly. It was made of adobe, some sixty feet by thirty, within huge walls several feet thick. The ceiling had fallen in, but even in decay Laura was impressed with its lofty grandeur. A few beams remained, showing crafts-manship that was skilled, if not fine.

"What an interesting pattern," Laura said, noting some diagonal adobe brickwork in one of the crumbling walls at the back of the church.

"Yes," Mr. Anderson said. "Inventive work for savages."

Laura smiled. "You don't believe they were savages."

"No," he said, smiling back.

The party scattered to wander among the rubble and explore. Laura strolled out into the sunshine along the side of the great church and stopped to gaze at a tangled patch of wild herbs inside the remains of a low adobe wall. "This must have been a lovely garden," she said to herself.

"Do you like gardens, Miss Howland?" Laura looked up to see Mr. McIntyre a few steps away. No one else was near.

"Yes," she said. "My father and I used to grow homeopathic herbs whenever we had a patch of ground to scratch on."

"Herbs? Not flowers?"

"Those, too." Looking toward the pueblo, she saw Dr. Connelly and Mrs. Canby picking their way among the crumbled walls. "We've fallen behind. Will you escort me, and prevent my tumbling into a pit?"

"Miss Howland—"

He would not be stayed from declaring himself, then. Laura's heart quickened, and she made an effort to breathe slowly. She raised her eyes to meet his, and found his gaze so intent that she had to steel herself not to turn away.

Please don't, she thought. Not just now.

He seemed to be searching her face, and for a moment he said nothing. Then he drew a breath and said, somewhat haltingly, "It would be my very great pleasure to watch over you." With these words he offered his arm.

Laura breathed a sigh. "Thank you," she said, favoring him with a smile. She laid her hand on his arm, and they walked away from the ruined church, hastening to catch up with the others.

9

We are getting very tired of being confined in a fort, and long to go into action; although some of us may never come out of it alive.

—Corporal Charles A. Shanks, 2nd Texas Mounted Rifles

"Hurry up, then," O'Brien said, leaning over Hall to peer at the page he was writing on. "I'll be late!"

"Take it easy," Hall said. "You want it to look nice, don't you?"

O'Brien paced away to the end of his quarters, glanced out the window at the cold morning, then turned his back to it. "All these papers—you should have been the captain."

"All you have to do is sign them," Hall said. "That's all the other captains do. Here, it's done."

O'Brien came back to where Hall was sitting and knelt by him, taking the pen. He stared at the report, tidy lines of script with a sprinkling of numbers. "What does it say?"

"It says all present for duty except Duncan who's in the guard house for drunkenness. Sign it. You're late."

O'Brien slowly scrawled his name at the bottom of the form. He was getting better at it, what with daily reports to sign; the quill hardly ever skipped now. "Thank you," he said, handing the pen back, and Hall's eyed flickered amusement.

"You're welcome. Go on ahead, I'll clean this up."

"Joseph—"

Hall looked up. It was hard, very hard, to be asking, but

at last O'Brien managed to voice the request he'd been thinking of for weeks. "Would you teach me my letters?"

Hall's eyebrows rose. "Sure I will, if you like," he said with a shrug, and began gathering up the paper and ink.

O'Brien felt as if something wrapped tight around his chest had just broken. He blew on the ink to make sure it was dry, and hurried to headquarters to hand his report in to Chivington.

"Late, Mr. O'Brien," the major said, accepting the page.

"Sorry, sir."

"Here— what's this? Did you even look at this, Captain?"

O'Brien glanced at the paper in Chivington's hand and swallowed. "Yes, sir," he said.

"Well?" Chivington said.

O'Brien felt as if the floor were sinking beneath him. The major was frowning; had Hall put some nonsense into the report? "Sir?" he said.

"You've got a hundred and two men here," Chivington said.

"Yes, sir," O'Brien said, trying to recall if that was the right number. He thought so.

"Well, hold your elections, man! Should have done it a week ago!"

Sucking air in relief, O'Brien nodded. "We'll hold them tonight, sir."

"Hold them before battalion drill," Chivington said. "I want your report after dress parade."

"Yes, sir."

"Promptly, Captain."

"Yes, sir," said O'Brien.

"Dismissed."

O'Brien hurried back to his quarters, where he found Hall standing over one of the new recruits—a farm boy, by his looks. He had bucket and brush and was scrubbing away at the floor.

"Better have the boys make you a table and chair, Red," Hall said. "I dripped ink on your floor."

"Never mind," O'Brien said. "Company drill, come along. You can finish that later, Private."

He and Hall turned out the men and placed the half-dozen recruits among them according to height. The farmer's son went on the left with the shorter men, and as they began to drill, O'Brien saw he would be a problem. He was clumsy and had to be told several times what to do. Franklin, on his right, took to prompting him. It helped, until Hall chose to stride down the line and shout. "Franklin! Breeden! No talking in the ranks!"

Franklin looked at him. "I was merely explaining—"

"I said no talking, Private Franklin!"

"You're not our lieutenant yet, Mr. Hall," Franklin said.

O'Brien saw Hall's eyes narrow and stepped up beside him. "Attention, Company!" he shouted. Franklin nudged the farm boy, who had shouldered his old squirrel gun. O'Brien pretended not to see the gun slide slowly back to the ground, glanced at Hall to make sure he had come to attention, and addressed the men.

"Company elections will be held at one o'clock in the first platoon's mess room. Be there as soon as you're done eating dinner. Now," he added, backing away a few steps, "company, right face!" He sighed as only half the men remembered to double. "Get back in line, you damn bloody trolls! Again!"

He worked them hard till the dinner call sounded, then got Hall to help him tear paper for ballots. The company gathered in a mess room that still smelled like sawdust, and O'Brien stepped up to its single, new-made table. He looked over the sea of faces turned toward him and realized he no longer knew all his men by name. The company had grown just as fast as the barracks.

"Here are your ballots," he said, as Hall started passing out paper to the men. "You'll have to share pencils. I need two volunteers to count the votes—all right, Denning—and McGuire." O'Brien handed the fiddler a box to collect the votes in.

"I'd like you all to remember that it was Mr. Hall who

suggested I form this company," O'Brien said. "Write your choice for first lieutenant, then second lieutenant, then first sergeant . . ." He went on down the list, then waited while the men conferred and scribbled. He noticed one of the newer men talking to Franklin, and Franklin nodding and filling in the man's ballot. O'Brien looked away, his face growing hot.

Hall came up and dropped his vote in McGuire's box, then leaned against the table next to O'Brien. "Looking forward to my new quarters," he said, grinning.

The men waited, chatting in low tones, while Denning and McGuire tallied the votes. O'Brien watched them pile up the ballots, then Denning frowned and went through them a second time. Finally he looked up at O'Brien and offered him the tally sheet.

"Read it," O'Brien said, nodding toward the company.

Denning looked uncomfortable. "There were one hundred and one ballots," he said. "Maybe we should send someone to get Duncan's vote?"

"The only thing he'd vote for the next couple of days is rye whiskey," Morris shouted, evoking a laugh from the men.

"No, it's his bad luck," O'Brien said. "Go on, then."

Denning licked his lips, and held the paper at arm's length. "Company I Officers. First lieutenant, sixty-three votes, Charles Franklin."

"What?!" Hall exclaimed.

O'Brien looked at Franklin, who seemed as astonished as Hall was, and none too pleased.

"Second lieutenant," said Denning, "thirty-two votes, Joseph Hall—"

"Hold on there!" Hall said. "I want a recount."

"We counted it twice," McGuire said.

"*I'll* count it, damn it!" Hall strode to the table and seized the ballots. Denning gave him a nervous glance.

"First sergeant by forty-one votes, Luther Denning." Denning paused as if expecting a challenge, then continued. "Second sergeant, thirty-seven votes, Hugh Ramsey. . . ."

As Denning continued, Franklin worked his way forward. "If you dislike it, Captain, I'll withdraw," he said quietly.

"Beg pardon, sir," said Morris, who was standing nearby. He turned to Franklin. "I voted for you, Charles. A lot of us voted for you because you're smart. We'll need smart officers when we go to Leavenworth."

"Sixty-three," McGuire said, as Hall slapped the final ballot onto the table, scowling.

O'Brien frowned. "Hall's just as smart as—"

"Leave it, Red," Hall said sharply. He came toward Franklin, smiling. "I'm content if you are, Chas."

There was something in Hall's eyes that gave the lie to his words. Franklin saw it, too, and hesitated.

"Come on, Charlie," Ryan said, joining them. "We want you."

Franklin shot him a glare. "Don't call me Charlie."

"Take it, Charles," Denning said. "Please." A number of others came forward and gathered around Franklin, who glanced at O'Brien, then at the hand Hall offered.

"All right," he said to Denning, a corner of his mouth turning up in a wry smile as he pulled off his glove. "I'll try not to disappoint you."

Franklin's hand was small, very white compared to his sun-darkened cheeks, and perfectly groomed, and it all but disappeared into Hall's great brown paw. Hall grinned, his eyes two gleaming slits. "I'm sure we won't be disappointed," he said, prolonging the grip. O'Brien wondered if he was trying to crush the lad's fingers.

"First Sergeant," O'Brien said, "write up the results and bring them to me. The rest are dismissed." O'Brien stood by the table, watching the men disperse, with Hall silent beside him. Morris slapped Franklin on the back as he pulled on his glove again. Franklin tossed a strained smile at O'Brien before letting Morris and the others lead him away.

"There's gratitude for you," Hall said. "After the fine bargain I gave them on their horses."

"Oh, aye, a fine bargain," O'Brien said. Hall glared, and O'Brien relented, saying softly, "I'll speak to the major."

"I don't want any favors from you, Red."

"Ah, now don't be off sulking. They like him because of his fine horse and all of his money, but when we're on the campaign, they'll be glad of an experienced leader."

Hall smiled reluctantly. "Well, by then it might not be an issue," he said, watching Franklin pass out of the room.

O'Brien glanced at his friend. "No trouble," he warned. "I don't want to see you in the guard house."

"You know me, Red," Hall said in a lazy drawl. "Trouble's the last thing I want." Hall's words were easy but as he strolled away his body was taut, and O'Brien saw his hand clenching into a fist.

Men swarmed over the cannon, sweating in the fall afternoon and cursing each other in their haste. The nearest crew to McIntyre was the first to finish the loading drill. Leaning against the adobe wall that surrounded Fort Marcy Post's grounds, he watched Anderson give a curt word of approval to the gunner, then jog down the battery line to advise the other crews. McIntyre sympathized with the frowning artillerymen. Until recently they had been cavalrymen—mounted rifles before that—and while willing, they appeared not to relish their new work.

There were two twelve pound field howitzers and two six-pounders, and providing their equipment had pretty well exhausted the department of field artillery supply. More had been sent for, but "more" was increasingly a futile request. Washington was preoccupied with its hopeful star, General McClellan, and had little interest in the remote Territories or their troubles.

McIntyre waited through the drill, all the while watching Anderson. He hadn't seen much of his friend since Captain Hatch's promotion and departure eastbound. Anderson had volunteered to take charge of the newly formed battery and was spending most of his time whipping it into shape.

"Dismissed," Anderson cried at last, in a voice gone hoarse from unaccustomed shouting. He trotted to where McIntyre was leaning against the wall and grinned, white teeth flashing. "What do you think? They're a bit awkward still, but they're coming along."

"Not bad for one month's drill," McIntyre agreed.

"Hatch made a good start with them. By the time we get to Craig they'll be in fine form." He took off his hat and mopped at his tanned face with a handkerchief.

"Looking forward to it?" McIntyre asked.

Anderson glanced at him, then gave a laugh as he returned the damp handkerchief to his pocket. "I suppose so. Yes."

"You liked being adjutant."

"I don't mind the change."

Anderson started toward the gate, and McIntyre followed him. "Let me buy you a drink."

"Oh, no thanks," Anderson said. "I'm behind on my correspondence—"

"Bull. You could write six letters in an hour. Nico's not half as efficient."

"He just starts out slow," Anderson said. "We started in the same class at the Academy, but I'm the one that was held back a year. He'll get the knack of it, you'll see."

"We miss you already, Allen."

Anderson stopped short and gave a startled laugh. "I suppose I've been trying not to think about it." He looked up at McIntyre. "I'll miss you, too."

McIntyre grinned. "Drink. I won't take no for an answer."

Anderson slowly grinned back. "Well, if I don't have a choice. . . ."

McIntyre flung an arm across his shoulders, and guided him toward the plaza.

The last Sunday before they were to march Momma fixed a special dinner in honor of Jamie and Captain Martin.

Emmaline met them on the porch, looking like a princess with her best Sunday dress glowing white in the twilight. She and Momma must have spent all day cooking. There were potatoes and beans and corn bread, sugar beets and carrots, a gigantic roast, and peach cobbler waiting on the sideboard. Martin took his usual place at Dan's chair beside Emma, and they all bowed their heads while Poppa said grace.

"Lord," he said, "we thank you for the bounty you have given us. We thank you for the friends, neighbors, and family with which you've blessed us, and we ask you to keep them safe through all their journeys. May God bless us all."

"And God bless Texas," Gabe added.

"God bless Texas," Poppa said, his voice wavering a little, and they all echoed him, then sat down to the feast.

Momma pressed Daniel's latest letter into Jamie's hand and asked him to read it aloud. Dan was with the Eighth Texas Cavalry, which had gone into Missouri. They still hadn't heard from Matt, but his name hadn't been on the casualty lists in the papers, and in his letter Dan said he'd heard Matt's company hadn't reached Virginia until after the battle at Manassas. Momma smiled when Jamie read that part.

Emma said very little over dinner. Martin planned to ask her tonight, Jamie knew, and he was quiet, too. When supper was over they all rose, and Martin gave Jamie a nervous smile.

"Gabriel," Momma said, her eyes on the captain, "you do the washing up tonight."

"That's Emma's chore!" Gabe protested.

"I'll help you," Jamie said. "Then we can have a game of checkers after. Give you a penny if you beat me."

"A half-dime!" Gabe said, his eyes lighting.

"Who taught you to be a sharp?" Jamie laughed. "Half a dime for two out of three." He started taking the plates to the kitchen, and saw Emma and Martin slip out to the porch. He and Gabe scrubbed and put away the dishes, then tidied the kitchen and set the kettle to boil for coffee. When they were finished Gabe skipped ahead to fetch the checkerboard while Jamie joined Momma and Poppa in the living room. Momma was knitting more socks—she was always sending socks to Matt and Dan—and Poppa was reading the paper. Gabe set the checkerboard on the floor between them, and Jamie made him work hard for his half-dime. Just as Gabe crowed in triumph at the end of the third game the front door opened and Emma came in, eyes shining and her fingers twined with Martin's.

"Momma and Poppa," she began, then seemed to choke on a big, silly grin and looked at Martin, who smiled back down at her.

"Mr. and Mrs. Russell, with your permission I'd like to marry your daughter," he said.

After a certain amount of whooping and hugging and back-slapping, everyone settled down to talk over the details. Jamie listened while he helped Gabe pick up the checkers, which had gotten scattered in the fuss. Martin outlined his family's background and his plans for giving Emma a home once he returned from campaigning. Emmaline was cheerful, insisting she didn't mind waiting. It would give her time to get her trousseau together, and besides, Poppa would need her on the ranch until one of the boys got back.

Momma smiled bravely and took out her big sewing basket. "I have something here for you, Jamie," she said, putting aside the cover. She reached into the basket and pulled out a jacket of gray wool, trimmed in orange for the mounted volunteers, with gold braid twining up to the elbows and a first lieutenant's bars on the collar.

Jamie whistled, and stood up to accept the gift. It was much finer than the plain gray shirt he'd been wearing and for which he had thought himself lucky. Uniforms were scarce, and most of the regiment was still in civilian clothes. He took the new cloth in his hands and rubbed it with his thumbs, noting the tiny stitches that had gone into it. Momma was proud of her needlework, and rightly so. A glance at Martin trying to hide a grin told him where the bars had come from. "It's beautiful, Momma," Jamie said, his chest getting tight. "You must have spent hours—"

"You'd best try it on," said Momma. "I used one of your old shirts for the size—you might have grown."

I haven't grown an inch in two years, Jamie thought. He shrugged into the jacket and smoothed the sleeves. "It's perfect," he said, and leaned down to hug Momma. "Thank you."

"My turn," Emmaline said. She got up from the sofa and went to Momma's china bowl on the mantel. From it she took two bits of metal, handing one each to Jamie and Martin. Jamie turned his over in his hand. It was a silver star, with a pin on the back.

"So you'll have a bit of Texas with you wherever you go," said Emma.

Jamie grabbed his sister up in a big bear hug, then turned her over to Martin while he sat down for one last checkers game with Gabe. A few minutes later everyone ignored the sound of the front door as the couple walked out.

The rest of the evening flew by, though not much really happened. Somehow the moves on the checkerboard had become awfully important. Jamie watched Gabe's hands and thought about how big they were getting, and wondered how big they'd be when he came back. He glanced up at Momma at work on her knitting again and at Poppa, who'd lit his pipe and sat rocking and staring at nothing. Maybe Sunday nights weren't much, but he would miss them sharply, he knew.

Time came for good-byes, and Jamie made them as fast as he could. Hugs all around, promise to write, good luck, keep safe. Jamie offered to fetch the horses, hoping to give Martin another minute alone with Emma, and Poppa said, "I'll lend you a hand."

They walked to the corral together, caught Cocoa and Martin's gray and saddled them up. Then Poppa looked at Jamie across the animals' backs.

"You be careful, Jamie," he said. "That's rough country."

"Sure, I will, Poppa."

"They give you a pistol?"

Jamie gazed at his father in surprise. "Yes, a Colt revolver."

"Good," Poppa said. "Keep it loaded. I want you to come back."

Poppa didn't say that sort of thing much, and Jamie felt like he'd been given a prize. "I will, sir," he said.

"Good thing you're a quartermaster," Poppa added, taking the reins of Martin's gray. "You probably won't have to fight."

Jamie frowned. He'd been thinking much the same thing not too long ago, but out loud the words sounded slightly insulting, though he was sure Poppa hadn't meant it that way. It wasn't like Jamie couldn't fight. He just had more important work.

Except that fighting was the most important work of the war, wasn't it? Fighting was the real work.

Jamie and Martin rode silently back to headquarters, each with plenty to think about. They had one day to finish organizing the train that would supply the regiment on its long march. They were called the 1st Regiment now, being the first of the three regiments in Sibley's brigade. They would also be the first to leave for Fort Bliss. The regiments would march a couple of weeks apart to give the springs along the way a chance to recover and to let the 2nd and 3rd finish mustering in.

Monday was madness. Rushing to get a few more wagons, assign teamsters, find extra herders for the beeves. Late in the morning an order came from General Sibley to distribute eight hundred pair of trousers to the regiment: trousers from the Federal uniforms left behind when General Twiggs had turned over the U.S. Army property after Texas seceded. Jamie commandeered a wagon to haul the clothing from the depot to Camp Sibley, a little way up Salado Creek. A few hours later he saw the trousers again when the regiment paraded in the Main Plaza.

It was well after dark when Martin finally sent Jamie to bed in the little room behind the office. Jamie lay on his back calculating how long it would take to get to Arizona Territory, and finally drifted to sleep thinking of bills to be paid. He woke before the sun was up, and pulled on boots and his new jacket over the clothes he'd slept in. Martin was up—or perhaps hadn't slept—writing to Captain Harrison, the brigade's chief quartermaster who had gone to New Orleans to fetch money for the payroll. Jamie leaned over his shoulder, watching him sign the letter.

"How come the men who have 'acting assistant' before their titles are the ones who do all the work?" he asked.

Martin laughed. "Would you mind scrounging up some coffee?"

Jamie nodded, wishing his future brother-in-law wouldn't act so normal. This was not a normal day. He opened the pot-bellied stove and poked life back into the dregs of yesterday's fire, then put the kettle on and went downstairs and outside.

The sky glowed like a deep, blue jewel. San Antonio was still asleep, but there was a sound on the breeze unlike any he'd heard before, something like a herd of cattle but deepened by the rumble of dozens of wagon wheels. He strolled north up St. Mary's Street until he could see past the buildings. A dark column was approaching from Camp Sibley; the 1st, all mounted, three wagons with each company to carry the gear.

It's really happening, Jamie thought. Strange to think that he was part of that awesome mass of soldiery. He had made it to the camp to drill with the regiment less than a dozen times, but he knew every piece of a soldier's equipment, how much it weighed and how much it cost and how long it would probably last.

Heading back, he met Sergeant Rose outside the Vance House. Rose had just transferred to the Q.M.D. a couple of weeks earlier. Jamie liked him, partly because he was younger than himself and partly because he was quick and clever with his hands. Rose was a carpenter's son, and had built Martin a portable field desk in only two days. Then he'd overseen the construction of a dozen more in response to the instant clamor of the headquarters staff.

"Pack up the office?" Rose asked as they climbed the stairs. Jamie nodded, and the two of them started to sort and pack papers while Martin tied up the loose ends. They finished just in time to get down to the Military Plaza and take their place with the staff as the 1st Regiment formed.

Jamie smoothed the orange cuff of his new jacket, and searched the crowd for familiar faces. Seemed like all of San Antonio had turned out to see the 1st off in the cool of the morning. He spied Mr. Webber watching, and Gabe beside him. Farther back, he saw Poppa's wagon in the line of carriages and carts, with Momma and Poppa on the seat, and Emmaline standing behind in the wagon bed. She waved, and Jamie had to keep himself from waving back.

Colonel Reily gave a stirring speech and his own daughter presented the regimental colors: the Lone Star, and the Stars and Bars. Jamie felt an odd tug at his chest when the flags were displayed. Those colors were the regiment's tie to home and would not be taken from them except at the cost of blood.

General Sibley made a speech, too, and though he didn't speak as well as Reily, he looked so fine in his gold braided uniform, surrounded by crisp staff officers, that Jamie didn't care what he said. Sibley was splendid, plain and simple. He had the bearing of a hero with his tall, erect frame and handsome side whiskers. Jamie was proud to be following such a general.

Then the speeches were over, the regiment was marching west out of town, and the three quartermasters were scrambling to the depot. Wagons choked the streets, and Martin and Jamie shouted themselves hoarse getting things moving. By the time the train finally rolled out in the regiment's wake, the sun was well up in the east.

As they neared Russell's Ranch, Jamie saw Martin look toward the house. Jamie heard nickering from the barn, then saw Smokey trotting out with a rider on his back. Too tall for Gabe, not big enough for Poppa. Jamie smiled and guided Cocoa toward Emmaline, who fell in with the column.

"We got a letter from Matt yesterday," she said, grinning at him. "He hadn't got ours yet. He said tell you to keep watch over the beans and coffee."

Jamie grinned back. "Tell him I am," he said, and with a last hug across horseflesh, he moved off again to let Martin get in a final word of farewell.

The last day of October was mustering day, and also O'Brien's birthday. The morning began with an icy sky and a dim, glowing halo 'round the sun: a sign of change, probably for the worse. O'Brien tucked his hands into his armpits to warm them, wishing he'd paid the extra money for a pair of gloves along with his new uniform. He joined Hall on the parade ground where Company I was beginning to assemble. Hall nodded approval.

"You look right official, Red. How do you like mine?"

"Very smart," O'Brien said.

"Tell you who's smart, it's that damned tailor in Denver City. Must be making a fortune. Had to sell Hambleton another horse to pay for this."

O'Brien nodded in sympathy. He had given most of his money to the tailor himself, keeping only a few dollars for lean times. He had not yet been paid—none of the men had. It was only by means of his Treasury drafts that Governor Gilpin had been able to feed and equip the regiment.

"Here comes Chas," Hall said. "Ain't he a picture?"

O'Brien looked up and saw Franklin coming toward them, looking crisp in a blue coat that fit him exactly. He wore new gloves—cavalry style, soft leather with big bell cuffs—and a plumed hat, and as he approached took a small book from his pocket with unconscious grace. The combined effect sparked sudden resentment in O'Brien. All the oppressors of wealth, birth, and schooling—all the things he didn't have and whose lack kept him in his place—stood

before him in Franklin. He could knock them down with
one blow if he chose, but the depths of his instinct
restrained him. To strike unawares would be to yield any
claim to honor and confirm himself a peasant in every
sense. He held off, not for Franklin's sake but for his own.

"Good morning, Captain," Franklin said. "Mr. Hall."

"There'll be no reading on the parade grounds, Lieutenant," O'Brien said.

Franklin looked surprised. "It's the manual of tactics,
sir. I thought I should—"

"Not on the parade grounds!" O'Brien snapped, and
with a swift movement knocked the book out of Franklin's
hands.

"Yes, sir." Franklin's startled eyes held O'Brien's,
watching warily. The book lay in the dust at their feet, and
Hall stooped to pick it up.

"Think this book'll teach you how to fight, Chas?"

Franklin's gaze flickered to Hall as he flipped through
the pages. A card slipped out, and Franklin's hand moved
swiftly toward it, but Hall stepped away.

"What have we here?" Hall said, peering at it. "This
you, Chas?"

Franklin reached for the card again, pale with anger.
"No," he said as Hall held it out of his reach.

"Brother and sister?"

"That's right," said Franklin.

"Isn't that sweet?" Hall brought the portrait to O'Brien.
"See, Red? Sis looks just like Chas, only a sight meaner."

O'Brien glanced at the worn image. The woman in it did
resemble Franklin, as did the man.

"All right, give it back," Franklin said.

Hall handed the book to O'Brien and waved the picture
tauntingly at Franklin. "Fight you for it," he said, grinning.

"No."

"What's the matter, Chas? Afraid to dirty your pretty
new clothes?"

"No—"

"Or are you just a coward?" Hall said this loud enough for

some of the men standing nearby to hear. His eyes had narrowed to gleaming slits, and his grin was becoming a sneer.

Franklin lifted his chin. "I volunteered in order to fight Confederates," he said, "not—"

"I was born in Mobile," Hall said. "That good enough?"

"Not while you wear that uniform."

"I'll take it off, if it makes you feel braver."

Franklin's fine nostrils flared. "Don't bother," he said coldly. "It would be unseemly of me to strike a man of lesser rank."

Hall's grin vanished, replaced by an ugly scowl as he lunged toward Franklin. O'Brien stepped swiftly between them, grabbing Hall by the shoulders. "Chivington," he hissed in Hall's ear.

They all came to attention as the major approached. "Trouble, gentlemen?" he said.

"No, sir," O'Brien said.

"I was just showing Mr. Hall a carte-de-visite, sir," Franklin said.

Chivington's eyebrows went up, and he took the card away from Hall. After a glance he handed it to Franklin, who tucked it into his coat. "Colonel Slough has ordered all company commanders to report with muster rolls," he told O'Brien, then glanced at Franklin and Hall. "Save your blows for the secessionists, gentlemen."

Chivington moved on. Hall glared at Franklin and spat in the dust at his feet. Franklin stood silent, eyes cold and a stubborn set to his jaw. A bugle call signaled assembly.

"Get the company formed," O'Brien said to Franklin, tossing the book to him. Franklin caught it, stared at O'Brien for a moment, then saluted and stalked away.

"Coward," Hall said softly to Franklin's back.

"Stow it, Hall." O'Brien held out his hand. "Give me the muster roll."

Hall took out the paperwork and handed it to him. "Here," he said, "and a little something in honor of the day." A slender flask glinted under the paperwork, silver, brand new by its finish. O'Brien glanced over his shoulder to make sure Chivington wasn't watching, then opened it and smelled the ambrosia scent of old Irish whiskey.

"You're a true friend, Joseph," he said, breaking into a grin as he slipped the flask into his pocket. He clapped Hall on the back, then hurried into the general dining hall where the muster would take place. Tappan, now lieutenant-colonel of the regiment, sat at a table with pen in hand, much as he had on the day O'Brien had first arrived with his fledgling company. Behind him stood Slough and the surgeon who would examine the men.

"F Company," Tappan said as O'Brien entered. "Captain Cook."

O'Brien got in line behind Captain Marion of K Company, a quick, dark-haired fellow from Central City. Sam Logan, who had replaced Tappan as captain of Company B, came over to join him.

"Felicitations, Red," Logan said. He tapped O'Brien's muster roll. "Many happy returns, eh?" He laughed heartily.

O'Brien shook his head, sighing. "You'd joke with the Devil," he said.

"If he gave me the chance," Logan said. "Hear about Springfield?"

O'Brien shook his head. "What about it?"

"G Company," Tappan said. "Captain Hambleton."

"Frémont whipped some Rebels there last Friday," Logan said. "News came over the telegraph, and when California heard they wired back offering a regiment. Amazing thing, ain't it? Crossing the whole continent?"

"The telegraph?" O'Brien asked. "Or the Californians?"

Logan chuckled. "Now that—"

"No!" came a shout, and the whole room looked up at Hambleton standing before Tappan. "We joined as mounted rifles," he said, "not infantry!"

"This is an infantry regiment," Colonel Slough said in a chilly voice. "And less than half of your company is mounted."

"We're not infantry!" Hambleton insisted, his color rising.

"Josiah," Sanborn said, "we've got to stick together here. You know I wanted my boys to be zouaves, but—"

"Zouaves?" Marion sneered. "What's a zouave but a fellow dressed up like an organ-grinder's monkey? If we muster as infantry we could lose our horses!" He strode forward and jabbed a finger into Cook's chest. "You should know better, Samuel! You got passed over for promotion, didn't you? Because of your horses!"

"Marion—" Cook began.

"You're out of order, Captain," Slough said.

Cook backed up until his lanky form came up against a table. Marion kept pressing him. "Want to see your boys dismounted?"

"No!" Hambleton shouted again, his bellow almost a match for Chivington's. O'Brien wished the major were present.

"Captain Marion!" Slough snapped, coming around the desk.

"Do you, Sam?" Marion demanded, ignoring the colonel. Getting no response from Cook, he turned to O'Brien, eyes glaring. "O'Brien, do you?"

"Captain Marion!" Slough said, before O'Brien could answer. "Stand at attention!"

Marion faced him, a wild glitter in his eyes. "I'll see you in hell before I muster my men as infantry!"

Slough's nostrils flared. "Guard!" he called, and the two privates outside the door ran in looking fit to soil themselves. Slough pointed at Marion, rage shaking hand and voice both. "This man is under arrest. Disarm him, and tell the officer of the guard I want him escorted to the city jail."

Tappan put down his pen, leaned back in his chair, and folded his hands. One of the privates, eyes wide with alarm, stepped forward and turned to Marion. "Captain, please surrender your arms," he said nervously.

Marion smiled sourly and gave up his pistol and sword. "If you want men to follow you you've got to give them good reason," he said to Slough.

"You will be silent, sir!" Slough ordered, brows drawing together until he looked nearly cross-eyed.

Marion gave a soft laugh. "And you'll be sorry," he said. "Wait and see."

The guards marched him off, door banging shut behind them, and no one moved for a moment. Then Tappan picked up his pen, dipped it in ink, and dabbed the excess on the mouth of the inkwell. "G Company," he said. "Captain Hambleton."

Hambleton stood in the middle of the room like a mad bull deciding what to run at. "We're not infantry," he said, but he sounded more sullen than sure.

"You are infantry or you are nothing," Slough said icily. "You're one step from prison yourself, Captain."

O'Brien moved forward, enough to attract Slough's glare. He was angry, as well, but he forced himself to speak politely. "We won't lose our horses, sir, will we? They're our own property—"

"I don't give a damn about your horses," Slough replied. "You will muster as infantry, or not at all!"

"Well, Captain Hambleton?" Tappan asked.

Hambleton stood frowning, then turned and, with a muttered oath, stalked out of the room. No one moved.

"H Company," Tappan said into the silence. "Sanborn."

Sanborn gave his sheet over without a word. Easy enough, for his men had always been infantry. O'Brien looked at the paper curled in his hands and thought of the effort he'd spent building his Avery trolls into a company. All hopes—theirs and his—for winning glory and riches would come to nothing if they were not mustered into the United States' service.

"I Company. O'Brien."

O'Brien raised his head and looked Tappan in the eye. Tappan was like cold marble, unreadable. O'Brien walked forward and turned in his muster roll, then signed his name at the end of Tappan's list. It was the best he'd ever written it, he noted as he gave the paper back.

Tappan accepted it, then shuffled his papers. "Mustering by company," he said. "A Company, Wynkoop."

The captains began to disperse. O'Brien stood watching Slough, whose jealous eyes followed each man through the door. When they turned on O'Brien he looked away and without a word followed the others, glancing up at the sun as he stepped outside. The grounds were abuzz with gossip. Wynkoop's men, filing in to be mustered, stared curiously at O'Brien as they passed. He ignored them and walked toward his own company.

"What the hell happened?" Hall asked, coming to meet him. "They've got Marion in the guard house!"

"He talked smart to the colonel," O'Brien answered. "Didn't want to muster his men as infantry."

"Well, I should think not!" Hall laughed. "They're cavalry, same as us." His smile faded when O'Brien didn't reply. "You're not mustering us as infantry, are you?" he demanded.

"There isn't a choice."

"I thought you wanted to be a gentleman, Red," Hall said. "You don't take his horse from a gentleman!"

"We'll keep our horses," O'Brien said, "if I have to whip Slough myself."

Hall gave a bitter laugh. "And be court-martialed? You don't whip a colonel, Red. If you want to get a superior officer out of the way, you arrange an accident for him."

O'Brien stared at his friend as if at a stranger. Hall was serious, and a more dishonorable plan he had never heard. A chill settled in his gut, and at that moment a crow flew overhead, croaking.

"We'll keep our horses," he repeated, and started toward the company, but a commotion near the gate attracted his attention. A crowd had gathered and angry voices rose as Marion was marched out of the camp under a heavy guard. Some of the men followed despite the guard's best efforts—men from K Company, O'Brien thought. The noise only increased after Marion's departure, and O'Brien spotted Franklin among the growing crowd. Guards were struggling to close the camp gates.

"Something's wrong," O'Brien told Hall. Some of his men had started toward the fracas, and O'Brien shouted, "Attention, company!" to bring them back in line. "Denning, call the roll," he ordered, then looked back toward the gate, which the guards had just succeeded in closing with the help of Franklin and several others. As he watched, Franklin started toward him at a run. From the look on the lieutenant's face, something was most definitely wrong. "Stay with the men," he told Hall, and jogged a few steps forward.

"Sir"—Franklin gasped—"the drafts have been denied!"

"What drafts?" O'Brien asked, frowning.

"The Treasury drafts! Governor Gilpin's drafts." Franklin's face was taut with dismay. "Washington has refused to pay them!"

10

By means of drafts on the U.S. Treasury, the Governor defrayed the expense of raising clothing and sustaining his Volunteers, though this irregular proceeding afterwards environed him with trouble and finally cost him his office.

—Private Ovando J. Hollister, 1st Colorado Volunteers

O'Brien stared at Franklin in disbelief. Men all around were shouting now; the word had spread through the camp like prairie fire, and a riot was building at the gate. O'Brien turned to his company at the very moment they broke and ran toward the fray.

"Couldn't stop 'em," Hall said, joining them with Denning beside him. "Is it true?"

"Come on." O'Brien started for the gate. He spotted a man from I Company squeezing beneath the fence rails. "Duffy!" he shouted. "Where do you think you're going?"

"Back to the mines," the private called. "How about you?"

O'Brien grabbed at his foot but the man was clear and hightailing it away from the camp. Plunging into the chaos by the gate, O'Brien and his lieutenants tried to collect their company, but it proved an impossible task.

"Silence!" a familiar voice roared, and out of habit the men fell still. Chivington stood at the front of the mob. "Men of the Colorado Volunteers," he said, his voice booming through the camp, "remember why we are here. Governor Gilpin built this camp, fed and clothed you and made soldiers of you for a cause—a sacred cause—the preservation of Union in Colorado! He has risked his position and reputation to do this. If there is a shadow over us today, it is not from want of noble purpose on our governor's part. Any shadow over us is caused by war.

"Great armies are moving in the East, and Washington's eyes are on them. We are small, and we are far away. The men in Washington do not yet see the importance of preserving our Territory, so we who do see it must hold our ground. There are those who would have the pestilence of slavery creep over this land and darken its fair skies. Do not allow it! Do not abandon the cause which brought you here! God has brought us together, he will see that we are given our just reward!"

Chivington spoke on, building up his passion as he did at the prayer services. O'Brien could see that he was pouring his whole soul into this entreaty, and couldn't help being moved. "If money is all that concerns you," Chivington said, "I cannot make you stay. If you have pride, if you have honor, if you have a sense of right, then you will remain and fulfill the trust placed in you by the citizens of Colorado." His gaze swept the crowd of silent men, then he nodded to the guard. "Open the gate."

A number of men poured out of the camp at once while others milled around the grounds grumbling and arguing. The muster had stopped short. Colonel Slough's carriage pushed through the crowd and flew toward Denver City. The Colorado Volunteers were crumbling. O'Brien's own company—what was left of them—gathered in front of their barracks to argue the question. He watched them, standing a little apart with Hall.

"What do you think, Red?" Hall asked, leaning toward him. "I'm half inclined to go out riding myself. Bet there'll be good money escorting people back to Kansas."

"They won't need to go if we're still here," O'Brien said, but his hope was fading even as the words left his mouth.

Franklin, who had been standing on the outskirts of the arguing men, came toward them. "Ramsey's trying to talk them into going to Leavenworth to enlist there, sir. If you could speak to them—"

"Nothing I can say will stop them," O'Brien said.

"I don't think it's the words that matter, sir," Franklin said. "They just want someone to tell them it's right for them to stay. Someone they know and respect." The youth looked up at him, and O'Brien saw something that fairly astonished him. Franklin, whose polished speech and manners O'Brien had resented from the moment they met, was deferring to him.

"Hopeless," Hall said. "They're already gone."

O'Brien frowned. "Not yet," he said, and stepped toward the men with Franklin at his heels. As they fell silent, he looked 'round at their faces. "Leavenworth, is it?" he said to them. "Leavenworth and back east. Well, if you're ready to drop all you've broken your backs for, go on then."

"What's there to stay for?" McGuire asked. "Governor can't feed us, much less pay us!" An angry chorus supported him.

"We can feed ourselves," O'Brien said. "I know you. Flannery—Kimmick—not a man of you isn't a bally fine hunter, and game enough up in the hills."

"Maybe we should go back to them hills," Bailey shouted.

"Go back if you like," O'Brien snapped. "Go back to your digging, you trolls! I didn't spend a month building barracks just to leave them for a hole in the ground!"

Temper, Alastar. You must win them, not drive them away. He glanced at Franklin, who was watching him with a worried frown. Trying to emulate Chivington's persuasive power, O'Brien threw back his shoulders. "I don't know what you men came to Colorado for," he said. "I came for a chance at something better than I could get in New York, and I'm not giving up! If you do, that's your own choice, but I'm telling you this—there's not a better lot of men in this camp than Avery's own trolls, and if you go it's a damned bloody shame."

The men shifted and glanced at each other. O'Brien glared at them while inside he was trying desperately to think of something more to say, a clincher that would keep them for sure.

"The captain's right," Franklin said, voice soft and eyes glinting. "We won't get another chance like this. When Colorado becomes a state, you'll all be heroes."

McGuire was staring at the ground now. The others had ceased their muttering. O'Brien was their captain again, he realized. To seal the bond, he gave them an order. "Company inspection in fifteen minutes," he said sharply. "Dismissed."

They drifted away, most of them into the barracks. A couple slunk toward the gate; O'Brien did nothing to stop them.

"Well done, sir," Franklin said beside him.

O'Brien looked up, suspicious, a half-formed question on his lips, but it died when he saw Franklin beaming at him.

"Very well done." Franklin snapped a salute, still grinning, and turned toward the barracks, leaving O'Brien to wait an eternal quarter hour to learn what was left of his company.

"¡Ándale!" Jamie called in a hoarse voice as the wagons splashed through the river yet again. The Tejano teamsters seemed not to have heard, but three weeks' march had taught him to urge them on anyway because if he didn't they'd stop altogether. Jamie licked cracked lips. The train was to press on to Beaver Lake today, no matter how long it took. At noon they had still been six miles away with the road growing steeper and rougher. It would be dark well before they were in camp.

Devil's River was beautiful, but Jamie had long since ceased to enjoy it. The stage road kept crossing and recrossing it, further delaying the train as the teamsters negotiated the fords. When it wasn't crossing to the river, the road was choked with dust kicked up by horses and wagons. In the haze ahead Jamie could see Martin's gray trotting toward him. He waved, then saw a second horse, a big chestnut, and groaned. Probably brass again, nagging them to move faster.

"My assistant, Lieutenant Russell," Martin said. "Jamie, this is Colonel Scurry."

"Sir," said Jamie saluting. He'd seen the Lieutenant Colonel at the review in San Antonio—it seemed like months ago—and had heard he'd been a delegate to the secession convention. The regiment's second in command, "Dirty Shirt" to his friends, was a sharp-eyed lawyer who missed nothing and rarely took no for an answer.

"How far back are the beeves?" Scurry demanded.

Oh, no, Jamie thought. He looked back though he knew the herd was well out of sight. "Two or three miles," he said.

"They've got to come up tonight," the colonel said.

Jamie looked at Martin, then at Scurry. "Can't do it, sir. Not if you want them to live."

Scurry frowned, but spoke quietly. "The regiment's marching ahead tomorrow, and they've got to take two days' rations of beef and bread." He looked expectantly at Jamie. Martin must have told him Jamie was from a ranching family.

"We could drive a few head forward faster, but they might start dropping, and either way they'd lose quality," Jamie said. "The only other thing I can suggest is to send some wagons back to the herd and slaughter what we need. They still wouldn't arrive before midnight," he added.

"That'll have to do," Scurry said. "See to it, then."

He galloped away, disappearing in the dust. Jamie sighed. The job of organizing the slaughter would doubtless fall to him. He closed his eyes wearily.

"Sorry, Jamie," Martin said. "I'll go round up some of the commissary's wagons. How many should I send?"

Jamie stared at the sky. "Two days' meat for the regiment, that's five or six beeves . . . better make it three wagons."

"Would you ride back to the herd and pick them out? I'll send the wagons and the butchers back to you."

"Yes, sir." Martin reached over to lay a sympathetic hand on his shoulder, and Jamie reluctantly smiled.

Company I stood ready for inspection. Of the hundred and one men who'd assembled for muster that morning, sixty-

four remained, including most of his first recruits from
Avery. O'Brien passed slowly along the diminished ranks
while Denning called the roll, nodding, trying to look
proud of his men when inside he was deeply depressed.

Others had gathered to watch. O'Brien gave a couple of
orders, and the snap with which his men obeyed seemed to
ring through the parade grounds. He heard Logan ordering
his own company out for inspection. Lifting his head,
O'Brien called out loudly, "Dress parade at five-thirty.
Company, dismissed!"

He stood watching as they fell out. No more arguments;
the men went about their business quietly, exchanging
nods, picking up where they'd left off that morning.
O'Brien heard a step behind him and turned to see Chivington approaching.

"Very good, Captain," the major said. "Your company's
in good order."

"What's left of them," O'Brien said.

"What's left will be the best of them," Chivington said.
"We've lost deadwood, that's all. The Pet Lambs will be
better for it." Chivington clapped him on the back, then
went off to offer encouragement in other quarters.
O'Brien looked at Hall, lounging on the boardwalk before
the barracks.

"Guess I might as well stay," Hall said.

Relieved, O'Brien grinned. He took out his new flask
and offered it to Hall.

"You first," Hall said. "It's your day."

O'Brien took a swallow, then in a generous mood turned
to offer it to Franklin, but the lad had disappeared.

"Has it occurred to you," Hall said, following his gaze,
"that Chas could have talked them into staying himself?"

O'Brien frowned. "No," he said, handing him the flask.
Hall took it, a smile on his face that was none too pleasant.

"He made you do it," Hall said. "He's quite a swell, our
Chas, but he don't like attention, have you noticed? Keeps
to himself a lot. Almost like he's afraid of something."

O'Brien leaned against the rail beside Hall. "A man likes to be alone, doesn't mean he's a coward."

"No," Hall said, passing the flask back again, "but it might mean he's a spy."

O'Brien stared at him, then burst into laughter. "A spy? Saints in heaven, what would a spy do out here?"

"There's a lot of secesh around here still. They were buying up rifles earlier in the summer. Wanted me to sell 'em some horses," said Hall.

O'Brien laughed, then frowned in puzzlement. "But what could a spy tell them about us? Half Denver City watches our dress parade!"

Hall shrugged. "When we're expecting orders. Escort details, scouts. There's a lot that might be useful."

"Oh, you're dreaming, laddie." O'Brien laughed. "I don't like Franklin, either, but you'll have to do better than that."

"He's either a traitor or a coward," Hall said, reaching for the flask. "I'd be willing to bet on it."

O'Brien squinted at the sun, still hazy as it hung over the mountains. "Ten dollars says he's not a spy."

"Done."

"How will you prove it?" O'Brien asked.

Hall shrugged. "Suppose I'll have to do some spying of my own."

"Well, stay out of the guard house. That's all I ask." He shook the flask—nearly empty. "Here's to the Pet Lambs," he said. "Saints in heaven preserve what's left of them."

"Amen." Hall laughed as O'Brien drained the last of the whiskey.

The commissary's butchers were efficient, but it still took two hours to get the beeves slaughtered, dressed, and loaded in the wagons. Jamie hated slaughtering; always had. Though Poppa had made him learn how and he'd killed any number of steers with his own hands, he'd never heard their frightened bellows without being sick at heart. He was glad when the little train moved away from the pile of skins and guts. It seemed a shame to waste the organs, but there was no time to clean them so they stayed in a grisly heap by the trail, a feast for scavengers.

The carcasses couldn't be hung, so the wagons dripped blood all along the road to Beaver Lake. When they caught up to the herd, the herdsmen, with a good deal of cursing, took the rest of the animals well away from the trail.

Late in the afternoon the stage rattled by on its way west. One of the outriders, bandanna over his nose to keep out the dust and, no doubt, the smell of blood, frowned as he passed. Jamie was unsympathetic; the stage would reach the lake in a couple of hours, while he was stuck with the slow-moving commissary wagons. He thought with envy of the regiment, in camp by now, resting, maybe bathing in the cool water. He took a sip from his canteen and glanced back at his wagons to make sure they were together.

As evening came on it grew cooler, for which Jamie could only be grateful. A hot night would have made their unappetizing cargo much more so. The teamsters needed no urging to hurry—each man of them wanted supper and bed—so Jamie stayed at the head of the little column to avoid the dust.

By the time they reached the lake, its surface reflecting campfires along the shore, he was tired beyond caring. Dark forms hurried forward to the wagons and urgent voices hung in the night air, but Jamie didn't register their words. He rode ahead to the largest fire in sight, hoping it was headquarters, and wasn't disappointed. An orderly took Cocoa and as he slid stiffly from the saddle, Martin was there with a mug of coffee. Jamie drank half of it at one pull. It was sweet, and warm all the way down to his stomach.

"Thank you," he said when he came up for air.

Martin smiled. "Come on, there's supper for you."

They sat looking out at the lake, Jamie digging into a plate of beans and fresh camp bread—no beef, thank you. Soon the whole camp was moving as the beef ration was distributed, and the smell of roasting meat rose from all the campfires.

"Why two days' rations?" Jamie asked, finally beginning to feel alive again.

"It's a hard march to the next water," Martin said. "Dry camp the first night."

"Oh." Jamie looked at the lake, feeling a belated fondness for the Devil's River.

"That's not all. They say the spring is twelve feet down, so the water has to be brought up in buckets. Draft animals and the herd will have to do without."

Jamie sighed. "There won't be an ounce of fat on those beeves by the time we get to Franklin."

"Skinny beef is better than no beef," Martin said with a shrug. "By the way, we got mail today." He reached into his coat and pulled out a letter, which he handed to Jamie. Holding his bread in his teeth, Jamie set his plate on the ground and eagerly spread open the sheet covered in Momma's spidery handwriting, holding it up so he could read it in the firelight. Matt had written. He was in camp near Dumfries, Virginia, standing picket duty on the Potomac and spoiling for a fight. The rest of the letter was a mixture of family chat and advice for surviving the rigors of the trail. Momma warned him to change his socks every day, and Jamie smiled as he read her promise to send him six more pairs by the next mail. She signed "all my love" and had left room at the bottom for a postscript from Emmaline: "Poppa read your letter twice through— write again soon and keep an eye on Stephen for me, love E."

Jamie looked up. "Did you get a letter?"

Martin nodded. "I've already answered it. Emma told me to take care of you. I wrote back saying I'm treating you like a slave instead."

Jamie laughed. "I'll tell her you made me butcher cattle to keep me humble."

"About the herd—they'll have stopped for the night?"

"Um-hm," Jamie said through a mouthful of bread. "Should get here tomorrow."

"We need to keep them moving."

Jamie shook his head. "If they have to go without water they'll need a day's rest and grazing here. Otherwise we'll lose them."

"Then the men will have to live on crackers after the first two days. Reily wants them at Fort Lancaster by Monday."

Jamie shrugged. "Can't be helped." He looked out over the lake. Fort Lancaster was another four or five days ahead and was not even halfway to Fort Bliss, their destination near Franklin, Texas. They would be marching for at least another month. Though Jamie had known this before they left, somehow he hadn't realized how wearisome it would be. The wagons, their bad-tempered drivers, plodding mules and horses and the occasional broken wheel, all were much more work to manage than a herd of cattle. Add to that the constant pressure from Colonel Reily's impatient staff officers, and the job of quartermaster began to feel like martyrdom. It wasn't the staff's fault, he knew. The colonel had been pushing the regiment hard ever since he'd received an urgent plea for reinforcements from Baylor, who feared that Canby, the U.S. Commander of New Mexico, was preparing to march two thousand men against him at Mesilla.

Jamie yawned. Tomorrow would be soon enough to worry about all that. He carefully folded up Momma's letter, put it in his pocket, and followed Martin to their tent, where he pulled off his boots and fell asleep the instant he was prone.

"Small apples this year," Mrs. Canby said, reaching up to hang another string of slices on the wall of her kitchen.

"There was not enough rain in the summer," Doña Isabel said.

Laura picked up an apple and handed the empty bushel basket to María, Mrs. Canby's maid, who gave her a full one in exchange. "They may be small but there are plenty of them."

"When my husband learned we were to come here, my mother told me it was a desert," Mrs. Josephy said. She was another of the many army wives Laura had recently met. She looked charming sitting by the fire with her infant son in her arms. "I cried for a week," she said, "because I thought I would have to live in a tent and haul water for miles like an Arab. But I never saw so much corn and potatoes as there are for sale on the plaza now. And the squashes! How do the Indians grow them and still roam about so?"

"The Pueblo Indians don't roam," Mrs. Canby replied patiently. "They have houses and farms. Have you not visited Tesuque?"

"Oh, no! My husband wouldn't like it."

"I wish I had," Mrs. Lane said as she sliced an apple. "I shall not have the time now."

"When do you leave for Fort Union?" Mrs. Chapin asked.

"In two days."

"So soon?" Laura asked. She liked Mrs. Lane, who had been staying with her two children in rooms loaned by the Canbys.

"Yes. We're going to Leavenworth with the men who were paroled at Fort Fillmore. My husband will ride with us part of the way, and then he must return to Fort Craig."

"Is Fort Craig a pleasant place?" Laura asked, thinking of Lieutenant Anderson and Captain McRae.

"Pleasant enough," Mrs. Lane replied. "The quarters are superior to many of the posts, but it is not considered a proper place for women and children just now."

"I should think not, with all those Texans in Mesilla and more coming," Mrs. Chapin said.

"You must dread leaving your husband," Mrs. Josephy said in an awed voice. "Why, you might never see him again!"

Mrs. Lane laughed. "The army has cured me of that. Captain Lane takes care of himself very well, and I do the same."

"María," Mrs. Canby said. "¿Puedes hacernos un té, por favor?" María nodded, picked up the kettle from the hearth, and carried it out to the well while Mrs. Canby hung another string of apples. "I think we have earned a cup of tea," she said. "We can try some of the apricot jam Miss Howland helped me put up."

"Miss Howland has been busy in your kitchen, Mrs. Canby," Mrs. Josephy said. "I never come here but she is with you."

"Mrs. Canby takes pity on me," Laura said. "I have no kitchen, and I'd much rather make jam than sit alone."

"Yes, how tedious you must feel at the fonda," Doña Isabel said. "With only one room, it is not like a home."

Laura smiled her gratitude, and the Spanish girl smiled shyly back. Laura was indeed getting tired of living in the hotel, and had become a frequent visitor to the Canby residence as a means of escape. It seemed less and less likely that she would leave Santa Fé soon. The mail had become erratic, harassed by Comanches. Even if she could somehow persuade her uncle to escort her, she knew she couldn't bear to travel with a military train as Mrs. Lane would be doing—they moved so slowly it would take months to reach Independence—and once there she would be faced with the problem of crossing a country at war.

"Have you heard from Captain Sena, Doña Isabel?" she asked.

The young lady brightened. "Sí, he sends a letter from Fort Union. He says they are coming well on the—the, digging, the—estructura, las fortificaciones de tierra, para el nuevo fuerte," she finished in a flurry.

"The earthworks," Mrs. Canby translated. "They're building a fortification."

"Like the one going up around Fort Craig?" Mrs. Lane asked.

"No, I believe it is separate from the post. A star fort, if I'm correct."

"Sí, un star fort," Doña Isabel said. "It sounds pretty!"

Laura laughed. "Hard work, with the ground so cold."

"The better to keep the men busy," Mrs. Chapin said. "Idle times bother them more than work."

Laura watched her exchange a knowing smile with Mrs. Canby and wondered if, privately, they felt more concern than they showed. Fortifications might be an interesting topic, but they represented war. What, she wondered, did Mrs. Canby feel as she watched her husband striving to build up New Mexico's defenses? Did she fear he would see battle? Would she be left behind for weeks, without word, while the colonel led the few troops he had to expel the Texans from Mesilla?

By the time tea was ready the ladies had finished five bushels of apples. The afternoon was fading, and further work was postponed until another day. The apricot jam was pronounced by all to be excellent, and the party broke up in good humor.

"Thank you for the tea, Mrs. Canby," Laura said as she took her leave. Her hostess followed her into the placita where Juan Carlos, María's husband, was waiting to escort her to her hotel.

"Thank you for your help," said Mrs. Canby.

"It's my pleasure, you know that," Laura replied, smiling. "Doña Isabel was exactly right, I am tired of the Exchange."

"How is your uncle?" Mrs. Canby asked. "I have not seen him lately."

"I see very little of him myself," Laura said, wrapping her shawl closer around her shoulders. "I believe he is well."

"You need a heavy coat for winter."

"Yes—I have not had a chance to shop for one."

"Laura—"

Laura looked up, and Mrs. Canby pressed a jar of apricot jam into her hand. "Remember me, if you should ever need a friend," she said, and with a fleeting smile returned to the house. Surprised, Laura stared after her, then followed Juan Carlos to the heavy gate that barred the passage to the street.

"What is it called again, please?" she asked, touching it.

He grinned, flashing white teeth. "El zaguán," he said, opening the door for her to pass through.

"Zaguán. Gracias." Stepping into the street, Laura glanced at the jam jar and smiled. Whatever else befell her, at least she had made good friends.

At the hotel she met her uncle in the placita with a large, paper-wrapped bundle in his arms. "There you are!" he said. "I've brought you a gift."

"I've been meaning to speak to you, Uncle. I need some warmer clothes for the winter."

"Yes, yes," her uncle said, ushering her toward her room. "I've got you some new things right here. Come and look!"

Laura opened her room, and Uncle Wallace went to her bed, where he proceeded to tear open his package. "Here we are!" he said, holding up a dress. A very fine dress, Laura realized, taking a step closer. He must have sent to St. Louis for it, for no Santa Fé seamstress could have produced this confection. It was made of silk the color of fine Wedgewood, cut in the latest style and trimmed with dainty ruffles and silk violets. The fabric whispered as her uncle held it out to her.

"You're very kind," Laura began, "but I cannot wear this—"

"Nonsense. It should fit you perfectly, I had one of your own gowns measured. Do you think it unbecoming?"

"The dress is lovely," Laura said, "but it would be unbecoming of me to wear it so soon after my father's death."

"Soon? It's nearly a year, isn't it?" her uncle replied, holding the gown up to her. Laura was obliged to take it from him to prevent his pressing it against her shoulders, and caught a whiff of liquor as he leaned toward her.

"We are invited to a party tonight," he said, reaching back into the torn wrappings to retrieve a pair of dancing slippers the same delicate blue as the gown. "You shall wear this dress."

"Thank you, but I don't wish to go out."

"You shall go, however. No arguments," he said. "I can't support you forever, you know. It's high time you were married."

"Uncle, I am not in a hurry to wed."

"That's obvious. You've done little enough to attract a husband. I suggest you start making an effort." He dropped the slippers on the bed and started out, then paused at the door. "Parker's carriage will pick us up at six. I'll come by at a quarter to, in case you need help getting ready."

The door snapped shut behind him, and Laura stared at it in disbelief. That had been a threat, she realized. Her uncle had not spoken to her in such a manner before; her father would never have done so. The irony was that her easiest means of escaping her unpleasant uncle would be to do as he wished, and marry, but she would not be rushed into marriage, by him or by anyone.

She looked at the silk in her hands. A year previously she would have been delighted by such a gift and showered thanks on its giver. How young she had been then. She laid the dress down, sat beside it on the bed, and reached out to touch the warm, polished wood of her father's clock. She felt movement under her hand and in a moment it began to chime. Laura smiled at it sadly, wishing it could give her more time.

11

No one need hang, drown, or shoot himself. If a man becomes disgusted with life, let him go to a fandango, raise a row, and be killed decently.

—Ovando J. Hollister

McIntyre led his dance partner to the sweets table and paid the old crone who presided over it twenty-five cents for an orange. This he gave to his señorita, whose name he did not know or care to know. She thanked him and rolled it between her hands, her brown eyes plainly inviting him to greater intimacy. Customs were different here than in the States; liaisons were common and the natives thought nothing of them except on occasion when jealousy intervened. McIntyre had found it thrilling at first, but lately he had begun to think what was so easily gained was not much worth having. He thanked his partner for the dance and turned away as the music began again. From the corner of his eye he glimpsed her returning to the table to sell his orange back to Abuela. He shrugged. It was customary, and it matched his mood well enough. The gift had meant no more to him than it had to her—it was merely what was expected.

The floor was crowded with twisting, spinning dancers. Dark eyes and white teeth flashed to the rhythm of guitar and violin. McIntyre moved toward the far room where Pigeon had tapped a barrel of wine from Chihuahua. A willowy señorita dancing nearby fixed her eyes on him and raised her arm in a slow arc, the cigarrillo in her fingertips glowing. McIntyre gave her a nod but moved on; wine attracted him more in his present mood.

Anderson had gone, driving his battery south to Fort Craig, and McIntyre missed him sorely. Nicodemus was not nearly as good company, especially since he'd just received his promotion to captain and was consequently full of his own importance. McIntyre watched Nicodemus dancing with a native girl no more than sixteen, and decided he was a fool. He passed into the east room, which was filled with a haze of smoke. The party was just warming up. It would be some time yet before the flow of wine and passion swelled to the level of possible ugliness, and even then a quick fight—and most of them were decisively quick—would hardly cause a beat to be missed in the music.

A half-dime bought a steerhorn cupful of red wine. By the cask a couple of soldiers were arguing over whether Canby should be replaced as head of the department.

"He's a do-nothing," one said. "A real commander would have chased Baylor out of Mesilla by now."

"Canby'll run him off," the other replied. "He's just waiting for reinforcements."

They were both wrong, McIntyre thought. What Canby was actually doing was writing letters: making excuses for not sending the Regulars—all of them, for the cavalry had now been recalled, as well—to Leavenworth; begging the War Department for badly needed funds and supplies; trying to make Washington see the urgent need for defensive forces here in New Mexico. Washington, so far, had been unresponsive. Canby felt his first duty was to protect Fort Craig and Fort Union against the Texan threat. Not a daring plan, perhaps, but it was prudent commanders who made the best use of their men—never wasting lives in needless conflict—and wise soldiers loved them for it.

McIntyre carried his wine to the main room and leaned in the doorway, watching the dancers. A bustle at the outer door heralded new arrivals. Phillips came in, followed by a couple of others. Then Wallace Howland appeared with his niece in tow, and McIntyre inhaled sharply. Of all the places he'd imagined Miss Howland, a fandango was not one. She held her black shawl tightly closed over a splendid blue dress, the hoop of which was causing a disturbance among the revelers. She was the only woman in the room in American dress—indeed, she was the only American woman—and she looked far from happy. McIntyre set his cup on a shelf and pushed away from the wall.

"What's your hurry, soldier?"

A hand caught at McIntyre's arm and he turned, knocking it away. The wine had made his limbs heavy. "Leave off," he said, then saw it was Phillips who'd stopped him.

"What's your hurry, army mule?" Phillips repeated, sneering.

McIntyre ignored him and pushed through to the door, but the Howlands had moved away. He spied them near the sweets table, talking to a native. The uncle appeared to be making introductions. Damn him for bringing her, she didn't belong here! McIntyre started toward them, determined to protect her from any unpleasantness.

"This is Señor Ortizz, my dear," Uncle Wallace said. "He—"

"Ortiz," the native corrected, bobbing his head and grinning at Laura. The sarape he wore smelled of lanolin, and the clothes that it covered were none too clean.

"Sí, sí," said her uncle, who was somewhat unsteady under the effects of a bottle of brandy he had shared with Phillips on the drive to Glorieta. He returned his attention to Laura. "Señor Ortiz is looking for a wife."

"Es muy bella, muy bella," Ortiz murmured, eyes sweeping Laura's form.

"He owns a great many sheep."

"I am very happy for him," Laura said, marveling at the ludicrous conversation.

"Willing to settle the whole herd on you."

"Uncle, you must know that is out of the question—"

"Has a house near Laguna," her uncle added.

"Laguna, sí." Ortiz nodded more vigorously. "Mi casa tiene tres cuartos."

"Says it's got three rooms. That's a good house, m'dear. Good as this one."

Laura realized her uncle was impervious to reason in his present condition, and changed her tactics. "Uncle," she said sternly, drawing her shawl closer around her shoulders, "I cannot marry while I am in mourning."

Uncle Wallace's brows rose as this seemed to penetrate his understanding. He conferred with Ortiz in Spanish, then turned to Laura with a triumphant smile. "He'll wait," he announced. Ortiz's head bobbed enthusiastically; clearly he approved of such propriety on the part of his chosen bride. He took a step forward and reached for her hand. Laura drew back.

"Go and dance with him, m'dear."

"No," Laura said firmly.

"Mr. Howland," came a voice behind her—a most welcome voice. Laura turned and saw that it was indeed Mr. McIntyre.

"Good evening," he said, addressing her uncle as he stepped into the small space between Ortiz and Laura.

Uncle Wallace peered at him. "Oh, good evening, Captain . . ."

"Lieutenant McIntyre. Lacey McIntyre, remember?"

"Oh, yes, yes. Good evening."

Señor Ortiz was looking displeased, but Mr. McIntyre appeared not to notice. "Rather stuffy in here, isn't it?" he said to Laura. "Would you like to get a breath of air?"

"Yes, thank you," she replied.

"We shall be just outside, sir," he said with a formal bow that was wasted on her uncle.

Uncle Wallace frowned as if trying to remember something. "All right," he said. "Come, Ortiz, I'll buy you some vino."

The lieutenant led Laura outside to the darkness of the portal. A few men were leaning against the pillars, their figures black shadows, the coals of their cigarrillos dancing like fireflies as they talked. Mr. McIntyre guided Laura a few steps away. The night was sharp, making her wish she had more than her shawl, but she was grateful for the pure air. She drew a deep breath and sighed. "Thank you, sir," she said.

"My pleasure," the lieutenant said. "If I may ask, why did your uncle bring you here?"

"You haven't guessed?"

"I did overhear some mention of sheep."

Laura had to laugh. "It·is too ridiculous," she said, but humor couldn't mask the distressing truth of her situation. Her uncle, on whom she was solely dependent, was a fool and a drunkard, and apparently wished to be rid of her.

The lieutenant came to stand beside her. "I am only a soldier," he said softly, "but I assure you I can offer you better than three rooms at Laguna."

Laura's heart gave a flutter. She looked down. "You're very kind."

"And if you want sheep I'll buy you some."

She put a hand to her mouth to smother a giggle. "Oh, dear. How am I to resist such gallantry?"

"I hope you won't," he said, moving closer. Laura peered into the shadows hiding his face, a strange tension rising in her chest. He reached up to caress her cheek, and she allowed it. His fingers had a clean-leather smell that was not unpleasant, and with gentle pressure they lifted her chin toward him. She realized he was going to kiss her, and turned her head. A faint smell of wine, and the touch of his lips on her cheek sent a tingling shock through her.

"Forgive me," he said, moving back. "I shouldn't have done that, but I've been wanting to, for quite a while."

Laura took a small step away.

"You are very beautiful tonight. Is that a new dress?"

"My uncle bought it. I should not have let him bully me into wearing it."·She leaned a hand on a pillar. "I do not intend to come out of black gloves before Christmas."

"I see." He took hold of her free hand, his fingers stroking it, warming it through the glove. "When I see you in white gloves, may I hope for a chance to address you?"

Laura shifted, her feelings a jumble. "I am not sure I want to remain in New Mexico."

"I could send you to my family—"

"In Tennessee?" she said softly. "I think I'm safer here."

He sighed. "Well, I won't press you."

"Thank you, Mr. McIntyre."

"Call me Lacey, please."

Laura glanced away, looking out at the cottonwoods across the road. The waxing moon cast just enough light to silver the dry leaves rustling and fluttering to the ground. "Tell me about your family, Lacey," she said, gently withdrawing her hand from his. "You are farmers?"

"My father has five hundred acres in corn and wheat," he said. "You want to know if we have slaves."

"Oh, dear." Laura laughed. "I thought I was being subtle."

The lieutenant's voice grew earnest. "We do," he said. "I can't do anything about my father, but when they come to me I'll free them if you wish."

Laura peered at him, wishing she could see his face better. "That's very generous of you," she said slowly. "Would you have freed them otherwise?"

He was silent for a moment. "I hadn't thought about it. I've only been interested in the army."

"Well," Laura said gently, "someday you'll have to choose."

"You have only to say what you want."

"What I want doesn't matter," she told him. "It's what you think is right that's important." Important to me, she thought privately. For all their pleasant conversations, Mr. Lacey McIntyre was essentially a stranger to her, and until she knew more of his character, she could not commit her heart to him. "I need time to consider my choices," she said. "So do you, I imagine."

"I've made my choice," he answered. There was an unsteadiness in his voice that made her think he might try again to kiss her. She was spared having to offend him by the opening of the nearest door. A man stood in it, music and laughter spilling out around him.

"Come on, missy," Mr. Phillips's voice said. "You ought to be inside."

"Miss Howland found the party uncomfortable," Mr. McIntyre said stiffly.

"Getting mighty comfortable with you, though, ain't she?"

Alarm poured through Laura as she sensed the anger in the lieutenant's response. "Please," she said as he took a step toward Phillips, "it doesn't matter."

"It ain't right for you to be out here alone with a soldier, missy," Phillips told her. "No telling what he might try."

"Never thought I'd hear you preaching morals, John Phillips," said Mr. McIntyre.

"I brought the lady here," said Phillips, letting the door fall shut behind him. "Up to me to take care of her. Come on, missy." He reached for Laura's arm, but Mr. McIntyre stepped between them, knocking his hand away.

"Mr. Phillips," she said in desperation, "I wish to go back to Santa Fé."

"I'd be happy to take you, missy!"

"You're not taking her anywhere," Mr. McIntyre said. He pushed Phillips back, and suddenly they were scuffling, bootheels scraping the earth. Laura backed away.

"Monsieur Vallé!" she called wildly.

"Me voici," came a voice. A little shower of orange sparks danced up as a cigarrillo hit the ground a few feet away. Vallé strode up, swiftly imposing his tall figure between Phillips and McIntyre. "Please, señors," he said. "You are frightening the lady. Is it Miss Howland?"

"Yes," Laura said. "Thank you, monsieur."

"I thought it must be, but mon Dieu! This is not a proper party for you, mademoiselle!"

"No, and I'm taking her home," Mr. McIntyre said. "Pigeon, can I borrow your wagon?"

"You ain't taking her—"

"Enough!" Laura stamped her foot angrily. "I'm not going with either of you!" She turned to Vallé. "Monsieur, I'd be happy to stay with Carmen in the kitchen."

"Ma chère, it is likely to be a long party. Will you allow me to drive you home?"

"I cannot take you from your guests."

"They will be here when I return," he said, and the humor in his voice calmed her feelings.

"Miss Howland?" Mr. McIntyre said in a contrite voice. Laura peered at his face, hidden in shadow. "Maybe Pigeon would let me drive you and Carmen to Santa Fé. Would that suit you?"

"Yes," she said slowly. "If he can spare her."

"Bien," Vallé said. "I will fetch her. Come with me, Phillips." Putting an arm around the other man's shoulders, he led the way into the house.

"I apologize," Mr. McIntyre said as soon as they'd gone.

"Heroines in novels may like to have men fight over them," Laura said. "I don't find it pleasant at all."

"I'm sorry. Phillips is a bad sort."

"I'm aware of that, sir." She immediately regretted her severity, and reached out a hand, which the lieutenant caught and bowed over.

Vallé returned with Carmen and a blanket for the ride, and one of his ranch hands brought out a mule-drawn wagon. "Please come and visit me again, mademoiselle," Vallé said as he helped Laura into the wagon, "only not at a fandango."

"I will. Thank you, monsieur," she said, sharing the blanket with Carmen and settling back for the long drive to Santa Fé.

Hall was waiting outside headquarters. O'Brien nodded as he stepped off the boardwalk, his boot threatening to slip on frozen mud. "They've been cashiered."

"Hambleton, too?" Hall asked as they started toward their quarters.

O'Brien nodded. "Insubordination." Which would surprise no one who knew Hambleton at all. O'Brien was sorry for the way in which Hambleton had been forced out of the regiment, and thought Slough had made a great mess of the matter, but he was not sorry to see the fellow gone.

"Marion's first lieutenant resigned, too," he added. "They've commissioned Sam Robbins for his company."

"They won't like it," Hall said. "They're none too fond of Slough as it is. He should have let them pick their own captain."

"Didn't want another mutiny," O'Brien said. He saw Sergeant Ramsey approaching and stopped. He didn't care much for Ramsey, a latecomer to the company who'd gone back to his fine home in Denver City the minute the trouble with Gilpin's drafts had occurred. O'Brien didn't know what a fellow like Ramsey wanted with soldiering, but he'd long since given up trying to understand all of his men.

Ramsey saluted and offered O'Brien a much-folded slip of paper. "Beg pardon, sir. One of the boys found this under his blanket. Said it must've been given him by mistake."

O'Brien unfolded the paper and peered at the scrawling handwriting. Hall had found little time to devote to his schooling, but he knew his numbers, and recognized "3:00." Then Hall twitched the page from his hand. Annoyed, O'Brien said "That's all, Ramsey."

The sergeant hesitated, a speculative look on his face. "It isn't true, is it, Captain?"

"That's a matter for the major to decide," Hall said. His lips had curled in a mirthless smile.

Ramsey reluctantly retired. O'Brien waited until he was out of earshot, then asked, "What is it?"

"It's a note from Chas. Shall I read it to you?"

O'Brien nodded.

"'Meet behind dining hall 3:00 A.M. Horses provided for journey to Texas. Pass along to fellow friends, C. Franklin.'"

A tingle ran down O'Brien's spine that had nothing to do with the cold. So Franklin *was* a Rebel agent. A mixture of feelings sprang up in him, of which the strongest was the need to move carefully. "You're right," he told Hall. "The major should see this." He took the note and started back toward headquarters with Hall beside him.

He had heard of attempts to seduce men away to the South. Captain McKee, an old Indian hunter, had been caught trying to lead forty men into Texas and was now in the Denver City jail. Other deserters had overpowered a Federal supply train near Fort Wise before they were captured. Company F had been sent out into a howling storm to escort them to Denver for trial, and was considered lucky to have drawn this duty, life in Camp Weld having become something of a living hell since the panic over Gilpin's drafts.

O'Brien's knock was answered by Lieutenant Shoup, Chivington's aide-de-camp. "The major's at supper," he said. "What's your business?" O'Brien gave him the note and his brows rose as he read it. "Where did this come from?"

"One of my men found it," O'Brien said.

Shoup frowned at the note. "Bring this man in for questioning," he said at last. "I'll notify the major."

O'Brien and Hall crossed the parade grounds with a few dry snowflakes blowing around their heads. In the hallway of Officer's Row, O'Brien stepped up to Franklin's door and listened, heard nothing. Light showed beneath the door, so without warning he threw it open and stepped in.

Franklin had been on his cot with a book, and jumped to his feet as O'Brien came in. "What is it?" He looked at O'Brien, dark eyes wide, and said, "Captain?"

"Shall I search him, Red?" Hall asked.

O'Brien nodded.

Franklin stepped back warily. "What's this about?"

"We've heard of your meeting," O'Brien said.

"What meeting? I protest—" Franklin exclaimed, pulling away from Hall, who had grabbed hold of his arm.

"Let him search your pockets, or I'll hold you while he does it," O'Brien said.

Franklin looked stunned, then angry as Hall pulled his coat off and went through its pockets, patted down his trousers, and made him remove his fine boots. The proud, handsome face flushed as he suffered Hall's handling in silence, all the while staring defiance at O'Brien. Hall tossed Franklin's knife onto the cot and then went through his wallet, finding only his commission and two portraits: one of Franklin and the one of his sister and brother they had seen before.

"Search his traps," O'Brien said.

"What am I accused of?" Franklin burst out. "And who accuses me—you, Captain? I demand to see Major Chivington!"

"Oh, you'll see him all right," Hall replied.

In minutes the room was a wreck. Franklin watched with crossed arms while his clothing was strewn on the bed, books rifled and tossed on the floor. In a little box Hall found some money and several pieces of jewelry. O'Brien picked up a dainty necklace of gold filigree with red gems—worth more than he'd scraped out of Avery's hills, he figured—and raised an eyebrow at Franklin.

"Gifts for my family," the youth said, but a tinge crept into his cheek.

"Where are your family's letters?" Hall demanded.

Franklin looked startled.

"There's not a letter in here anywhere," Hall said, getting to his feet. "Mighty odd for a man of literary tastes. Where've you got them hidden, Chas?"

Franklin gave him an indignant look, but no answer.

O'Brien gazed at Franklin narrowly, then tossed the necklace onto the bed. "Bring him to headquarters."

They went to Chivington's office, Franklin shivering in his shirtsleeves. There was no fire, the office was cold, and the major looked in a bad mood. He sat with his huge hands on the desk, the note spread between them, and glanced up at Franklin.

"What is your explanation?" Chivington asked.

"Of what?" Franklin said.

Chivington stood and shook the scrap of paper before Franklin's face. "Of this, sir!"

Franklin flinched, and stared at the note. "I've never seen it before."

Chivington gave it to him. Franklin read it, then looked up, eyes flashing. "I did not write this."

Chivington took the paper back. "C. Franklin. Have we another C. Franklin in the camp?"

"That's not my signature! I didn't write it, sir," Franklin said. "You can ask the men about my loyalty—"

"It was one of ours brought me the note," O'Brien said.

"It's a forgery," Franklin said fiercely. "That's nothing like my hand—"

"Anyone can disguise their handwriting," Hall drawled.

Franklin's gaze shifted to Hall, eyes narrowing. "Why would I disguise my writing and then sign my own name?"

O'Brien watched them stare off, noticing the slight flare of Hall's nostrils. Chivington gestured to Shoup. "Fetch the oaths of allegiance for Company I."

They all waited silently until the aide returned with a fistful of papers, which he handed to Chivington. The major flipped through the stack until he found the one he wanted, and held it close to the lamp on his desk alongside the note. He stared at both, frowning, then went through the signed oaths again and pulled out another. After a moment he looked up at O'Brien.

"You're wasting my time," he said.

Hall stepped forward. "There were no letters in his traps, sir."

"Perhaps Mr. Franklin doesn't write letters. He didn't write this one," Chivington said tartly. "Thank you, Shoup, that's all."

The aide went out. Chivington looked at them each in turn, then picked up the note again and held it in the light. "'Meet behind dining *hall*,'" he read. "You have a distinctive signature, Lieutenant." It took O'Brien a moment to realize he was talking to Hall. He glanced at his friend and saw his jaw working, danger in his eyes.

"Captain O'Brien," Chivington said, holding out the two pages. O'Brien took them and glanced at the scrawling lines. Right before "3:00" on the note was a series of loops that matched the end of the signature on the oath. Loops that meant "hall," he supposed. He handed them back to the major.

"I'm aware of the friction between your lieutenants, Captain," Chivington said, straightening the oaths. "I leave it to you to resolve. If this sort of prank comes to my attention again I'll hold all three of you responsible. Dismissed."

"Thank you, sir," Franklin said. He left the office without a glance at the others.

Chivington stood and took the chimney off his lamp, then held the note to the flame, letting it burn almost to his fingertips before tossing it into the empty fireplace behind him. "Good night, gentlemen," he said.

O'Brien saluted and left headquarters, hissing as he stepped into the sharp wind. Franklin was nowhere in sight. O'Brien strode onto the dark parade grounds. Footsteps scraped the frozen ground behind him, but he waited until he was well out in the yard before turning to face Hall.

"Don't worry," Hall said, "I'll settle him."

"No, you won't," said O'Brien. "You're to leave him alone."

Hall shook his head, a sneer twisting his lips. "I'm not satisfied. I'll leave you out of it if you prefer."

O'Brien seized him by the shoulders and gave him one hard shake. "You can't," he said. "You heard the major—any more trouble and it's all of us. I'll not lose my commission over a milk-whelp like Franklin. Leave be!"

"Seems you're forgetting who gave you that commission," Hall said with a sour smile.

"If anyone did it was Franklin," O'Brien said. "He's our twenty-fifth bloody man, remember?" He pushed Hall away. "You had the chance to command, and you turned it away. Well, live with it, laddie! I'm captain now, and I'm ordering you to stay the bloody damned hell away from Franklin!"

Hall's eyes glinted in the dim light, and his low laughter came out in clouds. "Yes, sir," he said with a careless salute, and strode away into the darkness.

A dog howled from the stables. O'Brien was angry, at Hall, at Franklin, at himself. He went back into Officer's Row and walked slowly down the corridor, pausing outside Franklin's room. Inside he could hear the lad setting his things to rights. On impulse, he knocked.

There was fury in Franklin's face as he opened the door, but it disappeared when he saw O'Brien, replaced by a wary look.

"Sir?"

O'Brien glanced in at the wreck Hall had made. "Sorry for all that," he said.

"You're not to blame," Franklin said.

"Be careful of Hall," O'Brien told him.

"You don't have to warn me." Franklin brought his hand from behind the door to reveal his pistol, which he uncocked. O'Brien looked from the gun to his face, saw the strain that he hadn't noticed before.

"Why don't you have letters from your family?" he asked suddenly. Franklin's eyes flickered, then a strange smile hovered at the corners of his mouth.

"They didn't want me to join the army," he said softly. "I'm in disgrace." In his eyes was a bitter loneliness. Caught off guard, O'Brien felt sorry for the lad. He'd always thought of Franklin as an arrogant, rich bastard, never as a young lad far from home and cut off from his people. Unable to think of comforting words, O'Brien put a hand on his shoulder.

A surprised smile flicked across Franklin's face, then he drew away. "Thank you, Captain," he said, reaching for the door. "Good night."

O'Brien nodded. After Franklin closed the door he stood in the hall for a long moment frowning, feeling he'd missed something. He walked slowly toward his own quarters. The memory of the necklace came to him, red jewel-drops dangling from his fingers. If Franklin wasn't writing to his family, why was he keeping extravagant gifts for them?

He glanced back at Franklin's closed door. Traitor or

coward, Hall had said. O'Brien had glimpsed something more, something that felt akin to his own struggles. It made no sense; they were worlds apart. With a shake of his head, O'Brien entered his quarters, wrapped himself in a blanket against the cold and phantoms, and slept.

Jamie held out four hundred dollars in Confederate bonds, but the Mexican merchant shook his head. "¡Ese dinero no sirve para nada!" he said.

"It's no use, Lieutenant," Judge Hart said apologetically. "None of the natives will accept anything but specie."

Jamie put away the bonds, holding back his anger. He glanced at the sacks of beans from Sonora, precious beans, sorely needed. Hart was speaking soothingly in Spanish to the merchant. Jamie walked away, looking out toward the Río Grande. Winter sunshine glinted from its surface.

"I've told him you have money coming," Hart said, rejoining him. "He'll hold the stores."

"Gracias," said Jamie to the merchant. "Volveremos." He shook hands, then climbed into Hart's carriage. Hart picked up the reins and started toward the ferry.

"We don't have money coming," said Jamie.

"Baylor has," Hart replied. "He cashed in the Federal drafts taken from Fillmore. I'll speak to him for you."

"Thank you, sir."

Judge Simeon Hart was a saint to all the quartermaster staff. He'd been stockpiling forage and foodstuffs from Mexico for weeks, and his own mill had ground out thousands of pounds of flour for Sibley's army.

Back on the Texas side of the river, the carriage rolled through the tiny town of Franklin toward Fort Bliss. Below the fort was the camp of the 1st Regiment, reunited after spending two months strung out along the Overland Trail. The camp dwarfed both Franklin and the fort. Jamie couldn't help feeling pride at the sight of crisp rows of white Sibley tents and the Lone Star flag snapping in the breeze with the brown mountains behind.

Hart stopped his carriage at the quartermaster's sally port and offered Jamie a hand. "Come to dinner tonight," he said. "Bring Captain Martin."

"I will, sir! Thank you again," Jamie said, smiling. He jumped down and waved as the carriage departed, then turned to go in, glancing up at the fish weathervane that topped the sally port, his favorite feature of the post. He nearly ran into Martin, who was on his way out.

"Good, we're late," Martin said. "Come on."

"I couldn't get them to take scrip." Jamie jogged after him across the dusty grounds. "Where are we going?"

"Staff meeting. I know, I didn't have any luck, either."

"Judge Hart's asked us to dinner."

"We may not have time," Martin said, ducking through the headquarters door. Jamie followed Martin back to the commander's office, a narrow adobe room where it seemed every officer in Franklin had gathered. Many were new to Jamie, some in uniform, most not. He and Martin edged their way to a place by the window just as General Sibley entered and went to his desk.

He was taller even than Jamie remembered, and dashing in his gold-crusted uniform. "Gentlemen," he said, glancing around the room. "We are on the eve of glory. Here are copies of General Orders No. 10, by which I have assumed command of all the Confederate forces here and in Arizona and New Mexico. Henceforth"—the general paused for effect—"they shall be known as the Army of New Mexico."

Sibley handed copies of the orders to Reily and Scurry, and gave the rest to the adjutant to pass around. "The Second and Third regiments will arrive by month's end," he said. "We shall then move up the Río Grande and should have little trouble taking control of all New Mexico."

Jamie sucked in a breath. Momma's face flickered through his mind, but he brushed the thought aside to listen.

"The Army of New Mexico is ample to seize and maintain possession of that Territory against any force which the enemy is now able to place within its limits," Sibley continued. "Our success is inevitable, but there is no need to stop at New Mexico. Northward lie rich fields of gold which our government dearly desires. We can take them. Westward lie ports in California, which no blockade of the Black Republicans can reach. We can take them." Sibley gazed at his staff with a confident smile. "Our watchword, gentlemen, is 'On to San Francisco.'"

"On to San Francisco!" Scurry cried, jumping to his feet, his eyes alight. The officers roared in agreement, and Jamie was caught up in the cheer. He glanced at Martin, who grinned back. They were going to war.

Squinting in the bright sunlight, O'Brien led his jaded horse to the river. Company I's horses were suffering as much as the men—there was not much forage to be had, and they lipped at the frozen stubble of grass on the riverbank.

"When are we going to march?" someone asked. O'Brien didn't bother to answer. It was a question everyone asked all the time. Orders would come soon from Leavenworth, the men told each other, but though mighty armies were gathering in the east, Leavenworth was silent.

Desertions and arrests for thievery were bleeding away the regiment's strength. O'Brien's company now numbered sixty-one, and that was a miracle, all things considered. As his nag lipped at the icy water, O'Brien looked down the bank at the line of ragged Pike's Peakers with their thin ponies. Even Franklin's beautiful bay was looking gaunt. O'Brien saw Franklin frown as he leaned against the horse, his face paler than usual under the dark curls, then the frown became a grimace and the youth put a hand to his gut.

"Sick, are you?" O'Brien asked.

Franklin started, and the look in his eyes as he raised them to O'Brien's was, for an instant, naked fear.

"No," he said, standing up straight and smoothing the bay's mane with a gloved hand. It was a lie, sure as heaven. O'Brien stepped closer and saw sweat on Franklin's smooth jaw. Idly, he scratched at the short beard sprouting on his own chin.

"You don't look well," he said. "Best report for the sick call."

"No, I'm fine, sir," Franklin said, red-faced. "I'll be fine tomorrow. Must've had a bit of bad beef."

O'Brien stared narrowly at his lieutenant. The lad was a coward, he thought. Or a spy. The oddest things frightened him—the surgeon among them, it seemed. Now, what would a spy have to fear from the surgeon? Discovery of some secret document? But such a thing could be hidden elsewhere before sick call.

"Report to the surgeon tomorrow," O'Brien said, watching for Franklin's reaction. "That's an order."

"Please, Captain." Franklin's voice was almost a whisper. "It's nothing, I assure you. It will pass."

The dark eyes pleaded, making O'Brien think of younger brothers and sisters at home. He had not meant to soften, but something in Franklin's eyes touched whatever shred of Christian charity was left in him.

"Report to me after the morning stable call, then. If you're still sick you go to the surgeon."

"I won't be," Franklin said. "Thank you, sir." He moved off, leading the bay back toward the corral. O'Brien watched him away, musing.

"He won't last the winter," Hall said, coming up. His gray horse tossed its head and flattened its ears at O'Brien's nag. "Pneumonia'll get him. Always hits the weak ones."

"Then he'll be no more trouble."

"Oh, he won't trouble me another day," Hall said with a grin. "I'm transferring out."

O'Brien gave a snort of laughter. "To Leavenworth, I suppose?"

"No," said Hall. "To Dodd's company. They're heading to Fort Garland to muster in."

O'Brien turned to stare at him, and realized Hall's horse was saddled. He was leaving, then, truly? O'Brien felt like he'd been punched in the gut. "Dodd's?" he said stupidly.

Hall nodded. "Shoup's got the paperwork ready. Would you mind coming to H.Q. to sign off?"

"Yes, I'd mind," O'Brien said. "Why is it you never mentioned this before?"

"I just got the word," said Hall with a brittle smile, "I'm following your orders, Red. I'm keeping away from Chas."

O'Brien frowned. "Stay. Hall, I need you."

"You've got Chas," Hall drawled. "I'm sure he'd be happy to obey your every command."

"Damn you, Hall! I don't give a bloody damn about him—"

"But you want to keep your straps. I understand. But you see, if I stayed I expect I'd have to kill him."

O'Brien stared. Hall wasn't joking. "Why?"

Hall shrugged. "Can't explain. Something's not right about him, that's all." He laughed. "Or maybe it's just cabin fever. This camp's driving me crazy, Red. I've got to get out." He checked a stirrup leather. "They're saying Dodd's will be Company A of the 2nd Regiment. He'll be promoted, most likely, and so will I." He turned a cool gaze on O'Brien, who realized there was no more to say. O'Brien turned his horse out in the corral and walked to headquarters with Hall, where he signed the transfer papers.

"You'll promote your first sergeant?" Shoup asked.

O'Brien nodded. Not that it mattered.

"And the others in turn, I presume. I'll inform the major," said Shoup.

They left the office. A sky silvered over with clouds seemed to reflect the thin layer of snow on the parade grounds. "Well, that's that," Hall said, and O'Brien stood watching him tighten his saddle. He tied off the leathers and turned to O'Brien with a smile. "Good luck, Captain," he said, as he held out his hand.

O'Brien stared at it. Hall's hand had brought him good news and bad, whiskey and comfort. It had led him here. He shook it at last, feeling helpless and angry. "I hear Garland's a hell hole," he said.

"At least it'll be a change." Hall grinned. "Be seeing you, Red."

Don't go, O'Brien thought. He watched while Hall trotted away toward the gate, leaving a trail of brown hoofprints in the virgin snow. A final wave of the hand—he was gone, and O'Brien was alone.

12

An army under my command enters New Mexico, to take possession of it in the name and for the benefit of the Confederate States.

—H. H. Sibley

Christmas morning dawned cold and clear. Jamie walked up a hill overlooking the 1st's camp at Willow Bar, a riverside grove of leafless trees that were fast being consumed as firewood. The Río Grande glistened in the chill sunlight, and a sharp breeze blew Jamie's frozen breath away over the foreign hills. They were in New Mexico. Arizona, actually, though the new Confederate territory was still unconfirmed, but it was foreign country as far as Jamie was concerned. Forage was poor, mostly scant patches of buffalo grass. In the camp below, soldiers sat huddled in their blankets around fires that smoked and snapped from green wood. They had been here five days, and Jamie figured another week would strip the place.

Wind carried the sounds of slaughter to his frozen ears. Skinny beeves for Christmas dinner. Jamie wrapped the scarf Momma'd sent him around his head to block out the sound and the cold, sat down on the hilltop, and settled his notebook on his knee to write a letter home. He tried to keep it cheerful, leaving out the frustrations of his work and anything that might frighten Momma, such as the fact they were about to begin a full-scale invasion of New Mexico. Instead he described the country he'd come through, and passed along some anecdotes of camp life. He put in a word about Martin for Emma's sake, though he didn't mention how strained the captain was looking lately. Jamie was feeling the pressure himself. Supplies stockpiled from Mexico had to last until the army could capture the Federal depots up north, and it was hard saying no to men who were cold and hungry. He thanked Momma for the scarf and the socks, telling her he'd passed along a couple of pairs to friends in need. In fact, he'd kept only one extra pair, giving the rest away to the men.

As he paused to blow on his numb fingers he noticed a commotion in the camp below. Pulling the scarf away from his ears, he caught the sound of the assembly call. Jamie stuffed his writing things into his pockets and scrambled down the hillside, getting into camp just in time to take his place as the regiment came to attention. The ranks had been reduced by some few dozen men who, struck down by smallpox or pneumonia, had gone to the hospital at Doña Ana. The rest stood with shoulders hunched against the cold, their eyes on Colonel Reily, his silvered beard muffling his neck and a woolen overcoat shielding him from the bitter wind. Jamie sighed, wishing he could give such a garment to every man here.

"Soldiers of the 1st," Reily said, "I commend you on your gallant march from San Antonio. I have great pride in you, and I regret that I will not be with you at your future victories. Diplomatic duties call me to Mexico, so I must leave you, but I do so knowing you are in competent hands and will go on to win honor and glory. As Colonel Scurry is at headquarters in Franklin, I now give temporary command to Captain Scarborough. May God bless and keep you all, and bring you as merry a Christmas as you can have this far from hearth and home."

The regiment gave him three cheers, then hurried back to their blankets and campfires as the colonel went to his carriage escorted by his son, Lieutenant John Reily, commander of the artillery battery attached to the 1st. Jamie exchanged a glance with Lieutenant Lane, the adjutant, who shrugged. Ellsberry Lane was a friend of the younger Reily's; they had both transferred from the 2nd Texas Mounted Rifles in the fall, Lane joining the Regimental

Staff while Reily took command of the new artillery corps. They were a few years older than Jamie, who liked their easy ways.

"What diplomatic duty?" Jamie asked, nodding toward Reily's carriage.

"Sibley's sending him to the governors of Chihuahua and Sonora," Lane said. "Establishing relations."

Jamie nodded, watching the younger Reily trudge toward them as his father's carriage headed for Franklin. The colonel was a fine old gentleman, a good choice for diplomatic work.

"Guess it's Dirty Shirt for us," said Lane with a grin as Reily joined them.

"He should do," Reily said, smiling. "Clever of Father to head for Mexico during the winter."

"Care for some coffee?" Lane asked.

"Yes," said Jamie and Reily together, and the three of them hurried toward regimental headquarters—a Sibley tent—where a pot of water was already simmering on the stove. Jamie and Reily rubbed their hands over the flames while Lane used a river-smoothed rock to crush coffee beans in a tin plate. They were alone in the tent, clerks and orderlies being off-duty in honor of Christmas. Captain Martin was in Franklin scrounging for more supplies. No doubt he and Scurry would sit down to a comfortable Christmas dinner in snug quarters at Fort Bliss, Jamie thought.

"Why do they call Colonel Scurry 'Dirty Shirt'?" Jamie asked.

"From his lawyer days," Lane replied. "He loved giving speeches off the cuff." He paused to throw the ground coffee into the pot. The brew boiled up for a moment, emitting a cloud of coffee-scented steam, and Lane stirred it with a peeled willow stick. "One day he drives an ox wagon into Shreveport and finds they're having a fair or something, with a lot of politicians giving speeches. Scurry can't resist giving one himself, so he jumps straight off the wagon onto the platform, covered with dust and all, and gives such a speech that everyone is spellbound. Then someone in the back yells 'Go it, dirty-shirt!' He's been called that ever since."

Jamie smiled. "How'd we wind up with so many politicians for commanders?"

"Power," Lane said simply. "It's like honey to the bee. And they figure being a war hero can't hurt in the next election."

Jamie glanced at Reily, wondering if he'd been offended by the question. Colonel Reily was quite a politician himself, and Jamie was a little envious of John, who'd traveled with his father on diplomatic duty to Russia. The more Jamie saw of the army and the men who comprised it, the more he realized how little he'd seen of the world.

Lane peered into the briskly boiling coffee. "This is ready. Bring the cups."

Jamie and Reily held tin mugs while Lane poured the coffee. Reily produced a flask from his breast pocket and added to each cup a splash of brandy, then raised his steaming mug. "Merry Christmas, boys," he said.

Jamie covered a pang of homesickness with a smile. "Merry Christmas." He swallowed deeply, hoping to burn away the feeling along with the cold.

"And a Happy New Year in Santa Fé," Lane added. The tin mugs clicked together while the wind howled outside the tent.

O'Brien came out of his quarters and frowned at the dingy snow piled by the porch. Not as deep as in Avery, he reminded himself, but that was small comfort against the dreary cold and boredom of Camp Weld. Nothing to eat but crackers, nothing to do but drill or scrape snow or stand guard. Christmas day was different from other days only in that the regiment had been excused from drill and were expected to attend a special prayer service to be conducted by Major Chivington that evening.

As O'Brien stepped into the sunlight, a ragged cheer

drew his attention. He turned toward the noise and saw his men gathered around a cart, which they were quickly relieving of its load of live turkeys, laughing and arguing over the birds. Fearing trouble from the merchant, O'Brien strode toward them. Only Lieutenant Denning saw him in time to salute.

"What the hell is all this?" he demanded.

"Christmas dinner for the boys, sir." Denning grinned. "Franklin did it." He nodded at Franklin who was paying off the poulterer. Franklin put away his purse and accepted two fat and squirming geese, which he carried up to Denning.

"Here's yours, Luther," he said, handing him one. He turned to face O'Brien and, with a crooked smile, offered him the other goose. "And this is for you, Captain. Merry Christmas."

O'Brien stared at the bird. He did not want to accept a gift from Franklin—he'd nothing to give in return. But to turn down a fresh goose when all he'd had for two months was hard crackers and rotten bacon was more than could be expected of human flesh. He took the bird, saying, "Thank you."

"Charles, won't you help us eat it?" Denning asked, laughing as his goose tried to struggle out from under his arm. "Mary'll scold me if you don't."

"No, it's all for your family," Franklin replied. "Give Mary my thanks anyway." He shouted after the men, who were fast disappearing with the turkeys, "Remember to cook them first!"

"Well, God bless you," Denning said. "Merry Christmas!"

"Merry Christmas," Franklin said as Denning hurried off, showing signs of losing his battle with the goose. Franklin turned to O'Brien in time to see him snap his own bird's neck. The youth recoiled slightly though he tried to hide it. Never had to kill his own supper, O'Brien thought.

"Good of you to buy food for the boys."

"I thought it best," Franklin said. "The man was bound to lose his birds today—he might as well be paid for them."

"Good of you," O'Brien repeated, then added a bit stiffly, "I've no family. Will you share this with me?" It was all he had to offer, and though he didn't much care for Franklin, he wanted to prove he could behave gentlemanly, and he thought a gentleman would offer what he could.

Surprise and something else flicked across Franklin's face. "Thank you, sir," he said, "but I've already accepted an invitation to dinner in town."

O'Brien looked down. The white feathers of the dead goose fluttered against his fingers in the cold breeze. Stupid, he thought to himself. Of course he won't take supper with you. He's off to dinner with his grand friends in Denver City. And even if he weren't, you're not fit to share a table with him. You're not his kind.

"Thank you all the same," Franklin repeated in an earnest voice. "Merry Christmas, sir."

"Merry Christmas."

O'Brien took his goose to the officers' mess and bribed Captain Logan's cook to roast it for him. Then, wrapping cold fingers around a steaming cup of coffee, he went to the fire, where a few other officers chatted. He sipped at his coffee and wondered if he would have bought his men turkeys had he Franklin's wealth.

"Say, O'Brien," Logan said, "did you hear Dodd's company's being sent south?"

"Are they?"

"That's where Hall went, isn't it? Dodd's?"

"Yes."

"Well, they're marching to Santa Fé. Ford's, too, I hear. Guess Colonel Canby's getting his reinforcements. Hell of a time for a march, though," Logan added, and a couple of the others laughed. "Glad it isn't us."

O'Brien sighed, thinking of Hall marching through snow, sheltering in a tent, huddling near a campfire. He imagined Hall must be delighted.

The Exchange's office was cold, and Laura paced back and forth to keep her feet warm. Her uncle had not seen fit to purchase more for her than a cloak of rough wool and a new pair of half-boots that were not thick enough to keep out the chill. She refused to be depressed, however, and glanced out the window toward the plaza. At any moment Lieutenant McIntyre would arrive to escort her to the Canbys' for Christmas dinner.

It was to be a small party, the obligatory social rites of the season having been satisfied at a Christmas Eve fête in the Governor's Palace the night before. Laura's uncle had, as usual, been included in tonight's invitation and, as usual, declined in favor of more lively entertainment. He was hosting a card party in his room.

"Pretty bonnet, Miss Howland," Phillips said, lounging in the door to the cantina.

"Thank you," Laura said coolly.

"Awfully cold, ain't it?"

Laura didn't bother to answer.

"Seems a nice lady like you should be somewhere warmer. Maybe you ought to go south."

The tone of his voice made Laura narrow her eyes. "I believe I'll step outside," she said. "It can hardly be colder, and the air is so much fresher." She went out without looking back, though she thought she heard Phillips chuckle.

The plaza was quiet, most of the natives being at home with their families or in church. Smoke twined from chimneys, scenting the air with piñon. The parroquia was aglow with candlelight against a blue-gray twilight. Behind it the Sangre de Cristos lay sleeping under a blanket of snow. Laura pulled her cloak closer about her shoulders and ventured across the street to peer in the window of Seligman Brothers' Mercantile. All the shops were closed, which was just as well for she had no money with which to purchase the tempting luxuries of gloves, scent, and candy on display. She had made one or two inquiries about hiring out her services as a seamstress or teacher, but there was small demand for such skills in Santa Fé. Perhaps she should approach the sisters at the convent about helping with their school.

Hearing steps behind her, she turned and saw Lieutenant McIntyre approaching in a blue military overcoat. "What are you doing out here alone?" he said, frowning.

"I was restless," Laura said. "Don't scold."

"Well, let's get you inside."

They hurried across the silent street and through the plaza. "Candles," Laura said, noticing a light in every window, an uncommon extravagance.

"They're to guide the Christ child," McIntyre said. "So are the luminarias." He pointed to a small bonfire beside the street, tended by two native youths and an old man. Laura noticed more fires here and there in the town. "They'll keep watch all night," the lieutenant told her. Laura paused to stretch out her hands to the flames, exchanging silent nods with the vigilants and watching the smoke and sparks climb upward in the fading light, before hurrying on to the Canbys'.

"Welcome, Miss Howland," Mrs. Canby said, meeting her at the door with an embrace. "Oh, you're chilled through! Come in to the fire."

"Thank you," Laura said, untying the strings of her bonnet. She handed it to Maria, and unfastened her cloak, blushing a little as she let it slide from her shoulders to reveal the blue gown her uncle had bought her. She glanced up at Mr. McIntyre, whose smile was warm enough to make her turn away.

In the parlor Colonel Canby was standing by the window with Captain and Mrs. Chapin. "Miss Howland!" he said as they entered. "You look delightful."

Laura dropped him a curtsey. "Thank you, sir. Merry Christmas."

"Did you see the procession around the plaza yesterday evening?" Mrs. Chapin asked.

"I watched a bit of it from the window."

"We went to the midnight mass afterward," Captain Chapin said. "Most impressive."

"They're going in." Mrs. Chapin nodded toward the dining room where the Canbys were passing through the door.

Mr. McIntyre offered Laura his arm. "That dress is even prettier than I remembered," he said softly.

"It's the best dress I have," she replied. The others were beginning to get threadbare.

Mrs. Canby and María had prepared a sumptuous feast: pickled oysters, posole, currant jelly, scalloped onions, roasted crane, and chiles stuffed with macaroni. Champagne sparkled for the Christmas toasts. Laura found herself thinking how lucky she was to have such good friends as the Canbys. They were more like family than her uncle—at least, more like the family she wanted. The meal was topped off with hot coffee, molasses pie, and plum pudding, after which everyone retired to the parlor.

"I was sorry to hear of Prince Albert's death," Laura said. "Poor Queen Victoria."

"Sad news for Britain," Mrs. Canby said. She glanced up at her husband. "Will it soften their stand on Mason and Slidell, do you think?" The Federal navy's seizure of the two Confederate envoys from the British mail packet *Trent* in November had not been well received abroad.

"No," Colonel Canby replied. "Britain wants them released, and I expect they'll have them. We can't afford a conflict in Europe."

"Why not?" Captain Chapin asked flippantly. "McClellan's army doesn't appear to be busy."

It was true that there had been no activity to speak of in the war back east, nor was any likely now that winter had set in. Missouri had begun to settle down somewhat under Major General Halleck, who had recently replaced the radical Frémont, but news of skirmishing at Independence, in Kansas, and in Indian Territory was disturbing to those who depended on the Santa Fé Trail for communication with the East.

Before long the Chapins rose to make their farewells. Laura felt she should also go soon and leave the colonel to enjoy a few precious free hours with his wife, but not just yet. The fire was so comforting, and she was a little afraid of speaking privately with Lieutenant McIntyre. It seemed her best choice would be to marry him, but she still hoped—irrationally, she knew—to return east. Staring dreamily at the glowing embers, she listened to the men talking of the war back at home. A soft knock on the door made her glance up.

It was María, with a letter that she offered to the colonel. He took it, frowning, and opened it to find a second letter enclosed.

"That looks like Henry's hand," Mrs. Canby remarked. Her husband glanced at her and strolled a few steps away as he broke the seal. Laura sat up, watching him. The furrow on his brow increased as he read.

"Richard?" Mrs. Canby said softly. "Is it from Henry?"

Colonel Canby finished reading the brief message and folded the sheet. "Yes," he said.

"What does he say?"

The colonel stood silent a moment. "He wishes us a Merry Christmas," he said finally, and moved to put the letter on the fire. Mrs. Canby rose to intercept him. Their eyes locked, then with a nod he gave her the note. Laura envied them, sensing the bond of silent trust between them. The moment rang with a clarity brighter than crystal; such, she realized, was the bond she wanted—a deep understanding, needing no words for expression—nothing less would satisfy her. She glanced toward Lieutenant McIntyre, wondering if such a bond grew over time. It was not a matter on which she was willing to gamble.

Mrs. Canby calmly returned to the sofa and read the note through while the colonel leaned on the mantel and gazed silently at her. When she finished reading she looked up.

"Yes, you're quite right," she said, handing the letter back to him. "It should be burned. How foolish of Henry to write such stuff." She smoothed her skirt and took out her sewing with an air of unconcern, but Laura noticed that her fingers trembled a little as they pushed the needle into the cloth.

The colonel, with a ghostly smile of admiration for his wife, tossed the note into the flames where it writhed for a moment before blackening to ash. "Will you excuse us, Miss Howland?" he said, gesturing to the lieutenant, who stood up. "I'm afraid this message requires an immediate response."

"Of course," Laura said. She watched them stride out, nodding as Mr. McIntyre threw her an apologetic glance, then looked back at Mrs. Canby, who had let the needle fall from her hand and was frowning into the fire.

"You met Henry Sibley, didn't you, Miss Howland?"

Laura nodded. "Briefly. At Fort Union."

"Yes, I thought so. He and Richard were once great friends. He's a Confederate general now." Mrs. Canby's voice was so gloomy that Laura was surprised; she had never seen her friend so troubled. Mrs. Canby looked up at her. "Do you still plan to return to Boston?"

"Yes."

"Best go soon," Mrs. Canby said. A sob escaped her. Alarmed, Laura put an arm around her. Strange to be comforting this lady who was such a pillar of strength in the small American community in Santa Fé. The older woman dabbed at her eyes with a handkerchief. "What an idiot you must think me," she said.

"I think you must have had some bad news," Laura said lightly, "so I wouldn't dream of going to Boston now."

Mrs. Canby laughed. "How ridiculous. No, you must go." Her face became serious again. "Henry's brought his army near Fort Craig. He plans to march up the Río Grande. He was warning Richard to send me to safety."

Laura's lips parted in surprise, and Mrs. Canby nodded grimly. "You must go now," she repeated.

"I can't," Laura said. "I have no money for the fare."

"Your uncle will see the need, won't he?"

Laura stared at the fire. "What will *you* do?"

Mrs. Canby straightened, as if the question had given her strength. She picked up her needle again. "Stand by Richard," she said, pulling the thread to its length. "I always stand by Richard."

Laura smiled softly. "May I help you with that?" she

asked, reaching for another square of the quilt, and the two of them stitched silently while the fire burned down to embers.

McIntyre shrugged into his overcoat as he hurried to keep up with the colonel. Canby was silent and McIntyre knew better than to ask questions. They went into headquarters, and McIntyre lighted lamps and laid a fire in Canby's office while the colonel went to his desk and began to write.

"Who's in town tonight?" Canby asked without looking up.

"Besides Chapin? Nico, I think, and Evans. Maybe D'Amours. Shall I fetch them?"

"Not yet. Find them before you retire, but first I need you to write to the chief of ordnance at Leavenworth. Tell him it's imperative we receive our annual supply at once."

"Yes, sir," McIntyre said, rummaging in the adjutant's desk for paper and ink. He began to write, his spirits sinking as the messages Canby ordered him to pen revealed what his commander hadn't taken time to explain: Sibley was in southern New Mexico, had reinforced Baylor with, he claimed, three regiments of Texans, and was threatening Fort Craig. McIntyre kept thinking of Sibley's beguiling manner and of Owens's farewell at Fort Union.

"You'll ride at dawn," Canby said as McIntyre sealed the dispatches. "Go find the rest of the staff. Tell them to meet here at five. Then get some sleep."

"Yes, sir," said McIntyre on his way to the door. He glanced back to see Canby put another log on the fire and begin to pace, unlit cigar in his mouth.

Hurrying away from the palace, McIntyre stuck his head into Consuelo's and spotted Nicodemus dealing cards to three noncoms. He went in and put a hand on his friend's shoulder, saying, "Pious work, eh, Nico?"

Nicodemus jumped. "Don't walk up on a man like that, Lacey. Thought you were off courting."

"I was. Canby got news, and he wants us to meet early tomorrow—"

"But it's Christmas!"

"Sorry, colonel's orders."

"Hell," Nicodemus said. "I was just starting to win." He tossed the deck on the table and went with McIntyre to the door.

"Where's Evans?" McIntyre asked.

"Don't know. Having dinner somewhere or other."

"Do me a favor and see if he's in quarters, and if not try to find him. And pass the word to the others. Canby wants the whole staff at five A.M."

"Hell," Nicodemus repeated, heading toward the post.

McIntyre hurried back to the Canbys', where he found Miss Howland on the point of leaving with Juan Carlos. She accepted his escort instead and, except for one searching glance, acted as if nothing unusual had happened. McIntyre marveled at her composure—his own heart was pumping pretty fast. When they were halfway across the plaza, surrounded in darkness and the bare, bony branches of cottonwoods, he stopped and took her hands in his.

"I'm leaving tomorrow morning," he said. "Not sure when I'll be back."

She nodded, her face pale in the starlight, framed by the black bonnet. The cloud cover had cleared off, leaving the winter sky glittering cold.

"Can you tell me where you're going?" she asked.

"I don't know yet. If I'm not back in a few days I'll write to you."

"All right."

She was so good. Her calm made him feel stronger, made him want to live up to her confidence. "Miss Howland—"

She reached up to press her fingertips, sheathed in worn black gloves, against his lips. "Not in haste," she said. "When you return." His heart flamed and he knew an impulse to cover her face with kisses, but he mastered it and instead led her slowly toward the Exchange. They paused before the doors.

"Good night, Miss Howland," he said, squeezing her hands. "I shall be thinking of you."

"And I of you. Merry Christmas," she said softly, looking up at him with a shy smile. Warmth filled his chest. He bent to kiss her hand. As he straightened her lips brushed his cheek, then she was saying good night, slipping inside, gone. Through the window he watched her pass out of the office toward her room. McIntyre's gaze met that of the hotel clerk, Phillips, grinning back at him. He turned away, knowing he'd get little sleep that night.

13

We have no fears of any armed force that Texas can send against this Territory.

—Henry Connelly, Governor of New Mexico Territory

Laura's cheeks were hot as she walked through the office. The look Mr. Phillips had given her when she entered the hotel had made it clear he'd watched her farewell to the lieutenant. She held her head high. She'd done nothing shameful, though she did regret having been observed. She opened the door to the placita and stepped onto the portal, her bootheels clicking sharply in the night air. The garden was frozen in sleep. Snow lay beneath the bare canes of the rosebushes. Laura hurried to her door and had already turned the key when the sound of a heavier tread registered in her awareness, and she looked up to find that Phillips had followed her. She took a step backward, key in hand, and the door of her room swung open.

"Evening, Miss Howland," The clerk said, smiling. "Such a cold night, ain't it?"

Laura was silent, watching him warily.

"Pretty lady shouldn't be alone on a cold night," he said. "Ought to have someone to keep her warm." He leaned against the door frame and glanced into her room.

Laura felt anger rising along with fear. "You're offensive, sir," she said. "Good night."

"Oho! Now I bet you wouldn't say that if I was Mr. McIntyre there," Phillips said. "You'd like *him* to keep you warm, I reckon."

"What I'd like is for you to leave."

"Now, now! If you don't want fellows to be friendly, then you shouldn't go a-kissing soldiers on the street."

"If you do not step away from my door at once I shall complain to Mr. Parker," Laura said.

Phillips's smile faded into a nasty sneer, but he moved away from the door, his eyes on her the whole time. In two quick steps Laura was inside and had shut the door behind her, locking it. She leaned a hand against it and stood listening, aware she was breathing shallowly. After a long moment the scrape of Phillips's boots reached her; she stayed frozen as his steps faded down the portal, followed by the snap and rattle of the far door.

The lamp cast a faint glow from the little table by her bed. Laura turned up the wick, and the smell of lamp oil increased briefly as golden flame chased the shadows back into the corners. She sat on the bed and reached a shaky hand up to untie her bonnet. Her clock chimed softly once, and she glanced at it. Half-past eleven; Christmas was almost gone. She set her key on the table and reached for the image of her father in its little silver frame. The metal was cold. She cradled it in her hands as if to warm it, and gazed at her father's face. Memories of Boston flooded back to her, of happy Christmases and of last year's, which had been so desolate.

A tiny scraping sound made her look up. Laura frowned, looking for the source of the noise, and heard a small *click*, then another. Then the handle of her door began to turn.

She was on her feet in an instant, snatching up her key from the nightstand, ignoring the bonnet that tumbled from her head as she ran to the far door, the one she always kept locked, the one that opened onto the street. The key jittered against the door in her shaking hand but she somehow fitted it to the lock, then she was out in the sharp night, flying up the street while the door banged behind her. Her boots slipped on frozen mud; she gasped cold clouds as she rounded the corner heading for the north side of the hotel and her uncle's room. The Spanish church loomed before her, its windows like two pairs of burning eyes. She found her uncle's door and banged her fist against it, still clutching her key.

"Uncle Wallace! Uncle—"

The door opened and Laura nearly fell into the room. Cigar smoke stung her eyes and nostrils. She coughed, suddenly conscious of what must be her odd appearance: hatless, with a key in one hand and her father's picture in the other. Before her, half a dozen men formed a tableau of interrupted revelry. Two had risen, a third—Mr. Parker—held the door open, his hand on the hilt of his pistol. Her uncle stood up, leaning fingertips against the baize-covered table for balance, and said in an unconcerned voice, "Laura, m'dear. What brings you here?"

Laura gulped a breath and tried to steady herself. "Someone—I believe Mr. Phillips—was attempting to enter my room," she said. "He—he—" She swallowed, unable to go on.

Parker's eyes widened. "He's there now?"

Laura nodded.

"I'm very sorry, ma'am," Mr. Parker said. "I'll get rid of him. Jimmy, Hank, Royce—you go cover the back door of number four. Vic and I'll go to the front. Howland, you stay and watch your niece. We won't be long."

Uncle Wallace nodded blearily, and Laura, with a flutter of mingled pleasure and fear, watched the brief flurry of gun-checking and shoulder-squaring that preceded the men's departure. Alone with her uncle, she felt both relieved and a bit foolish.

"Shouldn't have Phillips in your room, m'dear," Uncle Wallace said as he plopped back into his chair. "No prospects."

"I didn't invite him," Laura said tartly, though it was ridiculous to respond to such a remark at all. She sank into a chair at the table. She had suddenly started to tremble, and she gazed unhappily at the cards and coins scattered across the green cloth. The door opened; she looked up to see Mr. Parker with a bit of paper in his hand.

"I apologize, Miss Howland," he said. "Phillips won't trouble you again. He had this, I'm afraid." He handed Laura the Canbys' invitation to Christmas dinner.

"Thank you," she said numbly, smoothing the crumpled note. Her uncle leaned toward her to peer at it, wheezing whiskey fumes that made her turn her head.

"What'd he want with that?" he asked. "Not worth anything."

"I don't know, Mr. Howland, but it's certainly none of his business," Parker replied. "I took away his keys. He won't be working here any longer."

Uncle Wallace sighed dismissively, leaned back in his chair, and closed his eyes.

"Are you all right, Miss Howland?" Mr. Parker asked. "Did he hurt you?"

"No," Laura said. "I'm all right."

"Let me fix you some coffee. Maybe a little soup."

"Thank you."

Mr. Parker offered his arm and as she rose and took it, her uncle roused enough to say "Damned lot of bother. Broke up a good party." Then he sighed and began to snore. Laura raised her chin as she left the room, gathering what dignity she could from her own sources, for it was clear that her uncle had none.

Fort Thorn was about as miserable a place as one could be on a cold January day. Jamie got off of Cocoa and gave her reins to the quartermaster sergeant to hold, and stood frowning at the crumbling fort. The doors and some of the roofbeams had been carried off, giving it a forlorn appearance.

The 1st Regiment had moved upriver, both to safeguard Baylor at Mesilla and to make room for the 2nd and 3rd, which were creeping up the Río Grande at a snail's pace. The 1st's new camp was a couple of miles north of Fort Thorn, and Jamie and Sergeant Rose had come down with Captain Owens of Sibley's staff to see if the old fort could be put to rights.

"Looks pretty bad," Jamie said as they walked along the square of deteriorating buildings.

"Hasn't been used for three years," Owens replied in the soft Georgia drawl Jamie found so intriguing. He watched Owens covertly, trying to decide if it was more the captain's voice or the lazy grace of his movements that marked him as the son of a Southern lord. "That swamp," Owens added, pointing to where the ground sloped gently into a marsh as it neared the Río Grande, "breeds fever in the summer. I had the bad luck to camp here for a month, and I was sick the whole time."

Jamie looked at the swamp, which was now merely chilly—he couldn't call anything damp in such a dry country—and depressing. He peered into one of the buildings. Something small and fast scuttled deeper into the structure. Jamie grimaced and looked at Sergeant Rose, who shook his head.

"Might as well burn it down and start fresh," Rose said.

"No time for that," Owens told him. "The general wants to move headquarters here as soon as the 2nd gets into camp."

"What if we plastered the insides?" Jamie asked. "Would it hold?"

Rose cocked an eye at the walls. "Not long."

"A few weeks?" Owens asked.

"Maybe," the sergeant admitted.

"Let's do it, then," Jamie said. "Tell the carpenters to come down and figure out how much help they'll need. We'll use that mud plaster the Mexicans make—one of Coopwood's men will know how."

"Yes, sir," Rose said without enthusiasm.

Jamie led the way back to camp, where he sent Sergeant Rose to start organizing the work detail while he and Owens joined Martin, Lane, and Coopwood around a small fire.

Captain Coopwood had become a regular fixture at headquarters, his spy company helping locate forage and supplies in the sparse countryside. Jamie was somewhat in awe of Bethel Coopwood, who was ten years his senior and had studied and practiced law. The captain was staunchly devoted to his San Elizario Spies and Guides, almost all Mexicans but of a stamp braver and more loyal than most Jamie had seen. They had been tested twice in clashes with the enemy, at Mesilla and Cañada Alamosa, and they were as true to their captain as he to them.

At the moment Coopwood was wrapped in a blanket and huddling near the fire. He coughed as Jamie and Owens joined the group.

"How's Fort Thorn?" Martin asked, handing Jamie a canteen of water. Jamie took a deep swallow before answering.

"Wretched." He passed the canteen to Owens. "It'll take some work to put it in order."

"Good," Lane said. "Give the men something to do besides drink and brawl."

Martin sighed and poked at the fire with a stick. "They're fine when they can't buy liquor. It's too bad the sutlers caught up with us."

"How about them Indians?" Lane asked, eyeing Coopwood. "Time for another scout?"

Coopwood shrugged and sniffed, wiping his reddened nose on his blanket. "If you like," he said. "But we never catch any."

"You sound worse, Bethel," Martin said. "Did you see the surgeon?"

"No," Coopwood said. "Got his hands full. There's half a dozen sick just in my company."

Footsteps made Jamie look up. Two men were approaching the fire, one of whom Jamie recognized. Charles Pyron owned a cattle ranch south of San Antonio and competed, on friendly terms, with the Russells. Back in April he had raised a volunteer company that Matthew had wanted to join, and there'd been a fearful row with Poppa. Now Pyron, a major, had been given command of Baylor's troops as well as his own. There had been some misunderstanding between the self-appointed military governor of Arizona and General Sibley, though Sibley had left Baylor in office. Lane would know the whole story, Jamie thought as he watched Pyron come up.

A shuffling began; Martin was already on his feet, but Pyron gestured to the others to stay where they were, saying "At ease, gents." They stood up anyway, Coopwood pulling the blanket closer around his hunched shoulders.

"Major Pyron." Owens nodded. "Welcome to nowhere."

"Howdy, Owens," Pyron said, breaking into a grin. "I see you're already making up to the quartermasters." He turned to Jamie. "You're Earl Russell's boy, aren't you? Used to work at Webber's?" he asked.

"Yes, sir." Jamie nodded.

"Thought you looked familiar. How's your daddy's ranch?"

"They're managing," Jamie replied.

"That's as good as you can ask." Pyron gave Jamie a friendly nod, then turned to his civilian companion. "Boys, this is John Phillips, down from Santa Fé."

Jamie eyed the stranger as he shook hands. Phillips had hard eyes and his face seemed pinched into a permanent sneer.

Pyron continued. "He's been tracking those Apaches that stole some mules from the camp at Willow Bar."

"Any luck?" Lane asked, and Jamie heard a dig in his voice.

Phillips glared at the adjutant briefly. "No."

"Maybe you could use a man like him in your spy company, Captain Coopwood," Pyron said.

"Possibly," the captain replied coolly.

"Well, he knows the Territory," Pyron said. "So, Captain Quartermaster, you make sure he gets rigged out with everything he needs, and find him a place to stay, all right?" Not waiting for an answer, Pyron clapped Phillips on the back and headed off toward where his battalion was settling into camp.

There was a moment's uncomfortable silence. Jamie took the canteen back from Owens.

"What you got there, sonny?" Phillips asked, eyes suddenly sharp. "Whiskey?"

"Water." Jamie offered the canteen.

"Water?" The sneer deepened. "No thanks."

"We're short on tents," Martin said quietly. "You can share with me and Jamie if you like."

"That'll do," Phillips said. "Got a gun for me?"

"There were some rifles captured at St. Augustín. Jamie, did the lancers take them all?"

"We have a few left," Jamie said reluctantly.

Martin gave Jamie a glance and a tiny nod of understanding. "Come on, I'll get you fixed up," he said, leading Phillips away from the fire.

A green twig snapped in the flames. "Going to let him join your spies, Captain?" Lane asked softly.

"No," Coopwood said. Hearing the harshness in his tone, Jamie glanced up and saw Coopwood was frowning.

"Even if he knows Santa Fé inside out?" Lane said.

"I expect what he knows of Santa Fé is its underbelly," Coopwood said. "The man's a brigand."

"Oh, I don't know," Owens said casually. "Heard he fought an honorable duel at Fort Marcy last summer."

"And I heard he stabbed a man in the back at Mesilla last week," Lane said.

"I was there," Owens said. "He didn't start the fight."

"He didn't stop it, either, and a man died," Coopwood replied. A fit of coughing took him. "Try the surgeon again," he said in a strangled voice, nodding to the others as he left.

"He didn't kill the fellow," Owens said to his back, but Coopwood made no sign he'd heard.

"Still and all," Lane said slowly, "I wouldn't want to be his bunkmate. You keep an eye out, Jamie."

Jamie nodded, watching Martin and Phillips disappear among the wagons while at his feet the fire hissed agreement with the warning.

"Have you heard from the colonel lately, Mrs. Canby?" Mrs. Josephy asked.

"Two days ago," Mrs. Canby replied. "He has set up his headquarters at Belen. The Texans are still eighty miles from Fort Craig."

"Too close," Mrs. Williams said gruffly. Laura liked her, a good-hearted woman, the wife of a soldier in Ford's company of volunteers, and laundress for the company. She had marched from Colorado with her husband and two small children, only to be left behind in Santa Fé while the company returned to Fort Union.

Laura set a finished bandage roll in the basket with the others and reached for another strip of muslin. Mrs. Canby had organized the ladies in Santa Fé to make preparations against the possibility of a battle, and Mr. Parker had kindly donated some old sheets to be made into bandages. Mrs. Chapin glanced up at Laura with a reassuring smile, which Laura did her best to return. Captain Chapin had gone with the colonel and his staff, and was now acting as adjutant. A staff officer did not stand in line facing enemy guns, Laura knew, but he risked himself just as much riding alone to deliver orders.

"I'll be glad to get home to Connecticut," Mrs. Josephy said.

"Alice!" Mrs. Canby exclaimed. "You're leaving, too?"

"My husband wants me to take little Adam home to meet Grandma and Grandpa," Mrs. Josephy said in an apologetic voice. "And I confess I'm afraid to stay. I have nightmares—"

"Is Lieutenant Josephy going with you?" Doña Isabel asked.

"No, the colonel can't spare him, and we're spending all our savings as it is. I'm taking the servants, and Manny has a pistol. We should be all right. Shouldn't we?" She turned pleading eyes to Mrs. Canby.

"Of course you will," Mrs. Chapin said briskly. "The mail has a military escort all the way to Leavenworth. No sense indulging in horrible fantasies."

"When are you leaving?" Laura asked slowly.

"On the next coach," Mrs. Josephy said. "Monday, if it's on time."

"Do you know if there are any seats left?"

"No, I don't know."

"Are you thinking of returning east, Miss Howland?" Mrs. Chapin asked.

Laura glanced from her to Mrs. Canby and knew they were thinking of Lieutenant McIntyre. She felt a pang for his sake, but a surprisingly small one. She had made him no promise, after all. Home was what she wanted.

"I've been wanting to go for some time," she said, "but I have no escort. Would you be willing to let me join your party, Mrs. Josephy?"

The younger woman's face brightened. "Of course! I'd be happy to have you!"

Her enthusiasm sparked hope in Laura. "Then if you'll excuse me, I'll go to the post office right away and inquire about a seat."

"Take Juan Carlos with you," Mrs. Canby told her.

"Yes, thank you," Laura said, putting her bandage roll aside. As she hurried to the post office, her brain was at work on the problem of money. She would ask her uncle for the fare; she expected he would refuse, but perhaps he would give her something. Her friends in Santa Fé were all connected with the military, and the soldiers had not been paid for months, so she could not borrow money. Regretfully, she decided the only course left was to sell her jewelry. She would arrive in Boston penniless and threadbare, but free. With higher spirits than she'd felt in many days, she entered the post office.

"Help you?" the clerk asked, gazing at her from beneath thick eyebrows.

"I would like to book a seat on Monday's mail," Laura said.

"You taking the greaser with you?" The clerk nodded toward Juan Carlos.

"No," Laura said coldly. "I will be traveling with the

Josephy party. Miss Howland," she added as he scribbled on a much-altered waybill.

"How far?"

"Independence."

"Two hundred eighty dollars."

Laura was shocked. "That is far too high. Last spring my fare was one hundred fifty dollars."

"That was last spring," he said. "There's a war on."

Laura swallowed, then lifted her chin. "Will you reserve a seat for me please? I'll bring the money to you today."

"I can hold a seat till tomorrow morning," said the clerk.

Laura nodded and stepped briskly to the door. "Thank you, Señor," she said pointedly, as Juan Carlos held the door for her. Outside, she handed him a penny which she'd been fingering inside her pocket. "I'm sorry that man was so rude," she said.

"Gracias, Señorita Howland. But I do not pay any attention to gringos estupidos." Laura smiled, and they parted at the doors of the Exchange.

Two hundred eighty dollars, and more to get from Independence to Boston. She would have to sell every bit of jewelry, and her beloved clock, and possibly the silver frame that held her father's portrait. Mr. Seligman would give her a fair price, she knew; she had already parted with a small ring in order to purchase a few necessities, including a wicked little knife that comforted her against the threat of any more unwelcome visitors to her room. She was halfway through the office when she remembered her intent to ask her uncle for money. She stopped in the hallway, debating whether it was worth the attempt.

In a little niche in the wall a statue of the Virgin Mary gazed calmly back toward Laura. The gold paint had flecked away from the edge of her blue mantle, but she still possessed dignity and grace. Laura took a deep breath. Fare back to Boston was the least her uncle owed her. She went back out and down the street to her uncle's room.

"Come in," was the answer to her knock. Laura opened the door and found her uncle at the table, idly casting dice.

The remains of a late luncheon had been pushed to one side, chicken bones jumbled on plates smeared with gravy. An empty wine bottle stood beside the wreckage, and her uncle was opening a second bottle as Laura entered.

"Laura!" he said. "Come in, m'dear, come in! Have some wine!"

"No, thank you," she said, shutting the door. "I have a favor to ask of you. I have booked passage on the east-bound mail, and I wish you to give me the money for my fare."

"Now, Laura," her uncle said, "we have discussed this. It is not safe for you to travel alone—"

"I will be traveling with the Josephy family. They are going to Connecticut."

Wallace Howland pursed his ample lips and frowned. "It is a great expense," he said. "I do not have such a sum by me."

"How is that possible?" Laura asked, gesturing at the sumptuous apartment.

"My funds are—tied up in investments," her uncle said, pouring wine into his glass. "My dear, I think it would be best if you married. Ought to have someone to look after you."

"*You* were supposed to look after me!" Laura said. "Have you forgotten what you wrote?"

"Well, m'brother's memory, you know. Thought I should offer. Didn't think you'd come."

Aghast, Laura watched him set down the bottle and raise the glass to his lips. "What were you thinking?" she whispered.

The wine trembled in the bowl of the crystal, then the glass slipped from his grasp and fell, staining the table-cloth with a dark pool. Her uncle buried his face in his hands. "I'm sorry," he said in a muffled voice, and to Laura's astonishment he laid his head down in the wine and burst into tears.

Laura felt panic rising. "Your gold mine?" she said.

"Played out," he moaned. "Couldn't sell it."

"Your other investments?"

He raised his blotched face to look at her with pleading eyes, like a whipped dog. "I've always been lucky at cards," he said, sniffling. "Just a bad patch, my dear. I'll recover."

Laura stared at him, struggling to control her anger. Instead of rising to a challenge, instead of providing her with the means to get back into civilized country where she could at least earn her own living, he could do nothing but weep for his own folly. She could find no civil words to address to him, so she left, pulling the door tight behind her, and hurried to her room. She pulled off her cloak as she stepped in and was about to toss it on the bed when she realized something was wrong.

The room was silent.

She hurried to turn up the oil lamp. Her clock was missing. Her clock, her father's portrait, her silver-handled brushes and comb; she turned and saw that her trunk was open and its contents jumbled, her jewelry box broken and empty on the floor.

"No," she whispered. She stood staring at the ruin for a stunned moment, then she was in motion, running out of the room, back down the portal and into the office.

"Mr. Parker!"

The proprietor looked up from his desk as she burst into the room. He had just handed a key to a man in a huge overcoat with a valise beside him on the floor. "José, muéstrale al señor la habitación número siete," Parker said to his new clerk. Laura waited until they were gone, then stepped up to the desk.

"My room has been robbed, Mr. Parker. By someone who had a key, for I just unlocked it," she said.

Parker was on his feet. "Show me."

She led the way back to her room, and Parker frowned as he gazed at the wreck. "None of my people would do this," he said.

"Your new clerk?" Laura asked.

"No. I made sure of him before I hired him. I'm deeply

sorry, Miss Howland," Mr. Parker said. "I'll send for the marshal at once. And we'll give you a different room, if you like."

"Thank you," Laura said stiffly. She pulled the door closed and locked it, though there was nothing left to protect, and walked with him back toward the office. Her mind was flying in several directions at once, seeking the best way out of her predicament.

"Mr. Parker?" Laura felt her color rising, but this was no time for scruples. "May I inquire how far in advance my uncle has paid for my room?"

"Through the end of this month, ma'am," he replied, holding the office door open for her. "But please don't worry. You won't be turned out."

"That's not why I asked." Laura swallowed. "Is there any possibility you could refund me the balance?" At Mr. Parker's surprised expression, she added, "I intend to return to Boston."

"Oh. Well, then I'd be happy to give you a refund. It would come to fifty-one dollars."

"Thank you," she said. "Please excuse me, I shall be back shortly." She walked briskly through the hotel to the plaza, crossing the street to Seligman's, heedless of curious glances. Inside the shop she withdrew her gold neck chain from her bodice. The little gold watch was now all she had left, that and the chain, which would fetch a few dollars. She stepped up to the counter.

"I'd like to speak to Mr. Seligman, please," she said. "I have an item to sell."

"Go on back." The shop clerk nodded, and Laura went past the counter to Mr. Seligman's office at the back of the store, where she had met with him before to sell her ring. The door was ajar, and swung a little farther open as she knocked on it.

"Mr. Seligman?" she said. "It's Miss—" She stopped, frozen, as she saw her clock sitting on the desk inside.

14

I shall, with my mounted force, push for Santa Fé, and hold the country until the arrival of General Sibley.

—Lieutenant-Colonel John R. Baylor, Texas Mounted Rifles

Mr. Seligman came to the door, a cheerful smile beneath his bushy mustache. "Miss Howland, come in! Your uncle was just here this morning."

Laura stepped inside and involuntarily reached out to touch the clock. Her father's clock. Guardian of her hours. "He brought you this?" she asked softly.

"Yes, it's a fine piece."

"He had no right to sell it," Laura said. "It's mine."

An uneasy look came into Mr. Seligman's face. "He's your guardian, isn't he?"

Laura sat down and placed her watch and chain on the desk. She did not want to jeopardize her chances of selling them by making the merchant uncomfortable. "How much will you give me for these?"

Mr. Seligman took a seat and examined the watch with a practiced eye. "Fine work," he said. "Seventy-five dollars."

Laura's heart sank. "Is that all?"

"Eighty then," Mr. Seligman said. "And three dollars for the chain. You won't get more than that anywhere in town."

Eighty-three dollars. Added to Mr. Parker's refund, it came to just over a hundred and thirty, less than half what she needed. Laura felt numb. She was trapped in Santa Fé, trapped in a town whose civilized population was melting away from the threat of a Texan army. She shook her head to chase away the voices of fear. There was a chance—if

Mr. Seligman would help her prove her uncle had stolen the clock and her other belongings—of retrieving the money, though it was unlikely to happen before Mrs. Josephy left on Monday's mail. Drawing herself up, Laura said, "Thank you. I'll take it."

Mr. Seligman nodded and opened his desk. Laura cried out as she saw her father's portrait sitting inside. The merchant glanced up, his hand poised over the cash box.

"Please," Laura said humbly, "please may I have the portrait? The frame is yours, I understand, but you cannot want the image."

Mr. Seligman followed her gaze and picked up the portrait, handing it to Laura. She ran her fingers along the silver frame as he counted out eighty-three dollars in gold on the desktop. "He had no right," she whispered, and suddenly felt tears threatening. She blinked them away and began to open the frame.

"Keep it," he said, handing her the gold. "Keep the whole thing. Miss Howland, you know I had no idea these things were yours—"

"Of course not," Laura said. "I don't hold you to blame. Will you tell the marshal that my uncle brought them to you?"

Mr. Seligman shifted in his chair. "I've already sold the jewelry—"

"That doesn't matter. I was going to sell it to you myself. But please, will you tell the marshal?"

"Yes, all right," he said.

"Thank you." Laura unhooked the watch chain and removed her keys, and was reminded that her uncle had a key to her room. She pushed the thought of him aside. "This belongs with the clock," she said, holding out the heavy brass key. "Wind it ten turns once a day. And please take good care of it," she added. The words sounded foolish in her ears.

The merchant took the key. "I am sorry," he said.

His sympathy brought her tears up again, and she hurried out of the office. One hand clutched her father's portrait, the other guarded the money in her pocket. All her worldly wealth held thus tightly, she crossed the street back to the Exchange.

McIntyre put up a hand to shade his eyes as he neared Fort Craig. There were men on the unfinished earthworks, watching his approach. One of them scrambled down the steep slope and stood waiting for him at the bottom.

"Lacey," Anderson said, as McIntyre reined in. "I thought it was you." Anderson grinned and reached up to shake hands.

"Now you're an engineer, are you?" McIntyre said.

"Like it?" Anderson laughed. "It's my design."

McIntyre glanced at the fortification, an impressive barrier that stood ten feet high and extended on both sides of the sally port. To the west it formed a small bastion, and work was in progress to extend it.

"You should have stuck to artillery. Less work."

"And more glory," Anderson said. "What dragged you away from scenic Belen?"

"A dispatch for Colonel Roberts."

Anderson was suddenly alert. "From Canby? He'll want to see it at once. Go on in." He stepped back from the horse, and McIntyre spurred to a trot. "Tell 'em to put your gear in my quarters," Anderson called after him.

The January sun was hot, bleaching the adobe buildings to a honey color, brilliant against the dark looming mesa across the river to the northeast. McIntyre rode through the sally port and saw that wooden barracks had been thrown up between the adobe ones to accommodate more troops. He slid from his saddle, turning his horse over to an orderly before approaching the commander's quarters.

An aide stood up from his chair on the porch. "Help you, sir?"

"Dispatch for Colonel Roberts from the department commander," McIntyre said.

"He's in a meeting. If you'll wait just a moment. . . ." McIntyre nodded and the aide disappeared into the house.

In less than a minute he returned to usher McIntyre into a parlor where Colonel Roberts—a fine old gentleman with bushy side whiskers—sat behind a weathered desk. With him was Colonel Carson, the famous scout who'd taken over the First New Mexico Volunteers for St. Vrain. Chaves and McRae were there also, as well as a blue-eyed fellow whom McIntyre didn't recognize. The latter had his boots up on Roberts's desk, reminding McIntyre so strongly of Nicodemus he had to suppress a smile.

"Lacey McIntyre, sir," he said to Roberts, coming to attention. "Department headquarters. I have a dispatch for you from Colonel Canby."

"Thank you, Lieutenant," Roberts said. "Sit down."

McIntyre took a chair and waited while Roberts tore open Canby's letter. The fire on the hearth popped, spitting a tiny coal across the floor, which the blue-eyed man lowered a booted toe to extinguish.

Roberts set the letter aside. "How soon does Colonel Canby mean to arrive here?"

"The colonel hasn't told me his plans, sir," McIntyre said.

"Has he told you when we can expect reinforcements?"

The tension with which the four superior officers waited for his response told McIntyre something was wrong. Someone shifted, gentle scrape of a bootheel on the floor.

"I don't know, sir," McIntyre told them. "Colonel Canby's sent requests to Washington, Leavenworth, Colorado. Even California. So far as I know he's had no positive response—"

"What about pay for the men?" Chaves asked. "Uniforms?"

"The paymaster was detained at Leavenworth. The colonel's requested—"

"Requests!" Chaves stood and strode away from the desk, pacing like a greyhound. "Your government laughs at requests!"

"Manuel," Carson said calmly. "Aguate, mi amigo."

"I'm sure we'll hear something soon," McIntyre said, looking uneasily at Roberts.

"They're marching north, you see," Roberts said quietly, and the words sank into McIntyre's gut like a fist.

He stared at the commander. "The Texans?"

"Twenty-five hundred of them," Chaves said accusingly, as if McIntyre could somehow prevent their advance. "And half of my men are unarmed!"

"Twenty-five hundred?" McIntyre repeated stupidly.

"Thereabouts," the blue-eyed man said.

McIntyre looked at him, and he took his boots off the desk. "We haven't met," he said, leaning forward to offer a hand. "James Graydon."

"Oh, Captain Graydon," McIntyre said, numbly shaking hands. "We've heard good things about your spy company."

"Kind of you," said Graydon. "I'm just sorry we haven't got good things to tell you. Sibley's marching up the Río Grande with two full regiments and part of another."

McIntyre swallowed, looking at Roberts. "And you have—"

"Four hundred regulars, a thousand volunteers—"

"Half-trained volunteers," Chaves added.

"—eight guns and Graydon's spies," Roberts said, leaning back in his chair.

"And Dodd's men," McRae said.

"Yes, and one company from Colorado."

McIntyre stood up. "The colonel should be informed—"

"Easy, son," Roberts said. "I've already sent him an express. What we want to know from you is how soon he'll get here and how many men he can bring."

McIntyre frowned, trying to remember the disposition of troops. They'd been moving around so much—Canby jealously trying to guard all the passes into the Río Grande Valley—and he was sure there were more than two thousand, but not sure how many could be spared from the garrisons to assist Fort Craig.

"Does Colonel Canby still have the men he took north from here with him?" Roberts asked.

McIntyre nodded. "At Belen. They could be here in three or four days."

"So could the Tejanos," Chaves said.

"They're not moving that fast," Graydon stated. "Only making ten miles a day."

"Five or six days, then," Chaves said. "It does not matter. We cannot be ready in time."

"Enough," Roberts said, and the others fell silent. "We'll just have to do our best." He stood up, signaling that the meeting was at an end. The others rose, too, and filed out.

McIntyre followed them, asked the guard where to find Lieutenant Anderson, and was directed to the adjutant's office. He walked to the building in the opposite corner of the fort and went in. Anderson looked up from his desk, smiling. "Starved?"

"Yes," McIntyre said.

"Your cure awaits." Anderson led the way to his quarters and gave McIntyre a plate of cold beef, fresh bread, and a mug of lager. McIntyre took a pull at the latter.

"Good," he said in a surprised voice.

"Sumowski keeps a good store," Anderson said. "Wish all sutlers were as good, and as decent. Makes my work easier."

"You're back to being adjutant, eh?" McIntyre said. "When you're not building earthworks, that is."

Anderson nodded. "McRae's got the battery now. He's good at it. Really good." He reached for the mug, took a pull, and passed it back. "How is Miss Howland? Am I to congratulate you?"

McIntyre swallowed a bite of beef. "Not yet," he said. "We left town in a bit of a hurry."

"I see. Well, it won't be long, I'm sure," Anderson said. "You should see the battery. We've scraped up two more guns, and the men are much improved."

McIntyre ate while Anderson rattled on about earthworks and native volunteers. He himself was not so sure of his chance of success with Miss Howland. She had kept him from making the proposal she'd agreed to hear. Perhaps, he thought unhappily, she had decided to await the outcome of events in New Mexico, which looked more and more like war.

"Do you think there'll be a fight?" he asked when Anderson refilled the mug. Anderson didn't reply at once, but finished pouring and carefully stoppered the jug.

"Yes." He set the jug aside and leaned his elbows on the table. "Graydon sent one of his Mexicans into the Texans' camp selling apples, and he found out everything he wanted to know. They plan to take the depot at Union, then march into Colorado. They want the Pike's Peak gold fields."

McIntyre sucked in a breath. That would put a crimp in the war effort. "They'll have to get past Craig first," he said.

Anderson nodded. "Or capture it." He gave a halfhearted laugh. "All those theories we studied at the Academy— siege tactics, all that—I never thought we'd really use them."

McIntyre took a swallow of beer and passed him the mug. "Looking forward to it?"

Anderson turned the mug round a couple of times in his hands. "Not really," he said, glancing up with guilty eyes.

McIntyre felt a flood of relief. "Neither am I."

Anderson broke into a grin and raised the mug, and they passed it back and forth until it and the jug were dry.

It was near dusk when Jamie crested a hill and saw the army's camp ahead. The smell of burning mesquite came to him from fires glowing all along the river. Wearily, he urged the train forward, thankful to have caught up at last. The united Army of New Mexico had broken camp at Fort Thorn several days before. Jamie had been placed in charge of the supply train while Martin stayed behind to do some last-minute scrounging in the Mesilla Valley, and he did not relish the responsibility. All along the way he'd been plagued with messages to hurry forward with the train and the beef herd, which had dwindled to just over a hundred head. Now hungry soldiers came to meet the train, and Jamie had to issue some sharp commands to prevent a free-for-all with the commissary stores.

A horseman trotted up and Jamie smiled. "Hello, Ells!"

"About time you got here," said Lane, grinning back. "The men are threatening to boil their boots. Come on, I've got a place for your park." As Jamie brought Cocoa abreast of Lane's horse, he added, "Where's your mascot?"

Jamie grimaced. "Still at Fort Thorn. He's organizing his own company of spies."

"Coopwood wouldn't have him, eh?"

"Coopwood's oblivious. He's in the hospital with smallpox."

"Poor fellow!" Lane said. "So Phillips figured he'd like to be a captain, is that it?"

"Just about," Jamie replied. "He's collected a handful of Santa Fé gamblers and named them the Brigands. Only they're not to be sworn in, just employed."

"Employed? By whom?"

"By the quartermaster department, naturally," Jamie said in disgust. "We have to pay them soldiers' wages without having any military authority over them."

"Oh, poor Jamie." Lane laughed. "Was this Martin's idea?"

"No, he doesn't like it any better than I do. They're Pyron's pets, and Pyron gets what he wants."

They reached a level area scattered with a few mesquite bushes. "Here you are," Lane said. "The horses are right over there, and you're near the guard."

Jamie gave orders for the wagons to be parked, and soon the commissary was handing out flour, with the sounds of slaughter a little way off promising fresh beef. Lane threw a sack of flour across his saddlebow and led Jamie toward the 1st's camp.

"Where is Martin, anyway?" Lane asked.

"With Sibley. Foraging."

"Well, the general better hie himself up here, or he'll miss the party. Colonel Green's straining at the bit."

Jamie sighed. "Sometimes I think we'll never see a fight."

"Oh, we'll see a fight," Lane said, and the unexpected seriousness of his tone made Jamie glance at him. "Scouts have been flirting with the Federal pickets," Lane added. "They're falling back to Fort Craig. That's where they'll make a stand."

They turned out their horses and headed for a collection of tents huddled around a firepit that had burned down to embers. Voices came from one of the tents; Jamie recognized Colonel Scurry's. Lane led him into a smaller tent where stacks of correspondence covered a field desk and a few empty chairs were gathered around a Sibley stove. The canvas walls held in a little of the warmth. Jamie sat down in a rickety camp chair, stretched out his tired legs, and sighed.

"I'll take this to the colonel's cook," Lane said, hefting the flour. "Maybe he can manage some biscuits for us."

Jamie flapped a lethargic hand as Lane left. He moved his chair closer to the stove and pulled his last letter from Momma out of his coat to read it again. In two weeks he'd perused the pages so often they were threatening to tear along the creases. Happy birthday, Jamie, and many happy returns of the day. The ranch was surviving, Poppa, Gabe, and Emmaline all well and happy. Daniel had been the first to see battle, riding with Terry's Texas Rangers into the fray at Woodsonville, Kentucky, on December 17, and riding safely out again—to Momma's agitated relief—though Colonel Terry had not been so lucky. Matt still on picket duty and things fairly quiet. Miss you, love you, write soon.

Jamie carefully put away the letter, wondering if Matt had received his yet and whether he chafed at Daniel's news, stuck in winter quarters in Virginia with nothing to do but stare at the Potomac. Why, he suddenly wondered, were he and his elder brothers scattered across the continent in armies that seemed to have little or nothing to do with each other? He tried to recall the fire of patriotism that had burned in him last summer, but felt only weariness. If he was offered the choice of leaving the army tomorrow he'd take it, he knew, and the thought shamed him.

Good thing you're a quartermaster, his father's voice echoed. *You probably won't have to fight.* He remembered how angry those words had made him, but he was too tired to be angry now. The romance of soldiering had faded as he came to realize the enormous work involved just in moving an army from place to place. He took off his hat, running his fingertips over the silver star that pinned up one side.

"Emmaline," he whispered. Emmaline would have understood. But she wouldn't have sympathized, he thought with a sudden grin. Too bad Martin hadn't just married her and brought her along. Jamie suspected she'd make a better soldier than himself. Laughing softly, he leaned back in his chair, dropped the hat over his face, and slept.

"Dealer folds," Shaunessy said. "You're called, Red."

O'Brien laid down his hand. "Straight."

"All blue," Morris said, showing a handful of spades. He grinned as he gathered in the pile of coin. "My turn to buy the whiskey. I'll be back in two shakes."

O'Brien nodded and glanced round the room to make sure all his lads were behaving themselves. Colton's Saloon had been busy of late, the result of passes issued to the Pet Lambs. Though Chivington disapproved of the carousing in town, a bit of ordained revelry went a long way toward stopping absenteeism. Where the lads got the money for whiskey was truly a mystery to O'Brien, but money they found, and the liquor flowed freely.

In the corner McGuire played along with the piano, the old rusty fiddle still true. O'Brien leaned back, enjoying the song and the whiskey, imagining himself back in Dooney's, with never a care in the world. He enjoyed his lads, too. They were his kind, the Avery Trolls, and so long as they minded their orders he set less store on his rank than they did. They kept his glass full and he kept a mellow eye on their exploits, keeping them from shooting at the bottles behind the bar, and sitting in judgment over all disputed properties, including the dance girls.

"You know," Shaunessy said, shuffling the cards, "it's St. Valentine's day."

O'Brien glanced up to see Shaunessy watching a girl who was laughing with two of the lads. "Thinking to buy yourself a sweetheart?"

"It's been a long time, hasn't it?" O'Connor said.

That it had, but O'Brien shook his head. "Stick to the crùisgean lan," he said, picking up his glass and draining the last of his whiskey. "Makes you just as giddy, and can't give you the pox."

"Look at her hair," Shaunessy said. "I knew a girl in Derry had hair like that."

"You'd have to sell your boots, lad," O'Brien said, "and I'll have no barefoot Irish peasants in my company."

Shaunessy's answer was cut off by a cry of "Attention!" O'Brien looked up, but his view was obscured by the men standing in front of him.

"Fall in," the voice said, and he knew it was Franklin. "I Company will return to camp at once. Sergeant Morris, get them out of here in five minutes or you're on report."

O'Brien stood up. "Never mind that order, Morris," he said, and strolled slowly through the crowd toward Franklin. The lieutenant had on his dark overcoat and looked windblown, cheeks bright from the cold.

"Sir," Franklin said, straightening into a salute. "I've been looking for you."

"Have you now?" O'Brien asked. "Or were you just looking for someone to order around?"

The room fell silent behind him. O'Brien knew it was whiskey talking, but he didn't care. But for Franklin, Hall would never have left. Anger stirred in him like a waking beast. "Go along, Chas," he said. "This is our place. You'll want the Criterion."

The lads gave a murmur at that. O'Brien watched

Franklin, whose face went from hurt to indignant, and settled into determination. "Captain—" he began. Their eyes locked, and the hint of fear O'Brien saw was like a flag to a bull. Abruptly he swung at the boy, who dodged, stumbling backward. The lads let out a whoop and instantly formed a ring round them. Two of them kept Franklin from falling and pushed him back toward O'Brien.

"I don't want to fight you, sir!" Franklin cried, real panic in his voice.

A gentleman wouldn't do this, came the faint protest in the back of O'Brien's mind, but it only made him angrier. He would never be a gentleman, gentlemen held themselves above his kind, just as Franklin did. Just as he was doing now.

"Too good to strike a lesser man, are you?" O'Brien said. "Well, I'm not!"

With a quick stride forward he aimed another punch at Franklin's jaw. The youth ducked again but not in time to save himself a gash across the eyebrow. Franklin's gloved hand went up to the cut and came back red. He stared at the bloodied fingertips in fascinated horror, then looked up at O'Brien.

"You're in the army, laddie," O'Brien said. "If you want to stay in the army, you'd better learn to fight!" On the last word he planted his left fist in Franklin's stomach, and the boy went down with a *whouf.* O'Brien backed away. The men yelled, and Franklin slowly got to his feet, glaring now, his anger finally awakened. O'Brien beckoned him with a jerk of his chin. Franklin, pale but erect, shook his head. O'Brien rushed at him, aiming to grapple, but the lad was too quick—a sidestep and O'Brien fell heavily, tripped by an elegant boot. The men booed the trick while O'Brien got his hands under his shoulders and raised his chin from where it had made painful contact with the wooden floor. Franklin was on his knees beside him. O'Brien felt a light hand on his shoulder.

"I'm sorry, sir," the youth was saying. "Major Chivington sent me to find you."

O'Brien shook his head to clear it and looked up at him. "Chivington?"

"Yes," Franklin said, and O'Brien noticed the strange brightness of his eyes. "We've received marching orders from Leavenworth."

15

Hurrah for the road.

 —Ovando J. Hollister

Stillness. Then Company I began to cheer. Hats were thrown in the air, dance girls caught up like children and hugged without mercy. O'Brien looked at Franklin, who offered a hand to help him up. Grudgingly he took it and staggered to his feet. The room swayed and Franklin steadied him.

"I'm sorry, sir—"

"Shut up, Franklin." O'Brien walked back to his table, picked up his money, and slipped it into his pocket. "You heard the man," he shouted over Company I's riot. "Fall in!"

The lads bade farewell to the girls and scrambled for their hats and coats. In less than five minutes they were mounted and riding back to Camp Weld. "Leavenworth" was on every tongue. Some thought they'd be shipped from there to Washington by rail, others argued Kentucky was the logical destination. O'Brien, riding at the column's head with Franklin, didn't care. Anywhere was better than camp.

The parade grounds were buzzing with activity. O'Brien ordered his men to their barracks to start organizing their traps and went with Franklin to report to headquarters. They found Major Chivington at his desk, signing papers with Shoup hovering at his elbow. Colonel Slough sat beside him, and looked up at O'Brien and Franklin with a haughty stare.

"You took your time, Lieutenant," Chivington said, glancing up. He frowned at Franklin. "What happened to you?"

Franklin again touched his eyebrow, now clotted with blood. "Stupid horse threw me, sir," he said. "It's just a scratch."

Gentleman, O'Brien thought unwillingly.

"Here are your orders," Chivington said, handing a paper to O'Brien. He looked down at it, made out the numbers "10, 1862" but the rest was meaningless. A glance told him Slough was watching, and instinct warned him to hide his weakness from this man. He wished for Hall, who would have read it to him outside.

"May I, sir?" Franklin said softly.

O'Brien gave up and handed him the page, bracing himself for humiliation. Franklin glanced at the orders as if merely curious. "Marching in two days. That's good news," he said carelessly, and gave it back.

O'Brien stared at him. Hadn't he tried to force a fight on the boy not an hour before? What had prompted this courtesy? And how the devil had Franklin known?

"How long will it take us to reach Leavenworth, sir?" Franklin asked.

"We're not going to Leavenworth," Chivington said, handing a stack of papers to Shoup and starting on another. "We've been ordered to support Colonel Canby in New Mexico. It seems some Texans have got a whiff of gold."

"Come and stay with me, then," Mrs. Canby said.

Laura held her cloak tightly closed and tried not to think about the cold as they walked to the Sunday church service. Her boots scraped against patches of ice in which dirt and small pebbles had been embedded by many feet and wagon wheels. The bright sun, which forced her to keep her eyes on the ground, did little to warm her.

"Thank you," she said, "but I don't wish to impose on you."

"Nonsense," Mrs. Canby replied. "We have plenty of room. You'd be most welcome."

Laura smiled briefly. "If I can find some employment that will enable me to pay for my lodgings—"

"Laura." Mrs. Canby stopped at the door to the Governor's Palace, where the Episcopalian services were held, and Laura looked up at her, blinking against the sun.

"Your company will be a greater advantage to me than any rent you might pay," Mrs. Canby said. "Do not think you will escape being put to work! There's much more to do to prepare for a possible battle." She smiled as she spoke, but her eyes seemed haunted by sadness.

Laura swallowed her pride, and said, "Thank you. You are very good." Mrs. Canby nodded, and together they went in.

The congregation was smaller than usual. The few other stalwarts who had braved the frozen morning were mostly military families, come to ask God's protection for their loved ones. Many Americans had left town, including Mrs. Josephy and her party. Even Doña Cabeza de Vaca had whisked her daughter away to the protection of the family's remote hacienda. Santa Fé was becoming a ghost town.

Laura and Mrs. Canby sat on one of the plain pine benches and shared Mrs. Canby's Bible. The minister stepped up to the wooden music stand he used as a pulpit, the pages of his sermon rustling softly.

Laura bowed her head, giving thanks for the kindness of her friend. She would not impose on Mrs. Canby a moment longer than necessary. When the colonel and his staff returned, it was possible that her troubles might resolve themselves. Having failed to escape Santa Fé, she might at least escape her uncle by marrying Lieutenant McIntyre. The thought did not fill her with immediate joy, but she was fortunate to have his regard, she told herself, and offered a silent prayer for his safety.

McIntyre grunted as he and Captain McRae helped a handful of artillerymen wrestle a Quaker gun into an embrasure. When it was in place he paused to stretch and look eastward, where tents dotted the gentle slopes nearly all the way down to the river. Fort Craig was crawling with troops, so many that they spilled outside its walls and the growing earthworks. Almost immediately after McIntyre's return to Belen, Colonel Canby had moved army headquarters down to the fort.

"One more," McRae said, recalling McIntyre's attention to the task at hand. Captain Graydon's spies had reported fifteen cannon in the Texans' train, and McRae's six guns, plus a second battery of two twenty-four-pound howitzers, were all that Fort Craig had to oppose them. To improve these odds, McRae was mounting the Quaker guns—logs carved and painted to look like cannon—in the fort's empty embrasures.

"Rider approaching, sir," a sentry called to McRae.

McIntyre leaned forward on the false cannon and peered out of the embrasure. Riding toward the fort was a solitary horseman carrying a white flag. McIntyre scanned the plain south of the fort but saw only a small escort party waiting on a ridge. Three days earlier the Texans had demonstrated in force on that plain, but Canby had refused the invitation to fight, though he had lined up several companies of nervous New Mexico Volunteers south of the fort's walls to counter the demonstration. The Texans had shivered blanketless through a night of snow—most of which quickly vanished into the thirsty ground—then apparently decided Craig was a beehive they didn't care to poke, and retreated downstream in a howling, two-day sandstorm. Their camp could be seen from the roof of the post sutler's store, the haze from their morning cookfires drifting over the river.

The horseman—a staff officer, splendidly uniformed— galloped up the short rise approaching the fort, then swung west, heading toward the gate. McIntyre admired the rider's richly plumed hat, the gold braid gleaming on his sleeves, the way his flag snapped smartly as he turned his horse. "Must be from Sibley," he said, grinning. "He always insisted things be done with style."

"Sibley's a traitor, son," McRae said.

McIntyre glanced down at the painted log beneath his hand, feeling the blood rise into his cheeks.

"Take Budagher with you and go meet the fellow," McRae said.

"Yes, sir," said McIntyre grateful for the escape. He tapped one of McRae's artillerymen and led him to the stables. In moments they were mounted and at the front gate to receive the Rebel messenger, who reined to a halt a few yards outside. McIntyre rode forward at a walk to meet him.

"Well, well!" the envoy said in a familiar drawl. "Just like old times!"

Owens. McIntyre caught himself smiling at the elegant Georgian. We are enemies now, he reminded himself.

"Still a lieutenant, I see," Owens added, and McIntyre realized the three bars on his collar must mean captain.

So Sibley had made good on his promise. McIntyre was suddenly conscious of the grimy condition of his uniform. "What's your business, sir?" he said awkwardly.

Owens retrieved a letter from inside his coat. "Message for Canby from General Sibley. How is the colonel?" he added as he handed it over.

Unable to think of a safe reply, McIntyre began to turn his horse toward the gate.

"Mac," Owens said softly. "I'm to wait for an answer."

McIntyre stopped and glanced up at Owens. For a moment their gaze held, and silent understanding passed between them. Somehow, inexplicably, they were still friends.

"Take him into the guard house," McIntyre said to his escort. "Give him some coffee." Feeling about to burst, he spurred his horse toward the sally port.

"Thank you, Mac," Owens called after him with a laugh. "That's mighty white of you."

Without looking back, McIntyre rode into the fort and hurried to headquarters. He heard voices in the commander's office, and knocked on the closed door.

"Come," Colonel Canby called.

"—only the respect that is due them as officers," Colonel Chaves was saying as McIntyre entered.

"No one intends them disrespect, Colonel," Canby said. "But when they cannot speak English—hello, what's this?" Canby reached for the letter, which McIntyre handed him.

"From Sibley, sir," he said.

Canby's face hardened to a neutral mask. He tore open the page with a swift movement and read it silently, then handed it to Chaves with a small smile. "He's demanding our surrender."

"Hah!" Chaves said. "What he wants is for us to come out and fight him on open ground."

"We can't do that," Canby said. "His force is stronger."

Silbey's force stronger. McIntyre felt a sinking in his gut. He shifted and Canby glanced up at him. "Sir, the messenger is waiting for an answer," he said.

"All right." Canby reached for paper and pen. "Colonel Chaves," he said casually as he wrote, "would you kindly have your fastest rider saddle up?"

"Certainly, Colonel." Chaves saluted crisply, then nodded to McIntyre and left.

McIntyre was silent, listening to the scratch of Canby's pen. The colonel folded the page and sealed it, then handed it to McIntyre and reached for a fresh sheet of paper.

"Sir—" McIntyre began.

Canby looked up, his grey eyes coolly inquiring. "Yes, Lieutenant?"

McIntyre wanted an answer, but he couldn't compose a question. "Nothing, sir," he said miserably, and left.

Owens was lounging in the front room of the guard house with a sergeant standing nervously in the doorway. The Georgian stood up as McIntyre came in and handed him Canby's letter.

"I'll see you out," McIntyre said.

They retrieved their horses, and Owens glanced around as they mounted. "Interesting little resort you have here," he said. "Still betting on the Union?"

McIntyre was silent and they rode slowly out of the fort. Outside Owens paused. "It's been nice seeing you, Mac."

McIntyre struggled to answer. "Yes," was all he managed.

A wry grin turned up one corner of Owen's mouth. "Be a good soldier, now," he said, then clicked to his horse and was off at a canter, the white flag fluttering behind him. McIntyre watched him go, wishing things were different, or at least over.

Hoofbeats made Jamie look up from the fire where a few of the staff were huddled. The wind was falling off at last, but occasional gusts still stung their faces with sand and battered the faltering fire. Jamie traded a glance with Lane as Captain Owens rode up to Sibley's tent.

"He's not in there, Captain," Lane called.

"Oh?" Owens came toward them. "Where then?"

"In that ambulance," Lane said, pointing to a vehicle parked at a short distance, its canvas sides lashed down against the wind. "He's indisposed."

With a grimace, Owens dismounted and headed for the ambulance. Jamie nudged a log into the fire with the toe of his boot. Beside him Martin took out his last letter from Emmaline. Jamie had seen him read it at least once every day. Lane was cracking pecans and tossing the hulls into the fitful flames. He handed a nut to Jamie, who glanced toward the ambulance.

"What's ailing the general?" he asked.

"Didn't say," Lane said. "Just told me to send for Colonel Green."

"We can't afford to sit here much longer," Martin said, returning Emma's letter to his pocket. He stretched his feet toward the fire, the soles of his boots inches from the coals. Jamie noticed tired circles under his eyes.

"Tenshun," Lane said suddenly, and the men hastily stood to salute Colonel Tom Green, commander of the 2nd Regiment, who pulled off his gloves and held his hands toward the fire.

"At ease." The colonel nodded. "You sent for me, Mr. Lane?"

"General Sibley did, sir. He's unwell and has turned command over to you."

Green blew out his cheeks and squinted north toward Fort Craig. Owens, returning from the ambulance, snapped a salute as he joined them. "General Sibley's respects, sir, and he said to give this to you." He handed the colonel an open letter, which Green read with a frown.

"How are we fixed for supplies, Captain Martin?" Green asked.

"No more than ten days' rations, sir. Plenty of ordnance."

"You were at the fort?" Green asked Owens, who nodded. "How many guns do they have?"

"At least a dozen," Owens said. "They're good for a long siege."

Green shook his head. "We'll have to turn the fort. Lane, bring me a map, and get ready to write some orders."

Jamie traded a glance with Martin while the adjutant ducked into a tent. Moving at last! Lane returned with a board he settled onto his lap for a desk.

Green frowned at the map. "The army will ford the river and camp tonight at Paraje. Then we'll march north, circle this table mountain, and recross at Valverde," he said. "They'll either have to come out and fight, or watch us cut off their supply lines."

Martin nodded. "I'll send out scouts right away," he said, and strode off toward Pyron's camp. Jamie hid a smile. Martin was always ready to send Phillips's Brigands on scout duty. The less time they spent in camp the better he liked it, and he was determined to make them earn their pay.

A gust of wind threatened to scatter Lane's papers, and Green took him into Sibley's tent to finish the orders, leaving Jamie alone with Owens.

"Might I trouble you for something to drink, Mr. Russell?" Owens asked, settling into Lane's chair.

Jamie reached for the coffee that was sitting on a rock at the edge of the coals and filled a tin cup, which he handed to Owens. "How was the general?" he asked.

Owens blew across the hot liquid and sipped. "I'm no

surgeon," he said, "but if you ask me he's suffering from an overdose of rotgut." Jamie glanced up in surprise, and Owens laughed. "You are an innocent, aren't you?" he said.

"I just don't think it's appropriate for the commander of an army to be drunk," Jamie said with dignity.

"That makes two of us." Owens smiled. "Where are you from, Russell?"

"San Antonio."

"Like Texas?"

"Yes." He had never been anywhere else, until now.

"Like the army?"

Jamie opened his mouth but couldn't think what to say. With a laugh, he shrugged again. "I don't know."

"You haven't really seen anything yet," Owens said. "Wait till we get past that mesa. Likely we'll get some action then."

"Have you ever been in a battle?" Jamie asked.

"A few skirmishes with Indians. How about you?"

Jamie shook his head.

"Never seen the elephant, eh?" Owens said. "Wondering what it's like?"

Yes. No.

"My brother was in a fight in Kentucky," Jamie said.

Owens smiled lazily, understanding in his eyes. "Don't worry, Lieutenant," he said. "You'll get your chance."

The echoes of cannon fire brought activity in Fort Craig to a standstill. McIntyre stood with Canby and several of his staff on the porch of the commander's quarters, watching while the 2nd New Mexico Volunteers, sent across the river to block the Texan's northward march, were thrown into utter confusion by artillery shells exploding in their midst. True, the Texans had higher ground and were making good use of it, but a more disciplined troop would have kept their ranks under the largely harmless barrage. McIntyre, scanning the higher ridge, saw sunlight flashing from the brass instruments of a band and could almost imagine he heard strains of "Dixie." He handed his field glasses to Nicodemus and glanced at Canby.

"Tell Roberts to bring them in," the colonel said to Chapin beside him, "before it gets any worse."

With a nod Chapin was off the porch and sprinting to his horse. McIntyre looked back at the skirmish. Even without the glasses he could distinguish Colonel Chaves's black charger storming along the shattered line, Chaves no doubt trying to rally his men. They were hopelessly mixed with the cavalry and artillery that had been placed to support them. Canby was right—it was useless.

"Colonel Carson," Canby said, "do you think your men can behave a little better than the Second?"

"They will, sir," Carson said sternly.

"Post them along the east bank of the river. Keep the Texans off that high point, and deny them the water."

"Yes, sir," Carson said, saluting. McIntyre looked back at the ridge where the Texan guns were still firing. The sun was already setting, turning the puffs of smoke an incongruous pink. Anderson was out there somewhere. He wondered if Owens was, too. He heard pounding hooves and saw Captain Chapin galloping for the river with Canby's order of retreat. A disappointing day, he thought, trying not to think about tomorrow.

It was well after dark when Jamie arrived at the campsite, bone-weary and parched. The supply train had followed the army up a mile-long ravine filled with sand in which wagons sank up to their hubs. Double and triple teams were necessary to haul them out. Teamsters and soldiers had laid shoulders to the boxes, straining to push and drag the vehicles up the gully. The artillery had had similar trouble, but got out in time to create a ruckus firing from the ridge ahead. Jamie hadn't paid much notice—his attention had been confined to the struggling train.

Now, on the dark, windswept plain, Martin chose a place for the wagon park and gave instructions to the exhausted teamsters, while Jamie led Cocoa to a makeshift corral of staked ropes. When he asked about water, the herders laughed and invited him to walk up the ridge and admire the enemy picket line that stretched along the Río Grande below, gleaming fires marking the curves of the river. Jamie sighed and shook his canteen, which gave a hollow splash. He took one sip and poured the rest into his cupped hand for Cocoa. "Sorry, girl," he said as she licked the last drops from his palm and nickered softly for more. He stroked her neck to comfort her, then turned her into the corral and hefted his saddle onto his hip. The camp had an unfamiliar smell as he passed the small, fitful fires. Jamie realized it was the smell of melting lead. The soldiers were casting bullets, talking in hushed voices of the battle to come. If the Federals attacked it would be at the ford near Valverde, a tiny Mexican village north of the mesa, where the army would try to cross the river tomorrow.

Jamie found the headquarters fire, a miserable affair built of greasewood, all that could be found for fuel on the barren plain. Several officers were crouched around the feeble flames.

"Hallo, Jamie," Lane said, making room for him in the circle. "You missed the party."

"Was it fun?" Jamie asked, plopping down and leaning against his saddle.

"You should have seen them run," Reily said, his grin flashing white in the darkness. "One shot, and they broke ranks! If that's all Canby can offer, we'll be celebrating Easter in Denver City!"

"Russell, I don't suppose you have any water in those supply wagons?" Owens asked.

Jamie shook his head. "We were dry before dark."

Owens sighed. "No matter. We'll get to the river tomorrow, though we may have to trample some abs along the way."

"Abs?" Jamie asked.

"Abolitionists," said a cavalry captain with a fierce black mustache. "Where you been hiding, boy?"

Jamie frowned. "They're just soldiers—"

The captain's eyes flared. "They are abolitionist scum, and they're trying to take away our rights!"

"Stow it, Gardner," Owens said. "Who's the invading army here?"

"Who's going to be fighting tomorrow?" Captain Gardner countered. "I don't need any lip from a damn quartermaster!" He got up and stalked away. Jamie swallowed and stared into the flames. The smoke stung his eyes and he blinked.

"Never mind him," Owens said softly. "He's never seen a battle, either."

Jamie glanced at Owens with a grateful smile. "I wish I could fight tomorrow," he said ruefully.

"Well," Reily said, "it's only five miles to the ford. Maybe once you've moved the wagons, you and your men could give the artillery some support. We could use it."

"Excellent suggestion," Martin said, sitting down in the space left by Gardner. "After today, the teamsters will think it's a vacation." He smiled at Jamie and winked.

Jamie laughed and grinned back. Suddenly an echo of the old excitement was there. Maybe by this time tomorrow they'd be writing to Momma and Emma, telling of the battle they'd fought and won, describing it in words that would be relayed to Kentucky and Virginia. Daniel would be proud, Matt would be wildly jealous, and Poppa would know that all of his sons had mettle. Jamie smiled at the flickering fire, and curled up to sleep.

"Come on, Lacey!" Nicodemus said pulling at McIntyre's sleeve.

McIntyre groaned, his dreams interrupted. "What now?"

"Come on!" Nicodemus insisted in a hushed voice.

Anderson rolled over. "Go to sleep, Nico," he said in a weary voice. "It's nearly midnight."

"Not me," Nicodemus said. "Captain Graydon's getting up some fun, and I want to see it!"

"If you're smart you'll steer clear," Anderson said. "Paddy Graydon's half crazy."

McIntyre sat up and glanced at Anderson's dark shape. He had returned from the skirmish exhausted and exasperated with the volunteers' poor performance. The experience of being under fire seemed not to have changed him, but McIntyre still felt a bit chagrined at having watched it all from safety.

"What sort of fun?" he asked Nicodemus.

"I don't know, but come on, or we'll miss it!"

McIntyre threw back his blankets, shivering as he reached for his coat. He shoved his feet into his boots and followed Nicodemus out to the stables, where several of Graydon's men stood gathered around two old mules. Some were packing a wooden box with dark shapes that looked like howitzer shells, while others strapped a similar box to the back of one of the mules. McIntyre looked around and saw Captain Graydon watching the operation, the stub of his cigarrillo glowing in the night.

"Are those army mules?" McIntyre asked.

"No, they're old breakdowns. Got 'em from a farmer up the river," Graydon replied. "Close it up, now," he told the men, going forward to see that the boxes were fixed to his liking.

As McIntyre watched, a man approached him in the darkness. "Mind if I join the party?" the newcomer asked, with a hint of Alabama in his voice.

"I'm not in charge," McIntyre said. "Captain Graydon is."

"Suits me. I like Irish captains." The stranger offered a hand. "Joe Hall," he said. "Dodd's Company."

"Lacey McIntyre. This is Will Nicodemus."

"Come on along," Nicodemus said, shaking hands. "More the merrier."

Graydon's men had finished loading the mules and began to mount up, so the three of them did likewise and followed the little troop, with the mules going quietly along, out of the fort and toward the river.

"What's he going to do?" McIntyre asked.

"Stampede the Rebs' beef herd," Nicodemus said, grinning. "They won't stay long without their grub."

Hall laughed. "Wish I'd come down to New Mexico sooner!"

"We wish you had, too," McIntyre said, thinking of Canby's repeated pleas to Governor Gilpin for troops.

They forded the cold, swift river and passed through the picket line. McIntyre's nape crawled as he realized they were heading straight for the Texans' camp. He peered into the darkness, straining to see movement, listening for a sound above the muffled tread of the horses. They advanced cautiously, Graydon waiting for his scouts to report before moving their party ahead. McIntyre glanced at the ridge above, which that afternoon had bristled with cannon. All was silent.

Graydon circled north and climbed the rise, following a little arroyo to the top of the ridge. Campfires glimmered to the south. Slowly they approached the dark, moving masses of the herds, keeping a sharp watch for guards. When they were within a hundred yards of the animals, Graydon and a couple of his men dismounted and huddled by the two mules, talking in hushed tones. McIntyre saw a tiny flame spark, and a moment later Graydon aimed the mules toward the herd and slapped their rumps. The animals trotted off, and Graydon and his men hurried back to their horses. "Home," McIntyre heard him say. Glad to obey, he urged his pony to a brisk trot as they headed back for the shelter of the arroyo. He was sorry he'd come—if he had known what fate awaited the old mules he'd have stayed behind, but it was too late now. He glanced back and, to his horror, saw the mules trotting calmly along behind him.

"Captain!" he said, strangling a shout.

Hall, riding beside him, turned, and said, "Shit!"

Graydon's horse turned, and in an instant the captain had seen the mules. He kicked his horse so hard it reared, and as he clung to its neck Graydon yelled, "Run for it, lads!"

McIntyre jabbed his heels into his pony's sides and whipped it with the reins, galloping for his life. A shout from somewhere far behind told him the Confederates had noticed them, but it hardly mattered. They would have noticed soon enough, as soon as the fuses ignited the shells in those two boxes. Graydon's men were cursing, driving their ponies on while the mules did their best to keep up. Hall let out an insane, laughing whoop beside him as McIntyre stared at the arroyo ahead and prayed he would make it that far.

16

---

*Wounded and dead horses were stripped, and those that
were able to move were turned loose to feed around or to
shiver and die till the battle was over.*

—Sergeant Alfred B. Peticolas, 4th Texas Mounted
Volunteers

The explosion jerked Jamie awake. Martin was already on
his feet; men were running and shouting. Jamie staggered
up, stamping his right foot, which had fallen asleep. Scurry
burst from his tent. "What the hell was that?" he shouted.

"Came from over there," Martin said, pointing northward.

Jamie heard the shrieks of frightened animals, and suddenly feared for Cocoa. "Are they attacking?" he asked.

"The train!" Martin said, and together they broke into a
run, heading for the wagon park. They found it intact, the
guards wide-eyed at their posts. The camp was now under
arms, but no more explosions had followed the first shat-
tering blast.

"Can I check on Cocoa, sir?" Jamie asked. "Please?"

Martin nodded and Jamie hurried toward the corrals.
The animals were agitated, running back and forth, pushing against the ropes. Jamie heard the herders cursing as he
whistled for Cocoa. She answered with a high whinny,
coming to him through the mass of milling horses, and
stood trembling while he petted her and murmured to
soothe her.

A rider swung down from his horse, turning it out in the
corral without unsaddling it. "Go home, sonny," came
Phillips's voice. "Show's over."

Jamie bristled, but curiosity won. "What was it?" he asked.

"Some abs trying to blow us up," Phillips said with a shrug. "Nothing you need to worry about. Go on back to your wagons."

Frowning, Jamie watched him stride toward the camp. The herders' shouts were getting frantic. There was a rumbling sound that Jamie suddenly realized he'd been hearing for a few minutes, getting louder. He knew that sound, and it made his heart sink. Squinting into the darkness, he made out shapes moving beyond the corral—mules, at the gallop. Jamie led Cocoa out, jumped onto her bare back and rode toward the stampeding herd with his fingers twined in her mane. Another rider joined him, the wagonmaster on a big pinto. Voices of others came to him across the stampede, but there were not enough to stop the panicked mules. The leading animals went over the ridge and down toward the river. Jamie and the drovers managed to cut off the last two or three dozen. The wagonmaster rode on, trying to head off the herd, and disappeared over the ridge.

"Whoa, girl," Jamie said. Cocoa stopped at the crest, her sides heaving. Jamie peered down the slope. Too dark to see much, but sharp voices told him the wagonmaster had been caught by the Federal pickets below. Jamie could make out a dark swarm of mules at the river's edge, crowding eagerly into the water to drink. The pickets had already started to herd them across. Helpless and angry, Jamie nudged Cocoa back toward the camp. He rode along the corrals to make sure no more of the animals were threatening to break loose, and encountered the trampled ropes that marked the start of the stampede. As luck would have it, the escaped mules belonged to his regiment. Lieutenant-Colonel Scurry was at the corral with Martin, cursing the herders.

"How many got away?" Martin asked. Jamie had never seen him look so grim.

"Near two hundred," Jamie said, half choking on the words.

"Go back to the train and start consolidating the wagon loads," Martin said quietly.

"And you," Scurry told the herders, fury vibrating in his voice, "get back to your posts. If we lose another mule you get to do his work yourselves!"

Am I dead?

McIntyre tried moving, shifting his arm from under his head. Pain answered, and so did an anxious voice nearby.

"Get up!"

It was the Colorado fellow, Hall. McIntyre raised his head and made out the shapes of Nicodemus and his pony, horse and rider both knocked senseless by the explosion. "Nico," he said, reaching over to shake his friend's shoulder. Nicodemus stirred.

"Hurry, they're coming after us," Hall said. "You hurt?"

McIntyre slowly stood up, stretching protesting muscles, finding no serious damage. He helped Nicodemus to his feet while Hall got the horse standing.

"He's cut his knee," Hall said, looking at the pony's foreleg. "Not too bad, though. He should do."

Nicodemus grunted as he bent to examine the wound. McIntyre spied his own horse nearby and caught the reins. Graydon was prowling among the men, cursing and ordering them to get up. Shouts and the pounding of hooves from the Texans' camp spurred them on. By great good luck Nicodemus's horse was the only injury, and the party were soon slinking back down the arroyo. McIntyre sighed with relief as they reached the pickets at the river. They splashed cold water on bruises and cuts, and were told by Carson's men that they'd won some mules for the Union.

"Don't talk to us about mules," Hall said.

"Amen," McIntyre said. He was bruised and shaken, ears still ringing from the explosion. The others were in more or less the same condition. No one spoke until they were back at the fort and stabling their horses.

"You boys care for a drink?" Hall asked.

"I'd better fix this up," Nicodemus said, feeling his horse's foreleg. "Another time, thanks." He led his mount away.

"How about you, Lacey McIntyre? Something to settle the nerves?"

"I could use it." McIntyre nodded, and Hall led him out the sally port to where the Colorado Volunteers were camped north of the fort. For men who had recently made a forced march through bitter weather, they were considerably rowdy. Hall led the way to a large fire where tin cups were passing around as fast as they could be filled from a small keg.

"Gentlemen," Hall said, "I'd like you to meet Mr. Lacey McIntyre. Oh, excuse me," he added, peering at McIntyre's uniform in the firelight, "*Lieutenant* McIntyre."

"Have a seat, Lieutenant," said a man with captain's bars on his shoulders, making room on a cottonwood log. McIntyre and Hall squeezed in and stretched hands and feet to the fire.

"This is Captain Dodd," Hall said. "Our gallant leader."

"Teddy," said Dodd, offering a hand. "Class of '53."

"Oh!" McIntyre said, brightening. "I'm '59."

"What's your company?" asked Dodd.

"G, Fifth Infantry," said McIntyre, "but I'm with department headquarters at the moment."

"Oho! One of Canby's dandies!" a Volunteer said.

"What's it like up in heaven?" another asked.

McIntyre grinned. "Beans and bacon, same as down here."

"That where you've been all night, Hall?" a soldier asked, handing him a cup. "Brown-nosing the H.Q. staff?"

"As a matter of fact, Mr. McIntyre and I have been on a mission of major importance, behind enemy lines," Hall replied.

"Well—" McIntyre said.

"Or close to, anyway." Hall took a swallow from the cup and passed it to McIntyre, who detected the distinctive smell of Taos Lightning. He drank, letting the liquor sting his tongue and dull his senses while Hall recounted the story of Paddy Graydon's exploding mules. By the time Hall had reached the awful moment of discovery, McIntyre was sufficiently mellow to laugh at his own terror. The Colorado men toasted him and Hall as heroes, and only the knowledge that Canby would expect him to be sharp in the morning made him quit the party. He was sent forth with claps on the back and a full cup of Taos Lightning, a ward against phantoms of mules. He paused inside the fort to gaze up at a sky spattered with stars. The laughter of the Pike's Peakers carried clearly in the still night air. McIntyre stared at the heavens as if he might suddenly lose contact with the ground and fly into their icy depths. Was that where heaven was? He didn't usually think about such things, but he had recently feared for his life. There was so much he didn't know of the world, and what he knew, he scarcely understood.

Drunk, he realized. Good thing, too. Never sleep otherwise. He found his way into Anderson's quarters where Nicodemus was already snoring, took a last swig of liquor before carefully setting the cup on the floor, and crawled under his blankets without even removing his boots.

Flames blazed angrily in the Confederate camp, reaching orange tongues toward the cloudy dawn. Jamie felt the heat tightening the skin on his face, though he stood well back from the bonfire. He licked dry lips and stared bitterly at the jumble of burning wagons, some still loaded with clothing, regimental records, blankets that were sorely needed but could not be moved without mules. Martin came to stand beside him and silently handed him a strip of dried beef. Neither had slept.

"What a waste," Jamie said.

"Better than leaving it for the Federals," Martin said. "Don't take it personally, Jamie. War is a business, too."

Jamie couldn't help smiling. "How come you always know how to make me feel better?"

Martin shrugged. "Guess I always wanted a little brother," he said softly. "Come on, it's time to start."

They collected their horses and went to the head of the train, where the 1st Regiment had formed to cover the advance. Sibley, recovered from his malady, was back in the saddle and had ordered the Second and Third to march at dawn, west toward the river in a feint. At the same time Pyron's battalion had set out to take control of the ford at Valverde, north of the mesa. No one doubted that one way or another there would be a battle. As the long serpent of wagons rumbled to life, Jamie looked forward to the fight and a chance to vent his frustration.

They'd been marching an hour when a horseman came thundering toward them. Jamie recognized Phillips, who sought out Scurry. In minutes word traveled back through the ranks; Pyron's men had met the enemy at the ford, and more Yankees were marching from Fort Craig. The 1st picked up a trot and soon outstripped the heavy wagons. Jamie fretted and took out his impatience on the teamsters. Nervous and excited, he checked his pistol though he knew it was loaded and ready, and wondered what Matt and Daniel were doing. From ahead came the distant boom of cannon.

"Not long now," Martin said.

Jamie glanced at him, calmed by the quiet words. Martin smiled, and Jamie could tell that the captain knew everything he was thinking. He relaxed and grinned back, reaching up to his hat to touch Emma's star for luck. Martin nodded and did the same. Then they turned eyes and thoughts north.

"They're withdrawing," Canby said, handing the field glasses to Chapin. McIntyre, though his eyes were a bit bleary, didn't need the glasses to see that Canby was right. The Texans who had advanced toward the river were now falling back. A rider kicked up dust amid the scrub as he galloped toward the small group of mounted officers. Canby waited, wearing his favorite gray woolen shirt, an unlit cigar dangling from his lip, the cold breeze ruffling his hair. He sat his old horse Charley, the mount he'd ridden in Mexico, with the ease of a gentleman of leisure preparing to ride out for a picnic. McIntyre, stiff from the previous night's adventure, waggled his shoulders in a futile effort to make them comfortable. The rider— Nicodemus, he now saw—slowed to a trot and picked his way through the Volunteers' empty tents to where Canby and his staff waited.

"Colonel Pino's respects, sir," Nicodemus said, tossing off a salute. "He believes the enemy is retiring."

Canby took the cigar from his mouth. "Thank you, Captain Nicodemus," he said. "When you've caught your breath, please return and tell the colonel to bring his men back to this side of the river and await orders."

"Yes, sir," Nicodemus said, accepting the canteen offered by McIntyre. He took a strong pull at it, coughed once, and looked back toward the river. The Texans were turning north. They would pass behind the mesa and join their comrades at the ford, where Colonel Roberts waited with the bulk of Canby's troops.

"Mr. McIntyre," Canby said, putting the cigar in his pocket.

"Sir?"

"My compliments to Colonel Roberts, and inform him that I'll be taking command in the field shortly."

"Yes, sir."

"Would you also tell Captain McRae to expect the third section of his battery? Thank you."

McIntyre saluted and guided his horse down the slope, cutting cross-country to the wagon road. Once on it he spurred from a bone-jarring trot to a gallop, and was soon approaching the bend in the river that marked the north ford. The sky was heavy with silent, gray overcast that promised snow. Cold air burned his face and lungs. McIntyre found Colonel Roberts on the west bank, gazing intently toward the leafless cottonwoods of the bosque that lined the river. Above the ford McRae had four guns, silent at the moment, trained across the water. Sporadic small-arms fire echoed against the mesa to the south.

Roberts received Canby's message in silence. "Very well," he said. "Would you do me the favor, Lieutenant, of crossing the river and asking Captain Selden to prepare to advance?"

"Sir." McIntyre saluted crisply and turned toward the ford. His mount splashed through the cold, muddy water and up the eastern bank into the bosque where the regular infantry were in line among the trees. "Where's Captain Selden?" he called to the men.

"Up with the Pike's Peakers," a soldier said, waving north.

McIntyre picked up a trot. It had begun to snow by the time he reached the left end of the Federal line. Dodd's company were in front of the grove of barren trees, facing low sand hills across a stretch of flat. Behind the hills Texans were making their presence known with occasional rifle shots. Captain Selden and Anderson stood with Captain Dodd and Lieutenant Hall, who broke into a grin as McIntyre dismounted.

"Come to help avenge the mules?" Hall asked.

McIntyre managed a laugh, and raised an aching arm in salute. Selden turned, as did Anderson. McIntyre nodded, glad to find his friend well and whole.

"Captain Selden," McIntyre said, "Colonel Roberts asks that you prepare to advance."

"Good." Selden turned to his bugler. "Sound the recall. Allen, take the word to Wingate—" Selden and Anderson strode off down the line with Dodd following.

"Could you spare some water?" McIntyre asked Hall.

"Fire water or river water?"

"Either."

Hall handed him a canteen. "Here's the whiskey. Otherwise you can wring out my trousers, and be thankful you're mounted."

A shout made McIntyre look up. Three columns of horsemen were pouring from the sand hills to the south, driving straight toward Dodd's company, the blades of their lances glinting. McIntyre glimpsed Dodd charging back to his men shouting "Form square! Form square!"

Hall took up the cry. "Form square," he yelled, drawing his pistol. "Fix bayonets!"

"Christ!" McIntyre said, flinging away the canteen and reaching for his saddlebow. With a grunt he forced stiff muscles to heave him into the saddle. The Pike's Peakers were hastily converging into an infantry square, bayonets bristling toward the oncoming charge. Hall and Dodd stood in the center shouting orders. The lancers raised a blood-curdling yell and McIntyre spurred his horse, while the infantry on Dodd's right loosed a volley into the horsemen crossing their front.

"They are Texans," he heard Dodd shout behind him. "Give them hell!"

McIntyre left the square at a gallop, flying past the ranks of men just before they closed, and made for the river. Deeper here; he hissed as cold water poured into his boots. Drawing his pistol to keep it above the water, he slid out of the saddle while the horse swam, floating alongside until they got to firmer footing near the west shore. He got back in the saddle and they scrambled up the opposite bank, where McIntyre found himself in the midst of McRae's battery, the men all staring across the river. Turning his horse, he was just able to make out the fight through the bare branches of the bosque. The lancers were evaporating, shattered by rifle fire. Dodd's men stood firm against the remnants of the attack. It was terrible and glorious, and McIntyre couldn't look away. Rifles rattled. Bayonets flashed, some lifting doomed lancers from their saddles. The squeals of wounded horses tore the air and made McIntyre's mount sidle nervously.

"By God," McRae said at his knee. "Those Pike's Peakers are sound! Refreshing, after yesterday."

His voice recalled McIntyre to his duty. "Captain McRae," he said, and cleared his throat to get rid of the quaver in his voice. "Colonel Canby is sending your third section up to you."

"Looks like we'll need it," McRae replied. "Lacey," he added as McIntyre started to turn his horse, "are you all right?"

No. "Yes. Must go," he said. There was an ache in his chest that had nothing to do with being knocked silly the night before, and everything to do with the gallant cavalrymen who were spilling their blood across the Río Grande. With feelings as muddy as that river's waters, he turned away from the battle to find his commander.

"Start another one," Martin said.

Jamie and Martin stood back while the quartermaster's hands finished shoving a bottomless half-barrel into the hole they'd dug, then moved a few feet away to dig a second pit in the dry streambed. Men reached eagerly into the barrel, which had welled up with silty water, to cup the precious liquid to parched lips.

The 1st had fought stubbornly all morning but had been slowly pressed back and had finally gone into an old riverbed, an excellent natural line of defense. A lull had fallen in the battle. Men lay exhausted under the shelter of the bank, chewing dried beef and hardtack. Now and then a cannon boomed to remind them the enemy was still at hand, and the number of fallen mules and horses east of the riverbed attested to the deadliness and superior range of the Federal sharpshooters. The animals, tied to trees and bushes, had been unable to escape when the Federals opened on them, and only recently had the fire diminished enough for the men of the 1st to set the remaining mounts free. Jamie looked away from the sad corpses, thankful that Cocoa was safe with the wagon train.

"Bring those canteens over, Rose," he said. He had brought a ladle from an empty water cask and started dipping it into the seeping hole and filling the canteens. "Take over," he told Rose, and he and Martin began handing out the filled canteens. Word had traveled fast; men gathered from all along the line for the first water they'd had in over a day.

"One to a company," Martin said. "Bring back empties."

Jamie gave away his last canteen, then found a full one thrust into his hands. He looked up at Martin. "Forgot," he said with a grin, and sipped, then drank deeply. The water was bad, but it tasted sweeter than anything he'd ever drunk before.

"Hey, Russell!" Lieutenant Reily called, trudging toward him. "Heard you found water. Can I have some for my men?"

"Have some for yourself first," Jamie said, handing him the canteen. "Enjoying the fight?"

Reily guzzled, then paused to breathe and dragged a sleeve across his mouth. "Lost a gun," he said in disgust. "Carriage splintered, had to leave it on the field. And we're out of action for now. My little howitzers don't have enough range."

"You'll come around."

"How about you?" Reily asked. "Seen any fighting?"

Jamie shook his head. "We just finished getting the wagons in." He watched Reily pull greedily at the canteen again. "What's it like?" he asked.

Reily laughed. "Search me," he said. "All I could see was a lot of damned smoke. My boys are doing good work, though. Only lost a couple so far."

The thud of hooves announced Captain Owens, who reined in, spattering them with sand. "Where's Colonel Scurry?" he asked, reaching for the canteen. "Anything left in that?"

Reily handed it to him. "I saw him with Major Lockridge earlier," he said. "Up that way." He gestured up the line.

"What's the news?" Jamie asked.

Owens had drained the canteen and grimaced as he tossed it back. "The general's ill again," he said scornfully. "He's gone back to his ambulance and left Green in charge."

Jamie and Reily exchanged a glance. "Heaven help the righteous," Reily said. "I wish my father were here."

"So do I," Owens said. "Canby's pressing our left. We'll be in trouble before long." He picked up his reins.

"Wait a minute," Jamie said, and ran to the water hole, returning with two full canteens. He gave one to Reily and handed the other up to Owens. "For the colonel."

Owens slung it over his shoulder. "He'll be grateful," he said with a nod, and was off again.

A cannon discharged nearby, then another, followed by a shower of spent minié balls that made Jamie flinch. Reily grinned. "Heating up for a duel, sounds like," he said. "Let's have a look!"

Reily crept up the dry bank to peer westward. Jamie followed him and cautiously raised his head. Captain Teel, whose battery had been part of Baylor's command before Sibley's advent, had two long field guns aimed at the Federal line. The crews had taken a beating. Jamie could see Teel himself helping to serve the pieces. Cannon fire was now almost continuous, from both in front and farther down on the left of the line.

"The Yankees must have brought their guns across," Reily said. "Getting hot up there."

As he spoke a shell exploded beneath one of Teel's guns and Jamie heard the yelping voices of the cannoneers as the grass nearby caught fire. Two of them hurried to drag the limber out of danger while others beat at the flames with their jackets.

"I'd better give them a hand," Reily said. "Thanks for the water." With a wave he scrambled up the bank and hurried up to Captain Teel.

Jamie sighed and slid back to the streambed, returning to oversee the distribution of water from the second well while the hands started on a third. Minié balls now began to sing overhead. One struck a private in the arm, and he screamed as his friends dragged him to shelter under the bank. Jamie swallowed and kept working. All his enthusiasm had drained away again. He kept thinking of his sister's peach cobbler for some reason, and it made him homesick. He could see himself writing his next letter home: "There was a battle. I filled canteens."

A commotion made him look up to see Colonel Green trotting along the line. "Boys," he said, "we must charge that battery. I'm looking for volunteers." Men jumped up to offer their services. "Form here and wait for Major Lockridge's order," the colonel told them, and rode on down the line.

"Line up here, boys," Captain Shropshire yelled, holding up his sword. He grinned, blue eyes flashing at Jamie. "Coming?"

Jamie felt a tingle in his hands. If he was to get into the fight, this was his chance. He stood, looking for Martin. The captain caught his eye, came toward him, then nodded.

"Sergeant Rose," Martin called over his shoulder, "you're in charge of the train." He clapped a hand on Jamie's back and smiled. "Time to show what a quartermaster can do," he said.

McIntyre let his horse jog along after Canby's as the staff rode down the river's west bank. They'd spent the last hour repositioning troops in preparation for an advance. Canby planned to pivot his forces and enfilade the Confederate line, a maneuver that would have been sure of success had his men all been seasoned soldiers. They were not, however. Fewer than half his force were Regulars, and of the Volunteers, only Dodd's company and Carson's regiment had proven themselves reliable.

It was getting late; another hour of daylight, two at most. Even Nico was silent, too tired to do anything but follow orders. McIntyre was numb from a long day of hard riding. He wondered where Anderson was, hadn't seen him since the lancer charge. He wished the whole business were over.

Rifle fire continued, hotter in some places than others, joined by the deep boom of cannon at either end of the line. Canby aimed his field glasses south where the Federal right ran against the mesa. "I believe," he said slowly, "they are forming to charge Hall's battery. Chapin— where's Chapin?"

"With Colonel Carson, sir," Nicodemus said.

"Then you, Nico," Canby said. "Go to Ingraham and tell him to support Hall's battery. Colonel Chaves, would you ask Colonel Pino to cross your reserves to the east bank and stand ready to support Selden?"

Chaves nodded grimly. "They have crossed the river twice already, sir."

"I'm sorry," Canby said with gentle firmness. "They're not the only ones who are wet, if that's any comfort."

Chaves gave a silent salute and turned his horse south.

"McIntyre?" Canby said.

"Sir?" McIntyre roused himself.

"Go to McRae and Dodd, tell them to hold firm. They're the anchor for our pivot. D'Amours, go and find Wingate—"

McIntyre urged his tired mount to a trot and rode away from the staff, northward, back to the ford. He'd lost count of the number of times he'd crossed the river with messages to and from the commanders in the field. A minié ball flew past with the peculiar whiz that in the morning would have made him cringe, but he hardly noticed it now, he'd heard so many. If a ball was meant to get him it would, and there was nothing he could do about it.

The bosque was thick with smoke and McIntyre's eyes began to sting as he entered it. McRae stood watching his men feed the hot mouths of his six cannon with clockwork economy of movement. McIntyre left his mount tied to a tree near the artillery horses, having learned earlier in the day that if he tried to ride up to the roaring guns the beast would do its best to throw him. He came up on the battery from the right. The ground was bad, too rough, with brush and fallen trees that would make it difficult to maneuver. Voices of tactics instructors echoed warnings in his mind.

"Alec," he shouted above the din of the guns, "Canby wants you to hold firm. He's going to pivot the line."

McRae threw a glance at the sand hills. "We'll hold," he said. "But we may need more support."

McIntyre nodded. "The reserves are crossing now." He peered into Dodd's company, now just behind and to the left of the battery. "I need to find Captain Dodd."

McRae nodded and returned his attention to the guns. As McIntyre started toward the infantry, a shower of musket balls made him duck behind a tree. The Texans were firing canister. That meant they were close. McIntyre tried not to think about it as he slunk through the trees toward Dodd's company. He found the captain sitting on the trunk of a cottonwood that had been felled by a cannon ball earlier in the day. Compared to the havoc around McRae's battery, the Pike's Peakers were on holiday, crouched behind trees just inside the bosque, with only an occasional ball hissing by.

"Hello, Lieutenant," Dodd said as McIntyre approached. "What's the news?"

"Colonel Canby wants you to hold firm," McIntyre said. "He plans to pivot the line on your anchor."

"Well, this is a nice spot, eh, Hall?" Dodd said as Hall joined them. "Don't see any reason to leave it, even if the neighbors are a little noisy."

"There are some Texans collecting behind that bank," Hall said. "I was just out for a walk, and one of them tried to redesign my hat." He showed them his hat, the brim of which had a ragged edge where a ball had grazed it.

"How many Texans?" McIntyre asked, frowning.

"Can't say," Hall shrugged. "More than before."

McIntyre stared toward the sand hills, disliking the silence. "Where were you when you saw them?" he asked Hall.

"I'll show you if you like. How much did you pay for your hat?"

They walked north through the bosque past companies of the Seventh, Tenth, and Fifth that formed the Federal left, then crept east, sheltered by scrub. Hall took to his knees and McIntyre followed suit, the back of his neck prickling as it had on the mule expedition. They elbowed their way up a soft, sandy rise and found themselves over-looking an old channel of the Río Grande that curved away to their right. A couple of hundred yards down, beneath the overhang of the west bank, Texans stood clustered with arms in hand while an officer paced their length.

"There's more now," Hall whispered.

McIntyre glanced around nervously, looking for pickets, but saw only the milling troops. He guessed there were two hundred in sight and probably more beyond the curve. "They'll charge," he said softly. "I have to tell the colonel." They backed down the slope and hurried to the Federal line.

"Put on your party clothes, boys," Hall called as they jogged into the bosque. "Company's coming!" He grinned, and waved farewell to McIntyre, who continued on.

The cannon fire had fallen off somewhat, and as he came toward McRae's battery, McIntyre realized with a sinking heart that it was because the Confederate guns had gone silent. He sought McRae, whom he found inspecting a damaged limber. The captain looked up as he approached.

"You're about to be charged." McIntyre quickly gave him the few details he had.

"Where are the reserves?" McRae asked, glancing back at Dodd's company.

"I don't know." McIntyre searched the bosque to the west. "They should have crossed by now. I'll go—"

A banshee howl filled the air, the yell with which the Confederates had begun all of their charges that day.

"Double canister!" McRae shouted to his men, who were instantly in a flurry of motion. Minié balls began to fly close, some sinking with sharp thuds into tree trunks.

McIntyre ran crouching through the trees to his horse, and rode away from the chaos toward the river. The horse stumbled and grunted, slowing momentarily until McIn-tyre's spur urged it onward and over the riverbank. He held reins and pistol in one hand, about to kick out of his stir-rups for the swim across, when the animal suddenly fal-tered and went down.

Icy water closed over his head. McIntyre nearly panicked as he struggled to free his boots from the stirrups. His foot touched the river bottom and he pushed against it to get clear of the horse, and found he was able to stand, the water just up to his chest. He gasped and coughed, spitting water. A thin red swirl in the muddy current explained his mount's fall; the animal must have been hit. If not already dead it would swiftly drown, and McIntyre abandoned it for lost.

The current was fast and threatened to carry him off his feet. He looked at the western shore. If he crossed over he'd be out of the nightmare for good, probably, and could walk along the road until a mounted officer found him. Then he glanced toward the east bank, the nearer of the two. He could hear the report of the cannon, and picture McRae standing his ground stubbornly. He might still be able to help if McRae would lend him a horse.

"Hell," he whispered, and struck out swimming for the east bank, hoping he would not be too late.

It was thunder and hell. Jamie's hands shook as he clutched the shotgun he'd borrowed from one of the teamsters. Out ahead the first line was getting shot to pieces by the Federal cannon and supporting troops. Some of them had gone into a stand of trees a little to the left, and Jamie caught himself wishing for a skinny cottonwood to hide behind.

Captain Shropshire, waving his sword over his head, strode on, and the second line followed. Jamie forced his feet to move and stared at the bosque ahead, where dark forms moved in the smoke like ghosts or demons. He glimpsed a laniard stretching away from its gun.

"Down!" Shropshire screamed, and Jamie dropped with the rest of the line, covering his head as the hail of balls shrieked overhead. He looked at Martin beside him, who grinned.

Major Lockridge came up, a bull of a man, shouting "Charge!" The line rose, and a wordless howl burst from them as they ran toward the Yankees. Men from the first line came out from behind their trees and followed. A wave of bullets hissed toward them, and the shouting of the Federal cannoneers promised another deadly round of canister. Jamie's throat and nostrils burned with the smell of powder. Someone let out a yelp of triumph, and Jamie saw that part of the Yankee line had fallen back behind the battery. Many bluecoats lay on the ground around the guns.

"Charge!" Lockridge's sword flashed in the smoky light and Jamie added his voice to the yell as they started forward, though he could hardly hear himself. He heard the whine of a minié ball and thought for sure he'd be hit, but it was Martin who suddenly stumbled to his knees.

"Sir!" Jamie reached toward him, glimpsing blood on the captain's shoulder.

"Don't stop!" Martin shouted, waving him on.

Jamie forced himself to face the guns again. Duty, do your duty, show you're a man. He hurried to catch up with the line and it seemed now he was marching straight into hell. The best thing, he decided, was not to think about it, not to think at all. With that decision came the release of anger, fear, and frustration all jumbled up together and he yelled as he hadn't yelled before, shrieking like a wounded animal, searching the Yankee line for a likely target.

Shivering, McIntyre ran from tree to tree as he made his way back to McRae's battery. The smoke was thick and the noise of the fight a continuous rumbling roar. Balls shrieked past. He glimpsed Anderson off to the left, sword in hand, yelling furiously at men—Regulars, damn them—who were running from the line. McIntyre kept on toward the battery looking for a mount, but all the artillery horses were down. One thrashed as he crept by, nearly kicking him. He searched among the cannoneers for McRae, saw a man using a flagstaff to ram his charge into his gun. Some of the Texans had reached the battery, and the guns fell silent as the cannoneers began to drop back to the limbers.

Then he spotted McRae, right arm hanging useless and streaming with blood, racing back to the guns with a line of infantry behind him. "Save my guns!" he shouted to them over his shoulder, waving them on with his good arm. McIntyre could see another line of Texans advancing just beyond the trees.

"Alec!" He scurried out from his shelter and caught up with McRae. The captain turned to him, his face a fierce scowl. McIntyre wanted to tell him to give it up, come away, save himself, but one look at the man's face told him McRae would not admit defeat. McIntyre clenched his teeth and followed him to the battery. When he reached for his pistol, his fingers scrabbled against an empty holster.

Gone. Dropped in the river. Feeling naked, McIntyre hung back at the limber while the infantry passed him and entered the battery.

"Alec!" he shouted again, but McRae didn't hear.

McIntyre glanced back to the left, where the 10th Infantry were retreating in disorder toward the water. Looking south, he saw Canby appear out of nowhere, shouting orders to a cavalry company on his right. McIntyre's heart rose at the sight of him, but the next moment the colonel and his horse went down, and McIntyre cried out.

"Surrender!" came a shout through the roar of rifles and pistols. The voice was familiar. McIntyre turned to peer into the smoke. Texans were swarming into the battery, grappling with the infantry support while the artillerymen defended themselves with swords and pistols. McIntyre picked up a sword from a fallen gunner and began working his way up to join McRae. He saw a Texan atop one of the caissons down the line, aiming his pistol at a cannoneer. As he watched, the man thrust a lighted fuse into the caisson, and the next moment a blinding explosion nearly knocked him down.

"Surrender, McRae!" the voice came like a whisper though McIntyre knew it was a shout. He looked up and found himself staring at Owens.

"We don't want to kill you!" Owens cried. McRae placed a hand on the butt of a twelve-pounder. At the same time a Texan major put his gloved hand on the hot muzzle and waved his hat.

"This is mine!" the major yelled.

"Shoot the son of a bitch!" McRae shouted to his men. At that instant rifles fired, seemingly from all around, and both McRae and the Texan fell across the gun, their blood hissing on its hot surface. McIntyre stared at them, horrified, then raised his gaze to Owens, whose face was a mask of grief. Owens looked up and beckoned him forward. With an anguished, inarticulate cry McIntyre threw down his sword, raised his hands in the air and ran toward Owens, the only friend visible in the maelstrom.

All was madness. Jamie ran into the Yankee battery, becoming just one more demon in hell. There were men in blue running among the trees, some toward him, some away. An artilleryman pointed a pistol at him; Jamie emptied his shotgun into the man's gut, then stepped over him looking for more. He passed through the battery and into the woods. Suddenly a giant in blue loomed over him and jabbed with a bayonet. Jamie parried clumsily with the shotgun, which the giant grabbed in one huge paw and wrenched out of his hands. The bayonet flashed again and Jamie jumped back, feeling the point catch at his jacket. He read his demise in the giant's grimace, then a gunshot close by stunned him for a second. The giant put a hand to his chest and looked from the blood seeping over it up to Jamie's face, his expression astonished chagrin. Then the man collapsed, still staring at him, mouth working. Jamie was appalled, even more so when he realized the shot had come from the pistol he didn't even remember drawing.

On the edge of his vision a Yankee rifleman was taking aim. The pistol fired again, and Jamie was drawn back into the madness.

From the direction of the battery a huge explosion sounded. Jamie glanced back and saw flames around the guns. The Yankees were giving way. Jamie followed, and suddenly he was part of a line again, his comrades chasing the Federals out of the battery with wild yells. The bluecoats swarmed into the river where the Texans shot them up horribly, staining the muddy water with blood. Jamie couldn't bring himself to shoot at the helpless men so he stood watching the slaughter until a blue-coated horseman appeared from the south, waving a white flag.

"Stop!" Jamie cried, but no one paid any attention. I'm an officer, damn it, he thought. He stepped in front of the line and held his pistol aloft, yelling "Hold your fire!"

The men in front of him lowered their weapons. Someone down the line repeated the order and the firing stopped. In strange silence the horseman approached. The Texans jeered at him but he paid no heed and trotted his blowing mount up to Jamie. The man was not much older than himself, Jamie realized, and at least as frightened. His eyes were wide open, whites showing.

"Where's your commander?" the rider asked.

"Dead, you son of a bitch!" one of the men yelled.

"Silence!" Jamie pointed his pistol at the soldier who'd spoken, then stared stupidly up at the enemy messenger, almost surprised to hear him speaking English. Footsteps caught his attention, and he glanced around to see Scurry hurrying forward.

"What's your business?" Scurry called.

"Sir," the messenger said, "Colonel Canby requests a cease-fire for the purpose of tending the wounded."

"Let me take you to Colonel Green," Scurry said.

The horse stepped forward. Ranks parted to let him through. It's over, Jamie realized. Suddenly he felt like crying. A soldier tossed his hat in the air and a general cheer went up along the line, then the men fell to plundering the Yankee dead. Overcoats, haversacks, rifles were snapped up. "Whiskey!" a soldier yelled, waving a canteen. He was instantly mobbed.

Sickened, Jamie began to walk slowly back through the woods. There was something he needed to do, only he couldn't remember—wasn't thinking straight. His eyes fell on a dead Confederate's belt buckle: the Lone Star.

"Martin!" he whispered, and began to run.

17

---

*We have had a most desperate and bloody struggle with the
Texans.*

—Captain Gurden Chapin, 7th Infantry

The light was going. McIntyre shivered in his wet clothes
and paced in an effort to get warm. He and a few other prisoners were being held in the dry streambed he'd spied on
earlier with Hall. Texan guards, lean and bearded, watched
with scornful suspicion. A rumble of wheels made him
look up. Mules had dragged the captured battery to the rim
above, and men stood arguing over the carriages. One of
the tubes was stained with blood. McIntyre squeezed his
eyes shut and took a deep breath to steady himself. Something brushed his back and he jerked away, heart racing.

"Easy, Mac." It was Owens, with a blanket. McIntyre
shuddered, then gratefully wrapped himself in the coarse
wool.

"Come on, I want to talk to you," Owens said. With a nod
to the guards, he led McIntyre away from the others and
handed him a flask. McIntyre pulled greedily at the liquor.
The cannon were being hauled south along the ridge.
Streaks of salmon-colored clouds filled the sunset sky.

"McRae—" said McIntyre.

"He's dead. So's Major Lockridge. Over that damned
gun."

McIntyre took another swig of whiskey. Owens led him
into the shadow of the bank, where they squatted in the
sand.

"Come over to us, Mac," Owens said softly.

McIntyre looked up, surprised. "I—I can't do that."

"You almost did before," Owens said. "All the more reason now. We're going to win, Mac. We've already won. Look what happened today." Owen's eyes were earnest and sincere. Friend of old. Comrade-in-arms.

McIntyre swallowed. "How can I?" he asked feebly.

"Same way I did," Owens said. "Resign. Sibley'll take you on your commission."

"Don't you think it's a little late?" McIntyre said.

"Would you rather spend the war in chains?"

"Of course not."

"Think about it then," Owens said. "Think about what your father would want."

"I don't know what he'd want," McIntyre said.

"Then what do *you* want?"

McIntyre sighed, set the flask in the sand, and ran his hands through river-plastered hair. What he really wanted was to sit down to a good meal with good friends and forget about all this.

"Hey, there, Tennessee!"

McIntyre looked up into a grinning face. With a shock he realized it was Hall, the Colorado man. He had shed his Federal jacket and somewhere found a grungy buckskin coat to replace it, and carried two haversacks slung over his shoulder and a loaf of fresh bread that had come from the ovens at Craig. He took a bite of it and said, "Going to join the cause?"

"I see you have," McIntyre said.

Hall shrugged. "I like to be on the winning side."

Owens stood up, looking Hall over.

"Val Owens, Joe Hall," McIntyre said. He picked up the flask and got stiffly to his feet as they shook hands. The whiskey was already at work. "Could I have a bite of that?"

Hall handed him the bread. "You are in sad shape," he said casually.

"Thank you, you look interesting yourself."

Hall laughed. "And here I was offering to let you wring out my trousers."

McIntyre almost choked on the bread and had to swallow a bite half chewed. A fit of giggles racked him and Hall joined in, laughing and clapping him on the back.

"What you need, boy," Hall said, "is a warm fire and a full belly." McIntyre saw him flash a look at Owens, who nodded.

"Yes," Owens said. "You can decide what to do tomorrow. Come on, they'll have a fire going by now."

Relieved, McIntyre pulled his blanket tighter as they started down the streambed. He didn't feel up to hard moral problems. A night's sleep would clear his head. He took another bite of bread and followed his friends into the Texan camp.

The battlefield was more horrible now than it had been during the fight. Then, smoke and fire had obscured the fallen, and the roar of cannon and rifles had blotted the cries of the wounded. Now, as Jamie wandered the field in the failing light searching for Captain Martin, he was surrounded by voices begging for water, for help, for an end to misery. Some could not form the words and instead moaned piteously or wept like children. Feeling a brute, Jamie passed them by. There were others at work to assist them; he had to find his friend.

The captured Yankee battery had been hauled away, but charred trees gave evidence of the fire. Jamie stood on the spot and tried to remember where he'd been in the fight. Here and there fires had been built and the wounded huddled around them, but Jamie searched their faces in vain. Men were starting to collect the ones who couldn't walk, their lanterns casting an eerie glow through the dusk. Jamie approached a man who was trying to move an unconscious soldier half again his size onto a makeshift litter.

"Excuse me," Jamie said.

"Hold this, will you?" The man thrust his lantern into Jamie's hands. "Sir," he added, and began to roll his patient roughly onto the litter.

"Has Captain Martin been taken to the hospital?" Jamie asked.

"Don't know, sir. Sorry," the soldier said between grunts.

Jamie sighed. His gaze fell on a form on the ground nearby that looked vaguely familiar. He held the lantern aloft and found himself peering at a Yankee who lay with eyes open and staring in astonishment. It was, Jamie realized, the man he had killed with his pistol an hour and an eternity ago. A wave of nausea gripped him.

"Hey, never mind that one, he's gone," said the litter-bearer. "Hold that light over here. I mean, please, sir."

Jamie turned his back on the corpse but could still imagine its eyes staring at him. He shivered and hunched his shoulders to get rid of the feeling. The man finished loading his charge and took back the lantern. Jamie followed him out of the trees, thinking he should check at the hospital. Likely Martin had been able to walk away and seek help on his own. In fact, he was probably with the train by now, wondering where Jamie was. Jamie hurried to catch up with the litter-bearer.

A silhouette caught his eye, a familiar hat. Its wearer was seated on the ground leaning against a small, scrubby bush. "Sir!" Jamie ran forward feeling a rush of relief. "I thought you were—"

No. The figure didn't move, gave no sign of having heard. It was dark now and Jamie had to kneel very close to see Martin's face. The captain's head was thrown back against the bush that had kept him from falling to the ground, and his hat had dropped forward over his eyes. It took Jamie a second to work up the nerve to touch his cheek. The flesh was cool.

"Sir?" Jamie said. "Captain Martin?"

Somewhere nearby a casualty sobbed in agony. Jamie felt his throat tightening. "Please, sir," he said. "Stephen." He shook Martin by the shoulders, and his right hand came away sticky-wet.

"Hoah." Jamie sat back on his heels, fighting down horror and grief. He swallowed, then carefully pulled Martin free of the bush. The hat tumbled away, Emma's star flashing a glint of lantern-light. As Jamie picked it up he realized he'd lost his own hat, Lord knew when. He put Martin's on his head and hefted the captain, struggling to lift him. By pulling Martin's arms over his shoulders he was able to drag him away from the battlefield. As he trudged on he heard the hiss of a minié ball, saw again the captain falling to his knees. Yes, there was the bush behind him. Why hadn't he remembered that?

The hospital tent was as bad as the battleground, filled with moaning wounded. Worse, the flickering lanterns made their agony visible. Jamie tried not to let his gaze dwell on any of them. He laid Martin down outside the tent and stood in the entrance looking for help.

"Move ahead, there!"

Jamie stepped out of the way and a litter was carried past bearing a soldier who'd been shot through the mouth, leaving only his eyes to express his anguish. A surgeon stopped to give the bearers some instructions, then came up to Jamie, who knelt beside Martin.

Please, Jamie thought as his gaze met the surgeon's, but the word wouldn't leave his lips. The surgeon nodded as if he'd heard anyway and looked at Martin, then put a hand to the captain's neck. Jamie knew for certain then.

"I'm sorry," the surgeon said wearily. He gave Jamie's shoulder a pat and turned away.

That's all?

Jamie gazed helplessly around. Men were digging nearby; the sound of shovels biting sand took him back to the dry riverbed and the makeshift wells that morning. *Start another,* Martin's voice echoed in his head. Biting his lip, he forced his weary arms to work, hefting Martin again.

Jamie found Sergeant Rose standing over a crew of quartermaster's hands who were digging a long trench. Bodies already lined one end while the hands extended the other, throwing their sand onto the corpses. Jamie laid Martin beside the trench, and Rose's eyes widened.

"Keller," Rose said sharply, and a clerk with a lantern and a handful of crumpled papers hurried up. "Captain

Stephen Martin, 1st Regiment, A.Q.M." Rose said in a dull voice.

The clerk set down his light, took out a pencil, and scribbled against his thigh. Rose, his brow puckered in a frown, nodded to Jamie. The bodies lay two deep, wrapped in blankets. Jamie thought of going back to fetch one for Martin but decided not to; the captain wouldn't want a blanket to go to waste. He searched Martin's pockets, found a wallet filled with Emma's letters, a silver watch with a ribbon and fob, and two gold five-dollar pieces sticky with blood. Putting all in his own pockets, he retrieved Martin's pistol and forced himself to remove the captain's boots, then stood up and watched while two of the gravediggers laid Martin's body beside the others. Jamie backed away and the plop of shoveled sand resumed.

I should pray, Jamie thought, but no prayers came to mind. Dear God, I'm sorry, was all he could think. Now was the time for tears but they wouldn't come. Jamie left the boots and the gun with Rose and walked away from the grave, feeling only numbness. Perhaps, he thought with strange detachment, it was because he didn't dare feel anything more.

He wandered on, not really caring where he was headed as long as it was away from the nightmare. In the darkness he tripped on something and stumbled a step or two.

"Hey, there! Russell?"

Jamie gazed around, bewildered. Three shadows came toward him. For a second his skin crawled, but they were real flesh—he could tell from the smell of liquor.

"Russell!" It was Captain Owens, grinning big enough for Jamie to see even in the dark.

"You're alive!" said Jamie, shivering with sudden joy.

"So far," Owens said. He grasped Jamie's shoulder, then drew him into a hug and slapped his back. Jamie's eyes suddenly spilled over while he gave a sob of laughter.

"I'd like you to meet a friend of mine," Owens said. "Lacey McIntyre. Mac, this is James Russell."

"Hello," Jamie said, shaking hands with one of the shadows.

"And Joe Hall." Owens indicated the other. "We're looking for the headquarters fire. Do you know where it is?"

Jamie shook his head and wiped at his face with both hands. "I haven't been there."

"Come help us find it, then. We've liberated three canteens of Yankee whiskey," Owens added as they trudged forward. "Want to help?"

"Yes," Jamie said, and a canteen was thrust into his hands, just as Martin had done that morning. He raised it to his lips but his hands were shaking and he didn't want to spill it. The previous moment's elation fled as fast as it had come. *Am I going insane?* he wondered.

There was music ahead, and they made for the sound, rounding a hill and coming on a huge bonfire where a crowd of Texans were clapping along with "Dixie," played by Baylor's brass band from Mesilla. In the firelight Jamie glanced at his new acquaintances. One looked like a mountain man; sly, Jamie decided. The other was young, good-looking and, surprisingly, wore a Yankee officer's uniform. He looked up, saw Jamie watching him, and pulled his blanket closer as he turned away.

"We can do better than that," Owens said. "Mac, remember that catch we used to sing? How'd it go?"

The Yankee gave a wavering smile. " 'He that will an alehouse keep must have three things in store—' "

Owens joined the song. " 'A chamber with a feather bed, a chimney and a hey, nonny nonny—' "

Laughing, they wandered campfire to campfire, hearing snatches of bragging and stories of the battle.

"—sitting with his leg shot off, loading and firing away."

"—greasers probably ran all the way to Mexico!"

"—shot into the magazine and blew them all to Jesus."

"I saw that," McIntyre said as they walked on. "I was standing in the battery just a few minutes before. . . ."

"What happened, Mac?" Owens asked gently.

"A man was up on the caisson shooting the cannoneers.

The last one had a lit fuse, and he shoved it into the ammunition box. Must have taken a dozen Rebels with him. I mean—"

" 'Rebel' suits fine," Owens said.

The Yankee dropped his gaze to the ground. They walked in silence for a few paces, then came to a cluster of men around a group of cannon. Jamie saw Reily among them and called to him.

"Russell!" Reily jogged up and grabbed him in a bear hug. "Hey, you're a mess! That's not your blood, is it?"

"No," Jamie said. Shying away from explanations, he introduced Reily to the two newcomers. "We're looking for headquarters," he said.

"I'll take you," Reily said, "but first you have to admire our trophies!" He beamed as he showed off the six captured cannon. Jamie noticed McIntyre frowning, and handed him the canteen. With a grateful look, the Yankee guzzled whiskey until he nearly choked. Coughing, he passed it back to Jamie who did the same. If he drank enough, Jamie thought idly as they followed Reily into the darkness, maybe he'd forget everything.

Daylight intruded on McIntyre's awareness. He turned over, pulling the blanket over his head in an effort to escape. It was hopeless. He was waking, and as he slowly became aware of his body he noticed several discomforts: ringing in his ears, stiff muscles, an ache in one ankle, and a dry, pasty feeling in his mouth left over from the whiskey. When he tried to sit up he added a stabbing headache to the list. He lay back and stared at the tent wall glowing gold-white where the sun hit it, marred here and there by smears of dirt. His breath fogged as he sighed. He shut his eyes again, hoping sleep would return. Instead the distant boom of cannon echoed in his mind, bringing him back to the battle, the fight in the bosque and McRae. McRae had died rather than surrender. Was that the right thing to do? If so, it was far too late.

A sough of moving canvas made him raise his head.

Owens had come into the tent carrying a steaming mug. "Morning, Mac," he said. "Brought you some coffee."

McIntyre propped himself on one arm, took the cup and tried a sip but was barely able to choke it down. Owens sat down beside him, produced his flask, and added a generous splash to the mug. "That should help."

It did. McIntyre drank two gulps, then set the cup down and rubbed his eyes. The cannon boomed again; he looked up sharply.

"Fort Craig," Owens said. "They're burying their dead."

"Oh." McIntyre relaxed and rubbed at his temples, trying to ease the pressure.

"He awake?" Hall asked, coming in with an armload of clothing. He fished out a brown coat, which he offered to McIntyre. "No graybacks," he said. "I checked."

McIntyre stared at the garment. He had not worn a civilian coat since he'd left West Point, nothing but Union blue. Owens had been to the Academy too, though, and was proud enough in gray.

Owens gave Hall a frowning glance. "General Sibley's out of sorts," he said to McIntyre, "but I talked to Colonel Green. He doesn't see any reason why you can't join us. Said you can be in the spy company."

McIntyre bristled. "What, go and spy on Canby?"

"No, no," Owens said. "Scout work, you know. Like last winter."

Memories crowded unbidden into McIntyre's mind. Riding treacherous trails through bitter winds with Owens and a company of infantry, searching for renegade Navajos. At night they would camp where they could and if the weather wouldn't let them sleep, they'd talk all night around the watch fire. It had been miserably uncomfortable and great fun. McIntyre realized he was smiling and glanced ruefully up at Owens, who nodded.

"Stay with us," Owens said.

Yes. That's what he wanted. To stay with friends.

"All right," McIntyre said, sitting up and running his hands over his face.

Hall produced a folded sheet of paper, which he smoothed out against his haversack, and offered ink and a poorly cut pen. McIntyre hesitated, wondering whom to write to. Canby was dead, for all he knew. He hated having to write this letter, but if he didn't he'd be a traitor indeed. He dipped the pen in ink and did his best to write neatly, though it was only a shadow of his usual fine hand. The nib skipped on the word "resign," leaving a small blot of ink. He ignored it, finished the letter, and addressed it to Commander, Department of New Mexico.

"There was a courier here from Craig," Owens said. "I'll see if he's still around."

He went out, and McIntyre sneezed and groped in his pocket for his handkerchief, ignoring its questionable condition. While Hall stowed his pen and ink McIntyre stood up, stared hard at the brown coat, then shrugged out of his jacket and put it on. It was a little too big.

"I know some good places in Denver City," Hall said, grinning up at him. "I'll show you when we get there."

McIntyre gave him a thin smile, then emptied the pockets of his Federal coat and slung it over his arm. He went to the doorway and flinched from the sharp sunlight as he threw back the flap. The camp was a mess, tents pitched helter-skelter on the battleground with horses grazing among the guy-ropes and company wagons parked at random. Fires sent waves of heat skyward, making the cold morning air shimmer. Looking at it made McIntyre queasy. He spotted Owens near a blue-coated horseman with a flag of truce across his saddlebow.

"Here he is," Owens said as he approached. The rider turned in the saddle.

Anderson. McIntyre's heart gave one heavy thud as Anderson's gaze took in his attire.

"Lacey, what are you doing . . . ?" Anderson stared first in disbelief, then with growing anger. McIntyre felt his cheeks starting to burn and considered changing his mind, but it was already too late. His choice was known, he'd hardly be allowed to take it back. He handed Anderson his letter of resignation and his Federal jacket.

"Hey—" Hall protested, but McIntyre silenced him with a glare and looked back at his friend. Anderson's face hardened into contempt. He turned his back and spurred toward the river.

"We could have used that coat," Hall said.

"No," McIntyre said quietly. "I'll give it up, but I won't dishonor it."

Hall's frown faded into a shrug. "Come on and meet the captain. He's a regular rogue, you'll like him. Want some breakfast?"

McIntyre shook his head, nauseous just at the thought of food. He followed Hall through the camp and up to a fire a little north of the sand hills, where eight or ten fellows of dubious appearance gave him curious stares.

"Captain Phillips," Hall called out, "I've got another recruit for you." A man rose from the circle to meet them, and McIntyre found himself facing the clerk of the Exchange Hotel.

"Well," Phillips said. "If it ain't Romeo himself. Come to join the Brigands, eh?"

McIntyre could not think of a better description for the sundry villains of Phillips's company, some of whom he recognized from Santa Fé's seedier haunts. He suppressed a sneer.

"I don't know, Hall," Phillips said, his eyes traveling McIntyre's form. "Don't seem the adventuresome type."

"But he is," Hall assured him. "He was with the mules."

A guffaw went up in the small circle. "Well, let me shake your hand, then," one of the Brigands said. "Ain't seen the camp that lively before or since!"

McIntyre clamped his jaw shut. He did not want to serve under Phillips, but he hadn't been offered a choice. He'd put up with it for now, and ask to transfer the first chance he got.

Phillips turned and snapped his fingers. "Initiation," he said. One of his men hurried up with a tin cup and a heavy brown bottle. Phillips filled the cup and handed it to McIntyre with an unpleasant smile. "All at once."

McIntyre stared into the cup as if reading his future there. A bit of grass floated in the bottom. No help for it, he decided, and tossed it back. Chile-spiked whiskey, too hot. He got it down and coughed, throat and stomach burning as he gasped for breath and angrily threw the cup into the fire, which earned him a round of applause from the Brigands.

"Welcome, Brother McIntyre," Hall said, throwing an arm around his shoulders.

"Wake up, sir, please."

Jamie groaned. Someone was shaking his shoulder and it was making his brain rattle uncomfortably in his skull. He batted an arm at the offender to make it stop, then slowly drew himself up and looked around. He was in his tent, on a blanket that someone had thrown down for him. His kit sat unopened against the wall, as did Martin's. Sergeant Rose was peering at him, his young face strained and anxious.

"Sir, there's a problem with the mules," Rose said.

Jamie grunted, then staggered to his feet and went out with Rose close behind. In the bright sun he squinted at the chaos of the camp, then looked toward the wagon park, reassured by its orderly lines. The sound of digging haunted him. Glancing toward the battleground he saw that the first grave had been filled in and mounded over with sand, and a second trench begun. Feeling sick, he wondered how many Texans had lost their lives the day before.

Three men came toward him, captains from the 1st. One of them—Captain Hampton, of Company C—had his arm in a sling.

"Coffee," said Jamie, and Rose hurried away.

"Any remounts available, Lieutenant?" Captain Buckholts asked.

"Not unless we captured a bunch of Yankee horses," Jamie said.

"Half my men are unmounted," Captain Nunn said. "We can't march like this."

"I'll see what I can find," Jamie told them, "but I can't guarantee—"

"Where's Martin?" Buckholts asked.

"Dead," Hampton said, before Jamie could speak.

"Hell."

The three men exchanged glances, gazing speculatively at Jamie. It made him angry, and he said with firm dismissal, "I'll do the best I can."

Nunn frowned and was about to reply when Hampton said, "Come on, boys. Let's get something to eat." Slowly the captains departed, to Jamie's relief.

Rose reappeared with a mug of coffee. "Colonel Scurry wants to see you," he said.

Jamie glanced at the bloodstains on his shirt. "I'd better change, then." He went into the tent and dug in his kit, thought about donning the jacket his mother had made for him, then decided to save it. It would be a shame to ruin Momma's fine handiwork. He put on his old gray coat, which had bars on the collar at least. If he had to manage the train, he'd better look something like an officer.

"Rose, find out how many mounts each company has and how many they need," he said, emerging from the tent and starting toward headquarters.

"Yes, sir," Rose said, following him. "The blacksmiths want to know if they can get more iron for horseshoes."

"There isn't any," Jamie said, gulping coffee. "Tell them to take shoes off the dead ones."

"Yes, sir," said Rose. "Sir?"

Jamie stopped. "What?"

"I'm sorry about Captain Martin, sir."

Jamie sighed and stared into his coffee, blinking hard.

"Was it bad?" Rose asked in an awed tone. "It sounded pretty awful from the train."

Jamie looked up at the sergeant and was suddenly reminded of Gabe. For the first time in his life, he felt old. He wondered how to answer—sound brave, protect the innocent? "Yes," he said finally, "but we got through." He gave Rose a halfhearted smile and went on to find Scurry.

Regimental headquarters was buzzing, mostly with clerks trying to bring order out of the chaos created by the battle. Jamie went to the commander's tent, where he found Scurry sitting in front of a fire, watching Major Raguet hobble around, one leg bandaged, using a stick for support.

"Ah, Russell," Scurry said. "You don't have any crutches, do you?"

"I don't believe so," said Jamie.

"Who needs crutches?" Raguet said, taking a couple of steps without the stick to demonstrate his mobility. Then he plopped down in a camp chair with a grimace. "Say, you should salute, you know," he told Jamie. "He's a full colonel now."

Jamie obeyed. "Congratulations, sir."

"Thank you." Scurry nodded. "You deserve congratulation yourself. I never did see such a charge as that one you boys made yesterday."

"Thank you, sir," Jamie said, feeling anything but proud.

"I heard we lost Martin," Scurry said gently.

"Yes, sir."

"Damn shame. He was a good man."

Jamie glanced down, unable to form a reply.

"How are you fixed for horses and mules?" Scurry asked.

"The train didn't lose any—any more," Jamie said. "But the regiment—"

"I know," Scurry said, "my commanders are all screaming. Do you have any idea if the other regiments can spare some mounts?"

"I doubt it, sir," Jamie told him. "If they could we'd have borrowed them yesterday to haul wagons, instead of burning them."

"Would you ask anyway?"

"Yes, sir." Jamie saluted again and turned to go.

"Staff meeting at two o'clock, by the way," Scurry said.

"Here?" Jamie asked, looking back.

Scurry shook his head. "Army headquarters." He gave Jamie an odd smile, then nodded dismissal. Jamie went back to his tent, where he found Rose arguing with a surgeon whose apron was covered in blood.

"We don't have any," Rose was saying.

"I've got men turning blue in that tent!" the surgeon said.

"What's the trouble?" Jamie asked.

"I need blankets. My patients are freezing—"

"I'm sorry," Jamie said, thinking of corpses now buried in sand, each wrapped in his own blanket. "We don't have any extra blankets."

"This is hardly the time for conservation of resources, Lieutenant!" the surgeon said tartly. "If I have to I'll go to the colonel—"

"We don't have *any* blankets," Jamie said. "We had to burn them because we couldn't move them."

The surgeon was silent. Jamie stepped to his tent, reached in for his own two blankets, and handed them to the surgeon. "Rose," he said, "see if the other regiments can spare any, but first have some men put a few buckets of coals inside the hospital tent. And tell the burial detail to keep back the blankets from now on."

"Yes, sir," Rose said, and hurried away.

The surgeon looked at the blankets in his hands with faint surprise. He seemed to have no more to say.

"Excuse me," Jamie said, and turned his attention to the train.

He was soon swamped—a permanent clot of men formed before his tent with problems, requests, and complaints of shortages. Some Yankee horses had been caught, it turned out, but the men had already appropriated them. The captains of the companies that had stayed to guard the train were protesting the battlefield plundering done by the men who saw action. Jamie sent a detail to comb the battlefield for small arms and any other useful items, though most of these had already been scavenged. He avoided the field himself, wishing to forget the battle and disgusted by the plundering of the dead. A tinge of color came into his cheeks as he remembered Martin's belongings, still in his pockets. It was different, though; he hadn't stolen them, only saved them from being buried with the captain. He told Rose to handle the complaints, then shut himself in his tent and took out the meager collection, spreading it across the camp desk.

Martin had no living family. The army had been his whole life up until he'd met Emma. Jamie picked up the bundle of her letters, realizing with a tightening chest that he'd have to write to tell her the news. He'd bring the letters back to her, he thought, running a finger along the edge of the stack. He noticed one in Martin's handwriting—his last message to his promised wife. Jamie closed up the wallet, careful not even to glance at such an intimate letter, and silently promised himself to make sure it got to his sister safely. It would be small comfort, he knew, but Emma was strong.

What about the rest? Jamie picked up the bloodstained coins. He didn't feel right about taking them for himself or even sending them to Emma. He would save them, he decided. Maybe use them to buy supplies.

Last was the watch. Jamie examined the little fob on the end of the ribbon, which turned out to be a locket. He opened it and found a portrait of Emma that Martin had never shown him; their secret, the two of them. Jamie felt tears starting and brushed them away. He couldn't afford to indulge in them, he had work to do. He laid his head on the desk and drew a deep breath.

I'm all right.

It had been like a thought, but the voice had been Martin's. Jamie opened his eyes and the captain was standing before him, head nearly touching the peak of their little tent, sunlight glowing through the canvas behind him.

Jamie sat up, staring. He tried to breathe but it came in ragged gasps. Martin, real as life, smiled at Jamie, then turned and walked away, straight through the wall of the tent.

Jamie stared at the blank canvas. He wanted to cry but found himself laughing instead. He got shakily to his feet.

No need to touch the wall; it was solid, he knew. I'm not crazy, he told himself. I'm not.

He heard a ticking sound, and glanced down at the watch in his hand. Two o'clock. With a start he stuffed Martin's things into his pockets. He leaned a hand on the desk, telling himself he was fine, then headed toward the tent door and plunged back into the world.

"Sir—" Rose said as he emerged.

"Not now, I've got a staff meeting," Jamie said, barging through the cluster of petitioners.

"Sir, the surgeons want another tent—"

"You handle it," Jamie called over his shoulder, jogging in the direction of army headquarters. He reached the circle of tents and wagons that defined Sibley's command center, and tried to be quiet as he slipped into the large tent where the meeting was already in progress.

The general was seated behind a rough wooden table with Scurry and Green beside him. He looked well, if slightly drawn. He spotted Jamie and raised his head. "Ah, Captain Russell."

Jamie had snapped to attention before the word "captain" had registered. His mouth dropped open. He looked at Scurry, who gave him a nod and a grin. Jamie shut his mouth, swallowed, and said, "Sir?"

"I hear you fought valiantly yesterday," the general said. "I'm promoting you captain and acting A.Q.M. You'll be overseeing all the army's supplies from now on."

18

I am sorry to be able to give no better account of the operations of our army. I had anticipated a very different result.

—Henry Connelly, Governor of New Mexico Territory

"Congratulations, Captain Russell!"

Jamie looked up from the morass of his desk to find Captain Owens at the door of the tent. The Georgian offered his silver flask, but Jamie shook his head. He managed a smile, saying, "Thanks. News travels fast."

"The staff knows all. I heard you sent some Yankees to Jesus yesterday."

Jamie glanced away and shrugged.

"Our gallant quartermaster!" Owens grinned. "How do you feel now you've finally seen the elephant?"

"I saw a lot of elephants after all that whiskey last night," Jamie said ruefully. "I only wish I could hitch them to my wagons."

Owens laughed and slapped his shoulder. "Sibley's giving a victory speech this afternoon. See you there?"

Jamie shook his head. "I have too much to do."

"Supper then. My tent, seven o'clock."

"I'll try," Jamie said.

"If you're not there by seven I'll send the Brigands to abduct you," Owens said cheerfully, departing with a wave and a smile. Through the tent door Jamie glimpsed the crowd waiting for him—company officers, ordnance and commissary men—all his problem now. He thought of the train, a hundred wagons left out of the four hundred brought from San Antonio. With Fort Craig between them and the depot at Fort Thorn, they had no chance of resupply unless Canby surrendered or was defeated in another battle. Jamie shuddered at the thought, and went back to work.

A thundering at the outer gate made Laura and Mrs. Canby look up. Their eyes met, and Mrs. Canby hurriedly wiped floured hands on her apron. Laura followed her out of the kitchen to the placita, running across the frozen garden. Juan Carlos was opening the zaguán to admit a courier whose overcoat was spattered with mud.

"Captain Chapin!" Mrs. Canby said as he dismounted. "Come in! No, never mind your boots. Come in and get warm." She hurried him into the parlor while Laura fetched some of the stew María had simmering on the kitchen hearth. Laura caught up a couple of tortillas and put them on a tray with the brimming bowl, a dozen questions humming in her mind.

"I can't stay long," Chapin was saying as she entered the parlor. "The colonel asked me to pay you a call on the way to Fort Union. He's fine, ma'am, though he took a spill when his horse was shot."

"Charley?" said Mrs. Canby.

Chapin nodded. "Afraid so. Poor old fellow."

"There was a battle, then?" Laura said.

"Yes," Chapin said. "It didn't go very well, I'm afraid. Oh, thank you! That looks wonderful!"

"Didn't go well? Do you mean . . . ?"

"The Volunteers were shaky," Chapin explained. "Most of Pino's men wouldn't cross to support the battery, no matter what he and Chaves did." The captain looked at his hands. "McRae died defending his guns. The Texans took them in the end."

Laura caught at the arm of a chair and sat down, eyes suddenly stinging with tears, remembering Captain McRae's teasing at a dinner party not so very long ago. She pressed her handkerchief to her face.

"Tell us everything," Mrs. Canby said quietly.

Chapin, between bites of stew, sketched the battle for

them. All had gone well until the Union center had evaporated—some of the men veering south to help repel a weak attack on the right, others failing to support McRae on the left—allowing the Rebels to overwhelm McRae's battery and the men who had stood by it. With darkness falling and his troops in disorder, Canby had broken off the fight. He'd sent the remnants of Pino's scattered Volunteers north to remove supplies from the depots at Albuquerque and Santa Fé to Fort Union.

"Was Lieutenant McIntyre in the field?" Laura asked, maintaining an even voice.

Chapin swallowed a bite of stew. "Yes. He hadn't come in when I left. But that doesn't mean anything," he added. "I was in the saddle almost before it was over. Probably he's fine."

"You must be exhausted," Mrs. Canby said. "We should let you get home to your wife—"

"I've already been to see her, ma'am, thank you. Now I'd best be on my way," he said, rising. "Thank you for the stew."

The two ladies saw Chapin out, then returned to the kitchen and their neglected bread. Laura felt oddly calm as she punched at the dough, though of course she was concerned about Lieutenant McIntyre. She hoped and silently prayed he was not in pain, that he was well and safe. Beyond that it was useless to fret. She must trust in God. Sensing Mrs. Canby watching her, she paused in her kneading and looked up.

"Miss Howland," Mrs. Canby said, her kind eyes full of sympathy and pride, "have I ever told you what a fine army wife you'd make?"

Laughter welled up, and with it relief. Smiling, Laura resumed her attack on the bread.

The stink of burning leather made McIntyre grimace as he rode into the abandoned campsite. Sibley had set his army on the move again after receiving Canby's flat refusal to surrender. With the army short on food, the general had decided against besieging the fort, hoping instead to capture government supplies farther north. A good third of the men were on foot, trading off carrying the wounded on stretchers made from cut-up tents, while those lucky enough to have mounts rode ahead. Only the wagon train hadn't started. McIntyre found the quartermaster staring moodily at a bonfire of saddles, old clothes, and lances. Behind him a handful of loaded wagons were parked by a sandy ridge.

"Why aren't we bringing those?" McIntyre asked, remembering belatedly to salute.

"No teams," Captain Russell said. "We'll send some back to collect them as soon as we can."

"And Canby'll surrender Fort Craig," said McIntyre. Instantly he regretted the words. The Q.M. didn't need any addition to his troubles. He was hardly more than a boy, after all, and his sergeant even younger. "Sorry," McIntyre said. "It's been a rough couple of days."

"That's an understatement," said Russell, coming away from the fire. "You my guide?"

McIntyre nodded. Russell mounted his horse and called out orders, and soon the train was lumbering along toward the ford. McIntyre pointed out the shallowest crossing, but even there it was difficult for the wagons, which threatened to stick in the sandy bottom. He and Russell watched from the bank while the teamsters cursed and whipped their jaded beasts across.

"You were in the battle?" Russell asked, so softly McIntyre almost missed it.

"I was there." McIntyre nodded. "Didn't fight." He was surprised at how those words stuck in his throat.

"Not at all?" Russell asked, then his cheeks reddened. "I'm sorry."

"If I'd had a weapon I would have. Lost my pistol in the river when my horse went under. I went back to ask McRae for another mount—"

"You knew McRae?"

McIntyre nodded, feeling his throat tighten. "He was a

good man. From North Carolina." He glanced at Russell, whose eyebrows went up.

"I didn't know," said Russell.

"Those guns cost us. . . ." McIntyre swallowed, unable to continue.

"I lost a friend, too," said Russell quietly.

McIntyre looked up and was caught off guard by the quartermaster's ghostly smile. Then Russell shouted to the teamsters, urging the last wagon up the west bank and starting the train northward. McIntyre fell in beside him.

"I have some good news for you, at least," he said. "There's a store loaded with goods up in the village." He didn't add that the store's owner was a captain in the New Mexico Volunteers.

"How far?" Russell asked sharply.

"About six miles."

Russell sighed. "The men will plunder it before I can get there. Damn!"

"Well, then confiscate the stuff," McIntyre said.

The quartermaster gazed at him, bemused. "I didn't think of that."

McIntyre smiled. "Hasn't come up before, has it? Question is, do you have some men tough enough to do the confiscating?" He glanced over his shoulder at the young quartermaster sergeant, who looked half asleep on his horse.

"As a matter of fact," Russell said, a slow, sly smile spreading across his face, "the Brigands work for me."

"Truly? I wasn't told that."

"It's true. Think they'd enjoy wresting plunder from the army?"

"I think they'd like nothing better," said McIntyre, laughing. "But you'll have to watch them, or you'll never see half of it."

"I have a friend in the company," Russell said. "Don't I?"

McIntyre grinned as he shook Russell's hand.

Armies, O'Brien realized with disgust, were not designed to move quickly. Pike's Peak was still to the south after several days' march. He put his last stick of wood on the fire, blew on the coals until blue-yellow flames began to lick at the fuel, and sat back, frowning up at the peak though it already hid in night's shadow.

A snail's pace they were making—not ten miles a day— and the regiment strung out all over creation by the end of each day. The Pet Lambs were used to hard living, but not used to marching. There were grumblings at night, and even O'Brien, whose men were all mounted, had to use a sharp word here and there to keep them in line. Short rations were no help, nor was the weather. It had started snowing again.

O'Brien hunched closer to his fire, using a twig to turn the stick so the other side would catch. A shadow approached, snowflakes sticking on dark-cloaked shoulders. It was Franklin, carrying wood and a kettle.

"I was wondering if I could use your fire to make some tea, sir," Franklin asked. "Would you like some?"

O'Brien swallowed. The thought of tea had made his mouth water, and he wondered what other luxuries Franklin had brought on the march. Not as many as Slough, who rode in his carriage and slept in a house every night, but doubtless more than O'Brien could command. He nodded, and watched Franklin add his wood to the fire, making a bright blaze that washed his face with warmth. O'Brien sighed, reaching toward the heat.

Franklin stirred some of the orange coals to one side and set his kettle over them, then pulled his cloak around himself and sat hugging his knees. He looked tired, O'Brien thought, watching him stare dully into the fire.

"I suppose you want to go home now," O'Brien said.

"No," Franklin said.

"You're a fine gentleman, you don't need the army. You don't even want to fight," said O'Brien.

"I'll fight when the time comes," Franklin said softly.

"Oh, you're eager, are you?" O'Brien said. "Then why didn't you think to enlist in New York?"

"Pennsylvania."

"Pennsylvania then. Wouldn't they take you?"

Franklin frowned into the fire and leaned forward to rest his chin on his knees. "My family don't know I've enlisted," he said with his odd smile. "They wouldn't approve, remember?"

"Oh, a fine patriotic family, eh?" O'Brien said.

Franklin's head came up at that. "They are patriots! My brother died at Bull Run!"

"Did he now," O'Brien said. "On which side?"

Franklin's eyes flashed real anger, and for a moment it seemed he'd attack, but he stopped and then laughed and sat back, stretching gloved hands toward the fire. "I'm Union, Captain," he said. "I'm here to fight for the ideals on which this country was founded, that all human beings are equal—"

"Equal? Are we equals, then, you and I?" O'Brien hadn't meant it to sound so bitter.

Franklin paused, and then lifted his chin. "Yes, I believe we are."

"Rot," O'Brien said. He glared at the kettle starting to simmer. "You've got money, fine clothes, education—"

"All things you could have—"

"I'll never have your *place!*" Getting angry, but O'Brien kept his voice down. "All the money on Earth wouldn't change the fact that I'm low and you're not!"

"That's Europe talking!" Franklin said, dark eyes burning with some inner fire. "In America we don't have to live by the old rules. I truly believe you can rise to any place you want."

"Looks a long, weary climb from down here, laddie."

The kettle boiled over, water spitting from the coals, and Franklin hastily moved it. He brought a small block of tea from his pocket and scraped it over the water with his knife. O'Brien inhaled deeply as the fragrant steam drifted his way.

"I have faith in you, Captain," Franklin said after a moment. He glanced up and smiled again—that strange smile, almost otherworldly—as he poured the tea into two mugs.

He's a changeling, that's it, O'Brien thought, accepting a mug. Sure, he takes more abuse than any normal man would. Ashamed of his ill humor, O'Brien turned his gaze away from those dark eyes, poking at the fire with his twig and wondering why Franklin didn't hate him.

Jamie closed his eyes, letting Cocoa's steady gait lull him. He rode with the vanguard, scouting ahead in search of supplies while Sergeant Rose remained to oversee the slow-moving train. Stapleton's store at Valverde had indeed been plundered, and while the Brigands had been effective in retrieving the goods, the grumbling of the men was enough to make Jamie determined to get to any future resources ahead of them. One shot from the cannon had served to disperse the New Mexicans guarding Socorro, where they'd taken a flour mill and its stores, some oxen to haul wagons, and a flock of sheep that had fed the army for two days. After lengthy discussion Scurry had reluctantly ordered the 1st Regiment dismounted and their remaining horses distributed among the 2nd and 3rd. As A.Q.M. Jamie was exempt, but he pitied his regiment, unaccustomed to marching as infantry and now without bread, only beef and beans left to feed them. Much of the captured flour had been left with the wounded at a makeshift hospital at Socorro. Albuquerque was their next objective; with luck they would capture the Federal depot there.

"Looks bad," McIntyre said.

Jamie opened his eyes to see they had topped a hill. The Río Grande Valley was visible for some miles, and a column of smoke was rising from a cluster of trees that marked a village.

"Oh, no," Jamie said. "Please, no."

Major Pyron had seen the smoke, too, for he ordered the battalion to advance at a trot. They rode fast and soon reached the southern outskirts of Albuquerque. Imposing mountains loomed to the northeast, with more distant blue hills in the north and the Río Grande sparkling its way through a wide bosque. Jamie paused with McIntyre and Pyron at the top of a rise overlooking the village. "Good girl," he said to Cocoa, patting her neck, and she nickered in response. At least, he thought gratefully, there was enough fodder for the horses. Corn tops a-plenty had been found in the villages along the river.

"Don't see any Yankees," Pyron said, field glasses in hand. The town itself was intact; the smoke seemed to be coming from one or two buildings. "What do your scouts say, Russell?"

"*My* scouts," Phillips said, riding up to join them, "say the Yanks left last night after torching the depot." He turned a cold look on Jamie. "Tough luck, sonny," he said.

"Well, let's go have a look," Pyron said.

The battalion rode down the hill toward the village of Albuquerque in full martial array, cannon to the fore. They met no resistance, and on Pyron's orders their tents were pitched in the plaza before the church, and the Stars and Bars were raised on the flagpole. Jamie tied Cocoa near a trough where she could drink her fill, and hurried to the smoldering ruin that had been the Federal depot. It had not completely burned, and from the scatter of debris in the street Jamie guessed someone had tried to put out the fire, and had dragged away some of the stores. There was nothing salvageable left.

"Never mind," McIntyre said, joining him. "There are merchants here."

"If they'll sell on credit. I have no way to pay them," Jamie said. As he spoke, the sound of breaking glass issued from a nearby building. Some of Pyron's men had broken into a shop where the Stars and Stripes were flying. Jamie and McIntyre hurried over to where the men were already carrying away armloads of clothing.

"Hey, you there! Fall in," Jamie called.

The men—a dozen or more—paused in their looting. A big fellow who was standing guard with a shotgun swung it casually in Jamie's direction. Infuriated, Jamie started to order him out, but McIntyre stopped him.

"Better let them be," he said into Jamie's ear. "You don't want to have an accident." He took Jamie's arm to lead him away.

"But that's insubordination!"

"Can't be helped," McIntyre replied. "They're starving and they're cold."

Jamie shook his head. "We'll regret this. We wanted these people to see us as liberators."

"And so we are," McIntyre said, though a slight frown had creased his brow. "There are a lot of sympathizers here. I know who some of them are. If you like I'll take you to them. Maybe they can help."

They reported the looting to Pyron, who sent a guard detail to put a stop to it. Then McIntyre led Jamie to a house that was unoccupied, or so it appeared; no one answered his knock. Albuquerque was largely silent and deserted on this fine Sunday afternoon, a fact that made Jamie dubious about the number of sympathizers they would find. McIntyre seemed unconcerned, and went on to another little adobe house next to a plot of corn stubble. This time he was answered by a Mexican woman who hid her face with her shawl and kept repeating "No tenemos nada. ¡Váyanse!"

"I'd better find the shopkeepers and see if they'll give us credit," Jamie said as they came away from the house.

"Hold on," McIntyre said. "Barela?"

A man walking toward them along the street responded with a wave and joined them. "Señor Lacey," he said, looking concerned. "You did not leave with the Federales?"

"I've—joined the Confederates now," McIntyre said. "This is Captain Russell. Manuel Barela."

"¿Cómo está?" the native said, nodding.

"We're looking for someone who will sell us supplies on credit," McIntyre told him.

Barela's eyebrows went up. "I can do better than that," he said. "When the Federales set the warehouse on fire, we saved many things. It is all in a barn, and I will show it to you."

Jamie's heart leapt. "Thank you, señor! I don't know how I can repay you—"

Barela frowned, then pulled aside his sarape and raised his cotton blouse to show them an ugly scar at the back of his waist. "The Federales wanted me to join the militia. When I told them I could not leave my farm, they stabbed me with a bayonet. Chase them out of the country and that is reward enough."

Jamie shivered, the sight of the scar taking him back to the battlefield at Valverde. "We'll do our best," he said.

The three of them walked down narrow tracks between farms until they came to a ramshackle adobe barn. "Here, señor," Barela said, opening the door.

Jamie stepped inside and for a minute he just stared, feeling ready to cry. The barn was stacked to the roof with piles of blankets, molasses, vinegar, candles, soap, and other supplies, enough to relieve the army's immediate distress.

"Thank you! Gracias," he said, shaking Barela's hand. "I'll get some wagons."

Barela nodded. "I will wait here."

When they got back to the plaza, Jamie hurried to Pyron's tent to tell him the news, and found Phillips was there ahead of him.

"Cubero," Phillips was saying. "About sixty miles west. Kavanaugh tricked them into surrendering. The depot is stuffed with food and blankets and medicine. All I need is twenty wagons and a company of cavalry."

"Well, Russell," Pyron said, "there you go. Seems you owe Captain Phillips and his scouts a debt of gratitude."

Jamie met Phillips's self-satisfied gaze and bristled. "I'm afraid the wagons won't be available until tomorrow," he said. "I need them to retrieve some goods here in Albuquerque. The natives saved quite a few supplies from the depot. It's all in a barn not two miles away." Jamie glanced at Phillips and was pleased to see that his smug smile had vanished. He expected Phillips would make him regret it later, but he was too annoyed with the chief Brigand to care.

Pyron's brows went up. "Well, that's good news. Take as many men as you need to bring it in." His shrewd gaze passed from Jamie to Phillips. "You may have your cavalry, John. I'll send a detail to hold Cubero until the wagons are free. Good day, gentlemen." He turned to the papers that had already accumulated on his desk.

As they walked away from the tent Phillips said, "I might've known you'd be ungrateful."

"Not at all," Jamie replied. "I'm very grateful. We need every bit of supply we can find."

"You didn't see fit to say that in front of the major," Phillips answered.

"And you didn't see fit to tell me about Cubero," Jamie said. He stopped and faced the older man, hoping he sounded calm. "I don't want trouble with you, Captain Phillips. There are more important matters for us both to attend to, so let me just remind you whose payroll you're on."

Phillips's mouth curled in a sneer. With a scathing glance at McIntyre, he turned and left. Jamie realized he'd been holding his breath, and let it out in a sigh. "I'm sorry," he said. "I should have done that when you weren't around."

"Doesn't matter," McIntyre said. "We never got along much."

Jamie glanced at him. "How long have you known him?"

"A year or so. He used to be a clerk at the Exchange. . . ."

Jamie saw McIntyre's face go pale, and wondered what the trouble was. "I owe you," he said, wanting to dispel it. "Let me get the stores moved and I'll buy you a drink."

"I'll help," McIntyre said.

With the aid of a detail from Pyron's battalion and a few extra wagons that Barela had borrowed from friendly citizens, they got everything moved by sundown. Flour was issued to Pyron's grateful men for the first time in nearly a week, and a detail set off escorting a small train of supplies back toward the army. As a conciliatory gesture

Jamie offered Phillips the rest of the wagons for a night march to Cubero, but Phillips had already turned his Brigands loose on the town, and they were raising hell before the sun had set.

Having done a solid day's work, Jamie concluded to follow their example if not their extremes, and he and McIntyre set off with Barela to the home of Judge Baird, some eight miles south of town. The night was mild, no wind and a cover of soft gray clouds overhead. The judge's house was brightly lit, windows glowing in the blue night. A small fire flickered and popped near the stables where several Mexicans stood chatting. Barela spoke to them while Jamie and McIntyre stabled their horses.

They went into the house and were engulfed in a sea of music and laughter. Candlelight set the whitewashed walls glowing, and the sides of the room were packed with men waiting for their chance with the ladies. Barela was snapped up by a plump, dark-eyed dama who spoke into his ear as she dragged him onto the dance floor. Jamie took a glass of wine, McIntyre whiskey, and they stood against the wall watching the dancing. It occurred to Jamie that he had not associated with any ladies since the army had left Fort Bliss, and he amused himself by comparing the beauty of the damas, deciding which of them he'd like to dance with. He settled on a handsome señora who cast a sly glance at him as she danced past. Her partner disapproved, but since at the end of the dance all the women were surrounded by swarms of men, Jamie was in little danger of creating further jealousy. He was not happy, however, to notice Phillips making his way through the crowd toward them.

"Why ain't you dancing, Romeo?" Phillips asked McIntyre. "Pining for your Yankee Juliet?"

Jamie glanced at McIntyre, who stared silently at Phillips.

Phillips smiled slyly. "I bet she won't kiss you now!"

Sensing response from McIntyre, Jamie laid a hand on his arm. McIntyre turned furious eyes on him, then subsided and moved away. Jamie was left facing Phillips, who looked him up and down, then crossed the room to where some of his Brigands were gathered.

Jamie joined McIntyre at the whiskey keg. "I could use some air," he said. "Care to come outside?"

McIntyre gave him a sullen look, then nodded and refilled his glass before leaving the table. Outside, with music drifting after them and the gray canopy overhead, they walked to the low adobe wall surrounding the house and sat with their backs against it. Jamie watched McIntyre take a long pull at the whiskey, then offered him a packet of tobacco and trimmed corn husks from his coat pocket. McIntyre took it, rolled two cigarrillos, and held one out to Jamie.

"I don't care for it," Jamie said. "I keep it to give to the merchants. Go ahead."

McIntyre lit up and leaned his head against the adobe, blowing smoke toward the stars. "Thank you," he said, "for keeping me from wasting my breath with that fool."

Jamie smiled to himself in the darkness. "How'd you like to transfer to the Q.M.D.?" he asked. "I could use you."

"I thought I already worked for you."

"As an employee," Jamie said. "If I swear you in, Phillips won't have any authority over you."

McIntyre paused. "Let me think about it."

"Fine." Jamie drew up his knees and laced his fingers together around them. "Who's Juliet?" he asked softly.

McIntyre sighed. "A girl—a lady—I was courting in Santa Fé." The tip of the cigarrillo glowed hot as he drew hard on it. "Phillips was right. She'll have nothing to do with me now."

Jamie heard the ache in McIntyre's voice, and wondered if he'd ever have to go through that particular hell. He'd never found time for being in love yet, and from what he'd seen it do to his friends, he wasn't sure he minded.

"I'm sorry," he said. "Do you wish you hadn't changed sides?"

"I wish there weren't any sides," McIntyre said.

"You could've just resigned."

"I want to serve my country," McIntyre laughed and the smell of tobacco drifted to Jamie's nose. "I'm just not sure which one it is."

Jamie could see only the silhouette of McIntyre's face, pale against the adobe. "Well, you can't really go back."

"No."

A sensation came over Jamie of suddenly realizing he stood at a cliff's edge and was about to tumble off. What were they doing in this strange country, outnumbered, isolated, vulnerable? Fighting for a dream that had seemed real enough when San Antonio's plaza rang with Colonel Reily's impassioned words, but that paled to a shadow against the realities of harsh country and battle. He shivered, wishing for home more strongly than he yet had. McIntyre's hand came to rest on his arm, comforting him until he saw the other hand slowly carry the cigarrillo to the ground and snuff it. Jamie strained eyes and ears, and caught the sound of a too-familiar voice.

"Phillips," McIntyre whispered.

"They came out here," Phillips was saying. "Check if their horses are gone."

Jamie's heart was suddenly thundering. McIntyre's hand gave his arm a brief squeeze, then let go. A moment later Jamie heard the small click of a pistol being cocked. He stared toward Phillips's voice and made out four men standing in the yard, shadows against the bright windows of the judge's house. Two more figures joined them. Three to one.

Moving with painful slowness, Jamie drew his own revolver. His hands were trembling and he was suddenly in a nightmare sweat. The pistol he held became a bayonet-tipped rifle, and beside him Martin sat propped against a scrub bush. He shook his head to clear it of phantoms. The navy pistol was cold and heavy in his hands, and Phillips was speaking again.

"Then they're still here somewhere. Spread out."

The shadows of the Brigands formed a skirmish line that

began a slow, steady advance toward the wall. Jamie swallowed, knowing he should take aim at the nearest one. He couldn't raise his arm, though. In fact, he realized with horror, he couldn't move at all.

19

You can imagine better than I can describe what I felt on seeing all our troops, and that banner under whose shadow I was raised, leave. . . . The terror which I felt is inexpressible.

    —Mother Magdalen Hayden, Convent of Loretto, Santa Fé

Hoofbeats thudded outside the wall. McIntyre could feel them through the earth as he waited, pistol ready, for Phillips to attack. One horse, slowing to a trot, then a walk.

"Captain! How do," a familiar voice called, and McIntyre felt a spark of hope. The sound of the rider dismounting, soft chink of spur and the slap of leather. A figure came into view leading the horse by the reins. As he moved past a glowing window, McIntyre glimpsed his face and sighed with relief. It was Hall.

"Heard this was the best shindig around," Hall said.

Now was their chance. McIntyre put up his gun and nudged Russell to his feet, then walked forward with calculated ease. "Joe!" he said. "Glad you're back!"

Hall turned to shake hands, and McIntyre risked a glance at Phillips. The Brigands' captain was frowning but there was nothing he could do. Safe for now.

"Good to see you enjoying yourself," Hall said. "Shaking off the sulks at last?"

McIntyre forced himself to smile. "Working on it."

"Well, you'll like this. I just came in from Santa Fé, and the latest there is that my old regiment's coming to town."

McIntyre frowned. "Dodd's company? I thought they were still at Craig."

"I said regiment, my friend, not company." Hall grinned. "None other than the Pet Lambs themselves!"

"Gilpin's Volunteers?"

Hall nodded. "The same. Word is they're three thousand strong, but if that's so, old Gilpin must have found some way to pay them."

"And that," one of the Brigands said, "means—"

"Plunder a-plenty, me boys!"

A gun fired and McIntyre flinched. More pistols went off as the Brigands cheered, then headed into Judge Baird's house to spread the news. Hall gave McIntyre a wink and a clap on the back, then wrapped an arm around Phillips's shoulders and walked away chatting low in his ear. McIntyre glanced over his shoulder and saw Russell standing behind him, pistol held in a limp hand and his face pale.

"Here, put that away," McIntyre said, taking the gun and replacing it in Russell's holster. "You all right?"

Russell turned bewildered eyes to him. "I couldn't do it."

"You need a drink." McIntyre reached for his arm. "Come on."

"No," said Russell, stepping back. Standing in the light from the open doorway, he looked sane enough, if a little spooked. "Let's go back now," he said. "While they're busy."

McIntyre glanced toward the fandango. There was nothing he needed there, he decided. Nothing he couldn't get elsewhere anyway. With a nod he followed Russell to the stables.

"I don't want to see him," Laura said.

"Very understandable," Mrs. Canby said, "but he insists it's important and says he is leaving town. Shouldn't you at least say good-bye?"

Laura frowned at the fireplace. Mrs. Canby was the soul of generosity. It would be mean indeed to accept her kindness and withhold the same from her uncle, so Laura got up and accompanied Juan Carlos to the door. Her uncle waited in the zaguán, a cold wind blowing the skirts of his coat about his knees.

"Laura! At last! Come with me at once."

"No," she said. "I—"

"My dear, you must!" Uncle Wallace said in a voice more determined and more sober than Laura could remember. "The governor's evacuating the city!"

"I had not heard that," Laura replied. "Only that he is moving the government to Las Vegas."

"It amounts to the same thing! Everyone's leaving. Have you looked at the plaza?"

Laura walked with him down the passage to the street and saw wagons parked every which way, frantic people loading them with goods from the shops or baggage and furniture from homes. Down the street a neighbor was digging a hole in the churchyard, presumably to bury a box that sat nearby. A long file of wagons from Fort Marcy Post was moving slowly down the Santa Fé Trail. As Laura watched, the flagpole in the plaza crashed to the ground, cut down by soldiers.

"Why did they do that?"

"To keep the Rebels from raising their colors," her uncle said. "Sibley's army is marching for Santa Fé. There's no time to lose! Fetch your trunk!"

Laura felt a stirring of alarm at the frenzy in the streets but was reluctant to place herself in her uncle's keeping again.

"Has there been another battle?" she asked.

"Eh? No. Canby's still in Fort Craig. He let the Texans just march past to Albuquerque, and now they're headed here."

"That is unjust," Laura said, quick to defend her friend. "If the colonel let them pass the fort, he must have a reason."

"Reason or no, they'll be on us tomorrow, now go and pack your things! Connelly's got a hotel in Las Vegas, and he said he'd put us up."

"That's kind of him." Still Laura hesitated. She had

wanted for some time to leave Santa Fé, but the thought gave her little pleasure. "What about Mrs. Canby?"

"Damnation, child!" her uncle cried. "I cannot stand talking all day! Mrs. Canby is a capable lady, I'm sure she can take care of herself!"

Laura glanced back at the Canby's house, uncertain what to do, but there was no time to think it through. She must choose. She turned to him. "Will you send me to Boston?"

"What?" said her uncle. "Rubbish. Your home's here."

"If you will send me on to Boston, I'll come," Laura said. "Otherwise I wish you good fortune."

Uncle Wallace stared at her, his eyebrows drawn up like a crooked arch. "Laura! I'm trying to help you, child," he said in astonishment. "Have I not done as much as I could for you?"

Laura refrained from commenting on the quality of his past care. "Send me home," she said, pinning her uncle with her gaze, "and you need never be troubled with me again."

Uncle Wallace frowned, and blinked, and looked genuinely puzzled. "Well, I'll see what I can do in Las Vegas."

Laura nodded, as much to herself as to him, and promised to be ready to leave in ten minutes' time. She watched him cross the plaza back to the Exchange, then went in to tell Mrs Canby of her decision.

"Home to Boston," Mrs. Canby said, nodding. "I understand. Let me come help you pack."

"Shouldn't you leave, too?" Laura asked. "The post is being evacuated. Won't the Texans take the town?"

"They won't trouble me," Mrs. Canby said. "These Spanish houses are built for defense, you know. Not that it should come to that."

"You are brave!"

Mrs. Canby smiled and hugged Laura. "We'll miss you."

By the time they had packed Laura's few belongings in the small trunk she'd brought from Boston, her uncle was waiting at the gate beside a private carriage. Juan Carlos gave the trunk to her uncle, and Laura turned to Mrs. Canby.

"Thank you for all your kindness," she said. "You've kept me from going quite mad."

The older woman smiled. "If my own daughter had lived," she said, "I'd like to think she'd have been like you."

Laura felt tears starting. She caught her breath and hugged Mrs. Canby tightly.

"Come along!" Uncle Wallace urged.

"Write to me," Mrs. Canby said, squeezing Laura's shoulders.

"I will," said Laura. "And. . . ." She paused, not wanting to mention Lieutenant McIntyre in her uncle's presence.

Mrs. Canby nodded. "I'll send you news when I can."

Laura yielded at last to her uncle's impatience and got into the carriage. "Good-bye," she called, waving from the window. She sat facing backward at the end of the velvet-covered bench and stared out of the window at the blue Sangre de Cristos topped with snow. She had become fond of them, she realized with surprise, as she had of the people she'd met, and even of the mud walls of Santa Fé. She tried to remember what Las Vegas was like, but her memories of the outward trip were dim and jumbled with a general sense of misery. She slipped a hand into her cloak pocket and ran her fingers over the frame of her father's portrait. Time had softened the wrench of his loss, though some small, jealous part of her wanted to mourn him forever. There was something she had not yet grieved over as much as was needed.

As the carriage splashed through the Río de Santa Fé, Laura gazed back at the town which, except for the stream of wagons, had lost the appearance of activity and become again a lazy Spanish village, smoke curling from chimneys and beehive bread ovens. The hills finally blocked her view and she sighed, settling against the cushions while the carriage trundled toward La Glorieta Pass.

When they reached Cañoncito, Laura leaned forward to look at Armijo's hill, where she had climbed with her three

lieutenants in the summer. How long ago that day seemed!
She missed them more sharply than she had expected.

By the time the carriage had crawled over the summit, it
was well past noon and everyone inside was glad to stop at
Pigeon's Ranch. The house was swarming with refugees,
Vallé and Carmen waiting on them as fast as they could.
Laura sat at the corner of a table near a fireplace, sipping
coffee and nibbling at a fresh tortilla. She smiled as Vallé
came up to her.

"Bonjour, Monsieur Pigeon," she said.

"Bonjour, ma petite colombe," he replied, eyes crin-
kling. "You would like some stew?"

"No, thank you. We're not stopping long."

"Ah. Your uncle is treating you better now?"

Laura could only shrug. "I'm hoping to go home."

Vallé nodded. "This is a hard place for you."

Laura was piqued that Vallé seemed to think her
defeated by the frontier's hardships, but she knew it was
kindly meant. She drew a few pennies from her pocket.
"For the coffee," she said.

"No, no, ma chère. Your uncle has already paid me."

"Monsieur Vallé, I know you to be an honest man,"
Laura said sternly. "Do not disillusion me."

"I would not take your money, Miss Howland," he said,
closing her fingers over the coins and patting her hand. He
smiled, but his brow creased a little as he gazed down at
her. "You are welcome here. Any time you like."

A burst of Spanish from across the room kept Laura
from answering. Carmen was beckoning to Vallé. "Ya
voy," he called, and with an apologetic smile hurried away.

Laura finished her coffee, then stepped out to the portal,
where she was struck again by the mad scramble outside.
Yet even now, with the trail choked with civilians fleeing
the Texans, Laura could feel the valley's peace enfolding
her. Glorieta was a little oasis where thoughts could be
sorted and weighed. She gazed at the gray cottonwoods
and felt lonelier than ever. Boston, she thought, trying to
cheer herself. Boston waited at the end of a long journey,

with friends to fill the emptiness and old familiar places to wander. To whom would she go first?

The question paralyzed her. What friend was so close she would take up an indigent orphan who would have to find some menial work to maintain herself? Society was a balanced thing, based on understandings of common ground, and Laura's ground had shifted. She was no longer the daughter of a respected speaker but merely another poor woman of no particular accomplishment. She would be relegated to the class of governesses and milliner's assistants, expected to smile pleasantly, work hard, and keep quiet. This struck her as singularly unfair, but to whom could she assign blame? Not those she had once called her friends. They had their own survival to see to. In fact, she realized, she had never before had as close a friend as Mrs. Canby, save for her father.

That was not the home she wanted to return to. A hollow ache came into her chest and she stood staring at the stone well across the trail. If not home, then what? She almost wished she could stay here, in Glorieta, and be lost from time forever. Her gaze traveled up the tree trunks to the bare branches above. One dry leaf clung to a twig, and as she watched a breeze carried it away.

"Laura! Where have you been, child? Everyone's waiting to go on," Uncle Wallace said, hurrying toward her.

"I was looking for you," she answered, and noticed her hands were trembling. She folded them together.

"Come along, come!"

He hurried her off to the waiting carriage. Laura got in, and as the carriage began to move she saw Vallé come out of the house. She leaned out the window in a most unladylike fashion and called to him. He saw her and raised a hand in farewell, and stood waving at the coach until the trail curved around an outcrop of rock and Pigeon's Ranch was hidden from Laura's view.

Snow and more snow. Everyone's mood was foul, from the lowest infantryman right up to Colonel Slough, whose carriage had bogged down and taken the better part of an hour for the men to dig free. O'Brien paced along the haphazard row of tents Company I was pitching beside Dry Creek. The light was failing and the tents had to be up before parade.

A horseman went by, his mount blowing and kicking up snow as it jogged along the path worn by the feet of the Pet Lambs. O'Brien frowned after him, then spotted Franklin wading toward him at the head of the firewood detail. Franklin's arms were full of wood and he huffed ice as he came up to O'Brien.

"Where shall we stack it, sir?" he asked. He looked all too cheerful, cheeks reddened by cold and exercise.

"You're not supposed to carry it," O'Brien said. "You're an officer."

"I like my comfort," Franklin said, grinning. "The more wood, the bigger the fire. Here?" He moved to a space the men had cleared in front of O'Brien's tent.

O'Brien nodded, and Franklin and the detail dumped their wood in a pile. The lieutenant squinted at the parting sun. "Time for one more load," he said. "Come on, boys—"

"No," O'Brien said. "Dress parade."

"In this?" Franklin laughed, gesturing to the snow.

"Slough's orders." O'Brien turned and went into his tent, not because he wanted anything there. Franklin's good spirits irked him. It was the snow, he decided, and sat down on his bedroll to watch the light coming through the white canvas fade to blue-gray. Then assembly sounded, and reflecting with pity on the poor bugler's lips, O'Brien hauled himself up and went out to join his company.

The sun had set, leaving the camp in a blue glow of twilight. O'Brien stood at attention in knee-deep snow and waited, thinking of a fire and a hot meal.

Colonel Slough came to stand before his men with a piece of paper in his hands. "I have just received this message from Lieutenant-Colonel Tappan at Bent's Old Fort," he said, and read: " 'Captain Garrison from Fort Union met us today with word of an engagement fought near Fort Craig on the 21st ultimo, at which Colonel Canby's forces were defeated by the Texan army.' "

The colonel paused, and O'Brien heard someone behind him inhale sharply. He stared hard at Slough, straining to absorb every word.

" 'The Texans are now marching victoriously up the Río Grande, having cut off all communications between Colonel Canby and the forces above. Santa Fé is taken. Fort Union will share its fate, and all its vast military stores will fall into the hands of the enemy, unless we reach there in time to prevent it. I am marching to meet you at the Purgatoire above Raton, but if you do not find me there, for God's sake, you must hurry on. Fort Union's only hope is in your timely arrival.' "

The colonel's hand fell to his side. Silence followed, with the creak of snow under shifting feet.

"Men of Colorado," Slough said, his thin voice ringing clear in the winter air, "are you willing to endure the fatigues of forced marches in order to save the honor and prosperity of the republic?"

"Yes," O'Brien shouted, and heard Franklin's voice mirroring his. A roar of agreement rose from the regiment.

"Major Chivington," the colonel said, "we will strike camp at once. Dismissed." Slough turned and strode to his carriage.

O'Brien turned to look at Franklin, whose eyes gleamed back in triumph. War awaited them, casting all pettier conflicts into insignificance. Their common enemy was assigned—they had only to vanquish him and reap rewards. Franklin nodded as if he understood O'Brien's thoughts, and led the men off shouting orders. The camp, which had hardly been pitched an hour, was struck again, tents packed into wagons along with the men's gear. Haversacks were filled with hardtack, there being no time to cook anything. Gnawing at a dry biscuit, O'Brien ordered his company to mount their tired horses and led them into place at the front of the column, then began the long ride into night.

The Exchange Hotel in Las Vegas stood on the plaza like its namesake in Santa Fé but was otherwise nothing like the old fonda. It was a two-story affair built of stone and wood, the ground floor being taken up with offices, dining room, and saloon, and the upper divided into boxlike rooms by partitions scarcely thicker than heavy paper. Laura was given one of these to herself, for which she was sure she ought to be grateful. Whole families of refugees were packed into similar rooms, and many more stood in the lobby pleading with the harassed clerks for shelter that was not to be had at any price. Some talked of taking rooms in the houses of the natives despite smallpox raging in the town. The overall mood was of desperation, quiet or blatant.

Laura sat on the mattress in her little cell, trapped like a stray fly in a honeycomb of angry buzzing bees. She was hungry and cold; there was no fire in her room, and she didn't dare step out of it to seek food. She hugged her knees and thought of Boston and Santa Fé, Santa Fé and Boston. Neither was her home anymore.

She reached for her trunk and took out her brushes— wooden ones from Seligman's, bought to replace those her uncle had stolen—then undid her hair. Starting with the ends, she eased out the tangles, working her way up until the tresses shone smooth and the brush scratched deliciously at her scalp. Sighing, she put it down and draped her hair around her shoulders. What would Lieutenant McIntyre think of her thus? she wondered. He would be captivated, of course. Laughing at herself, she gathered up her hair, twisted it back into decorum, and began to pin it up again.

"Laura?" her uncle's voice came from beyond the curtain that served as her door.

"Yes," said Laura. "Come in."

The curtain was pushed aside and Uncle Wallace

stepped in. "Ah, good, you've already tidied up. Governor Connelly has invited us to join him for dinner."

"How kind!" Laura got to her feet and smoothed her skirts. "Should I change?"

"No, no. Come along, they're already sitting down."

Laura secured her trunk and went out with her uncle, down the stairs past travelers sitting on their baggage and into a private parlor behind the office. It was handsomely furnished, and the stuffed chairs beside the glowing hearth looked inviting, but her uncle passed through to a dining room where Governor Connelly sat at the head of a crowded table. The governor, deep in conversation with an officer on his left, glanced up as Laura entered and beckoned to her.

"Welcome, welcome!" Dr. Connelly said, getting to his feet. "Miss Howland, everyone, and this is Mr. Wallace Howland. You know Major Donaldson? Do sit down."

The major bowed to Laura, and he and the other gentlemen took their seats again as Laura and her uncle squeezed into two chairs that occupied the space of one at the corner of the table. Not wanting to crowd the governor, Laura kept her elbows close to her sides and took cautious bites of her meal. Hot roasted duck glazed in marmalade with potatoes and onions soon cured the chill, and a glass of red wine soothed her spirits. Connelly and Donaldson talked of government matters—the major was the district quartermaster, Laura remembered—while her uncle flirted with the matron on his right, leaving Laura to dwell on her own thoughts until the governor turned to her with apologies.

"I'm a wretched host tonight," he said.

"Not at all, it's kind of you to accommodate us," Laura replied. "I'm not a very sparkling guest, for that matter."

"Poor girl," he said. "You must be worn out with all this uproar."

Laura smiled. "Not quite worn out."

The lady beside her uncle leaned forward. "I think it's *terrifying*," she said, her jet necklace dangling over her plate. "What if the Texans follow us here?"

"Then we shall retreat again, Mrs. Keeler," Dr. Connelly replied. "I feel no disposition to be taken prisoner, do you?"

The woman sat back, silenced.

"Will they follow us?" Laura asked.

"They want Fort Union," the governor told her. He glanced around the table at his guests, who had fallen silent, and put on a confident smile. "But don't fear. There's a regiment of Colorado men marching to our aid. With their help Colonel Canby can give the Rebels their own again, and glad I'll be to see it. I was never sadder than after the battle at Valverde."

"You were at the battle, weren't you, Governor?" Mrs. Keeler asked. "Tell us about it!"

Dr. Connelly exchanged a glance with Major Donaldson, then gave in to the inevitable. There was nothing new in his story. So many versions of the battle had circulated that Laura almost felt she had seen it herself. She had certainly heard more gruesome accounts; the governor edited his sketch for his company.

"It was all the Mexicans' fault," Mrs. Keeler declared. "They spoiled it all by running away!"

"Madam, that is partly true, but they were not alone. Major Donaldson here and Colonel Canby begged the Regulars to support McRae. Lord proved himself a true coward, eh, James?"

Donaldson's face had become stony. "Captain Lord refused to obey my order on the grounds that I was not in uniform," he said. "You may draw your own conclusion."

"I should not be surprised if he were court-martialed," Dr. Connelly said. "Major Duncan behaved badly, too. But enough of this." The governor rose. "I'm sorry to leave you, but I must attend to business. Please stay and make yourselves at home." He and Donaldson made their way toward the door.

Laura got up and followed them into the parlor, where she touched Dr. Connelly's arm. He turned to her, eyebrows rising. "Yes, Miss Howland?"

"I wondered," she said, feeling herself begin to blush, "if you had seen Lieutenant McIntyre after the battle?"

Dr. Connelly looked troubled. He glanced at Major Donaldson, then led Laura to one of the chairs by the fire. "Please sit down, Miss Howland. You haven't heard news of Mr. McIntyre?"

Such gentle treatment boded ill. Laura sat straight in the armchair and watched Dr. Connelly's face. "Only that he was in the battle," she said as calmly as she could. "Has he been wounded?"

The governor shook his head with a rueful smile. "It's not as easy as that. I'm sorry to tell you he has resigned his commission."

Laura blinked, frowning. Dr. Connelly took her hand and patted it, like a father soothing a child over a broken toy. "He sent a letter to Canby from the Texans' camp the day after the battle," he said. "I assume he's joined Sibley's army."

Tears brimmed in Laura's eyes. She swallowed and shook her head in disbelief.

"I am sorry, Miss Howland. Would you like a brandy?"

"No. Thank you, Governor," she said. "Thank you for telling me. I mustn't keep you from your business."

Dr. Connelly's eyes searched her face. "Are you all right?"

"Quite all right, thank you." To prove it Laura squeezed his hand and smiled. He smiled back, then left with Major Donaldson, telling her to call on his clerks if she needed anything, anything at all.

Laura slumped in the chair and tried to sort her feelings. Why, since she'd more or less given up on Lieutenant McIntyre, did his desertion hurt her so? She stared into the flickering fire, remembering all his little deeds of the past months and trying to find among them something that would cause him to forswear his oath to the Union. He was from Tennessee. It was all she could think of, and it was not enough, in her view, to justify his action.

She was no longer in danger of crying. In fact, she began

to be angry, and realized it was because she had trusted him to an extent, and nearly promised to trust him entirely, and now she felt a fool for doing so. Lucky, she thought, eyes hardening as she stared at the fire. Lucky to escape so easily. Then the tears returned, and since she was alone she let them come, indulging in the rare luxury of self-pity.

O'Brien's back ached and his legs were sore from hours in the saddle, but he knew he was fortunate compared to those on foot. Four days of hard marching had brought the Pet Lambs to the Raton Pass. Tappan's men had joined the column at the Purgatoire and the reunited regiment had attacked the snowy mountain in good spirits, but long marches on hardtack and water were taking their toll and the lads were beginning to grumble.

By midday the column had reached the summit of the pass, where it paused to let the horses graze on what they could find beneath the snow. O'Brien, Denning, Shaunessy, and Morris wandered over to where Captain Downing sat with his lieutenants. He was a lawyer, sharp-eyed and quick, but much friendlier than some of the commanders, and O'Brien liked him.

"Pretty spot," Downing said, welcoming them with a nod.

"Aye." O'Brien glanced around at the scenery: deep chasms, the snow-crusted Spanish Peaks to the northwest, and restless seas of cloud black with snow. As he peered up at them he saw a trio of eagles circling overhead. Others had seen them as well, and a murmur rose among the men.

"Think you can hit one, Red?" Morris asked. "I could fetch your rifle."

O'Brien stayed him with a gesture, shaking his head. "It's a sign," he said.

"Let's shoot 'em!" a soldier from D Company shouted.

"No," Captain Downing answered, standing up before his men. "These are the birds of liberty, and they betoken victory to us!" He smiled at O'Brien. "Let's give 'em three cheers instead!"

The men responded with cheers that rattled among the

peaks like thunder. With spirits much improved, they took up the march down the far side of the pass.

The hills closed in around them, blocking the views. The road was bad and repeatedly crossed a twisting brook that would, they were told, eventually lead them to the Red River. O'Brien began to wonder if he'd be better off on foot, his horse's every step jolting his spine as the animal picked its way down the steep, rocky path.

A scout came thundering back to the column. "There's an ambulance coming," he shouted, and Chivington called a halt.

O'Brien sighed and wondered if getting down to stretch his legs would be worth the pain of mounting up again. He glanced at Franklin, who was leaning forward in his saddle to stroke the neck of his big bay, murmuring to it as if it were a child. A sharp pang of envy struck O'Brien, for the beast had proven itself sound indeed. Ah, for such a mount. He looked down at his own poor nag, which was not doing well. Yes, he might walk for a while, he decided.

The ambulance appeared with its escort, sides lashed tight against the cold. Muffled voices came from within. The column moved aside to let it pass on the narrow track, but it halted when Colonel Slough, splendidly uniformed with a blue cloak flowing from his shoulders, came out of his coach and strode forward to speak with the driver.

"Where are you from?" he asked.

"Fort Union," said the driver.

"What's the word there?" Slough said.

"Ah, it's bad, sir. The Texans are bound to take it. There'll be no stopping them."

"Are they near the fort?"

"I heard two days ago they were in Santa Fé," the driver stated. "Probably in Las Vegas by now."

Colonel Slough looked both grim and a little pale. "Thank you. Drive on."

The driver flicked his whip over the heads of his mules. They pulled at the traces, and the ambulance started to creep up the mountain again. Slough went over to Chivington, who got off his saddle mule to talk with him. O'Brien eyed the mule, an animal never so flashy as Franklin's bay or even Chivington's big grays, but sure-footed, with stamina, and able to give a better ride than a horse on steep mountain trails.

Slough returned to his coach. Chivington summoned O'Brien and the other mounted commanders and, when they had gathered, said, "The colonel wants to make Union tonight."

The captains exchanged a glance. "It's still eighty miles or more," Logan exclaimed. "We'd have to grow wings!"

"Grow them, then," Chivington said. "The colonel insists we won't stop till we reach the fort."

"Easy for him," O'Brien said. "He's got a fine carriage to ride in."

"Have a care, Captain," Chivington said frowning. He wheeled his mule and trotted uphill toward the infantry.

Tired as they were, the men responded to Slough's call for more speed. O'Brien took the rest of the descent on foot, and soon they marched out of the canyon onto a plain bright with sunshine that glowed on the short yellow grass. Only scraps of snow here. To the west the mountains were an intense blue, and the pines scattered at their feet sharply green. By three o'clock the regiment had reached the Red River, where they halted to fill canteens with icy water and swallow more hardtack. After an hour's rest Slough ordered them to stockpile all their gear but their weapons, haversacks, and two blankets each. A corporal's guard was left with the rest, and the emptied wagons were packed fresh with soldiers, some groaning from blistered feet, some even fainting. Three or four hundred remained on foot, O'Brien included.

"Let's have a song, lads," he said. "McGuire?"

The fiddler took out his bow and struck up as the march resumed. The Avery Trolls took up the tune, defiantly cheerful.

"Proudly the note of the trumpet is sounding,
Loudly the war cries arise on the gale—"

O'Brien sang along for as long as it lasted, but by twilight the music and cheers had given way to grumbling and curses. By dark there was only the tramp of boots on hard ground, the animals' labored breathing, and the rattle of wagons. For hours they marched into dead night. Every now and then a man would fall out, to be picked up and stuffed in a wagon. O'Brien's boots had scraped his heels raw, and every step was a misery. Despite this sacrifice, his horse fared badly, and he wished they'd cross a stream where he could water it. His canteen, too, was almost dry. He put that thought away from him, knowing to dwell on it would only make him thirsty.

Trotting hooves came forward along the column, and the words "Company, halt!" began to ring in the brittle night air. Shoup came up with O'Brien, saying "Wait here a bit. One of the draft mules has fallen."

"Fallen?" O'Brien said. "On this flat?"

"Fallen dead," Shoup said, and rode on.

O'Brien halted his company and ordered them to dismount. He sat down to take the weight off his feet, and watched his lads hobble around hissing. From the looks of it, the mounted men were no more comfortable than he. He saw Franklin a bit apart from the company, leaning against his horse. The boy looked drawn. Not suited for such a march, but he hadn't complained, not a word. Stubborn, that's what he was. Like a mule.

The dead animal having been replaced, the Pet Lambs marched on. It was bad. No one talked. A man needed all of his energy just to stay in his tracks. In less than an hour three more beasts had dropped to the ground, and Chivington, after a few heated words with Slough, called for a halt.

The men built fires of willow brush and wrapped themselves in their blankets, cursing and muttering. O'Brien threw himself down by a fire but was unable to sleep. The endless clop of hooves drumming in his head warred with the throb of his feet, and the cold bit right through his two blankets. As he lay shivering and muttering oaths to himself, a crackling sound followed by a flare of light made him look up. Franklin was kneeling nearby, piling brush on the fire. O'Brien watched him, grateful for the warmth that began to seep into his front, though his back was still freezing despite the blankets.

"Thank you," O'Brien muttered through the covers.

Franklin glanced his way and gave him a small smile, then curled up in his cloak and lay staring at the flames. O'Brien watched the firelight flickering from the lad's eyes as he dropped into troubled sleep.

Laura woke to the sound of a woman's voice. "Señorita," came the whisper. "Señorita Howland."

Laura sat up and lit her candle. "Who is it?" she said.

"Perdón, señorita," the woman said, sticking her head through the curtain. Laura recognized her—a native who worked in the hotel as a servingmaid. "Your uncle, he want you."

Laura sighed. "What for? Is he drunk?"

The maid gave a helpless shrug. "Your uncle," she said.

"All right. Sí," Laura said.

The maid bobbed her head and withdrew it from the curtain. Laura got up and began to dress. Undoubtedly her uncle was drunk. He had spent most of his time that way since they'd arrived in Las Vegas. She knew from experience that it was easier to obey his summons than to ignore it, for he was quite capable of sending for her again and again until she came and answered whatever foolish question had seized his mind.

She smoothed her hair with her brush and drew aside the curtain, finding the maid waiting outside. It was very late. Neither music nor voices issued from the saloon, and the hotel had subsided to the restless nighttime shifting of too many bodies in too little space. Laura followed the girl to Dr. Connelly's private parlor, where several men sat around a card table covered with the wreckage of a long night's gaming. Uncle Wallace lounged in a chair, his cheeks flushed with drink. Dr. Connelly, though he looked a bit bleary, went to the trouble of rising at her entrance, and the other three—men she knew only as her uncle's drinking partners—merely stared at her rudely. Laura gave Dr. Connelly a curtsey, then turned a cold look of inquiry on her uncle.

"Well, you've taken your time, haven't you, miss?" he said.

"The maid said you wanted me," Laura replied.

"You shouldn't always believe what you hear from servants, my dear." He turned to his fellow gamblers and waved his hand in Laura's direction. "There she is, gentlemen."

"Mighty pretty," said one, stroking his chin.

"Mighty fine indeed," another said.

Dr. Connelly drew himself up in his chair. "All right, Howland, the joke's gone far enough—"

"I am a man of my word, Governor," Uncle Wallace said in a voice that was lofty, if a bit slurred. "Well, gentlemen? What am I offered?"

A sinking horror overcame Laura as she realized he was referring to her. The men exchanged speculative glances.

"Two hundred," one said.

"Oh, come now! I'll pay the preacher," her uncle replied.

"Preacher?" Another laughed. "Four hundred, if you leave the preacher out of it."

Dr. Connelly stood up, though he had to grip the table's edge for balance. "Howland—"

"Don't call him by that name!" Laura said with a scathing glance at her uncle. "He doesn't deserve it!"

Indignation freed her from paralysis, and she strode from the room, glad of her anger, for without it the mortification of the scene just enacted might have killed her. She ran up the stairs and commenced pulling her dresses from the pegs on the flimsy walls and flinging them into her trunk. The blue silk she held in her hands for a moment, then threw in disgust to the floor. She put on her cloak and her shabby black bonnet, checked that her father's picture and her little knife were still in her pocket, and seized the trunk's worn leather handle. It was light enough for her to carry, since it contained only clothing and the few necessities she had purchased since her uncle's theft of her valuables. The memory spurred her anger, and she strode into the hall and down the stairs, determined not to spend another minute under the same roof with him.

Angry voices argued from the parlor. She slipped past to the hotel's front door, and quietly went out.

Cold and still, the plaza was an empty hollow. With her back against the Exchange's door, Laura stared into the darkness. Where could she go? There was nowhere. Fool, she thought. A familiar helplessness rose inside her, but Laura refused—quite irrationally, she knew—to yield to it. Better to freeze in a ditch than submit any longer to her uncle's abuses. Taking a deep breath, she stepped into the plaza.

The town seemed abandoned, mud houses huddled together against the cold. Laura crossed the plaza and walked along a narrow street, searching for a window or door that betrayed a scrap of light, hoping to find asylum with other travelers in the home of one of the natives. As she got farther from the plaza, she began to notice other sounds. At first she thought them the echoes of her own footsteps, but they were too many and too scattered. Dogs, perhaps? A hopeful thought, but soon crushed by the mutter of a low voice. Laura clenched her teeth and hurried on, now certain she was being followed.

The trunk banged against her leg as Laura strained to recognize the voices behind her. If it had been her uncle and his cronies, he would have called out to her by now. She thought of confronting the strangers, or of knocking on the nearest door, but before she could do either the steps caught up and a man blocked her path. She couldn't see his face in the dark, nor those of the two others. She took a step backward.

"What you got in the box, missy?"

Laura was silent, glancing around for a way to escape. One of the shadows reached for her trunk. "Don't!" she cried, pulling away. Her hand crept into her pocket and she thought fleeting words of prayer as her fingers brushed her father's portrait.

"Easy now, we ain't going to hurt you," the leader said. His comrade grabbed at the trunk again, and Laura's hand darted out to greet his with the blade of her hard-clenched knife. She felt it catch in flesh.

"¡Ai! ¡Puta!"

"Get her!" the leader said, and she ran.

The alley was narrow and uneven. Her boots slipped and she thought for a heart-stopping moment she would fall, but she caught her balance against a house, bruising the heel of her hand rather than dropping the knife. Her hoops bounced as she ran and her trunk thumped against the walls, slowing her. She heard the men running and shouting behind her, and a part of her mind that was absurdly calm marveled that no one came out of the houses to investigate the noise. As she rounded a corner the trunk smacked a wall hard and was wrenched from her hand. She abandoned it, running lighter and faster, scurrying toward another turn. Glancing back, she saw shadows huddled where she'd dropped the trunk; her pursuers had stopped to investigate it. She skittered around the corner, anxious to get out of their sight, and was brought up short by a blank wall some ten feet ahead.

Trapped. Her breath came in short sobs. She heard a crack as the rogues broke the lock of her bag. There was nothing in it to keep them long, she knew. Moving toward the wall, she peered at it, hoping to spy a door. Instead she found a narrow passage leading off to her left, just wide enough for one person. She tilted her hoops and squeezed into it, praying her pursuers wouldn't notice, then leaned against the wall and tried to catch her breath. Angry voices reached her and she froze.

Can't stay here. Laura squinted toward the far end of the passage. Was it lighter beyond, or did she just wish so? She began to move forward as quietly as she could, hoops held with one hand and the other brushing the wall, ears straining for signs of pursuit. She was sure now she saw light, a soft glow on the corner of the wall. She paused again to listen and heard nothing. No—a scraping, a rustling sound. She flattened herself against the wall and tried to make her breathing silent. Glancing back she saw only the dim street, a half shade brighter than the passage. Turning her eyes again to the splash of light ahead, a glimpse of movement made her jump. Too small for a man. A low shadow snuffled around the corridor's end, some small creature looking for food. It stopped and raised its dark head as if peering at her. She let out a shaky sigh, and the animal moved on, displaying a flash of white tail. A skunk.

Laura let a minute pass before moving ahead again. She stopped just short of the passage's end, hovering in the darkness. No voices now; all was quiet. Edging her head forward into the light, she saw that it came from a high, narrow window in a building across the street from her hiding place. The building was taller and longer than a house, with a room protruding from the side. A church? Yes, there was the wooden cross atop a short tower at the end, like the crosses of the parroquia in Santa Fé. Sanctuary.

Emerging cautiously from the passage, she glanced around but saw no pursuers. She squared her shoulders and crossed the street, forcing herself to walk—not run—to the church door. With a low creak it swung inward at her push, and Laura gave silent thanks as she stepped inside and closed it again.

Candles glowed on the rough altar and in nichos along the walls, and the pungent smell of incense came to her. The bare earthen floor was hard and empty save for the kneeling forms of two old women at the front of the church. Before them a plain pine coffin rested across two barrels. Laura was suddenly conscious of the bloody knife in her hand. She wiped the blade on her cloak and put it back in her pocket. She felt she would be safer away from the door but did not want to disturb the mourners, so she moved toward the corner to her left, and quietly sat on the floor.

It was Sunday, she realized. Or had been. It was Monday morning by now. She'd become so jaded as to forget the

Sabbath. She was inclined to blame her uncle, but knew the burden was hers. No person or place, be they ever so savage, could ruin a true heart; witness Mrs. Canby, who had endured years among rough folk.

The altar with its candles would keep back the night. A Spanish church was as much a haven as any. At the end, Laura reflected, they are all houses of God. She pulled her cold hands from her pockets, folded them together, and began to pray.

20

O'Brien came slowly awake, robbed of sleep by the cold.
He opened his eyes and saw Franklin lying beside the dead
fire with his cloak pulled up around his ears, looking
absurdly young. O'Brien watched him for a bit, then sat up
and poked at the ashes with a stick, searching for a live
coal. There were none. His legs and feet ached, and he
wanted to sleep for a week.

A bugle pierced the freezing air. Franklin started at the
sound and looked up. O'Brien threw off his blankets and
got up as fast as his frozen joints would allow, hobbled
away from the camp to relieve himself, then began to rouse
his company. A hard biscuit for breakfast and they were
back in the saddle, ready to march. O'Brien looked carefully at his horse and decided it looked rested enough to
bear him. Besides, his feet were so raw he doubted he
could keep up with the column.

Slough's coach rumbled forward, and the men marked
its passing with muttered curses. O'Brien kept silent
though he agreed with them. The regiment crawled to life,
and as the sky lightened a sharp, cold wind rose to cut right
through clothing, coats, and blankets. Men and animals
alike bent their faces away as they marched into its bitter
flail. The wind increased to a demon's howl, worse than
any O'Brien remembered even in Avery. At dawn Chivington's grays fell dead in their tracks. An hour later his sad-

dle mule dropped. More and more animals fell, and as they did the ranks of the footweary swelled. O'Brien glanced back at his men and saw the same dull expression on every face. Even Franklin's smile had given way to a grim hollowness. Knowing there was naught he could do to relieve their suffering, O'Brien turned away again to face the gray miles ahead.

Santa Fé was a ghost town compared to when McIntyre had left it: silent, huddled against the mountains awaiting inevitable storm. As they crested the hill above town, the Brigands broke into whooping cheers and kicked up a gallop. McIntyre held his mount to a trot and watched the bedlam begin. He'd seen the same thing in a number of small towns where Phillips had led his men "foraging." The pillage had sickened him and he'd reported it to Russell, but the quartermaster seemed paralyzed, or maybe was preoccupied in finding water and wood for the army. Russell was afraid of Phillips, and with good cause, McIntyre thought. He watched the Brigands' captain rein in at the plaza and dismount, entering the Exchange with a pistol in either hand.

"Miss Howland. Dear God," McIntyre whispered. He spurred his mount so savagely it shrieked and tried to buck him off, but he wrenched its head around and set it tearing for the plaza. He jumped off, letting the horse go where it would, and barged into the hotel after Phillips, hurrying toward the placita that faced Miss Howland's room. Seeing Phillips in the open doorway, he drew his own pistol and cocked it. Phillips looked up at the sound.

"Too late, Romeo," he said. "Your Juliet's gone."

White rage filled McIntyre at the image of Juliet dead on her couch, but reason replied with cold fact—he had not heard Phillips fire. He strode forward to look for himself and almost laughed with relief at the sight of the empty room.

"Too bad," Phillips said. "I enjoyed my last visit to this little bower. How about you?"

McIntyre spun around and nearly yielded to the impulse to throttle Phillips. Not worth being tried for murder, he told himself. He stared at the ex-clerk and backed away, pistol aimed at his gut. Soon, McIntyre decided. He would find a way to rid the world of the vermin soon, and without suffering for it himself. He reached the office door and slipped through. Phillips's laughter followed him out of the hotel.

Two of the Brigands were smashing the window of Seligman's. All the plaza shops were being looted; the post office door lay swinging on one hinge. McIntyre saw his horse lapping at a puddle in the street. He caught its reins and on a slim hope crossed the plaza and headed down the street toward the Canby's quarters. His knock was answered by Juan Carlos's voice, high-pitched and shrill, telling him to "Vete o te pego con un tiro."

"It's Lacey McIntyre," he shouted through the gate. "I'm looking for Miss Howland."

Silence. He knocked again. "Juan Carlos, soy yo, Lacey McIntyre." He kept pounding until the big gate opened and Juan beckoned him in. McIntyre led his horse inside and shut the gate after him. In the dimness of the zaguán he made out a feminine form and his heart leapt, but the voice that greeted him was Mrs. Canby's.

"Lieutenant McIntyre," she said. "How did you get past the Rebels?"

McIntyre closed his eyes briefly. "Is Miss Howland here?" he asked.

"No," Mrs. Canby told him. "She left several days ago with her uncle." She laid a hand on his arm. "Do you have news from Fort Craig?"

A thumping commenced on the gate door. "Hey, Mac, you in there?" Hall shouted.

"Go away," McIntyre replied.

"That's not friendly, is it?" Hall said. "If you've found something good, you should share!"

McIntyre waved Mrs. Canby away from the door and opened it, pistol in hand. Hall and two others stood outside, already laden with plunder. "There's nothing here," McIntyre said, waving at the manservant. "Just some Mexicans and a chicken or two."

"Let's have a feast, then," Hall said, raising a jug. "We've got the wine!"

"Another time," said McIntyre, holding Hall's gaze. "Consuelo's is good. It's just down the street, other side of the plaza."

Hall's eyes narrowed while his grin widened. "All right, brother," he said. "But you owe me one."

McIntyre nodded and watched Hall lead his cohorts away, then helped Juan Carlos bar the door and leaned against it. His eyes were adjusting to the shadow. As Mrs. Canby stepped toward him again he saw a deep sadness in her face. "I won't trouble you," he said. "I'll stay here and keep them off."

"Nonsense," Mrs. Canby said gently. "Come in and have some coffee. You look as if you've been riding all day."

McIntyre sighed. "You're a saint, Mrs. Canby. I don't deserve it."

"Hush," she said. "You may tell me all about it in the parlor."

The Colorado Volunteers marched on, west into the teeth of the wind, skirting the mountains. Flurries of snow blew into their faces, small hard flakes that stung. They crossed several streams, headwaters of the Cimarron, and O'Brien had to drag his mount's head up to keep it from drinking too much of the frigid water. After a time they began to see cattle, a sure sign of civilization. With spirits a bit higher, they came to a larger stream where a ranch and a mill house were found. O'Brien took heart at the sight of the mill. Maybe they would get some flour.

Chivington called a halt. Colonel Slough, it seemed, had determined to allow the major to handle the regiment as he was accustomed to doing, for he stepped down from his coach and disappeared into the house with the rancher and Lieutenant-Colonel Tappan. As soon as they halted

O'Brien got off his horse, which immediately began to cough. He waited, hoping the beast wouldn't collapse. Other horses and some of the draft animals also showed the effects of the strenuous march; several fell, never to rise again.

"Can't keep driving them this way," O'Brien said, his voice cracked raw from the wind.

"Do you think it's much farther?" Franklin asked. He stood clinging to his stirrup to keep his shaking legs from buckling.

O'Brien shrugged. "Don't even know where we are."

Franklin grinned. "Maxwell's Ranch," he said.

"Now how in sweet Jesus' name did you learn that?" O'Brien exclaimed. "I swear, you're the Devil incarnate!"

Franklin laughed. "I had it from one of the cowherds. That fellow that went in with Slough was Lucien Maxwell himself. Owns the largest ranch in New Mexico Territory."

O'Brien glanced at the cattle covering all the hills in sight, and could well believe it. "Think he'd miss one or two cows?" he said wistfully.

In the late afternoon the regiment moved ten miles south to the Reyado, another ranch owned by Maxwell and built, so Franklin claimed, with the help of Frémont's former scout, Kit Carson. This was a Mexican place, with high mud walls round a scatter of houses in a square. Maxwell gave meat, coffee, and sugar to the regiment and let them camp inside the Reyado's walls for the night. There was room for several companies in the ranch houses, and the rest sheltered as best they could in the lee of the walls. Company I built fires on one side of the square and sat roasting bits of beef on the ends of sticks.

"Bugger this wind," Shaunessy said, wiping smoke-tears from his face.

"Bugger all of it," Morris agreed. "I wish I'd stayed back in Avery."

"In Avery you wouldn't even have a scrap of beef," Shaunessy said.

"In Denver City, then."

"In Denver City you'd be in the jailhouse by now."

"Oh, in Hell then, if you like."

O'Brien pulled his stick back from the fire to inspect the meat. Still raw, with a layer of ash for seasoning. He sighed and put it back, holding it lower in the flames.

Franklin came up and plumped a small sack on the ground. "Flour," he said proudly, taking his knife to the seam.

"Maxwell gave us flour, too?" Shaunessy said. "He is a rare gentleman."

Franklin shook his head. "I bought it. Enough for the company." He turned to call over his shoulder. "Denning! Where's that water?"

"We've nothing to mix it in," O'Brien said.

"Mouth of the sack," Franklin answered. He suited action to words, taking off his gloves. The hands beneath were slim and graceful, and he plunged them into the flour, mixing a double-handful with some of the water brought by Denning and kneading it into dough. At Franklin's bidding Denning added a pinch from a box of salt he had bought along with the flour.

O'Brien checked his meat again and found it was starting to sizzle. "Here, let it drip on this a little," Franklin said.

The hot grease improved the dough, which Franklin twined around a stick and gave to Shaunessy to bake. Denning had passed the word to the company and lads began gathering to collect their share of the flour, some with plates or bowls borrowed from the ranch. Franklin, his hands powdered white, beamed at them as he portioned it out.

"The company fund will repay you," O'Brien told him.

"Oh, no need," Franklin said with a quick smile.

"You shouldn't be feeding us," said O'Brien. The words came out sharpened by weariness, and he was sorry at once, for Franklin's smile faded.

"Yes, sir," the lieutenant said, offended. "If you insist." He finished distributing flour and picked up the near-empty sack. O'Brien watched him go away with Denning, to a fire at the far end of the row.

Shaunessy pulled the first twist of bread back from the fire and divided it. "That was a mite ungrateful, Alastar," he said softly, handing a piece to O'Brien.

"I didn't mean it like that," O'Brien said. He had actually meant to be kind, which surprised him as much as it probably would have surprised Franklin.

The smell of hot bread made his mouth water. He bit into it and closed his eyes in bliss. All other thoughts ended as he spent the next minutes enjoying his first hot meal in days. Bread and beef had never tasted so good. Franklin had made dough for each man at the fire; it was smoke-cured, but good, and by sharing it around they all had their fill. O'Brien licked the crumbs off his hands and sat back with a sigh.

"Well, all I've got to say is, God bless old Chas," Morris said. He pulled out some coffee from his haversack and looked about for something to grind it with.

O'Brien noticed something lying by the fire and reached for it. Franklin's gloves. He turned them over in his hands, plain cavalry gloves, a bit cleaner than most. A wry smile came over his face. A gentleman must have his gloves, after all. He got up and strolled past the row of fires to where Franklin and Denning were sitting. Franklin was gnawing at a tough bit of beef, but looked up as O'Brien stopped before him and held up the gloves. Franklin gaped and reached to his belt as if it was his sidearm he'd lost, then turned wary eyes to O'Brien. An odd reaction, O'Brien thought. Instead of handing over the gloves as he'd planned, he summoned Franklin with a jerk of his head and walked a little way apart from the others.

"Why is it you're so fond of gloves?" he asked.

"What a question!" Franklin exclaimed. "Why are you fond of your boots, Captain?"

O'Brien frowned. "Show us your hands."

A flash of something—fear, perhaps—went through Franklin's eyes before he lowered them. The lieutenant brushed at the flour on his cuffs, then held out his hands. They were roughened a bit but still neat like a gentleman's should be, the nails well kept and short.

"Over," O'Brien said, and Franklin obeyed, showing soft palms. O'Brien could see nothing wrong with them, saving that they were small. He glanced up at Franklin's face. "How old are you?" he demanded.

Franklin hesitated. "Nineteen," he said.

"You don't look it,"

"I'm older than I look."

O'Brien stared at him, dissatisfied.

Franklin stood his gaze for a moment, then glanced away. "Why do you hate me?" he said. His voice was so soft O'Brien scarcely heard, but the words were like a smack in the face.

"I never said I hate you."

"You don't have to say it," Franklin said. He gave a strangled laugh and shook his head. "Never mind."

"No." O'Brien reached out to grip his shoulder, and the lad's flinch made him frown. "I've been hard on you," he heard himself say, and stopped, words stuck in his throat. The eyes that met his took him back to Colton's, where Franklin had ignored unforgivable cause for a fight. *I didn't know him then,* O'Brien thought fleetingly. *Don't know him now.* Feeling awkward and hardly knowing why, he said, "I'm sorry."

Franklin's eyes widened, then he gave a crooked smile. Embarrassed, O'Brien stepped back and held out the gloves. Franklin took them. "Thank you."

"Get some rest," was all O'Brien could think to say.

Franklin nodded. "Thank you, Captain," he said in stronger tones. O'Brien could feel the dark eyes watching him all the way back to his fire.

"Alguien está aquí para verle, señorita."

Laura looked up from the woman whose brow she was sponging with wine to find Padre Martinez standing above her. She smiled up at his kind, crinkled face. The padre had been very generous to her since he had found her asleep in the church that morning. Instead of dragging her back to the hotel—which she had half feared he would—he had fed her a breakfast of eggs and tortillas, refused to take any money for it, and given her a room that she suspected was his own, in a small building next to the church. He spoke no English, nor she much Spanish, but they managed to communicate rather well, she thought. She had spent most of the day helping him care for smallpox victims in a nearby house that was being used as a hospital. There was little she could offer them but comfort; still, comfort was a blessing, and the eyes of her patients thanked her.

"Ven conmigo, por favor," the padre said, beckoning to her.

Laura put her sponge in the basin, wiped her hands on a cloth, and got to her feet. The padre led her to the kitchen, where a fire was burning and a man stood with his back to the doorway, gazing at the little prints of saints decorating the walls. He turned as they approached, and Laura stopped.

"Dr. Connelly!"

"Miss Howland," the governor said, coming toward her. "Thank God! I hoped it was you. Gracias, Padre."

The padre nodded and stood watching. Dr. Connelly reached for her arm but she slipped away and went to the fire. She was embarrassed at her foolhardy flight, but determined not to return to her uncle. "How did you know I was here?" she asked.

"We've been searching the town for you, ever since your portmanteau was found this morning. When we caught some ladrónes with your clothing we feared the worst."

"Thank you for your concern, but as you see I am quite safe," Laura said.

"My dear," Uncle Wallace said, coming into the room from a side door, "you must never do such a thing again! Think of what you might have suffered!"

Bitter anger filled Laura's chest. "Worse than being auctioned like chattel?"

He blinked several times in a baffled way. "Chattel?"

"You don't even remember, do you?" Laura said. She stared at the creature who called himself her uncle, marveling that she could ever have trusted him.

Uncle Wallace rubbed at his brow. "Never mind that now, my dear," he said vaguely. "You must come with me."

"I shall not go with you, ever again," Laura replied.

"But, Laura—"

"And I have nothing more to say to you."

"Don't say anything, just listen!" her uncle said. "The mails have stopped running. I've got seats for us in a wagon going to Kansas, but you must come at once."

"No," Laura said.

"It's our last chance," he said, grabbing her wrist. "The Texans will be here soon!"

Laura turned a furious gaze on him, and he released her.

"I'll take my chances," she said coldly.

Uncle Wallace's brows snapped into a frown. "Very well, if you choose to be wanton! You cannot say I didn't try to take care of you—"

"Get out," Laura said. His astonished expression pleased her. "Out," she repeated, and reached for a broom that stood in the corner. He made no further protest, but hastily retreated. Laura turned to confront Dr. Connelly, who stood, hat in hand, looking rather remorseful.

"May I offer—" he began.

"No, Doctor. Thank you, I prefer to remain here. Padre Martinez has been very kind."

"You should not be here among the sick," he said.

"I was vaccinated in Boston," Laura said. "My father was very progressive. He was not at all like my uncle."

Connelly smiled wistfully. "I think I would have liked to know your father."

Laura's throat tightened suddenly and she could not respond.

"Miss Howland," he continued, "I cannot tell you how deeply I regret what happened last night—"

"You were not to blame," she told him, though her feelings didn't completely agree.

"Still, I am sorry. . . ."

"Good-bye, Doctor."

He looked at her with a sad smile and glanced at the padre. "Ven a verme si ella necesita algo."

"De acuerdo," the padre said.

Laura watched Connelly follow her uncle away, knowing that a part of her life had just ended. Where her future lay she had no idea, but she was determined to spend it among honest people.

Up at first light again, O'Brien felt slightly less weary. The wind had died down during the night, and a few hours' sleep had much improved the regiment's mood. They had to gobble down their cold beef and coffee, for Colonel Slough had decided to assert his authority again, insisting on a final push to Fort Union. "Only thirty more miles," Chivington said. "That's nothing to you, my brave bullies."

"Nothing but another layer of blisters," Shaunessy muttered, but his tone was less acrid than it might have been. The Pet Lambs were hot for a fight, and there'd been no more news from Fort Union.

They started out at a good pace, but the ground rose steadily, and before long men and beasts began to lag. The men on foot were lost to sight before sunrise. The wagons straggled out in an ever-lengthening line, while the mounted companies' horses nearly dragged their heads on the ground. Slough's coach outdistanced them several times, to be found waiting beside the trail. As soon as they saw it, it would start off again before the regiment's dust engulfed it.

Round midmorning they began to meet refugees heading north, some driving stock, some with laden wagons that the Pet Lambs eyed hungrily. They could give no news save that the Texans had not reached Fort Union by that morning. Their mood, which bordered on the hysterical, caused Slough to order the regiment to march faster.

At the crossing of the Ocate the regiment halted for water. O'Brien took out a cracker and chewed on it while his horse drank. Without warning, the nag collapsed in the stream.

"Tanam an Dhiel!" O'Brien splashed into the icy water and swore as he fished out the reins. He managed to hold the nag's head above water while some of his lads tried to drag it to shore. Franklin and Morris waded in to lend a hand, and Morris bent to the animal's throat. "No use," he said. "It's dead."

"Hell and the devil," O'Brien swore. He reached down to untie his rifle and blankets, all soaked. They got the saddle free with some effort, and the bridle, and left the dead nag in the stream. O'Brien piled his sodden belongings on the bank and stood shivering beside them, staring at the corpse. Behind him the bugle called the column back to order.

"Here, sir," Franklin said, bringing him a dry blanket.

O'Brien took it gratefully. "Damn the bloody nag to hell," he said. "Why couldn't it wait ten more miles?"

"Take Duke, sir," Franklin said.

"Don't be an idiot," O'Brien snapped, then to soften it, "I'll not take your horse, Lieutenant."

"Ride with me, then," Franklin said. "He'll carry us both."

O'Brien glanced at him, and at the bay waiting quietly. The horse had stood the march well, it was true. "For a while, then," he said.

Franklin smiled and led the bay forward. O'Brien picked up his saddlebags and emptied them of soggy hardtack and cartridges, then stuffed his wet blankets into them as far as they would go and gave the mess to Franklin to strap to the saddle. He dried his rifle as best he could and tied it beneath Franklin's other blanket, and sent Morris off to put his saddle in one of the wagons.

"Go ahead," Franklin said, offering him the reins. "I'll ride behind."

"No, lad," O'Brien said. "It's your horse."

Franklin shrugged and mounted, offering the stirrup to O'Brien. With a grunt he hauled himself up. The bay was a world better than his poor, dead pony. He could feel the animal's strength in the muscles beneath his legs. He arranged the blanket to cover his wet clothes as much as possible and pronounced himself ready to ride. They rejoined the column, and O'Brien gave silent thanks the wind had not returned. He was cold, but Franklin's back warmed him.

The day dragged endlessly. Weak sun filtered through thin clouds, growing orange as it neared the mountains. One or two more horses failed, though their pace was so slow that most managed to keep on. O'Brien began to feel dizzy and put a hand behind him to steady himself. Sweet Mary, don't let the Rebels have the fort, he thought. He pictured the straggling column, exhausted and starving, facing a battle line of well-equipped Texans, and him with no ammunition. No, he thought angrily, and shook his head to get rid of the vision.

"Are you cold, sir?" Franklin glanced over his shoulder. "You could have my coat."

"I'd be splitting your wee coat in two, lad," O'Brien replied. "No, I'm not cold. Just tired."

"We haven't seen the colonel's coach lately."

"Likely he's gone ahead to have supper with the Texans."

"They're more likely to have him for supper," Franklin said.

"Ah, but he'd give them a bellyache, same as he gives us."

Franklin's shoulders began to shake and he gave a gurgle of laughter. O'Brien laughed, too, and being weary they fed each other's hilarity until the tears ran down their cheeks.

"Captain's having too much fun over there," Shaunessy said.

"Think I'll get me a ride on a bay horse, too," Morris said.

"Oh, it's the horse, is it?"

O'Brien felt Franklin's back stiffen. "Never mind them," he said softly, then turned to call out to Shaunessy. "Shall I come ride with you, Egan? I'll do my best to entertain you."

"Oh, thank you kindly, sir, but my horse is afraid of brass. He'd shiver and shake us all the way to Union. See, even now he's a-trembling."

"Oh, it's the horse, is it?" said O'Brien.

Franklin choked on a laugh. Shaunessy's mount chose that moment to stumble, nearly pitching him off, to the delight of the rest of the company. A short outburst of cursing, then horse and rider settled back to the march.

A rumble ahead made O'Brien look up. The front of the column had picked up a gallop. Chivington and Tappan were racing toward the crest of the hill.

Franklin glanced back at him. "Sir?"

This is it. Mary befriend us, O'Brien thought, and nodded to Franklin, who gave a whistle. The bay pricked up its ears and in three strides went from walk to gallop. Ah, what a horse!

Clinging to Franklin's shoulder with one hand and waving them forward with the other, O'Brien looked back at his company. "Come on!" he yelled, and they charged toward the hilltop.

21

To Col. G. R. Paul, Fort Union, N. Mex., Sir: I am instructed by Colonel Slough to acknowledge the receipt of your communication of this date, and to state in reply that the instructions of Colonel Canby are not only to protect Fort Union, but also to harass the enemy. . . . Thinking that the command assigned by you can be spared for the purpose named, the colonel commanding cannot consent to leave any portion behind.

—Gurden Chapin, Acting Assistant Adjutant General

Chivington had pulled up atop the rise and the men gathered round him, horses blowing and sidling. Franklin edged the bay into the crowd. A mule kicked, causing a brief fracas, and the bay flattened its ears. O'Brien kept a hand on the saddle behind him. By craning his neck he could see they had topped a small valley that descended gently from where they stood. A glint of light marked a stream. Near the valley's far side was an earthen fortification, with buildings beyond: Fort Union. A flag waved above the earthworks, too distant to make out. Tappan was looking at it through a spyglass. He handed the glass to Chivington, who peered through, then said, "Thank you, Blessed Jesus. We're in time."

A cheer rose, an inarticulate cry of exultation that O'Brien joined full force. The bay jibbed and Franklin's hand went to its neck. Chivington dispatched a rider to pass the news back along the column, and as the sun dipped below the mountaintops with a final gleam of light they rode down to the valley. A pair of horsemen came out from the fort bringing greetings from its commander,

Colonel Paul, and confirmed there'd been no sign of the
Texans. The weary Pike's Peakers raised cheer after cheer.

It was falling dark by the time they reached the earthworks. The stream proved to be stagnant, but the horses
didn't mind. O'Brien walked around to stretch the cramps
out of his legs while they waited for the wagons and the
men on foot to come up. Once all were together, a column
was formed.

"Here, sir, you need a mount," Franklin said.

"No," O'Brien said. "You take them in, Franklin. I'll
come along with the infantry."

Franklin's eyes filled with pride. "Yes, sir," he said, and
snapped off a salute before remounting his horse. O'Brien
watched him call the company to order and fell in with
Captain Logan for the march, gritting his teeth at the
reawakening of his blisters.

"Good lad you've got there," Logan said.

"Aye." O'Brien nodded. "He's well enough."

Drums appeared as if by magic, pulled out of hiding
from the wagons' boxes or unlashed from their ribs. The
drummers set up a martial beat, and with proud colors flying the Colorado Volunteers marched into Fort Union.

Jamie lit a fresh candle from the sputtering flame of the old
one and stuck it on top of the dying wick. He had sent Rose
to bed hours ago, and since he was the only one left in the
depot—actually a storehouse belonging to a Unionist merchant who had fled Albuquerque—the rest of the building
was in darkness. He didn't have to work so late, but the
more tired he was when he went to bed the less likely he'd
dream.

McIntyre was gone to Santa Fé. Lieutenant Reily was in
Albuquerque, but his eagerness for more action didn't suit
Jamie's mood. Lane was with Scurry and the majority of
the army in the mountains to the east, recruiting their
strength where there was plenty of wood, grass, and water.
A Federal supply train bound for Fort Craig had been captured, adding to Jamie's hard-won stores and bringing the

unwelcome report in a St. Louis newspaper of Crittenden's defeat at Mill Spring. It was the first setback Sibley's army had heard of, and did nothing to improve their feelings of security. Jamie had scraped together all the stores he could find along the Río Grande, sending details as far as a hundred miles away to bring back supplies from ranches and trading posts. Though he had about three months' provision on hand it still seemed insufficient, and he, like his comrades, turned his hopes north toward Fort Union.

The door creaked open and Jamie looked up from his paperwork. The light from his candle didn't quite reach the doorway, and he tensed, thinking of Phillips. "Yes?" he said.

"Hello, Russell," Captain Owens said, strolling forward. "Haven't seen much of you lately."

"I've been busy," Jamie said, relieved.

Owens held out a folded paper. "From the general."

Jamie read the note, orders for a supply column to accompany Major Pyron to Santa Fé. He set it aside. "General Sibley's working late, too, I see."

Owens yawned and pulled up a chair, leaning his elbows on Jamie's desk. "Yes, but he didn't get up till noon."

Jamie looked at Owens, wondering what he wanted. They had not spoken much since Valverde. He pushed the memory of that day aside. "I don't have any whiskey," he said, venturing a guess. "It all goes to the surgeons."

"Dear boy, I know where to satisfy my needs," Owens said with a lazy smile. "But I don't think you do."

"I'm all right, thank you." Jamie picked up his pen.

"No, you're not," Owens said conversationally. He leaned his chin on his hands, eyes following the movement of Jamie's quill. "Never talked about it, did you?"

Jamie felt his hand begin to shake. He set down the pen and laced his fingers together over the papers. "I don't want to talk about it," he said with as much calm as he could command, "or think about it. I want to forget it."

"You won't," Owens said. "It'll be with you forever." He leaned back in his chair and folded his arms across his chest. "Shall I tell you about my first fight? It wasn't nearly so grand as Valverde, but it scared me well enough." He went on without waiting for an answer. "We were tracking Navajos—"

"I really—" Jamie began, but couldn't continue. He tried to swallow the feelings that were rising. Must not lose control.

"Son, you can't run away from it," Owens said. "You can't hide behind all these papers and boxes. You're a soldier, Russell. You did your duty and you survived—"

"Stop it, please," Jamie said.

"You survived that battle but you haven't left it behind you. You're still walking on that field—"

"No!" Jamie didn't remember standing up but he was on his feet, staring at Owens's face, ghoulish in the candlelight. He turned away, walking to a shelf full of carpenter's tools, and heard the scrape of Owens's chair and his bootsteps.

"Tell me," Owens said. Jamie felt the other man's hand on his shoulder and for a second wanted to cling to him, crying, like he had when Daniel and he had found their favorite hound caught in a wolf trap. Instead he brushed the hand away.

"All right," Owens said. "It's your choice. But I'll tell you, you won't get the better of this until you face it. That's how it was for me."

Jamie stayed frozen by the shelf, listening to Owens's steps recede and the sound of the door closing. Then he leaned his head on his arm and shuddered, dry sobs but no tears to relieve him. Presently he grew calmer and was able to return to the desk and tidy his papers. He picked up the candle with a hand that shook only a little, and walked between stacks of crates and shelves laden with clothing, blankets, soap, candles, commissary stores. He could almost imagine it was Webber's, only bigger. He reached the back of the storehouse where he'd set up a cot for himself and quietly got ready for bed. Martin's hat lay on a shelf, the silver star tarnished a little now. Martin's letter to

Emma and all of hers to him were in his coat pocket, along with the two gold coins. Martin's watch he'd been using so much he almost considered it his own, but now all these things whispered to him of the friend he'd lost, and he put out the candle to silence them, lying in the blackness thinking of ledgers until he slipped into exhausted sleep.

"What's your bet, Red?"

"I fold."

The cards weren't with him tonight. O'Brien leaned back with a sigh and stretched out his legs toward the fire.

If six days' hard marching had been enough to wear out the Pet Lambs, ten days of idleness had not only restored them but had driven them half crazed into the bargain. There had been some diversions: new uniforms and arms had been issued, the Regulars in the fort who had been at Valverde told a hundred different stories of the battle, and what remained unplundered of the baggage left at Red River had come down. The regiment's women came with it—soldier's wives and laundresses—and were greeted with heartfelt enthusiasm. O'Brien himself had been glad to see them, to his surprise. There were some ailments for which a woman's smile was the best of cures.

While he himself was content for now with a nod from Mrs. Denning, some of the lads had taken to amusing themselves at a nearby Sodom called Lomé. The place had a bad effect. O'Brien had worried that his men were shifting back into the sullen mood of their winter at Camp Weld, but that afternoon's orders to prepare for a march to Santa Fé had lightened their spirits. They'd already cooked three days' rations and commenced to celebrate. Swarms of them had gone to Lomé, others went only so far as the post sutler's cellar, which they raided for liquor, oysters, canned fruit, and other delicacies. O'Brien remained in camp, turning a blind eye to such activities, playing badly at poker with some of the other officers and looking forward to getting his lads back on the march.

Just after tattoo Franklin approached. "An express just

came in from Canby," he said, reaching his hands toward the fire.

"What's the word?" Captain Ford asked.

Franklin shrugged. "Don't know. Colonel Paul took them into his office the minute they arrived."

"Well, sit down then and lose some of your gilt," Captain Downing said.

Franklin glanced at O'Brien, who nodded and made room for him on his log. The lad wasn't so bad, really. A bit stiff-rumped, but he was improving.

"I think we may hear something from Colonel Paul this evening," Franklin said, pulling a handful of coins from his pocket and setting them on the makeshift table. "He was not pleased about Slough's marching orders."

"I wondered about that," Downing said. "I'd have expected them to come from Paul."

"Slough's commission predates his," Franklin said. "I heard it from the sutler. Colonel Paul is said to be greatly put out."

"Christ help us. We'll have our own war right here." O'Brien shook his head.

"Deal," Downing said, and passed him the deck.

O'Brien watched Franklin, not having seen the lad play at cards before. Franklin followed the bet in three hands, losing each time, then on the fourth he quietly displayed a flush and raked in a handsome pot.

"Why didn't you raise the bet?" Cook said indignantly.

"You were raising it for me," Franklin replied with a shrug.

O'Brien laughed. "He's awake, lads," he said, handing the cards over to Franklin, who hid a smile.

The adjutant walked up to the group, and the chatter came to a stop. Captain Chapin, sent to Fort Union by Canby himself, had been a great help in settling the Colorado men in, and had thus won their respect. "Colonel Canby has sent an order to wait for instructions before marching," Chapin said wearily. "The orders issued this afternoon are countermanded."

Someone muttered, "Hell."

"Sit down a spell, Captain," Logan said. "Brandy?"

"I shouldn't," Chapin said, but a smile spread on his face. He joined the circle, a flask was placed in his hands, he raised it to them in salute, then drank a good swig and sighed.

"Slough is giving you grief, is he?" Cook asked.

Chapin glanced at him sharply.

"You have our sympathy," Logan said. "None of us can stand the old peacock either."

Chapin laughed. "If I'd known I'd be caught between Slough and Paul, I'd have asked Colonel Canby to send someone else. They're not speaking. They are writing notes back and forth, which I have the joy of carrying."

"Who countermanded the marching orders?" O'Brien asked.

"Colonel Paul."

"Slough won't like it," Logan said.

"Colonel Canby's orders are explicit," Chapin said. " 'Do not move from Fort Union.' He wrote them before he knew of your arrival, but that doesn't cut much wood with Colonel Paul." He took a last pull of whiskey and stood. "Thank you. I'd better finish my rounds. Doubtless Colonel Slough is composing another love note for me to write to Paul."

O'Brien and the others wished him good night, and after a few more hands, broke up to pass the counterorders along to their units. Near half of Company I were still absent from camp, and O'Brien decided to seek them in Lomé.

"You haven't been down there yet. Care to join me?" he asked Franklin.

"If you don't mind, sir," Franklin said, looking uncomfortable, "I'd prefer not."

O'Brien gazed at him, then shrugged. "Suit yourself."

He went to the corral for the mustang he'd bought off a Mexican rancher. The beast was half wild, and though O'Brien had worked every day to break it he still had to coax it and curse it along. By the time he reached Lomé his arms were aching from hauling against the reins.

The village consisted of saloons and shanties, all filled with soldiers drinking, gambling, and whoring. O'Brien had first visited the town shortly after arriving at Fort Union, but the whores all looked pox-ridden to him, so he'd passed them by. It wasn't a whore that he wanted, he guessed, though a little pleasant company was always welcome. Some day, when he'd made his fortune, and if he was lucky, he'd find himself a wife.

He rounded up his men and told them they weren't marching after all, cuffed and cursed the ones who were too drunk, then headed back for the fort with a few of his company straggling behind. The rest he left to their fate.

"Ah, I hate drilling," Shaunessy said, walking beside the mustang. "When'll we get to a fight?"

When indeed? O'Brien thought, and slapped the reins against his horse's neck in impatience.

Jamie's breath rasped as he rode ahead of the train to a hilltop overlooking Santa Fé. With Cocoa galloping free beneath him and the wind in his ears it was almost like home, except that the wind was cold and his ears wound up frozen. The mare was his only connection with home now, and he enjoyed being on her so much that he'd decided to go forward with the train and get away from Albuquerque.

Sibley was preparing a move and had ordered the bulk of the army's supplies to advance. It had taken four days to move the sixty-odd miles to Santa Fé, and now they'd arrived Jamie didn't much like the place. It was pretty thoroughly a Mexican town, with not much relief from the mud but a half-finished government building with snowdrifts in its roofless corners. The natives watched with sullen eyes from behind cracked doors as the train rumbled into town. Jamie got his wagons into the grounds of the army post, then as the day faded he sought out Major Pyron. Headquarters was in the Spanish governor's palace—a huge affair, more than twice the size of San Antonio's—where he found Pyron poring through some old military papers.

"Ah, Russell. Welcome to Santa Fé." said Pyron. He was smoking a cigar, and offered the box to Jamie.

"No, thanks," Jamie said. "Sir, I don't like the looks of the natives."

"I don't much like them either, son."

"I mean with regard to our supplies. I think the train would be safer out of town."

Pyron exhaled blue smoke. "Out of sight, out of mind?"

"Yes, sir."

"Oh, stop all the 'sirs,' boy. Sit down."

Jamie took a chair and waited patiently while Pyron poured two glasses of whiskey. He thought it would be rude to refuse a second offering, so he took a sip from his glass, though he had not cared for whiskey since the night after Valverde.

"It so happens," Pyron said, "that I'm planning to move toward Fort Union. Haven't decided when, but it won't be long. There's a ranch just this side of the pass, owned by a fellow named Johnson. You can put your train there with a picket."

Jamie nodded. "Shall I start now?"

"What's your hurry? Wait for daylight. Phillips can show you where it is. He's putting up at the Exchange," Pyron said. Jamie stood, and the major's sharp gaze followed him as he picked up his hat and gloves from the desk.

"I want you and Phillips to get along, Captain."

"I've done all my duty," Jamie said quietly, and left.

It was now falling dark. Jamie stopped a man who pointed out the Exchange, and walked across the plaza to its open doorway. Inside were a number of soldiers lounging on broken and battered furniture that had once been fine. A dice game was being conducted in the hotel office. A voice hailed him and he looked up to find Hall, bottle in hand, leaning in a doorway.

"Howdy, Russell! How're your cows? Heard the Federals gobbled some of 'em."

"You all gobbled the rest," Jamie replied.

Hall laughed and gave him a cuff on the shoulder. "Play bluff? We've got a game going."

"I'll watch a while." Jamie followed Hall into the cantina. "Is McIntyre in town?"

"Right here," Hall said, leading him to a table in the back corner. Cards and money were thrown down as Hall passed the whiskey around. McIntyre shared a bench with a pretty Mexican girl whose blouse barely clung to her shoulders. The girl smiled up at Jamie, flirting her dark eyes in a way that left no doubt of her profession.

Jamie looked at McIntyre. "I hoped you'd be here."

"You look thinner," McIntyre said. He made room for Jamie on the bench, nudging the girl, who made a mock protest. "Sibley send you ahead?"

Jamie nodded. "I need to take the train to Johnson's Ranch. Can you lead me there tomorrow?"

"It's right on the trail, but I'd be glad to go with you."

"Thanks." Jamie watched the poker game for a while. Most were men he knew—Brigands—a couple with local girls in their laps. "Are there other hotels in town?" he asked McIntyre.

"One or two."

"Where are you staying?"

McIntyre shifted, and Jamie turned to look at him.

"With a friend," McIntyre said softly. "I'm helping keep an eye on her property."

Jamie glanced at the Mexican girl.

"No, no," McIntyre said, laughing. "An old friend."

A door opened and half a dozen guns were cocked and aimed at it. Jamie's mouth went dry. He stared at the door and the man standing in it with a tray in his hands.

"You ought to be more careful, Mr. Parker," came Phillips's voice from the outside. "You know the boys don't like surprises. Go on in now."

The man with the tray entered, his shirtsleeves rolled up to the elbow. He looked harassed, and no wonder, for Phillips followed him in, toying with a revolver. He set the tray down on the card table, and a dozen hands snatched at slices of ham. "Mighgy fine, Miffer Pargher," a Brigand said around a mouthful.

"Looks like we're going to need some more," Phillips said, picking up the last piece. "Go fetch it, will you, Parker?"

"There is no more," Parker said uneasily. "You've eaten it all."

"Oh, there's got to be another pig around here somewhere. Or has your family all left town?"

The Brigands roared at this sample of Phillips's wit. Jamie exchanged a glance with McIntyre.

"You've emptied my larder and I've yet to see a penny—"

Parker stopped, Phillips having placed his gun against his chest. "You watch yourself, Parker. I can have you arrested if you like, you God damn Union scum."

The room was still. Parker gazed defiantly at Phillips, but made no move nor a sound. Finally Phillips holstered his gun, then picked up the empty tray and tossed it to Parker. "Go and bring us something to eat now, there's a good feller. Remember to knock this time," he added as Parker retreated. Someone handed Phillips the whiskey and the card game resumed.

"I think I'll be going," Jamie said quietly as he stood up.

"What's the matter, sonny?" Phillips said, his attention caught by the movement. "Don't like our hospitality?"

McIntyre rose beside Jamie. "We're just stepping out for some air."

The Mexican girl, pouting, went over to Phillips and twined her arm around his. Distracted, he looked down at her and grinned. McIntyre nudged Jamie toward the door and they slipped out while the girl squealed and giggled.

Jamie sighed with relief as the door closed behind them. They were in a small garden, and he caught sight of Parker at its far end. Jamie stepped toward him. "Mr. Parker?"

Parker stopped in the doorway of a kitchen that bore signs of destruction, waiting with wary eyes.

"You're the proprietor here?" Jamie asked.

"Yes."

"I'm the quartermaster. If you'll draw up an account and direct it to my attention, I'll make sure you're paid what's due you."

Parker raised an eyebrow. "Oh, I'll be sure and do that," he said, turning away.

"Wait." Jamie took out Martin's two five-dollar pieces. "Take this," he said. "A down payment."

Parker hesitated, but Jamie saw the sudden sharpness of his eyes. He pressed the coins into Parker's hand. Parker turned them over, then glanced up with a look of real gratitude. "Thank you, Mr.—"

"Captain Russell," Jamie said. "Send me your bill and I'll try what I can do." He nodded farewell, then followed McIntyre through a door to the office and back outside.

"That was good of you," McIntyre said as they crossed the dark plaza. "It's true he's a Unionist, you know."

Jamie shrugged. "He's a civilian. I'm sure Phillips has had more than ten dollars' worth from him."

McIntyre laid a cautioning hand on his arm. Jamie followed his glance back the way they'd come, but saw nothing. McIntyre led him across the street and down a few doors to a small cantina, spoke briefly to the owner, and sat at a back table with a view of the door. The man brought two cups of wine to their table, for which McIntyre gave him a coin. He saluted Jamie with his cup and drank.

"They watch me sometimes," McIntyre said in a low voice. "I have an arrangement with Señor Lopez. See, there." He turned away from the door, and Jamie watched one of the Brigands amble in and buy a drink. "Got any of that tobacco?"

Jamie brought out his pouch, and McIntyre took elaborate care rolling a cigarrillo. He lit it and leaned back as if settling in for a long evening. With a grin on his face that didn't match the look in his eyes, he said, "Still there?"

Jamie nodded and picked up his wine. It was harsh, but he took a good swallow and then fiddled with the cup. McIntyre's voice was barely audible. "I don't want them to follow me home, you see. Hall knows where I am, but the others don't."

"Hall might've told Phillips," said Jamie.

"We have an understanding. How long are you in town?"

"Probably just tonight."

"Camping out in this weather? You're stronger than I," McIntyre said.

"I wouldn't be comfortable here. Got a tent and stove."

"Q.M.D. always gets the best of everything."

Jamie grimaced and took another mouthful of wine as an excuse to glance at the Brigand, who had finished his drink. Jamie lowered his gaze to the table, and noticed that McIntyre's hand was within easy reach of his pistol. "Leaving," he said softly, watching the Brigand walk to the door.

"Gone?"

Jamie nodded. McIntyre glanced around the room. He seemed satisfied, for he put down his cup and got up. Jamie followed him to the bar, where he gave another coin and the rest of his cigarrillo to the proprietor, then slipped behind the bar and motioned to Jamie to follow through a storeroom and a door. Emerging in darkness, Jamie gazed up at the stars, then a touch on his arm and he was following McIntyre toward the shadowy bulk of the mountains, behind buildings, along a ramshackle fence and across another street. McIntyre went up to a gate and knocked, one, one-two. In a moment a door in the gate opened, and they were stepping into deeper darkness. A shadow moved past Jamie and he flinched, but McIntyre led him into an entryway lit by a single candle, which revealed the shadow to be a Mexican servant. From there they went into a parlor where a fire glowed in its middle age, occasional yellow tongues emerging from the coals.

Before the fire sat a woman. For a stunned moment Jamie thought it was his mother, but then he saw that she was thinner and had darker hair. She was rolling a strip of cloth, and looked up as they came in.

"Ma'am," McIntyre said, stepping forward. "This is a

friend who's in town for the night. Would you mind terribly if he shared my room?"

"Of course not," the lady said, smiling. She set aside her bandage and stood up, taller than Momma too.

"This is James Russell," said McIntyre. "Russell, this is Mrs. Canby."

Jamie's mouth hung open for a full three seconds before he realized and shut it. Mrs. Canby gave a soft laugh. "Won't you sit down—is it Lieutenant?"

"Captain." Jamie sat on the edge of the sofa she indicated, feeling like he'd stepped sideways into some strange dream. He glanced at McIntyre, wondering if it was an elaborate trap, but it made no sense that the enemy commander's wife would want to trap him in an occupied town. Even if she did, he could not for the life of him imagine what use she could make of him.

"The ladies have just left me," Mrs. Canby said, moving a basket of bandage rolls from a chair and inviting McIntyre to sit. "Mrs. Williams asked me to thank you, Lacey. She has not been bothered again."

McIntyre nodded.

"Shall I make you some coffee? Maria has gone to bed."

"No, we're fine." McIntyre glanced at Jamie. "We won't keep you up."

"Have you eaten?" the lady asked, her eyes on Jamie. He lowered his gaze, realizing that he hadn't. He'd gone straight from the saddle to Pyron. "I thought you looked hungry," she said, getting up. "Wait here—no, Lacey, I'll just fetch what's at hand, now sit down. I won't be long."

Jamie watched her go, then resumed his seat and turned an accusing gaze on McIntyre, who grinned.

"She's the soul of generosity," McIntyre said.

"Now I know why you don't want Phillips to know where you are," Jamie said.

"Only because I don't want him harassing Mrs. C. She wouldn't hear of me staying at the Exchange."

"She's very forgiving," Jamie said, then regretted it, for McIntyre's face went grim. "I'm sorry."

McIntyre leaned forward, elbows on knees, hands clasped, staring into the fire. "She talked to me a long while about that. She is forgiving. And she made me see where my duty lies. I can still play an honorable part in all this, and I intend to." He looked up at Jamie, blue eyes sharp. "I'll take you up on that transfer, if you still want me."

Jamie nodded, wanting to ask exactly what part McIntyre thought he should play. "I'll write to the general tomorrow."

"Thank you." McIntyre smiled ruefully. "I'm not cut out for a Brigand."

Mrs. Canby returned with tortillas and two bowls of Mexican stew that was spicy and savory. They gobbled it down, listening to her chat politely about matters of little consequence. The more he listened, the more Jamie began to admire her. Here she was, entertaining two of the enemy in her parlor, and perfectly calm and cheerful about the whole thing. It made some kind of sense, he decided. After all, she was both a civilian and a lady of prominence.

When he'd finished the stew he mopped at the bowl with a tortilla, and Mrs. Canby favored him with a smile.

"Where are you from, Captain?" she asked.

"San Antonio," said Jamie.

"I've heard that's a pretty town. It has a good deal of Spanish influence, does it not?"

"Yes, ma'am."

"So perhaps Santa Fé does not seem so strange to you. Would you like some more stew?"

"Oh, no thank you, ma'am," Jamie replied. "That was first rate."

Mrs. Canby smiled. "It's a good custom, keeping a stew on the hearth."

"We should turn in," McIntyre said. "Russell has to pitch a camp tomorrow."

Mrs. Canby turned to Jamie, one delicate eyebrow rising slightly. "A winter camp?" she said after a moment. "My sympathies. If you are ever in town again, please come to me. I'd be happy to put you up."

Jamie exchanged a glance with McIntyre. "Thank you, ma'am, but I wouldn't want to trouble you."

"It's no trouble. I would much rather house an officer—a quartermaster, perhaps—than be obliged to quarter troops." Mrs. Canby stood and picked up the empty bowls. "I'll just put these away and fetch out a mattress."

"Please don't trouble yourself, ma'am," McIntyre said.

"Hush, Lacey. If this is Captain Russell's last night indoors, he should spend it comfortably. Why don't you take him to your room? I'll meet you there."

Jamie watched her out, then turned to McIntyre. "I'm impressed," he said. "How'd she know?"

McIntyre grinned. "She doesn't miss much."

Jamie slept like a dead thing, and Mrs. Canby sent him off the next morning with a hearty breakfast and a packet of sandwiches. Before noon he and McIntyre had the train moving, and they rode on ahead to Johnson's Ranch, southeast of the town.

There was not much level ground, and Jamie decided the best place for the park would be down along the creekbed where the wagons would be easy to get to. He rode up the creek a little way and found a box canyon that could be roped off and used as a corral, then returned to the ranch house—a crumbling adobe with two rooms, deserted—where McIntyre was waiting.

"Where's Mr. Johnson?" Jamie asked.

"Probably taken his cattle up north," McIntyre replied.

Jamie raised an eyebrow. "You wouldn't happen to know where?"

McIntyre laughed. "Afraid not. There are dozens of meadows in the mountains. There could be twenty herds of cattle there—"

"And likely are," Jamie said.

"—and we'd never find them. Sorry, my friend."

Jamie shrugged. "All we have to do is get to Fort Union. How far is it?"

"About a hundred miles."

"And the garrison?"

McIntyre's face went grave. "I'm not up to date on that. Even if I were . . ."

Jamie wished he hadn't asked. "Never mind. Not my concern, I'm just a quartermaster." He sat on the porch and rested his elbows on his knees. "You know, Valverde was a month ago today." Just saying the words made him shiver.

McIntyre sat by him. "I know. I was thinking about that."

Jamie felt a lump starting in his throat. "Owens wanted me to talk about it."

"Well," McIntyre said slowly, "do you want to?"

Jamie shrugged, unable to speak. He hugged his knees. McIntyre touched him, then his arm went around Jamie's shoulders. Jamie swallowed and said, "I just want to be finished with it all and go home. Does that make me a coward?"

"No," McIntyre replied. "No, it doesn't. Any man with any sense feels the same way."

McIntyre squeezed his shoulders and let go. A moment later he was holding out a flask. Jamie stared at it. Yes, he decided, and tipped back the whiskey. It tasted good. He took another mouthful before returning it, combed his hair back with his fingers, and sighed.

"Here come your wagons," McIntyre said.

Jamie looked up to where the first vehicles were rumbling around the hill behind them. McIntyre rose and went to his horse, and Jamie followed him. "Thanks," he said.

"Any time." McIntyre swung himself into the saddle. "Don't get lonely out here."

"If I do I'll come look for Phillips," Jamie said.

McIntyre laughed and began to trot away, then turned his horse and shouted back. "Hey! What's your favorite dinner?"

Jamie broke into a grin. "Chicken and dumplings," he hollered, and stood watching from the ranch house porch until McIntyre disappeared around the hill.

In the morning "assembly" sounded early, and the merrymakers from Lomé looked a few years older by daylight.

All came to attention as Captain Chapin stepped forward and, much to the astonishment of O'Brien and his men, again read out marching orders. O'Brien cornered him after they'd been dismissed.

"What the devil's going on?" he demanded.

"Don't ask," Chapin said. "Slough overruled Paul. Better get your men together, he's heavy on the bit."

The march was a shambles at first. Men went out ahead to conceal or consume what they'd stolen from the sutler, and all day the command straggled from Union to Lomé to the Sepullo creek, a grand distance of eight miles, where they quit and camped for the night. On the second day they fared better, marching all the way to Las Vegas, which they reached as the sun was nearing the mountains. A huge corral was given over to them for their camp, and O'Brien set his men to pitching tents. The village looked like Maxwell's place at the Reyado on a larger scale, flat-roofed mud buildings and a central square. After a brief parade, the command was dismissed and proceeded to descend on the town looking for entertainment. O'Brien noticed a Mexican hurrying two women swathed in shawls away over a field. "Well, Franklin," he said. "Better get into town before the girls are all taken."

"Oh, no thank you," Franklin said hastily. "You go ahead."

O'Brien turned an eye on him. "Don't you like women?"

"Of course I like them." A slow blush crept up Franklin's neck.

O'Brien laughed. "Well, I'll be blessed! I've finally found something I know more about than you!" He laced his arm through Franklin's and said, "Come on."

"No." Franklin dug in his heels. "Really, I—"

"Faith, you've got to get baptized sometime, laddie. This'll give you something to live for when we get to battle! Don't worry, I'll make sure she don't have the pox."

Franklin continued to protest, but O'Brien enlisted Shaunessy, Morris, Dougal, and O'Connor to help him cart the lad into town, and made so much fuss about the initiation to come that Franklin fell into white-faced silence. On reaching the hotel, they found it overflowing. An occasional feminine squeal issued from the saloon along with the strains of a badly tuned piano. O'Brien provided himself with a torch and led the way down a street past huddles of staring Mexican men, poking his head into houses. He glanced back at Franklin, self-conscious, for though others were doing it, he knew a gentleman wouldn't invade even a Mexican house, but Franklin seemed lost in a daze and might well have fallen down if not for Shaunessy and Dougal supporting him. Mexicans wouldn't have understood if he did ask leave, O'Brien thought, and anyway he didn't see much to attract him. The houses were sparsely furnished, and the only ornaments were walls full of mirrors and a lot of cheap prints of saints in tin frames. He was near giving up when he opened the door of a tiny house next to a church and thrust his torch inside to see what was there.

This house had no ornament at all save for a wooden cross on the wall. Beneath the cross was a mattress, and on the mattress was a woman. No, a fairy princess—she had pale skin and large eyes, a firm chin, hair a bit tousled from sleep. He had waked her with the torch, and as she sat up, brushing a wisp of hair from her eyes, he saw that her dress was black. For a moment she looked bewildered, then she gave him a hesitant smile.

O'Brien's heart left his body. Here was all he needed in the world. He smiled in response, and stepped forward.

22

Man's inactivity is the Devil's opportunity.

—Ovando J. Hollister

Laura's smile faded as the strange captain entered the room. He was good-looking in a rough sort of way, but the expression in his eyes was too powerful for comfort. As soon as his body no longer blocked the door other soldiers followed, whooping as they saw her in a way that turned doubt into fear. In an instant she was seized and dragged to her feet.

"Give us a kiss, darlin'!" one said, grasping her waist.

"No!" Laura struggled though she knew she had no hope against a half-dozen men. Wild thoughts flashed in her mind: her knife in her cloak pocket, a hope that the padre would come to her rescue.

A higher voice rose above the soldiers' laughter, crying "Leave her alone!" but her attackers ignored it. The captain pulled one of them off. The others were laughing, grabbing at her clothes.

"No!" she screamed again.

A clap of thunder seemed to fill the room. Laura cried out, and the men holding her flinched.

"Let her go, damn you!" the high voice shouted.

Laura looked toward the doorway and saw a young man just outside, a smoking pistol raised skyward in his hand. He lowered it and stepped into the room. "Can't you see she's a lady?" he said angrily.

The next moment she was released. The torch came nearer, and the captain who held it stared intently at her. She looked back to the youth and saw lieutenant's bars on his shoulders.

"I'm terribly sorry, ma'am," he said, stepping toward her. "Are you hurt?"

Trembling, trying to catch her breath, Laura said, "No."

"Chas just wants her to himself," one of the men grumbled.

"Shut up, Dougal!" the lieutenant said. He looked around at the men. "That's enough fun for tonight, boys. Go try the saloon."

The men shifted, glancing at each other and at Laura. She looked away.

"Do as he says," the captain said roughly. "Go along."

They filed slowly out. Laura kept her eyes averted until the two officers were all who remained.

"You shouldn't be alone, ma'am," the lieutenant said in a gentler voice. "Not with the army here."

"I was not aware of the army's presence, nor that they were in the habit of invading private homes," Laura said tartly. She immediately regretted her tone, and looked up at him in apology. "Forgive me," she said. "I am in your debt."

"You are naturally upset," the lieutenant said kindly. "We won't intrude on you any longer, as soon as we're sure of your safety. Where is your family?"

"I have none," said Laura. None she cared to name as such.

"Is this your house?"

"It is Padre Martinez's house. He is giving a service."

The lieutenant looked perplexed. "You're really not safe alone, ma'am. There are a thousand soldiers camped in the town. This could happen again. Is there someone we could escort you to?"

Laura shook her head. "All my friends are in Sante Fé."

"Santa Fé?" the captain repeated, his green eyes boring into her as if he would like to eat her. "That's where we're headed. We'll take you."

"Sir, we can't—"

"I said we'll take her!" The violence of his shout made Laura jump. She glanced at the lieutenant, who was staring at the captain in amazement.

"Sir, the *Texans* are in Santa Fé! We can't take her there."

Laura felt a flutter of hope, and took a step toward the captain. "Can you take me as far as Pigeon's Ranch?"

"Where's that?" he asked.

"In La Glorieta Pass, east of Santa Fé."

Without taking his eyes off her, the captain nodded. "We'll take you there."

"Captain!" the lieutenant cried.

"What's your trouble, Franklin? Aren't officers supposed to help ladies in distress?"

"She wasn't in distress until we broke in here!" The lieutenant sounded exasperated. "Ma'am, I'm terribly sorry, but you can't come with us. The major will never permit it," he added, turning to the captain.

"We'll see about that. Do you need to pack anything up, miss?"

Laura shook her head.

"Sir, it'll take days to get there!" the lieutenant protested, his voice rising. "She can't march with us! She'd be better off here!"

"Mary Denning can look after her," the captain replied.

"But—"

"Shut it, Franklin! We're taking her!" Sudden fury marred the captain's face and sent fright chasing down Laura's spine. The two men stared off. Laura looked from one to the other. The lieutenant glanced at her, and his expression of anger changed to one of—hurt? Then he turned and, without a word, strode to the door.

"Franklin!" The captain's voice made her flinch, and brought the lieutenant to a halt in the open doorway.

"Best stay here, lad," the captain said softly. "You wouldn't want to leave this fine lady alone with an old troll like me."

The lieutenant turned slowly around, defeated. He did not meet Laura's gaze, but glanced resentfully at the captain, then stared at the floor. Whatever had passed between these two men was beyond her immediate understanding, she realized. It had to do with more than just her.

She glanced at the captain, who was smiling down at her, an expression almost tender in his green eyes. It was clear from his voice that he was Irish, and his lieutenant was just as clearly well bred. If she were to place her trust in one of them, she would prefer it to be the lieutenant, but it was the captain who, with an awkward bow, offered her his arm.

"Thank you," she said, and preferring not to take the arm of a stranger, fetched her cloak from its peg instead. She threw it over her shoulders and followed him out to the yard, passing the lieutenant, who fell in behind them.

Padre Martinez came out of the church and hurried forward in alarm. "¡No, no, señorita! ¡No vaya con ellos!"

"It's all right, Padre," Laura said. "It's all right."

"Tell him she'll be safe, Franklin," the captain said.

"Ella estara segura, Padre," the lieutenant said dully.

The priest, with troubled face, crossed himself.

"Gracias," Laura said to him. "Muchas gracias." She smiled and laid a hand on his arm to reassure him, then allowed the captain to lead her away, lighting their way through the streets with his torch.

Her spirits rose, though she was beginning to doubt the wisdom of this course. She should, she supposed, simply stay by the padre while the army was in town, or relent and forgive Governor Connelly, seeking shelter with him. It was what she should do, but not what she wished to do. She was weary of smallpox and hopelessness, and knew Las Vegas could offer no better for her. If she could get to Monsieur Vallé, he would look after her until it was safe for her to go to Mrs. Canby.

She shook her head, smiling at herself. What would Father have said? She reached into her cloak pocket, past her father's portrait, and grasped the comforting handle of her knife.

He'd run mad, that was surely what it was. No use trying to fight it, O'Brien thought as he guided the lady through the army's camp, with Franklin sulking a few paces behind. The lad's mood didn't concern him; he was busy working out how to make his lady comfortable and keep her safe in a camp full of hundreds of men. He glanced sidelong at her. In the torchlight she seemed a magical, frail thing. It was a miracle that he should have found her at all.

Oh, Alastar. This will lead you to trouble, it will.

Some of the lads had returned from the town, and sat round their fires singing and drinking, admiring new possessions acquired in Las Vegas. A few catcalls and ribald comments went up, which O'Brien silenced with a glare.

"See that?" Dougal said. "It was the cap wanted her to himself!"

"You shut your mouth, Dougal, if you want to see morning," O'Brien said. He whispered to the lady, "Don't mind them."

They had reached their camp, where the fire had burned down, having been left unattended. The Dennings' tent was dark. Franklin tossed a couple of pieces of wood on the fire and poked at it with a stick. Flames leapt up, bathing them in golden light. "She can have my tent," Franklin said moodily.

"No, mine," O'Brien said. "It's bigger. I'll share yours."

Franklin's head snapped up and his eyes flashed resentment, and something else, harder to read. "Yes, sir," he said, turning away. "I'll see if I can find some extra blankets."

As he started to leave, the lady caught his arm and said, "Thank you for your kindness."

Franklin moved on with only a nod. The lady pulled her cloak closer to her.

"Are you cold?" O'Brien asked. "I can put on more wood—"

"No, thank you," she said. "I'm quite comfortable."

O'Brien tossed his torch onto the fire and strode to the woodpile, hefting a good-sized log. He carried it back, set it upright, and offered it to her as a seat, then stood back, regarding her with awe.

"You're a fine lady, aren't you?" he said.

That made her laugh. "Not very fine at present, I'm afraid." She gave him a small smile. "Are you from Fort Union?"

He shook his head. "Colorado."

"Colorado! Then you're Governor Gilpin's men!"

"Aye."

"Oh, at last!" the lady exclaimed, her eyes lighting up. "How many are you? Are there Regulars with you?"

O'Brien's surprise at her questions dissolved in the warm glow her smile made inside him. His heart began to pound. "Aye," he managed to say.

"Are you marching to join Colonel Canby?" she asked.

O'Brien swallowed, trying to form an answer. Footsteps approached.

"Captain O'Brien, your company is—what the devil? Miss Howland?"

O'Brien looked across the fire at the adjutant. The lady jumped up and ran to him, laughing. "Captain Chapin!" she cried. "How glad I am to see you!" He caught the hands she held out, and O'Brien felt a stab of envy.

"What on earth are you doing here?" Chapin asked. "Where is your uncle?"

"Halfway to Kansas by now. He has washed his hands of me, and I of him. This . . . gentleman," she said, gesturing at O'Brien, "has offered to see me to Pigeon's Ranch."

"But that's at least three days' march!" Chapin said. "Miss Howland, you cannot travel with the army. I'm quite sure the colonel wouldn't approve—"

"She could be a laundress," Franklin said lazily.

O'Brien turned to see his lieutenant returning with two blankets under his arm. He set them down by his tent.

"A laundress?!" said Chapin.

"Ford's stayed behind in Santa Fé," the lieutenant said.

Chapin sighed, shaking his head. "You Pike's Peakers will be the death of me. What would your Bible-thumping major say?"

"He'd say 'Blessed are the merciful, for they shall obtain mercy'," said O'Brien, dredging up the words from childhood.

The lady laughed again, a musical sound that made O'Brien's heart leap. "You are answered, Captain Chapin."

"I'll look after her, sir," O'Brien added. "Mrs. Denning will help, if I ask her."

Chapin frowned. "Very well. She can ride with the wagons. If I hear of any trouble you'll answer for it," he added. "She's a personal friend of the Canbys."

"She'll be safe with us," O'Brien promised.

"Hm. Your company is on guard duty tomorrow." Chapin turned to the lady. "Stay in the officers' camp, Miss Howland. I'm at headquarters, if you need anything." He gestured up the row of tents, then moved on.

The lady raised an eyebrow at Franklin. "A laundress?"

"It was all I could think of," he said with a shrug.

"Are you certain you weren't moved by a desire to see me washing your shirts?"

Franklin's face darkened. "Certainly not."

Again she laughed. "I'm teasing you, sir. I will gladly be a laundress for a day or two."

"You won't like it," Franklin said. "It's hard work."

She regarded him silently for a moment, then said, "It's the least I can do to thank you for rescuing me."

Franklin shot a look at O'Brien, then shrugged again. "I only did what any gentleman would do," he said, a mirthless smile twisting his mouth.

"Nevertheless, I am grateful, Mr.—?"

"Franklin," he said. "Charles Franklin."

"Laura Howland," she said. Something in the way she looked at Franklin made O'Brien's heart give a heavy thump. As if he had heard, Franklin gestured toward him.

"This is Captain O'Brien."

O'Brien came forward, bowing and walking at once, which had a poor effect.

"I must thank you as well, Captain," Miss Howland said. "I'm grateful for your protection."

O'Brien nodded, knowing he should say something, but unable to find words. She glanced at his tent behind her. "Is this—where I'll be?"

"Yes," O'Brien said.

"Do you need to fetch anything before I go in?"

He shook his head. The lady glanced at Franklin. "Then I'll say good night. Thank you again."

"Good night, miss," O'Brien said, finding his tongue at last as the tent flap closed behind her.

Firelight glowed through the canvas. Laura spread out her blankets—not much of a bed—and sat down to unlace her boots.

"Go ahead, sir," she heard Lieutenant Franklin saying. "I'll find another place to sleep."

"No you won't. There's room in your tent for us both."

"Captain, I—"

"That's an order, Franklin."

"Yes, sir."

Laura sighed. The captain had clearly taken a liking to her. She could see she would have to take care if she was not to bring his wrath down on the poor lieutenant's head.

She stood up and went to the tent door, finding a tie on the flap that she double-knotted—a symbolic bar, but it gave her comfort. The blankets were woolen and rough, so she wrapped her cloak around herself, lay down on one blanket, and spread the other on top. With a sigh she snuggled into the cotton lining of her cloak and tucked its end into a knot around her feet.

As the wool began to warm she lay listening to the sounds of the camp: fire crackling, soldiers' laughter, someone singing. Dozens of voices kept her awake, and she found herself thinking over the past year. A year ago, almost to the day, she had left Boston. Since then the country had gone to war, she had met and lost a suitor, and had cut the last tie to her family. What, she wondered, would her reaction have been if on that chilly morning in 1861 someone had told her that in a year's time she would be destitute and sleeping in a soldier's tent? She chuckled to herself. Without a doubt, she would have been deeply insulted.

"Miss Howland?" The voice was barely audible. Laura sat up, listening. "Miss Howland, are you awake?"

Yes, it was Lieutenant Franklin's voice. Laura got up, untied the door flap, and peeked out. The youth's dark form was edged in gold by the light of the dying fire.

"I'm sorry to disturb you," he said, "but I thought you might want this." He held out a tin chamber pot.

The Laura of a year ago would have been covered in shame, but she had suffered too much recently to be squeamish. She was in the midst of a thousand soldiers; a chamber pot was no small gift, and she accepted it with real gratitude, saying, "Thank you! How thoughtful you are!"

The lieutenant stepped back. "Good night, ma'am."

Laura caught his hand and pressed it, trying to make him feel her esteem through the glove. "I can't thank you enough for rescuing me."

His dark eyes were very fine, glinting starlight. The frown he'd been wearing all evening eased. "Well—you rescued me, too, in a way," he said softly. "I'd say we're even."

Laura gazed up at him, unsure of his meaning. "I hope I have not been the cause of a war between you and your captain," she whispered.

He shook his head, and an odd smile flickered across his face. "No, the war started long ago. Some days are better than others."

Puzzled, Laura peered at him, trying to read his face. He gently removed his hand from her grasp. "Good night, Miss Howland."

She watched him disappear into the next tent, then retied the door and went back to her bed, setting the chamber pot nearby. She was sure the army did not carry chamber pots. He must have gone into the village to get it, and if she judged his character right he had paid for it, not stolen it. The more she thought of his kindness, the warmer grew her feelings. Here was a man she could admire on all points: well bred, considerate, honorable.

And attractive, she made herself admit. A bit younger than she, perhaps, though his demeanor was more mature than his looks. Laughing at herself, Laura curled up again in her cloak, happy at being free of Las Vegas and at the thought that Lieutenant Franklin lay only a few feet away.

O'Brien turned over as Franklin came into the tent. "That was the longest piss in man's history."

"I had an errand in town," Franklin said.

"Aye, I heard you. Fetching presents for the lady."

"A chamber pot." Franklin stood by the door a minute, then came forward. "I brought you another blanket," he said softly.

O'Brien spread the wool over his legs, annoyed at the thoughtful gesture. He did not want Franklin to be generous. He wanted justification for the anger that was growing in him again. More than that, he wanted himself to be the one that provided for the lady's comfort. He watched the lad remove his boots, hating him for thinking of a chamber pot. Franklin unbuttoned his jacket, then slid between blankets and leaned on one elbow, facing O'Brien. In the darkness of the tent, O'Brien couldn't see his eyes, but he could feel them.

"Captain?"

"What?"

"I don't think I've ever told you—how much I admire you."

Bloody hell. Just when I'm trying to be angry with the lad, he goes all starry-eyed.

Franklin's voice was low, and his words hesitant. "You might be surprised—"

"Did you tell Morris we're guarding the wagons tomorrow?" O'Brien said, rather unkindly.

"No—"

"Then you'll have to rise early and tell him."

Silence. Then he heard Franklin sigh. "Yes, sir. Good night." The lad wrapped himself in blankets and lay down facing the wall.

O'Brien turned on his back and stared at the canvas over his head. The young lady—Miss . . . he'd forgotten her name—Miss Laura. She wouldn't like him to call her that. She was not one of your city smarts too good to say thank you to an honest man, but she was a lady every inch of her, and if he wished to call her by her Christian name he'd have to win the privilege.

He closed his eyes. He wanted her. Had wanted her from the moment he saw her, but he wanted more than the pleasure her body could give him. He wanted her to smile at him the way she had that first second, the way she had when he told her they were come from Colorado. The way she smiled at Franklin.

Laura was awakened by blue dawn. She was stiff and cold from lying on the hard ground. It had taken her hours to get to sleep, surrounded by the sounds of the camp. She pulled the blankets tighter but still shivered, and in desperation she got up, hoping there would be a coal or two left of the fire.

Outside she found the sky gray, with only a smudge of pink in the east. The firepit was all ash, and she sat on the stump, huddling in her cloak and looking around at the camp. The town's corral—ordinarily a stopping place for wagon trains, coaches, and occasional flocks or herds—was completely filled with long rows of tents, and more spilled outside. Few men were yet stirring. Laura saw an officer walking up the row toward her, and realized it was Lieutenant Franklin, carrying a pail of water. With a smile, she hurried to meet him.

"Good morning," he said, stopping. "I trust you slept comfortably?"

Laura thought she detected a hint of irony in his voice. "Quite well, thank you," she said, determined to be cheerful. "Would you walk with me to headquarters?"

Franklin put the pail down by the smaller tent. "It's this way," he said, gesturing.

Laura hesitated. "Perhaps I should leave a note for Captain O'Brien."

A wry smile came onto the lieutenant's face, and he shook his head. "He can't read," he said softly.

Astonished, Laura looked up. "How did he ever become a captain?"

"He *wanted* to be a captain. When he wants something, he doesn't care much for any other considerations."

Laura gazed pensively into his dark eyes. "Are you trying to frighten me, Mr. Franklin?"

"I'm trying to warn you."

Laura glanced back at the ground, thinking of the captain staring at her, torch in hand, while soldiers rushed past him to mob her. She frowned. He had come to her aid, if belatedly.

"If you wish to return to Las Vegas, I'd be glad to escort you," Lieutenant Franklin said.

"No, thank you," Laura said, meeting his cool gaze again. "I wish to go to Glorieta."

The lieutenant shrugged, and started down the row of tents.

"You think me quite shameless, I suppose," Laura said, hurrying to keep up with his long stride.

"I think you unwise, ma'am. You are not safe here."

"Nor is my reputation. I'm aware of that, sir. In fact, I'm sure you'd agree that with the highest sticklers, my reputation is already in shreds."

He paused to look at her, frowning. "I don't see why it should be."

"Why, Mr. Franklin! I believe that's the kindest thing you've said to me!"

He started walking again, and Laura thought she saw some color rise into his face.

"It comes of living on the frontier, I suppose," she said. "I've all but lost my parlor manners."

The lieutenant gave a cough of surprised laughter. "That is headquarters," he said, indicating a large tent and not quite suppressing a smile. "I'll return to escort you back in a few minutes, if you wish."

"Thank you." Laura held his gaze. "Please understand," she added, "I am trying to do what is right, not what is safe."

A mixture of emotions washed across his face—surprise, annoyance—admiration? Had she won some small measure of his respect? She turned toward headquarters, feeling warmth rise to her cheeks, more than satisfaction alone would justify.

O'Brien rose and went out to build up the fire. Miss Laura wasn't up yet, it seemed. He found the water pail outside the tent, put some on the fire for coffee, and had the happy thought of heating some extra for her to wash with. He scrubbed a tin plate with pebbles until it shone. The water had just boiled when he looked up and saw her approaching with Franklin. A stab of anger went through him, but he swallowed and managed to smile. "You're up early, miss," he said, then shifted his gaze to Franklin. "Find Morris?"

"Yes," Franklin said, and dove into his tent.

O'Brien looked up at his lady. She came to the fire, saying "Good morning, Captain."

"Thought you might like to wash," he said, offering her the plate filled with steaming water.

"Thank you," she said, smiling as she reached for it, then pulled back her hand. "Oh! It's hot!"

"Sorry," O'Brien said. "Here, I'll put it on this." He set the tin on the log where she'd sat the night before and gave her the soap from his rations, then watched her gracefully sit on the ground and dip her fingers in the water. Don't stare, he told himself, and went back to tending the coffee.

First call sounded. The camp was coming awake. Some of the men were already striking their tents. Franklin came back out, and said, "Are you all right?"

O'Brien glanced up and saw the lady wiping at her face with her hands. "Yes," she said, laughing. "I'm just washing my face, only I haven't anything to dry with."

"Here." Franklin took a handkerchief from his pocket and handed it to her. "You're lucky, it's my last clean one."

"Well, I'll remedy that," she said lightly. "I must earn my way after all. Thank you."

O'Brien fumed, angry at himself for forgetting to provide her with something—saints knew what—for a towel, and at Franklin for solving the problem so easily. He stirred the coffee and glowered into the coals.

"That smells wonderful," Miss Laura said, coming to sit beside him. "May I be of any help?"

Surprised, he looked up into her large eyes and shook his head. Say something, fool. Anything.

"Would you like some?" he asked.

"Yes, please, if it's ready."

He filled a cup for her and held it to her with the handle first. "Careful, it'll be hot."

She folded Franklin's kerchief round the handle and sipped. "Lovely. Thank you." Her smile made his heart race and he couldn't help staring. "Thank you again for the wash water. I suspect you are trying to spoil me," she said in the same playful tone she'd used with Franklin.

"If you'll let me," O'Brien said. He'd meant to match her banter but it came out much too earnest, and she dropped her gaze to the cup in her lap. I've no skill for this game, he thought miserably. Glancing up, he saw Franklin staring at him with a queer look on his face. The lad turned away as their eyes met.

O'Brien glanced at the lady again. He wanted her, and while he lived Franklin would not have her, that was certain. How, though, was he to make her want him? He knew nothing of courting a lady, all he'd ever known were whores, apart from a few kisses stolen from farm girls near Racecourse. He remembered Franklin's words over a fire in Colorado—You can rise to any place you want—and huffed a silent laugh. Can I rise to your place in her eyes, laddie? We'll find out.

23

The question is not of saving this post, but of saving New Mexico and defeating the Confederates in such a way that an invasion of this Territory will never again be attempted.

—Ed. R. S. Canby

"It is your lead, Colonel Chaves," Laura said, holding her cards at an angle so she could read them in the firelight.

"I am aware of that, Miss Howland. You Americans are so impatient. There."

The colonel took the next three tricks, and Laura laughed. "Next time I shall keep my peace! Your game, Colonel. My partner and I are outranked." She glanced across the game at Lieutenant Franklin and saw a reluctant spark of laughter in his eyes.

"At least I can keep cards together," Chaves said, gathering the deck. Laura glanced up at him, surprised at his tone.

"It wasn't your fault, Colonel," Captain Chapin said.

Chaves looked at Laura with a bitter smile. "I brought what was left of my Volunteers with me, but most of them deserted once we passed Glorieta. They have gone home to prepare their fields for planting."

"Well, I agree," Laura said. "That was not your fault."

"No. They did not make good soldiers. We did not have the time to train them."

"Let it rest, Manuel," Chapin said.

"I tried to make them understand how important it was to fight, but so many of them do not even understand they are now Americans—"

"Colonel," Laura said, laying a hand on his arm. "I am sure you did everything you could."

"Colonel Chaves?" a deep, booming voice said. Laura glanced up and saw Major Chivington at the edge of the firelight: tall, broad-shouldered, a fearsome man who, in her opinion, well deserved the name of Fighting Preacher. Chaves and Franklin stood up to greet him, and Laura got up as well, to stretch limbs numb from sitting on the ground.

"Excuse me for interrupting," Chivington said.

"Not at all, Major," Chaves replied. "What may I do for you?"

"I'm in need of a guide. Colonel Slough suggested I ask you to find me one."

"I would be honored if you would accept my services, Major," Chaves said. "Where do you wish to be led?"

"The colonel and I are discussing an advance toward Santa Fé. He doesn't favor a general advance but has agreed to let me make a reconnaissance in that direction. I will come to you in the morning." Chivington glanced at Lieutenant Franklin and said, "Where's your captain?"

"Out for a walk," said the lieutenant.

"Well, tell him your company's marching with us tomorrow," Chivington said. He turned to Laura and gave her a swift, evaluating glance. "This is your new laundress, I take it."

"Yes," Franklin said. "Miss Howland, Major Chivington."

"I'm afraid you'll have to stay behind with the command, Miss Howland," said Chivington, his brows drawn together.

"I would prefer not to, sir," Laura said.

"No help for it. We're only taking a few wagons for the infantry. I doubt you'd want to ride with them, and I doubt there'd be room if you did."

"She can ride a mule." Captain O'Brien's voice came from behind her. Laura turned to see the captain emerge from the shadows between the tents. She was glad to see him. He had disappeared after she had suggested a game of whist, and she feared he might have been offended.

"Can she?" Major Chivington asked in a skeptical tone.

"Yes," Laura said, "if it has a saddle." A sidesaddle was too much to hope for, of course. She'd make do.

"I don't have any mules to spare—"

"I'll get her one," the captain said.

"And I don't much approve of women with the army," the major continued, his voice rising. "If they belong anywhere they belong in camp, not in the vanguard!"

"Major Chivington," Laura said, keeping a pleasant smile on her face, "I am only traveling to the home of a friend, to whom Captain O'Brien has kindly offered to escort me."

"He had no business doing so, madam!" Chivington said. "We are close to engaging the enemy."

"What friend, Miss Howland?" Chaves asked.

"Monsieur Vallé." Laura turned to him.

"Pigeon? Órale, he will look after you."

"So he once said."

Chaves faced Chivington and bowed. "Major," he said with courtly graciousness, "if the captain's duties prevent him from escorting Miss Howland, I will be happy to take her myself."

Chivington looked at Chaves, and Laura saw that he knew he had lost. "Very well. But she'll have to keep up with the column. And God help her if we meet the Texans!"

"I am sure God will help her, Major," Chaves said with another slight bow. "Gracias."

Laura smiled at him as Chivington left. "Gracias to you, Colonel." Her eyes fell on Captain O'Brien and she took a step toward him. "And to you. Can you truly find me a mule for tomorrow? I have a little money—"

"Keep your money," O'Brien said roughly. "I'll get the mule." He stared at her—the hard stare she'd grown accustomed to—and went away with long strides.

"A bit touchy, isn't he?" Chapin said.

Chaves smiled. "I believe he likes the señorita. I have threatened his good favor, eh, Miss Howland?"

"Only in his imagination, Colonel," Laura said. "Gentle-men, thank you. I have enjoyed this immensely, but if we are to march early I should retire." She bade each of them good night, and accepted the cards that Captain Chapin pressed into her hands.

"You may need them for Patience," he said.

"Colonel Chaves would say so," Laura said, laughing. "Thank you, Captain. Good night."

Left alone with Lieutenant Franklin, she turned to shake his hand as she had the others', but found he had crouched to poke at the fire. He glanced up at her. "I think I should wait up for the captain," he said.

Laura nodded. "What made him so cross all at once?"

He shrugged. "It happens now and then. It'll pass."

"Well, good night," said Laura, wanting to linger by the fire. "Thank you for being my partner."

"Sleep well, Miss Howland."

She paused in the door of her tent to look back at him, wishing he would meet her eyes, but he seemed not to notice her there so she left the flap fall. Nestling in her blankets, she struck a match to the candle he'd given her. She was not sleepy, though heaven knew she should be after jouncing all day in a wagon that inspired in her a new respect for mail coaches, and then scrubbing laundry till her arms ached. She had helped out with the washing for I Company in return for the use of Mrs. Denning's washtub. Mrs. Denning was friendly enough, though she had raised an eyebrow upon their being introduced. Laura could hardly blame her for this. There were three other unmar-ried laundresses with the regiment, all of whom she sus-pected of plying another trade after sundown.

She smoothed out the blankets before her and spread out the cards. They were worn and dirty, but a treasure to one who had few possessions. To amuse herself she called the royalty after her friends. The king and queen of spades were the Canbys, clubs were the Chapins, and diamonds Colonel Chaves and his wife, whom she'd not met. She drew the king and queen of hearts. The king was Captain

O'Brien, she supposed. That would make her the queen, but she liked the knave of hearts better than the king. She picked up knave and queen and held them together in one hand.

You are a silly fool, Miss Laura Howland, she thought as she swept up the cards and put out the candle.

It seemed only a few minutes later when a bugle startled her awake. In half darkness she fumbled with her boot laces, then got up, packed her few belongings and tied her bedroll. She put on her cloak and came out of the tent to find the sky was growing light. A kettle sat in the ashes of the fire, which still gave out some warmth. Laura held her hands over them.

"Good, you're up," Lieutenant Franklin said, emerging from his tent. "The captain found you a mount. He's gone to fetch a saddle for it. Forgive me, but I think you'd better wear these." He held out a pair of army trousers.

"Mr. Franklin," Laura said in mock reproach. "You do offer me the most embarrassing gifts!"

He laughed. "I am trying to *spare* you embarrassment. Hurry and put them on, he'll be back soon."

She went into her tent, removed her boots, and pulled on the trousers beneath her skirts. They were long, and she had to fold the ends up and tuck them into her boots, then tie the laces over them. When she emerged the lieutenant was gone and Captain O'Brien stood saddling a burro, its coat deep and wooly, chocolate brown, with a cream-colored belly.

Laura glanced at the captain, wondering if a night's sleep had improved his mood. "Good morning, Captain," she said. "What a sweet-looking donkey."

It seemed to her that his smile was grudging, but smile he did. "He's about as sweet as a bag of lemons," he said, "but he shouldn't throw you."

Laura laughed and put on a bright smile. "This will be an adventure. Would you lead him over here, please, Captain? I can stand on this rock to mount."

The burro, which looked half asleep, suffered itself to be

led. Laura grasped the saddle, gathered up her hoops, and swung her leg over the animal's back. She fought down a blush and managed to arrange her skirts more or less to cover her limbs, though the hoops rode oddly across her hips. Picking up the single rein, she discovered that a burro did not behave like a saddle horse. A touch of her heel evoked no response. Captain O'Brien, who had been watching with undisguised interest, handed her a stick. "Prod him with it," he said. "Don't hit. That's how the Mexicans train them."

"Very well." She applied the end of the stick to the burro's hindquarters with positive results, and soon had him walking up and down while the tents were being struck.

"You'll do," O'Brien said, as the bugle rang out again. "Where'd you get the trousers?"

"From a friend," she said, not wanting to raise his ire against Franklin. She saw the lieutenant walking toward them and called out to him. "What do you think of my trousers, Lieutenant? Shall I set a new fashion?"

"Are you thinking of wearing them in Boston?" he said, grinning.

"I just might," Laura replied saucily. "Would not Miss Bloomer approve?" She rode the burro up to the captain and offered him her hand. "Thank you. I did not want to be left behind."

He took her hand as if it were made of glass, hardly daring to touch it. The eyes he turned to her were as green as spring grass, and he looked so earnest and so hopeless that she had to smile. She made it a kind smile, and said, "You've been very good to me, Captain O'Brien. I am grateful."

His lips parted but he said nothing. Poor tongue-tied fellow. He merely nodded, staring up at her. Laura gently removed her hand from his and dismounted. Glancing up, she saw Franklin watching them with a peculiar expression. He looked away at once and began stirring the dregs of the fire.

"I couldn't find out anything at headquarters," he said, adding some wood. "Chivington and Slough are still arguing. We might as well have breakfast."

His voice sounded upset, but he would not look at her, and Laura could think of nothing to say. The captain tied her burro to a tree behind the tents, and they began preparing for breakfast. Bacon, flapjacks with molasses, and the last of Lieutenant Franklin's tea. Laura thanked him for sharing it, which drew a reluctant smile from him. By the end of the meal, his mood seemed somewhat more cheerful.

"Mr. Franklin," she said. "May I try a hard cracker?"

"Whatever for?" He laughed.

"I'm curious."

"Here." Captain O'Brien took a cracker out of his haversack and handed it to her with a bland face. She turned the square over in her hands and tapped it experimentally against a rock, which seemed to have no effect on it whatever. Looking up, she saw the captain and lieutenant both grinning at her. She applied her teeth to a corner of the cracker and broke off a small piece, but one large enough to exercise her jaws as she chewed it into submission. Next she tried dipping the cracker in her tea, which made the outer layer soft but left the inside as hard as ever.

"Here," Lieutenant Franklin said, offering her a tin plate with some molasses in it.

Laura dipped her cracker into the syrup and gnawed at it a little more. "I see," she said. "Clearly its purpose is to help one eat molasses when one hasn't a spoon." She left the cracker in the plate and handed it back to the lieutenant, but the captain picked up the cracker, bit off the corner she'd damaged, and put the rest back in his haversack. His eyes were on her as he chewed, and she thought she glimpsed the past hardship that had taught him to save part of a cracker even when he had plenty of meat. How different was his world from that in which she'd been raised. Not quite so different now, she thought, looking away.

The morning dragged on into midday and still no orders

were issued. In desperation Laura brought out her cards. "I will make a bargain with you, Captain. I will teach you to play whist if you will teach me to play bluff."

"That's not a lady's game!" Captain O'Brien protested.

"I won't play it for money," Laura said. "I merely wish to broaden my knowledge."

"Why don't we start with knockdown?" Franklin suggested.

It was a good compromise, a game that taught the principles of whist without the complexities of bidding. Captain O'Brien was a quick study and a ruthless player, and had beaten Laura and Lieutenant Franklin twice by the time Captain Chapin came up.

"Your orders," Chapin said, handing a note to O'Brien. "Chivington's got Slough's permission to march on Santa Fé."

Laura watched O'Brien's face and thought she detected a hint of color in it as he stuffed the note into his pocket. Lieutenant Franklin rose and started to break up the fire.

"Don't do that," Chapin said. "You'll be cooking two days' rations. I believe the major plans to march through the night."

Captain O'Brien muttered something Laura couldn't hear.

"I'll go draw the rations," Franklin said.

Laura picked up her cards as the lieutenant strode away. "A night march," she said. "That will be interesting."

"Miss Howland," Chapin said, "I wish you would consent to stay with the command. I'll pledge myself to take you to Pigeon's as soon as it's safe—"

"Thank you, but I think the sooner I go the better chance I will have of reaching the ranch. Do you not agree?"

Captain Chapin led her a little away from the others. "Miss Howland," he said quietly, "Major Chivington is marching with the intention of engaging the enemy. If that should occur, you will not only be in danger but you will endanger those who will naturally wish to protect you."

Laura bit her lip. She had not thought of it in that light.

She frowned, and said, "You will think me very selfish, Captain Chapin, but I will go nevertheless."

"I think you are very brave," Chapin said with a smile. "And a little foolish."

"More than a little foolish, no doubt," Laura said. "But not so much that I will not thank you for your concern. I am confident I will reach Glorieta. If luck is with us, perhaps I will get all the way to Santa Fé."

Chapin's smile grew wistful. "If you do. . . ."

"Of course," Laura said, squeezing his arm. "I will tell her you are well."

"How I wish I were going with you!"

"Can't you?" Laura asked.

He shook his head. "Colonel Slough wants me by him. I am an appurtenance to his status." He laughed, and gave a slight bow. "Stay close to your guardians, Miss Howland."

"I shall." Laura watched him walk off toward headquarters, then turned back to the fire. Captain O'Brien sat frowning over the written orders Chapin had given him. Pity rose in Laura's heart. She stepped toward him, but he glanced up and hastily put the paper away. Laura knelt on the blanket where they'd been playing cards and picked up the deck. "You're a very quick study," she said softly. "It's a pleasure to have such a talented pupil."

He made no reply, and she looked up to find him staring suspiciously at her. "If there is anything I could teach you in exchange for your kindness to me—"

A hurt look crossed his face, and she knew she had made a mistake. "No," he said roughly, getting to his feet. He strode to where the burro was nibbling on dried grass, and made a fuss of tightening the girth. Laura sighed and began to lay out a game of Patience.

"There is more pie," Mrs. Canby said. "Will you have some?"

"Oh, no thanks." McIntyre patted his full stomach. "I've got to ride this evening."

"At night?"

"Scouting."

"Oh." She let it drop, as she always did, for which McIntyre was thankful. Mrs. Canby was compassionate to a fault, and well aware of his sensitivity about his allegiance. She never questioned him. To her he was a friend and guest, no more.

"What about you, Captain Russell?"

Russell shook his head. "Thank you. It was wonderful. Everything was wonderful. Thank you, ladies."

The three other women at the table—all wives of Union soldiers—smiled and nodded. "You're welcome, Captain Russell," said Mrs. Chapin, who had made the dumplings to go with Mrs. Canby's chicken. There were now only seven hens and a rooster left. A number of Mrs. Canby's birds had been stolen by Pyron's men before Juan Carlos had been able to lock them up. McIntyre had made sure to let Russell know, though the Texan's gratitude needed no prompting. He'd declared the meal to be as good as any his mother ever served, which won the ladies' hearts at once.

"Shall we go to the parlor?" Mrs. Canby suggested. "María will bring coffee."

They adjourned to sit before the fire, where the ladies began to interrogate Russell about his home and family. McIntyre sipped at his coffee. Odd how enemies in some situations could be perfectly friendly in others. Though McIntyre was now to all intents her enemy, Mrs. Canby's parlor was still a haven to him. Thank God, he thought with a smile.

Weary miles had gone by, but Laura remained in good cheer. The burro gave a tolerable ride, much more pleasant than being confined in a wagon, and it needed no prodding to keep up with the horses. Laura smiled up at Lieutenant Franklin. "That is a splendid horse. What's his name?"

"Evelyn's Duke. What's your charger's name?"

"Heavens, I don't know," Laura replied. "Something Spanish which I would no doubt mispronounce." Mindful of Captain O'Brien's watchful eyes, she turned to him. "What about your horse, Captain? Does he have a name?"

He was silent for a moment, then said, "Not one I can say in front of a lady."

Laura and Lieutenant Franklin burst into laughter. The captain looked surprised, then laughed with them. They rode on through the bright afternoon and soon reached the camp of a party—Company F and three companies of Regular cavalry—that had spent the night a few miles in advance of the command. Tents were being struck as they arrived. During the brief stop Laura remained on her burro, and Mr. Franklin offered her a canteen of water, which she gratefully accepted. She sprinkled a little on her fingers to cool the back of her neck, which was becoming sunburned. She looked up and saw Colonel Chaves riding toward her with another officer.

"Miss Howland," he said, "may I have the honor to present to you Captain Howland?"

Laura blinked at the gentleman, aged thirty or so, who bowed in his saddle. "Well, sir," she said, "this is indeed a pleasure! I had become convinced you were a creature of myth. Are you one of the New York Howlands?"

"Rhode Island," he said, smiling. "The colonel here tells me you're heading for Pigeon's."

"Yes, Monsieur Vallé has offered me shelter."

Captain Howland nodded his approval. "I'm afraid I can't do any better for you, or I would."

"That's quite all right, Captain. I—well, I have lately considered myself not to have any family."

His face went grave. "I dislike Wallace Howland. I only met him once, and avoided him afterward. Had I known—"

"Please don't trouble yourself over it," Laura said. "I'm among friends now, and quite content, I assure you."

"Yes. Well, I hope you will call on me if I may be of service to you."

"Do you play whist?" Chaves asked.

"Yes," the captain said.

"Then you will undoubtedly be of service to her."

Chaves smiled at Laura. "I am to scout ahead, so I fear I cannot play cards with you tonight."

Captain Howland turned his head to glance at the men breaking camp. "I'd best get my fellows together. A pleasure meeting you, ma'am." He touched his hat and rode back to the Regulars, who were mounting up to join the column.

Colonel Chaves leaned toward Laura. "Do you see that man he is talking to?" he asked softly.

"Yes."

"That is Captain Lord."

Laura gazed at the man who had refused to advance at Valverde. He looked to her like any other soldier. Captains on all sides, she thought to herself, and all of them as fallible as ordinary men. Why do we make such heros of soldiers? And such villains of those who fail? She mused on the questions as the march resumed, happy to have something to distract her thoughts from dust and the plodding of horses.

The sun was starting to sink over a plaza strangely quiet. Pyron had moved his men to Johnson's Ranch that morning, leaving only a small guard in town to watch over the prisoners. Parker was among the latter, much to McIntyre's regret. Phillips, on a spree, had thrown his former employer in jail and then stormed the office of the *Gazette*. McIntyre wished he had never joined the Brigands, and said so as he and Russell picked up a quick trot south of the town.

"I haven't heard back from the general," said Russell. "Maybe when Scurry gets here."

McIntyre nodded. "It's going to be cold tonight."

"I've got blankets."

"You may feel me crawling under them," McIntyre said, and Russell laughed. They chatted on about nothing much until they came to the campfires scattered down the canyon near Johnson's Ranch. Hall and two other Brigands waited by the ranch house: Madison—whom Phillips had just promoted first lieutenant, probably to annoy McIntyre—and Thatcher. Pyron had assigned them and McIntyre to scout Glorieta Pass preparatory to moving his force into it the next day, as rumors had filtered down from the north that the garrison of Fort Union was on the march.

"Evening, Mac," Hall said. "You're running late."

"I have five till seven o'clock," McIntyre said checking his watch.

"Let's go, then." Hall turned away and started off at a trot followed by Madison, who had belatedly remembered he was supposed to be the leader of the scout.

"Good luck," Russell said. "Watch yourself."

"You watch your wagons, friend." McIntyre reached out to shake hands.

"Lacey?" Russell said.

"Yes?"

"Just—thanks."

McIntyre gave his hand a squeeze, then picked up a trot to rejoin Hall and the others.

"You're mighty friendly with the Q.M.," Hall said. "I hope you're not making any deals without including your compadres."

"I don't have anything to barter," McIntyre replied.

"No? Not even your influence with our dear captain?"

"Didn't think I had much of that," McIntyre said.

"You did once, my friend," Hall said. "And you could do again, but not by making up to the quartermaster."

McIntyre was silent, wanting the subject to drop. The moon wasn't up yet, and shadows closed around them as they rode through Apache Canyon. The walls were steep and high, making the canyon cold, and McIntyre hunched into his coat. There was ice in the Galisteo Creek bed. On the rocky hills the cedars and piñons looked stark green-black against dry winter grass. All around the land was silent, frozen in darkness, waiting. They scouted off the trail now and then, but saw no sign of any Federals all the way to Pigeon's Ranch, where they stopped for a cup of coffee. Pigeon did not come to serve them, which was just as well because McIntyre was not sure he would prove so forgiving as Mrs. Canby. Carmen waited on them, and if she recognized McIntyre she didn't show it.

They went on through the canyon, which gentled as they continued eastward. No camp evident along the river. No Federals at the Pecos ruin. Madison called a halt, and Hall turned to McIntyre. "You're the one that knows this route. Anywhere else they might be?"

McIntyre paused. "Just Kozlowski's."

"Where's that?"

"Another mile or so."

"All right," Madison said. "We'll go there, and if we don't find anything we'll start back."

There was a light burning in the ranch house when they arrived, so they dismounted and Madison knocked on the door. The rancher opened it a crack. "What do you want?"

"Seen any soldiers about, mister?" Madison said.

"No, I have not seen anyone."

Hall leaned a hand on the door. "You sure of that?"

"Leave him alone," McIntyre said. "He answered."

"Is that Lacey McIntyre?" Kozlowski asked.

McIntyre stepped forward. "Yes. Hello, Martin."

Kozlowski opened the door wider, revealing a bony frame. "I'm sorry," he said. "I thought it was maybe the Texans."

McIntyre opened his mouth but Hall kept him from answering, saying "Sure you haven't seen anyone?"

"No. Not a soul."

"All right. Thanks. Come on, boys," Hall said.

McIntyre stared hard at Kozlowski, whose eyes took on a shade of doubt. Hall pulled at his arm. "Good night, Mr. Kozlowski," he said, and went off with the others, hoping for the rancher's sake that Kozlowski had noticed his lack of uniform.

"We'll scout a little more in the canyon," Madison was saying. McIntyre glanced up at the eastern hills. It would be a long night.

* * *

Laura sat her burro with grim determination. Her legs were getting chafed despite the protection of the trousers. She silently thanked Lieutenant Franklin again for them. Setting modesty aside, without them she would have been rubbed raw.

It had been dark now for hours. Time had expanded into endless marching. The Santa Fé Trail seemed under some evil spell as it followed the river, now closer to the water, now farther, but never arriving anywhere. Laura had begun to think Major Chivington was a lunatic, and almost regretted insisting on going with the advance. She wanted to reach Pigeon's Ranch, she reminded herself, and if nothing else, she wanted to prove to the major that she was equal to his challenge. This spur of pride was enough to keep her erect in the saddle until a scout came galloping back.

"Major," she heard the man say, out of breath, "there's a ranch up ahead, and the rancher says there were four men there earlier, asking if he had seen soldiers!"

"Were there, by God? I'll speak to him!" Chivington said, spurring his horse to a trot. "Shoup, we'll halt at that ranch," he called over his shoulder, for which words Laura breathed a sigh of thanks.

The column crossed the river and stopped near a small cluster of buildings. Laura recognized Kozlowski's Ranch, the last stage station before the trail entered Glorieta Pass. She peered at the shapes of men and horses moving about her, listening for any familiar voice. The waning moon gleamed overhead, casting a little light. Finally she saw a slender figure approaching, and smiled though she doubted Lieutenant Franklin could see it.

"There you are, Miss Howland," he said. "Do you need help getting down?"

"Thank you," she replied. She could have dismounted alone but instead let him steady her, and was glad of his support for her knees threatened to buckle once she was on the ground. Her legs were sadly chafed, and she couldn't suppress a small moan.

"Poor lady," the lieutenant said. "You're not used to hard riding."

"Do not patronize me, Mr. Franklin. After you marched four hundred miles in thirteen days, you cannot think this is hard."

"You've marched twenty-five miles in one day," he said. "That's hard enough for a start."

The kindness in his voice warmed her. He took the burro's rein and led her toward the house. Moonlight glinted on the river, and though weary and aching, she was happy.

"We may have to leave you here," the lieutenant told her.

"But we're almost there!" Laura protested.

"Those four men were probably pickets. The Texans may already be in the pass. Please understand," he said, "I am only concerned for your safety."

Laura's smiled in the darkness. "I'm grateful," she said, "but I am not entirely helpless, sir."

The lieutenant was silent for a minute, then in a soft voice he said, "A woman alone doesn't have many choices, I'm afraid."

"I am not alone now," Laura said. "I have Colonel Chaves to protect me, and Captain O'Brien. And you." She looked at him but could not read his expression in the darkness. "Are you married, Lieutenant?"

"No," he said, with a surprised laugh. Laura was glad he could not see her blush.

They reached the ranch house, where light gleamed from all the windows and doors. A tavern nearby was open and doing brisk business. Major Chivington came out of the house with a lieutenant at his heels. "Where's Shoup?" he demanded, stopping on the porch, and his eyes fell on Laura. He frowned.

"Here, Major," Chivington's aide said, hurrying up.

"We'll rest here while a detail brings those pickets in," Chivington said, turning to the lieutenant beside him. "Nelson, you and Franklin here take twenty men and go catch them, quietly if you can."

"Yes, sir," Nelson said, and Laura heard Lieutenant Franklin catch his breath. She stared at Chivington in cold anger, sure he had done it to spite her. The major left the porch, giving more orders to Shoup as the two of them walked away.

Lieutenant Nelson looked at Franklin. "Ten from each company?"

"Yes," Franklin agreed. "I'll meet you back here in half an hour." Laura could hear his excitement in his voice. He turned to her. "Let me take you to the captain."

She bit back a bitter reply and allowed him to guide her through the milling soldiers and horses to where Company I waited for orders. Some of the men had built a fire, and Lieutenant Denning beckoned them toward it, inviting Laura to sit on a saddle on the ground.

"No, thank you," she said. "I might never get up again."

"Denning, can you take care of Miss Howland?" Mr. Franklin asked. "I've got to go—"

"Where?" Captain O'Brien said, coming up to the fire.

"Major Chivington has ordered me to go after the Rebel pickets, sir."

The captain's eyes narrowed, then he nodded.

"I'm to take ten men with me. May I pick any ten?"

"Take Shaunessy and Morris," O'Brien said. "Leave Carter, he's coming down with a chill."

"Yes, sir. Thank you," Lieutenant Franklin said, excitement writ on his face. "You'll look after her?" he asked, nodding toward Laura.

"Aye," the captain said. "Go on."

Shoup came up to them, saying, "We're to pitch camp. All your horses into the big corral." Denning took charge of Laura's burro, and Company I followed him with their horses, leaving her alone with O'Brien and Franklin.

She turned to the lieutenant. "Must you?"

Firelight glinted from his dark eyes. "This is what I'm here for," he said. "Don't worry, I'm not a fool."

"I am," she said. "Take me with you. You can drop me at Pigeon's."

He laughed and shook his head. "Miss Howland, you're intrepid, but you have to stop somewhere. You don't want to be caught in a war."

"I am stronger than you think," Laura said.

His eyes rested on her and a slow smile broke over his face, so full of delight that it made Laura giddy. "Of that I have no doubt," he said.

"Franklin!" The fury in the captain's voice made her jump.

"Sir?" the lieutenant looked up.

"A word," the captain said, with a jerk of his head toward the river.

Mr. Franklin glanced back at Laura, gave her a fleeting smile, and followed the captain away. She stood by the fire, watching them walk into the darkness, chilled by the anger in the captain's eyes.

O'Brien was fighting a battle as he led Franklin away from the camp. It was a battle he'd fought off and on since the first day they'd met: anger and fear against trust, wisdom against instinct. Instinct was winning just now. It had been a long day and he'd tired of watching Franklin flirt with the lady he, O'Brien, regarded as his own. When they reached the river's edge he turned and grabbed Franklin by the shoulders. "Listen now, Chas," he said. "I found her. You keep your bally hands off."

Franklin laughed. "I wouldn't touch her—"

"You're a lousy liar, laddie," O'Brien said, pushing him away. "What was all that just now?"

"I'm only concerned for her safety."

"Concerned, is it? At home we've another name for it."

Franklin stood half in shadow, but O'Brien could tell he had made a wry face. "Sir," he said, "if you knew. . . . You won't win her by sparring with me. If you want her you must earn her trust—"

"Must I then?" O'Brien said, goaded by this advice from a mere stripling. "Well, that'd be a sight easier if you weren't around!" With no further warning he swung his fist, and had the satisfaction of feeling it connect and hearing the lad's startled cry as he fell to the sand. He'd misjudged the distance in the dark and had not hit full on, but had hit well enough.

"Get up," O'Brien ordered, pulling off his overcoat and tossing it aside. "Get up and fight, then, you coward!"

"I won't fight over her," Franklin said from where he lay. The lad's voice was annoyingly calm, and O'Brien let go of any last charitable thoughts.

"Won't you, then? he said. "Ah, but you'll fight all the same!" With a lifetime's frustration breaking loose in him, O'Brien fell on his rival and grappled with him in the darkness.

24

Battle brings all speculation to a point.

—Ovando J. Hollister

O'Brien's hands were closing on Franklin's throat when a thump at his back sent him sprawling. Kicked, he realized as he rolled to his feet. It was the first blow Franklin had ever offered him. He laughed, peering through the darkness at the shape that was Franklin shedding his overcoat, half crouched.

"So you do have some fight in you!" O'Brien laughed.

He launched himself at Franklin and received a punch to the ribs that knocked his breath from him. Surprised, he took a step back. This was a Franklin he hadn't met before. He could hear the lad's breath fast and sharp and knew he had him rattled. He closed more cautiously, aiming another swing at Franklin's head, which he could see dark against the silvery river. Franklin saw it coming and dodged, glancing his own blow along O'Brien's jaw. O'Brien's hand went up and found blood.

"That was the hilt," Franklin said. "Don't make me use the blade."

O'Brien went cold with rage. "Bloody bastard." He thought of the wicked little knife with which Franklin had fended off some fool at Camp Weld—brought back the sight of it—right hand. O'Brien charged, knocking the lad's arms aside and landing them both in the river, where he found Franklin's wrist and twisted it until he dropped the knife. Franklin aimed a kick at his crotch that missed, and tried to thrash away but O'Brien had him by the wrist and got behind him, both of them on their knees in the river. O'Brien grimaced with pleasure as he bent the lad's arm up behind his back, forcing his head slowly toward the water, wanting Franklin to break and grovel and admiring him for not doing so. The boy's struggles became wilder as his face went into the river. O'Brien laughed softly, pressing him ever downward.

"Stop it! Stop it at once!"

Startled, O'Brien turned his head, bringing Franklin out of the water coughing and sputtering. The captain stared into the furious eyes of Miss Laura, standing at the river's edge with a burning brand in one hand and a knife in the other, beautiful and dangerous, fire and ice.

"Let him go, Captain," she said, her voice low and angry. "Let him go or you'll have to fight me, as well. The two of us together might equal you."

Fight drained away into shame. O'Brien released Franklin, who crawled from the water and knelt gasping. She took a step toward him, but Franklin held her off with a gesture and staggered to his feet. O'Brien stayed where he was.

"I want no more of this," Miss Laura said. "If you cannot behave decently to each other, I shall leave you and go to Captain Chapin!" She spoke as if she were scolding both of them, but her eyes were on O'Brien. When he didn't answer she turned to Franklin, who stood shivering with his arms across his chest. "Are you all right? You should come to the fire—"

Franklin shook his head, wet curls plastered to his brow, and reached down to pull his satchel out of the sand. "Got to go on the scout," he said, slinging it over his shoulder.

"You're not still going!" she exclaimed. "After this?"

Franklin's eyes went from her to O'Brien. "No one can say I haven't done my duty." He turned and picked up his coat, then stalked away toward the camp.

O'Brien sloshed to his feet, and the lady turned on him, knife glinting in torchlight. He stopped and raised his hands to placate her, dripping, knee-deep in the river. Her eyes remained hard and she slowly backed away, then turned to follow Franklin.

Left in darkness, O'Brien had nothing to do but regret his actions and think of all the ill that might come of them. He'd attacked Franklin. The lad could have him court martialed and likely cashiered. That was bad, but it meant nothing beside the way Miss Laura had looked at him. She despised him, would hate him forever for setting his hands on her beau. Thrashing himself with these thoughts, O'Brien slogged out of the river and headed straight for Kozlowski's tavern.

When she reached camp Laura found her tent half pitched and the men who'd been working on it standing around Lieutenant Franklin. She dropped her torch back into the firepit.

"Let me come with you," Denning was saying.

"No, we can't both go," Mr. Franklin said. "I want you to watch Miss Howland." He glanced at her, then back at the men. "Denning, would you go to the house and tell Lieutenant Nelson I'll be there soon? Morris, get the lads mounted up."

Denning left at a jog, and several others headed for the corral. "Go on, finish with the tents," Mr. Franklin told the rest. He looked up at Laura and came toward her. She had to clasp her hands under her cloak to keep from reaching out to him. "Thank you," he said with a wry smile. "I'm in your debt." He sat down by the fire and pulled off wet gloves, then took his pistol from its holster and began to empty it of soaked charges. Laura found her bedroll on the ground nearby, pulled a blanket from it to drape around the lieutenant's shoulders, and knelt beside him, watching him dry and reload his gun.

"I wish you wouldn't go," she said softly.

"Maybe you should go to Captain Chapin."

"Your hand is bleeding," Laura said.

Mr. Franklin glanced at his knuckles. "Just skinned," he said. "Miss Howland, I have a favor to ask of you."

"Of course," said Laura.

"It'll sound ungrateful," he said, his strange smile curling his handsome mouth. Slender fingers set new caps in place on the pistol barrel. "Don't be quite so partial to me."

Laura looked down at her hands gripped together in her lap. "I had no idea he would—"

"It doesn't matter. Trust me, you'll be doing yourself a favor, as well."

She raised her head. "Do you mean that you cannot like me?"

Franklin finished with his gun and looked up at her. "I like you, Miss Howland," he said. "Very much. But that's all."

Laura felt her eyes begin to sting. She looked at the fire and laughed. "You must think me a great fool."

"No," the lieutenant said. "I think you are a delightful young lady, and deserving of a man who is worthy of you. I admire you a great deal, Miss Howland."

"Admiration?" she said. "Some couples start with less."

He gave an exasperated laugh. "If you knew me better you would not find me so attractive."

"Give me the chance to decide that for myself," Laura said, meeting his eyes. They were full of mirth and, yes, admiration. If he could bear adversity with laughter, so could she. "I challenge you," she said lightly, "to a duel of admiration. Shall we see who is the winner?"

He grinned. "It'll have to wait. I've got a prior engagement with some Texans." They got to their feet, the lieutenant shedding the blanket, which Laura gathered up.

"Be careful," she said, laying a hand on his arm. He took it in his and gave it a squeeze, his eyes glinting silent laughter.

"I am always careful, Miss Howland."

With the crooked smile she'd become so fond of, he shrugged into his overcoat and strode away toward the corral. Laura became aware of the men staking tents nearby, and blushed at having addressed him so boldly before them. Lieutenant Denning returned and gave her a respectful bow.

"Are you hungry, Miss?" he asked. "I have some cold meat, or I could fetch you something from the tavern—"

"No, thank you." Laura felt unsteady all of a sudden. "I think I'll lie down," she said, reaching for her bedroll.

"I'll be nearby if you need anything."

Laura went into her tent, tied the flap behind her, and spread out her bed. Exhaustion and worry conspired to make her hands shake as she unlaced her boots. Don't be a ninny, she told herself. There are twenty men against four. If you insist on loving soldiers, you will have to live with the dangers they face.

Laura stopped, realizing she had not before admitted to herself that what she felt for Lieutenant Franklin was love. With a politician's cold objectivity she analyzed her emotions, comparing what she felt now with her response to Lieutenant McIntyre, whom she had practically forgotten. That had been a pleasant association despite having gone awry, but it was nothing like her feelings now. She had no caution now, no reservations despite obvious disadvantages; she was playing the fool, she acknowledged, and how delicious and perplexing it was. Perhaps the excitement and uncertainty of the last few days had addled her senses, and restoration to her friends would cure her. She doubted it. Lieutenant Franklin—Charles Franklin—had taken a grip on her heart whether he liked it or no.

Laura shook her head, amazed at herself. Perhaps she belonged in a soldier's camp. Her recent behavior had certainly not been very ladylike. Well, she could make amends for that. She would not annoy the lieutenant. She would be patient and good, and hope to change his mind. She said a brief prayer for his safety, then wrapped up in cloak and blankets, and slept.

O'Brien was out of whiskey. He roused himself, gazing at his surroundings and slowly comprehending that he was in the yard near the ranch house, seated against a wall opposite the tavern, which had closed. It was dark. The remains of a fire nearby were down to orange and gray. Snores from a body lying near. O'Brien got to his feet and stumbled along to the tavern. He banged on the door a few times, but no answer. He turned round and leaned on the door, squinting up at the blue-black sky. No moon, not from where he was anyway. All darkness for him. He raised his bottle to his lips and let the last drops chase down its neck to his tongue, then threw it away to clatter against the wall. Dead soldier, he thought, and chortled.

Somewhere away down the hill were some fires, so he headed toward them. If there was a man awake who had liquor, O'Brien would have it of him. He saw a sentry near the corral and went up to him asking for whiskey.

"Sorry, sir," the guard said. "If I had any I'd have drunk it by now."

O'Brien scowled at him and went away toward the fires, most of them burning low. He trudged from one to the next looking for someone awake. He came across two tents in front of a fire with a few yellow flames still licking about the coals. Before the smaller tent lay two bedrolls. One was his, he could tell from the singed corner of a blanket. The other must be Franklin's.

Franklin. He had tried to throttle Franklin, he remembered, and then his lady had stopped him. A great sadness overwhelmed him. Why had the lad gone and angered him? He tried to remember how the fight had started, but couldn't think of anything except the boy's frightened breathing and how that had waked the hunter in him. He was sorry for it now. Franklin was not such a bad fellow, if only he would leave off the girl.

He looked up at the larger tent that was his. Where was Franklin? Inside? Would she have let him? Anger started to burn in O'Brien's belly. He licked his lips, frowning. There was something else—Franklin had been going somewhere—he couldn't remember. Maybe he'd been and come back, and was lying with the girl even now.

"No!" he said under his breath. He ground the heel of his hand into his eye, trying to think through the whiskey haze. Franklin was still gone, he told himself, or he'd have put his gear in the tent. She wouldn't have let him in, would she?

He thought of her lying there, there in his tent. Alone? Shouldn't be alone on a cold night. How he wanted her! He'd warm her soon enough. She shouldn't flirt with Franklin when it was he who had found her. She should save her smiles for him. Well, if she wouldn't, maybe he would just take them.

He walked up to the tent and reached for the center pole in front, grasping its top with one hand. The tent ropes creaked as the pole took his weight.

Gentleman. Gentleman wouldn't. He stood staring at the canvas as if he could see through it if he looked hard enough. She was his lady—he had found her—and all he wanted was just to look at her and maybe touch her hair. He wouldn't hurt her, even though she'd been proud and cold. He would never hurt her.

He closed his eyes. He was very, very drunk, but even so he knew that if he entered her tent at that moment he would lose whatever chance he had left of winning her trust and forgiveness. Better to act like a gentleman, even if he could never be one. He would pay for his sins, and maybe she'd forgive him someday.

He let go the tent pole and backed away, almost stumbling into the fire. With a muttered curse he kicked at the coals, then went into Franklin's tent. It was empty. He had left his bedroll outside. He would get it in a minute, but he had to sit down now, he was dizzy, and so tired. He sat on the hard ground and then leaned on one elbow. In a minute he would get up. He just needed to rest his head for a bit. Just for a minute.

Laura sat motionless, blankets clutched to her bosom, not daring to breathe. She was sure it was Captain O'Brien's shadow she'd seen, cast on the canvas by the dying fire behind him. She listened, but he had not come back out of the other tent.

Had he just mistaken her tent for Franklin's? Forgotten he'd loaned it to her? She did not believe it. She chided herself for not finding out where Captain Chapin was camped. Perhaps he was up at the ranch house. She could seek him there, but by now everyone was asleep; she'd have to rouse the whole house, all because a shadow had frightened her.

He had not come in. She took a shaky breath, then froze again as she heard a sound from nearby, half moan, half sigh. The captain had fallen asleep. No, she would *not* cry. She bit her lip and slowly felt down the length of her cloak until she found the pocket. Slipping her hand into it, she withdrew first her father's portrait, then her knife, and with one in each hand she lay back down, staring at the last flickers of firelight on the canvas, for sleep had deserted her.

25

---

*I am persuaded there are but few brave men by nature.
...Many, whose patriotism is unaffected and pure, would
flinch at the last moment but for self-respect. That I
believe is the only boon more precious than life.*

— Ovando J. Hollister

There were no lights at Pigeon's. McIntyre glanced eastward, where a sliver of moon was rising, and figured it was
nigh on four o'clock. He grunted as he helped Thatcher
haul up another bucket from the well and set it down for
the horses.

"We go back when I say we go back," Madison said.

Hall sat on the low stone wall of the well. "Madison,
you're a damned bloated toad. If there were any Yanks
around we'd have found 'em."

McIntyre kept out of it, strolling a few steps away.
Phillips may have promoted Madison to spite him, but it
looked like he'd missed his aim; Hall was more annoyed
by it than he. He gazed at Pigeon's house across the road,
thinking of a fandango and Miss Howland in a pretty blue
dress. He wondered where she was now. Far beyond his
reach, no doubt.

"We're going to keep scouting the pass until I say it's
clear," Madison said.

"Fine," Hall replied. "Well, since we've scouted the east
side twice already, what say we give the west another good
scout? Come on, Thatcher," he said, getting on his horse
and taking out a flask. Thatcher glanced at Madison, then
followed Hall.

McIntyre had no sympathy for Madison, who deserved

to be called a Brigand as much as any of his comrades. "We'd better stay together," he said, and mounted his own horse, leaving Madison no choice but to follow them back in the direction of Santa Fé.

Hall handed his flask to McIntyre as he caught up. "I'm for finding a spot to catch some shut-eye. Think your quartermaster friend'll put us up?"

"Would you be grateful if he did?"

Hall laughed. "Oh, I suppose so. If he could provide a girl to warm the blankets, definitely."

"He's always complaining that he can't keep them in stock," McIntyre said, which earned him a hoot from Hall.

They topped the pass and began descending the other side. A little farther on, Madison insisted on investigating an old shack that stood by the canyon wall behind a screen of pines.

"There's nothing in it but corn and flour." McIntyre had helped Russell stash the supplies there, but Madison insisted so they rode cautiously toward the building. They dismounted at the pines and left Thatcher holding the horses while they moved slowly into the shadows. Madison took the lead, pistol in hand. McIntyre glanced at Hall and saw him raise a hand to his face, then slip off through the trees to one side. Keeping silent, he watched Madison while trying to decide where to stand to avoid being shot. Madison had reached the door and listened at it, started to move and then froze.

"There's someone outside" came a muffled, high-pitched half whisper. "Get the gun, Walter!"

Madison jumped and then pointed his pistol at the door. Even from ten feet away in dim moonlight McIntyre could see his hand shaking. "Come out with your hands up!" he said.

A shuffling step preceded the appearance of Hall at the corner of the building. Madison jumped again and aimed at Hall, and for a heartbeat McIntyre thought he would fire.

"Get the gun, Walter!" Hall cried in the same falsetto,

eyes wide. Then he started to laugh, and McIntyre laughed, too, while Madison cussed. McIntyre walked forward and pushed open the door, revealing sacks of flour piled to the ceiling. Still cussing, Madison sat in the doorway and took a long pull at the flask Hall handed him. Thatcher came up with the horses, demanding his share of the whiskey. They passed it around until it was gone, then got back in the saddle and rode west again. There were no more excursions to scout the pass. They stayed on the trail, heading for the first warm bed available.

Light was growing behind them as they entered a narrow gap between two hills. A short distance ahead was a party of maybe two dozen on horseback, riding toward them.

"See?" Thatcher said to Madison. "Major Pyron's already got his men in the canyon."

It felt wrong. McIntyre reached out toward Hall but Madison had already ridden into the opposite group. McIntyre saw a pale strip of gold on a shoulder. Panic gripped him. He pulled back on his reins, about to turn and spur, but a voice said, "Don't move! Hands away from your weapons, now, nice and slow."

It was over. McIntyre let go the reins and slowly raised his hands. His career was over, and he hadn't even fired a shot in combat.

The larger party surrounded them and began to take their weapons. In incredulous tones another voice said, "Hall?"

"Hello, Chas," Hall said, and his right hand made a sudden move toward his gun.

McIntyre flinched, expecting to be riddled with bullets, but the stranger said, "Don't, Hall!" and at the sight of a dozen rifle barrels Hall thought better of it. They were disarmed and their hands tied in front of them—a courtesy to let them use them for balance—but their reins were taken and they were led, surrounded by soldiers, eastward back through the pass. McIntyre wondered why he was not more upset. All he felt was a kind of numbness. Who was the man who had recognized Hall? Hall had only been in the Territory a few weeks. It must have been someone who knew him before. . . .

In Colorado. The back of McIntyre's neck began to prickle. Colorado men in Glorieta Pass? There'd been no word the Federals had been reinforced. If he wished to be a hero, he could try to break free and ride back to Johnson's Ranch—it wasn't far—and warn Major Pyron. Hall would have done it, but Hall didn't try. Perhaps he didn't realize how important the information was. McIntyre shifted in the saddle, glancing at the soldiers surrounding him. He stood a good chance of losing his life if he tried to escape. Did he care enough for the Confederate cause to lay down his life in its service? Apparently not, for he rode quietly on, over the pass, beyond Pigeon's Ranch, losing faith in himself with every plodding step of his horse.

Sorry, Russell, he thought. Sorry Owens, and Pyron, and even Phillips. Sorry everyone. I've failed. Again.

Streaks of pink were streaming up from the east. McIntyre was thirsty but no water was offered and he didn't ask. They turned south at the Pecos, and McIntyre knew they were headed for Kozlowski's. He would be imprisoned there, to languish through the coming battle—for there would be a battle, no doubt—and await transportation to a guard house, either at Fort Union or Santa Fé. If the Texans won, he might be released. If he was he'd resign—well, no, he had no commission to resign. He could leave, if they freed him, just up and disappear back to Tennessee. Become a farmer, which was maybe what he should have been all along.

As the sun rose over a mass of tents between Kozlowski's and the river, all hope of freedom faded. Several hundred men were camped at the ranch, at least as many as Pyron had, McIntyre guessed, and Scurry was two or three days' march away. No, not likely he'd be rescued.

Their guards led them up to the ranch house. One of them must have ridden ahead, for a whole clot of officers were waiting on the steps, and McIntyre didn't recognize any of them. No—that was Manuel Chaves. McIntyre dropped his head, not wanting to meet Chaves's eyes.

"Good work, Nelson," said a loud voice. "Bring them inside."

Their captors helped them dismount and the two Colorado lieutenants led them into the house. Bacon was frying back in the kitchen. McIntyre tried to ignore the smell, but his stomach was already growling. Martin Kozlowski stared from a doorway, and McIntyre gave him a rueful smile as they passed. He was in for it now—he was so tangled up he had no notion where he would end.

One of Kozlowski's rooms had been made into headquarters. They were pushed inside and left standing in the center of the room while the officers arranged themselves around the walls. The door was closed. McIntyre glanced at the two lieutenants who had led the party that captured them, standing guard with pistols drawn, and at the big man in a major's straps who sat behind the table and was obviously their commander. "Good morning, Mr. Hall," the major said. "Would you care to explain yourself? I don't suppose we'll find Captain Dodd's company in Santa Fé."

Hall smirked and said nothing. McIntyre swallowed. The major did not sound like a forgiving man.

"Señor Lacey," a voice he knew said. "¿Qué haces con estos hombres?"

"Do you know this man, Colonel?" The major sounded surprised.

McIntyre looked up at Chaves, who was regarding him with doubtful eyes. "He was a member of Colonel Canby's staff," Chaves said.

The major stood up. "*Two* traitors? We seem to have made a fine catch! A staff member turned traitor," the major said, coming around the table to shout in McIntyre's face. "By God, sir, you will hang for it!"

"I resigned!" McIntyre said, unable to keep from cringing.

"Resigned, did you?" The major turned to Hall. "And I suppose you resigned, too?"

"Never mind him, Mac," Hall said in an insolent voice. "The reverend here can spit brimstone pretty well, but he can't hold us. Soon as Scurry comes up we'll go free."

You stupid fool, McIntyre thought.

"Scurry—that's—"

"A lieutenant-colonel," Chaves said. "Commanding one of the Texas regiments."

"He's a full colonel now."

"Shut up, Hall," McIntyre said.

"Where is your Colonel Scurry?" the major asked.

There was a pause, then Hall said, "Right the other side of the pass."

McIntyre stared at the floor. He heard Chaves murmuring something to the major but couldn't catch the words. They questioned Thatcher and Madison, got little out of them, and returned to Hall who went on lying, boasting of a force at Scurry's command larger than what Sibley had fielded at Valverde. Maybe they would believe him, but McIntyre doubted it. The major encouraged Hall's braggadocio and McIntyre listened in despairing silence while he dropped bits of gold among the chaff: Pyron's departure from Santa Fé, Sibley's presence at Albuquerque, Scurry's route from Tijeras on the Galisteo road. If the Colorado major didn't know the value of that information, Chaves surely would. Finally the major tired of Hall and turned his harsh gaze on McIntyre.

"A staff officer," he said. "Whose staff are you on now?"

"No one's," McIntyre said.

"He works for the Q.M." Hall said with a laugh.

"You're in the quartermaster department?" the major asked.

"We all are." McIntyre glared at Hall. "We're guides."

"How much ordnance do you have?"

"I don't know," McIntyre replied.

"How many guns?"

"Don't know."

"Where's your supply train?"

"Santa Fé." That was an important lie; Russell's safety

might depend on it, not to mention that of Pyron's advance guard. McIntyre tried not to move, tried to stay relaxed, and prayed that Hall would keep his mouth shut. The Colorado major stared hard at him for a minute, then walked back to the table.

"Shoup, detail a guard, find someplace to lock them up. Then tell the commanders to prepare to march." The major glanced up at the prisoners again. "Take them away."

McIntyre sighed with relief as he left the room. Their guards took them outside to wait, and McIntyre sat on the ground, rested his head on his bound wrists, and closed his eyes.

"Congratulations." A woman's voice spoke from nearby. "I imagine you're starving."

McIntyre raised his head and confirmed his amazement. "Miss Howland!"

She was handing bread and bacon to one of his captors—the lieutenant who'd recognized Hall—and both of them turned to look at him in surprise. Chagrin flooded him as her gaze hardened.

"You know this man?" the lieutenant asked.

"Somewhat," said Miss Howland.

McIntyre was unable to look away from her. She wore a dusty cloak and no bonnet, her hair a wispy tousle. She was sunburned and lovelier than ever.

"I'm sorry," McIntyre whispered.

"Yes," she said evenly. "I imagine you are."

He swallowed, trying to wet his parched throat. "Would you do me a favor? Tell the colonel I'd like to be exchanged, if it's possible?"

"I don't think my word would bear any weight with him," she said, her eyes softening. "But I will tell him, if I see him."

"Thank you." McIntyre continued to gaze at her, wondering how she came to be here in the midst of an army. Had she married some other soldier—his captor, perhaps? McIntyre envied him, though he couldn't help but wish for her happiness.

She removed a canteen from her shoulder, which she opened and offered to McIntyre. He drank greedily while she held it for him, then smiled his thanks. She smiled back, that brief smile he remembered, but she was not the same reserved girl from Boston. She was both stronger and gentler than before. He watched her give water to the others, wishing he had been with her to see the change, feeling he had missed something important.

The Colorado officer returned, and the prisoners got to their feet and were led toward the back of the ranch. McIntyre glanced at Miss Howland with a last rueful smile. "Give my best to Mrs. C.," he said. She made no answer, but stood beside the young lieutenant with unbearable pity in her eyes, and McIntyre stared back at her until the buildings came between them.

Something was wrong. Jamie poured out the cold coffee in his cup and refilled it with hot. He'd built up the fire when he finally went to bed, and the coals were still plenty warm when he rose again, but McIntyre and the others hadn't returned. The guard hadn't seen a sign of the four scouts and were tired of being asked. Pyron had sent out four more to look for them at dawn, and was now pacing up and down in front of his tent. Something was definitely wrong.

"Where'd they go, sonny?"

Jamie started at Phillips's voice, spilling coffee over his hand. He hissed and wiped off the scalding liquid, then looked up at the Brigands' captain who stood across the fire with thumbs hooked suggestively in his gun belt.

"How should I know?" Jamie said.

"You're the last one that saw them," Phillips replied. "You and your Yankee friend came from Santa Fé late. He plan this?"

Jamie shook his head, impatient with Phillips's suspicions. "They were going to scout the pass. If he had any other plans he didn't tell me. And he wasn't the only Yankee in the party."

Phillips's face got more sour and Jamie knew he should have kept silent. "Where were you and him in town?" Phillips asked.

"Having dinner with a friend."

"His Yankee lady friend?" Phillips gave the sneer that was as close as he got to a smile. "Think we're stupid? We watched him. Turn coats once, he could do it again. What did you boys talk about with old Mrs. Canby?"

"Nothing," Jamie said, watching Phillips stroll around the fire toward him. "We never talked military matters."

"She get any letters from her husband?"

"Do you think she'd tell us if she had?" Jamie said.

Phillips shrugged. "She might. Did she?"

"No. Not that I know of."

"Sure about that?" said Phillips, sitting on the ground next to Jamie. He took out a pocket knife and began to pare his dirty fingernails. "Maybe your memory needs jogging."

"Phillips, you're fishing in a dry well," Jamie said. He finished his coffee and stood up to look over the camp. He'd pitched his tent on the hill up by the ranch house, partly to keep an eye on the house, and to give him a view of the train.

"Maybe the Yankee lady'd remember more."

Jamie stared down at Phillips, crouched on the ground like some nasty little animal, and wanted to kick him. "You leave her alone," he said. "She doesn't know anything."

"Like her a lot, do you? She do you any special favors? Got a pretty maid, maybe, and a spare bedroom?"

"You're disgusting," Jamie said, turning away. Climbing the hill toward him he saw Major Pyron, who waved aside his salute.

"Phillips, get your company together," Pyron said. "We're marching."

The Brigand got up, dusted his filthy leathers, and ambled away with a last sour glance at Jamie.

"Do you want the train, sir?" Jamie asked.

"No," said Pyron. "We're just going to secure the pass until Scurry comes up."

Jamie wanted to ask about the scouts, but he knew from Pyron's frown what the answer would be so he kept silent. He gazed out toward the craggy hills through which McIntyre had gone, still hoping to see him riding back.

"Don't worry, son." Pyron's voice was so gentle Jamie looked up in surprise. "We'll see the inside of Fort Union in a few days."

Jamie gave Pyron a smile he didn't feel and watched the major tramp back down to the camp. Fort Union and then what? he wondered. Colorado? San Francisco? Every victory took him farther from home. He should write Momma, he thought for the hundredth time, though there was no way to mail a letter just now. But if he were going to write to anyone it should be Emma, and he hadn't yet found the courage to start that letter. If he put it in words on paper then Martin would truly be gone forever. As it was, Jamie'd been mostly able to pretend he was just out foraging or scrounging up more transportation. Except at night. That was when he felt most alone. He shivered, and went down the hill to distract himself with wagons and mules.

O'Brien felt half dead, although he'd been up for some hours. He regretted the fight near as much as the whiskey, and rode in silence, glancing now and then at his lady or at Franklin. The lad had said nothing. Maybe he was waiting for the chance to press charges, and O'Brien would know when the guards were upon him. Or maybe he'd forgotten the row in the flush of his scouting success.

Hall was taken, a prisoner back at the army camp, shamed. It made O'Brien angry: at Franklin, at Hall, at himself. That his friend could have gone to the enemy was too bad to think of, and in his muddled state he refused to think of it, turning his mind instead to matters nearer his own heart.

Miss Laura. An ice maiden, riding through the army's dust with silent patience. I Company had the rear guard today, with the Regulars and F Company before them, and the infantry in front of all. The choking dust did nothing for O'Brien's mood.

The road wound into the hills and eventually came to a glen where the infantry halted near an adobe building. O'Brien saw Laura prod her burro to a trot, heading toward the house.

"Halt and dismount," O'Brien said to Denning, then kicked up his horse and went after Laura with Franklin behind him. The column was falling out, breaking out rations for lunch. Miss Laura reached the house and jumped down from her burro as a tall man came out of the building.

"Miss Howland?" he said. "Qu'est-ce que c'est?"

"I am throwing myself on your mercy, monsieur," said the lady, smiling as she met him. "Am I still welcome?"

"But of course!" The tall man caught her in a hug that would have boiled O'Brien's blood had the fellow been younger. Franklin dismounted and went up to them, and O'Brien followed.

"May I introduce my friend, monsieur?" she said. "Charles Franklin, Alexandre Vallé."

Franklin shook the man's hand. "Mademoiselle m'avait dit que vous êtes un bon ami," he said.

"Elle n'a pas trop des amis," Vallé said with a smile.

"C'est vrais," Miss Laura said.

O'Brien stood by, feeling a fool. The tall fellow looked at him with raised eyebrows, and O'Brien feared he'd start babbling in some foreign language. He was about to leave when Miss Laura turned toward him. All thoughts fell away as she raised her eyes to his for the first time that day.

"And this is Captain O'Brien," she said, "Captain, this is Monsieur Vallé."

"Call me Pigeon, if you like, Captain," said the man, shaking O'Brien's hand. "I am glad to see this army. The Texans, they are making trouble in Santa Fé."

"Not for long," O'Brien said.

Pigeon smiled. "Miss Howland, I like your friends."

"I like them, too," she said. "I shall miss them." She

glanced at O'Brien again, and he felt as if he'd been struck. She was saying good-bye. He must leave her. Though he'd known she would stop at this ranch, he'd not faced it, and a great wrench it was to think she'd ride with them no longer.

Wild thoughts raced through him. He wanted her more now than ever, enough to bind himself in marriage for her sake, and give her all his poor fortune. If he threw himself down at her feet, would she take pity on him, forgive him?

"You'll look after her?" Franklin was saying.

"Certainement," the rancher said.

Franklin turned to the lady, who gave him her hand. "Keep safe, Miss Howland."

"Laura," she said, and O'Brien clenched his teeth. Franklin smiled, saying nothing, and turned to his horse. O'Brien waited to see if Miss Laura would offer her hand to him as well. She did, but her fingers slipped from his almost at once. "Good-bye, Captain," she said. "Thank you for your protection."

Words choked in his throat. He'd been dreaming to think she might have him, a poor Irish soldier. Dreaming to think she would ever forgive him for harming her dear Franklin. Such things happened only in fairy tales, and she was no fairy, however like one she might look.

"You must come back soon," Pigeon said. "Miss Howland's friends are always welcome."

O'Brien glanced at him and could only nod. He bowed to the lady, touching his hat, and managed to tear his eyes from her. Two strides took him back to his horse. He was in the saddle and kicking the beast to a trot before he had time to feel the loss of her. It was pain, that loss, real as any wound, and he gritted his teeth as he rode back to his company.

Denning handed him a strip of dried beef. O'Brien dismounted and bit off a piece, but it was dust in his mouth. Looking up, he saw Franklin watching, a strange sadness in his dark eyes. With a shock O'Brien knew, sure as Franklin had spoken, that no assault charge would be filed.

The next instant the lad turned away, leading his horse down to chew the grass in the dry creekbed.

O'Brien drew a breath. Strange forces flying today, he could feel it. The gray, leafless trees hid invisible spirits, weaving cobwebs of magic too fine for mere humans to see. A destiny day, his mother would have called it.

O'Brien caught his horse's reins and led it after Franklin. The lad had sat down on a rock, but rose as he approached. In his hand was an image, the one O'Brien had seen before, of his sister and brother. O'Brien let the horse go to grazing, and met Franklin's eyes. "I'm sorry for last night," he said.

Franklin glanced down, a smile twisting his mouth, and gave a curt nod. "You love her very much, don't you?" he asked softly.

What a question! Before O'Brien could form a reply, the lad spoke again.

"You have nothing to fear from me, Captain," he said. In his voice was a sadness, a hollowness. O'Brien did the only thing he could think of, which was to pull out his flask and offer it to Franklin. The lad gave a soft laugh as he looked at the silver, then took it and raised it. "Your good fortune, Captain O'Brien," he said, and drank, then passed the flask back.

"Alastar," O'Brien said, offering his hand.

Franklin coughed slightly and looked at it, then smiled his odd smile. "Alastar," he said, and shook hands. O'Brien could feel the warmth of his hand through the glove. Heaven knew why, but the lad seemed to like him, in spite of all his abuse. And in spite of himself, he liked Franklin. When he wasn't furious with him.

Bugles called them back to the road. The column was forming to march, and they brought their horses away from the streambed to join the company.

Chivington had doubled the pickets. O'Brien could see them disappearing over the hilltop a half mile ahead. The column moved forward. All the way up the hill O'Brien resisted looking back, but as they began descending he let himself glance at the ranch house just before it was out of sight. There she was, standing on the porch with the rancher, watching them over the hill. To hell with it—he would be in a battle by tomorrow. He'd come back and find her tonight and offer her his heart and hand. Then if she refused he could die bravely, for he'd have little reason to live.

They marched down a long slope between thick stands of pine. Before they had reached the bottom the sound of thundering hooves made O'Brien look up. The pickets were charging back toward them, yelling and whooping. The infantry was already closing ranks and O'Brien spurred forward. Now he could see that one of the pickets had a man prisoner, and as he galloped up to the column he shouted, "We've got them corraled this time! Give them hell, boys!"

"Hurrah for the Pike's Peakers!" Morris yelled, throwing his hat in the air.

Over the din of answering cheers came Chivington's voice ordering the cavalry into open orders by fours. O'Brien passed on the command, and the column began to advance at the double-quick. Elation washed away all other feelings. They were going into battle at last, and O'Brien grinned with glee.

The infantry shed knapsacks and coats and canteens by the roadside. All eyes looked eagerly forward, all hearts raced. The column rounded a bend in the road and found two cannon, not two hundred yards off, facing straight at them with a clot of men surrounding them. Beside the cannon was a red flag bearing a white star—Texas.

Chivington ordered the infantry into the hills on either side. The Regulars parted and fell back, leaving the mounted Pike's Peakers to face the guns. O'Brien cursed the Regular officers, who were plunging about and shouting to no purpose, and brought his men into line beside F Company. A glance at Cook, who nodded, and O'Brien resumed his grim smile.

"So that's what Rebels look like," he said to Franklin, gazing at the line behind the cannon. Then a crash of fire and smoke sent the first shell screaming over their heads.

26

That tremendous event, the burden of history and song, a battle, *burst on our hitherto peaceful lives like an avalanche.*

—Ovando J. Hollister

Laura's head snapped up and she nearly dropped her coffee cup as her eyes met Vallé's. A second explosion brought both to their feet, running for the door. Nothing could be seen, but a crackling sound echoed from the valley's rock walls. Laura realized it must be the sound of rifles firing.

"Go back inside, Miss Howland," Vallé said.

Laura shook her head, eyes on the hilltop where she'd watched the Colorado men disappear a short time before.

"Please go in, mademoiselle. I will go and see what is happening, and come back to tell you."

"Take me with you," Laura said.

"Mon Dieu! That is madness!"

"If you don't I'll follow you."

An incredulous smile broke over Vallé's face. "Ah! Someone has set you on fire! Bien, we will go then." He looked at his watch. "Wait here, I will bring the horse."

Instead Laura fetched her cloak and followed him to the corral to catch her burro. She would not be carried before his saddle like a sack of meal. The burro heaved a sigh as she threw the blanket and saddle over its back, and she had to poke it in the belly twice with her stick to make it exhale while she tightened the girths. She was ready as soon as Vallé looked for her, and together they trotted up the hill. Laura expected to see the battle from the top of the pass, but as they reached it there was no one in sight but a few stragglers on horseback. They rode on through the hills toward Apache Canyon, the noise of the fighting increasing. As they crested a hill, Laura gazed in wonder at the scatter of discarded clothing and equipment that lined the Santa Fé Trail as far as she could see.

"This way," Vallé said, leading her off the road up a steep hill. Before they reached its summit he stopped by a stand of cedar. "Wait here, I will find a place where it is safe to see."

"I will wait five minutes, monsieur," Laura said.

"Patience, mademoiselle! I swear I will return for you. Stay behind the trees."

She watched him walk his horse from tree to tree until their screen concealed him. Laura stared at the dry, brown leaves of a scrub oak. Impatience made her drive her nails into her palms. The noise of the battle seemed to increase with each passing minute, steady boom of the cannon and a continuous snapping of rifles. She thought of Lieutenant Franklin and prayed he would not be harmed. Why, she wondered, had God put such a strong heart into a fragile body?

The cannonade ceased abruptly. Laura was about to leave her shelter and pursue Vallé when he appeared at the hilltop and beckoned to her. "The Texans are retreating," he said. Laura urged her burro after him to a spot near an outcrop of rock that gave a view of Apache Canyon below. A straggling column of men were disappearing down the trail, and Chivington on horseback was preparing to follow them. As she watched they took up the march, with cavalry before and behind the infantry. Laura peered at the officers, trying to spot Lieutenant Franklin. Yes, there he was near Chivington, with Captain O'Brien and the officers of F Company. Her heart gave a sickening thump to see him at the front of the advance. She would much prefer him to be in the rear, but the Regulars seemed to have made up the rearguard; she could see Captain Howland. They appeared to be in no hurry, and Laura sensed a deep misgiving. She watched Lieutenant Franklin ride out of view and turned to Vallé.

"Let's go on."

"I should take you back to the house," he said.

For answer Laura prodded her burro forward. As they went down into the canyon they began to see trees whose limbs had been ripped and torn by cannon fire and peppered with musket balls. A deep gully on their right and a steep hill to the left forced them to descend onto the trail, and Laura began to have second thoughts about pursuing. Vallé pointed out where the Rebel cannon had stood, trampled dust blackened with soot. A little distance away lay a dead man, fallen in an unnatural heap of twisted limbs, blood pooling beneath him. Laura stared at him, surprised at how similar death looked on a battlefield as in a coffin. Nothing would bother that young man again.

They rode until they came up with a body of horses standing in the road, clumped in groups of three or four held by a soldier. Among the trees Laura spied their riders and the infantry swarming up the hills to either side of the road. Vallé led her up a small rise and they dismounted behind scrub bushes, holding the mounts' reins while they watched the men climb the steep hills. Farther down the road Laura saw men on horseback, the two mounted companies from Colorado, with Chivington conspicuous in their front. Beyond them was a bridge over the gully—or rather there had been, for she could see that the Texans had pulled it down—and beyond that the trail swung around a curve out of sight. In front of the curve were two cannon, aimed straight back up the canyon.

"They are there," Vallé said, pointing. "Across the arroyo, in the trees."

Laura followed his gaze and saw rifle barrels glinting on the hillsides past the bridge and above the cannon. As she watched, smoke began to puff among the trees and rocks, and answering rifles clattered from the forces in blue on the nearer hills. Laura moved closer to Vallé, her hand finding his, fear singing in her veins as she watched the men on the hills move forward and Chivington gather his mounted troops together.

*   *   *

"Hospital!" Jamie shouted, riding Cocoa into the midst of the hands who had run toward the pass when the cannon started up again. A rider came scrambling out of the canyon and galloped off in the direction of Galisteo.

"Get those supplies up there," Jamie said, pointing to Johnson's house. "Go on, there's nothing to see!"

He followed the grumbling hands back to the camp. Cocoa's warm body beneath him was comforting—he hadn't had time to saddle her—and he stayed on her while he oversaw the transfer of bedding and medical supplies to the ranch house. All the while his heart was pounding as painfully as if he were facing the guns himself. From the sound of it the battle was not more than a mile off, though the echoing hills might deceive. Jamie left Cocoa by his tent and returned to help carry. Walking into the hospital where the surgeon was preparing took him back to Valverde, and he set down the pile of blankets with shaking hands. "Please, Jesus God," he whispered, though for what he was praying he did not know.

O'Brien glanced at the hillsides where Union men had nearly flanked the Rebels. The Regular cavalry, whose officers had failed to follow Chivington's order to charge the retreating cannon, had been dismounted as punishment and sent to help the infantry.

Chivington, with a pistol in either hand and two more tucked into his belt, chewed his lips and frowned as he peered down the canyon at the two guns planted in the bend of the road. The Texans held a strong position and were pumping shells from their cannon as fast as they could load.

O'Brien glanced at Franklin—pale but calm, a heroic knight to make the maidens swoon—and fought down a pang of jealousy as he turned in the saddle to look over his company. The first shells had thrown the Pet Lambs into confusion, causing them to crowd behind some rocks for shelter, but they were steady now.

Chivington raised up his right hand, and yelled out, "Charge!"

The canyon was narrow, forcing them to attack in column right in the face of the cannon. F Company led the way, with cannister from the cannon and minié balls from the men on the hillsides raining about them. Cook was hit but kept riding, then fifty yards farther his horse stumbled with him and went down. O'Brien rode past—glimpsed Cook squirming away from the deadly flying hooves—then the world was down to hoofbeats pounding and the balls shrieking all around. Franklin's bay thundered beside him. The mustang tossed his head and screamed at the smell of blood. The Rebel cannon had disappeared down the road, and ahead the gully gaped. F Company's horses were leaping it where the bridge had been pulled down. One animal didn't make it and tumbled with its rider into the ditch. With a roar O'Brien spurred the mustang to fly across the gap. As one, mustang and bay hit the far side and were in among the Texans, charging through their line and scattering them.

O'Brien slashed about him with his saber, lost it and fired his pistol into a man's face. Many of the Texans had retreated after their cannon. Those who remained sought the shelter of trees, rocks, and a building or two from which they poured lethal fire. The Pike's Peakers charged back and forth among them, cutting them down and driving them from their hiding places. As they turned to charge again, O'Brien paused to aim at a sharpshooter and was nearly dragged from the saddle by a Texan armed with a long Bowie knife. He clubbed at the man's head with his pistol, but it was a shot from nearby that made his attacker fall slack. O'Brien looked up to see Franklin on foot, gun in hand, staring wild-eyed. The lad ran up to his horse and grabbed at the stirrup.

"Are you all right, sir?" Franklin shouted.

"Yes," O'Brien answered. "Where's your horse?"

"Shot. Go on, sir!" Franklin hopped out of the way of the mounted men surging back toward the Rebels, and

O'Brien lost sight of him as the mustang plunged into the charge.

Paralyzed, Laura watched the horror unfolding in the canyon. When an officer had gone down as the cavalry charge began she'd cried out in fear, then a moment later discerned it was Captain Cook, and almost wept with relief. Poor Cook was hobbling painfully back toward them, blood running from a wound in his leg. Beyond him, past the gully, all was chaos as the clash of steel joined the gunfire. Smoke drifted up and over the hills. The cannon were gone and most of the mounted men after them. The infantry descended from the hillside to secure the remaining Texans, and battle died down to a few pockets here and there. Laura felt a chill of fear when a group of thirty or forty Texans rushed across the gully that separated them from her side of the canyon, but they were cut off by the infantry and made prisoners. She searched for Lieutenant Franklin, saw a bay horse lying on the ground past the gully but no sign of its rider. Light was failing. The sun was already behind the high hills, and she felt a gentle tug at her hand.

"Come, mademoiselle," Vallé said in a sad voice. "It is over, and you should not be here. En fait, I should not have brought you."

Laura saw the wounded captain sit down beside the road, unable to walk farther. "We ought to help—"

"They are still fighting," Vallé said. "They will bring the wounded ones to my house, it is the closest water. Come, we must make ready to receive them."

She allowed him to lead her, back to her burro, to the trail and on until the hills hid the battleground from view. So this is war, she thought. The very war she was supposed to have left behind in the States. This was the darkness that men hid away from the polite surface of the world. She had glimpsed the secret of fear and idealism and righteousness degenerated to pure rage, and was horrified to have found an answering echo within herself.

They reached the ranch house and Vallé took the burro's rein as she dismounted. "I will see to him," he said. "Please ask Carmen to make coffee and hot water. Soup, also."

Laura nodded and went to the door. The house and valley seemed so still: no noises now save the gentle sounds of horses in the corral and a bird singing somewhere outside. Evening fires were not yet lit. The world was all shades of blue and gray. She walked back to the kitchen and found Carmen lighting lamps. The little señora looked up at her and without a word put down her matches and caught Laura's hands. Tears started and Laura took a gulping breath to stop them. There was work to do.

"Halt!" Chivington pulled his cavalry up in the road, and O'Brien followed his gaze to where the last few Texans were fleeing on foot between tall hills.

"We can catch them, sir," O'Brien said, but the major shook his head.

"It'll be dark soon," Chivington said, "and they may have reinforcements. We'll come back when the regiment is with us."

He led them back to the battlefield where the infantry were standing guard over seventy or eighty prisoners. Chivington gave orders for collecting the dead and wounded, and the Union force began to withdraw. O'Brien and Cook's two lieutenants rode with Chivington. As they passed slowly across the battlefield O'Brien gazed at the shattered bodies sprawled like puppets in the wake of a child's tantrum. His eyes fell on a familiar form propped against a boulder, and he stopped, then muttered, "Tanam an Dhiel."

"What's that, Captain?" Chivington frowned.

"Sorry, sir. Looks like I've lost my lieutenant."

"Well, pick him up then, or have one of your men do it."

O'Brien dismounted and led the mustang over to where Franklin lay. The lad had a hand across his belly, and the glove was stained with blood. O'Brien bent to see if he was dead, and Franklin opened his eyes. A glance of fear turned into recognition. Franklin smiled.

"Alastar. Finish it," he said. "Please."

Damn the lad. O'Brien reached to pick him up.

"No—leave me if you won't finish me."

"No secesh'll get their hands on an officer of mine," O'Brien said fiercely. They had made a peace, and he could not leave the lad to die on the field. Lifting his slight frame, O'Brien placed Franklin in his own saddle where he drooped, openly weeping. "Sit up," O'Brien commanded. "Hold the saddle." Franklin obeyed, though O'Brien wouldn't have bet against him fainting before they reached camp. He took the reins and led the mustang into the retreating column, shadows climbing the hill before him to the pass.

Pots of water were on the boil and Carmen was making soup. She had given Laura some old sheets to tear into bandages, and Laura took them outside, sitting under the portal with a lamp hanging from the eaves above her and her eyes turned toward the pass. Men were coming over the hilltop now. She could see them in the blue twilight, and they'd soon reach the ranch. A gray pall came with them out of the west, promising snow.

Captain Cook was the first man brought in, carried by two of his company and placed tenderly on one of the mattresses Vallé had laid out in the main room. The tables had been pushed to the walls and both fireplaces were roaring. Laura followed the men inside with her jumble of bandages, and watched Vallé carefully cut the trousers away from the captain's thigh, revealing four wounds—one large, three smaller—oozing blood.

"Buck and ball," the captain said, grimacing. "Damn close range, too."

"Where is your surgeon?" Vallé asked.

"Back with the command," Cook replied.

"Do you wish me to cut it out?"

"I'll wait," Cook said. "He should be up tomorrow. Could you take off my boots, though? I've got another one in my foot."

This procedure took longer than Laura expected. Not only had the captain a ball in one foot, his other ankle had been badly sprained when his horse fell on him and was now swollen. Vallé finally had to cut the boots away, causing him immense pain in the process. Laura sat beside the captain to comfort him, giving him her hand, which he squeezed so hard it made her bite her lip. He smiled all the while, though, and joked with his men who came to stare at him like frightened children.

Others had been carried in: a boy who had wrenched his knee and then taken a Texan captain prisoner, another with a wound to his face and one in his arm. Lieutenant Marshall had come through the battle unscathed, then while breaking a prisoner's musket he'd accidentally shot himself, receiving a horrible wound. Laura helped Vallé arrange them on the mattresses and bind their hurts until the main room was filled and they had to start putting men in the west room. One poor boy was shot in the head and chest, his breathing a ghastly wheeze. The private who had brought him in knelt talking quietly to him. Vallé was just lighting a fire and the room was cold still, so Laura brought an extra blanket for the wounded man. As she laid it gently over his bloodied chest, his friend looked up at her. His face was calm, but grief had chased all triumph from his eyes.

"What is his name?" Laura asked.

"Dutro," the soldier said.

"Dutro," she said softly, looking at him. She saw he had been shot quite badly through the head, and marveled that he was yet alive. Feeling a little sick, she rose and went to the window to regain her composure.

Outside men were lighting camp fires. The whole valley was filled with moving men and horses. She searched for a slender youth, but didn't see him.

"Miss Howland, please?" Vallé said. Laura turned to see him bandaging Dutro's head. "Would you go to the kitchen and tell Carmen I need another bottle of whiskey?"

Offering her escape. It was kind of him, and she gave

him a brief smile and a nod. She would go to the kitchen, certainly, but she would bring the whiskey herself.

Franklin had fainted sure enough. O'Brien pulled him from the saddle and checked to make sure he was still breathing, then carried him into the house. Pigeon called to him from the next room and directed him to put the lad down by the fireplace.

"I have no more mattresses," Pigeon said, tying off a bandage. "I will bring some straw."

"Tell me where it is and I'll get it," O'Brien said.

"By the canyon wall behind the ridge, that side." Pigeon gestured.

O'Brien started toward the door and met Miss Laura coming in with a bottle and glass in her hands. "Captain O'Brien!" she said. "Are you hurt?"

O'Brien glanced at Franklin's blood covering his coat and hands. "No," he said, gazing down at her. He wanted to keep her from the room, to spare her pain, or at least make it easier for her, but no words of comfort came to him and finally he just stepped aside. She made a sound—a little broken gasp that tore at his heart—and ran into the room, thrusting the bottle and glass into Pigeon's hands on her way to Franklin's side.

"This must be her young man," Pigeon said softly, pausing beside O'Brien to watch her. The words stung, and O'Brien turned away and went out for the straw.

It had started to snow—big, wet flakes drifting down through the night. All their tents were back at the river, but the men were too excited to care. They sat round their fires feasting on rations they'd picked up from their abandoned gear on the way back to the ranch, enthralling each other with tales of bravery and comic misfortune. Reinforcements had arrived from Kozlowski's, and the heroes' adventures were fast growing in the retelling.

O'Brien unsaddled his mustang and turned him out in the corral. He took out his overcoat, carried it to the straw pile, and filled it. This he took back to the house, where

Miss Laura was kneeling by Franklin, tenderly bathing his brow. She'd took off her gloves, and her hands glowed fairy-white in the firelight. O'Brien spread the straw on the floor and found Franklin a blanket, and was rewarded with a tearful smile from his lady. His heart gave a mighty squeeze, and he stood up from making the bed with the dizzying realization that her feelings were more dear to him than his own, and he would do anything for her. Anything, including giving her over to Franklin. Including letting her go.

She was getting up, trying to lift Franklin. O'Brien scooped the lad up—sure, he weighed next to nothing—and set him on the bed. Franklin stirred and muttered, and Miss Laura wiped at his face again, which brought him awake and struggling.

"It's me," she said. "It's me, Laura!"

Franklin stopped fighting. "Laura. Angel of Mercy." He sank back, exhausted, and she reached for his hand but the glove was soaked in blood. O'Brien watched her pull it off and take Franklin's pale fingers in hers.

"Such fine hands," she said.

Franklin laughed softly and closed his eyes. "Stay with me," he murmured.

"Yes," she said.

"Long as you're with me I'm safe." Franklin sighed, and a moment later was asleep. O'Brien picked up his overcoat, brushed the straw from it, and laid it round Miss Laura's shoulders. She looked up at him, brows knit, eyes pleading. O'Brien silently nodded and went away, leaving her with her beloved.

Fires on a battlefield again. Jamie stayed on Cocoa, clinging to one so vibrantly alive, for death was all around him. He looked in vain for McIntyre's brown coat, and gave curt orders to the men gathering the wounded. The dead were left to lie till morning. No more could be done for them, and the darkness hid them. Jamie rode Cocoa up and down the canyon with one of Pyron's men for a guide, searching the shadows, listening for a moan or a pleading voice, calling his hands over when he found one. The two wagons he'd brought weren't enough. He sent them to camp filled and had them return for more. It seemed to have been dark for days. No time passing here, only souls. Jamie shuddered and put a hand on Cocoa's warm neck.

At last there were no more feeble voices, and Jamie sent the wagons and men back to camp. He stayed behind, watching them out of sight, not knowing why for he hated a battlefield and never wanted to see another. Cocoa sidled, wanting to follow the others, but Jamie made her stand until they were gone around the bend. It was only then that he noticed the snow, though it must have been falling some time for it was already sticking to the ground. He had so loved to see snow, back in San Antonio.

Home. Home was all he wanted now. Friends came and went too easily, but he would always have his family. Wouldn't he? Standing on this field of death, he wondered if even now Dan or Matthew might be lying on some similar ground, with snowflakes melting in the last warmth of their bodies. Everyone dies. Everyone knew that, but Jamie had never before thought of death and his family together. What would his world be like without Momma, or Poppa, or Emma?

It was too much. The tension in his chest burst forth in an inarticulate cry of anger and grief. The sound echoed back to him from the hills, and Cocoa grunted in response. Silence fell again like a blanket of snow. Jamie closed his weary eyes, feeling the feathery touch of the flakes on his cheeks.

Nothing had been decided here. They would go on and, with Scurry's men, overrun the Federals and those terrifying Pike's Peakers, and spill more blood until they took Fort Union. Sibley's army was a machine made of men grown insensible of horror. It would roll on through the Rockies and westward till it reached the sea, and it would be Jamie's fate to see that the monster was clothed and fed and to gather up its broken leavings. It would be best to grow insensible himself, if only he knew how. He could not find a way to be callous with the memory of Martin's kind face forever in his thoughts.

Martin had come to him after a battle. Icewater seemed to pour down his spine; there were ghosts all around him here, freshly dead and wondering where to go. He clicked to Cocoa and galloped her back to camp, leaving them to fend for themselves.

Laura leaned against the warm adobe of the fireplace, watching Lieutenant Franklin sleep. It was quiet in the ranch house now. The lamps had been turned down and those still awake spoke in whispers. A soft moan might be heard now and again, but the wounded were as comfortable as they could be made with water and blankets and food for those who could take it. Vallé came and pressed a bowl of soup into Laura's hands.

"Thank you," she said softly, "but he's asleep."

"It is for you, ma fille."

"Oh." She smiled at him and picked up the spoon while he went to add wood to the fire. It was a good soup, but she had no appetite and could swallow only a couple of spoonsful. She looked up at the private still sitting by his wounded friend. "Would you like some?" she said, offering the bowl.

He shook his head. Laura set the bowl aside and gazed down at Lieutenant Franklin. In sleep he seemed younger still, all the lines of his face softened. She smoothed his hair back from his brow, then got up to stretch her legs. She took her cloak down from the peg where she'd hung it—Captain O'Brien's overcoat was long enough to trip her, and she added it to Lieutenant Franklin's bed—then sighed and went over to kneel beside Dutro with her fellow vigilant.

"How is he?" she asked.

"Slipping away, I think," the private said. "Every time he wakes he's farther off." He spoke calmly, but Laura could see the strain and sorrow in his face.

"He is fortunate to have such a good friend."

"Thank you, ma'am," the soldier said with a fleeting smile. "How's yours?"

Laura glanced over her shoulder. "Asleep still. Not surprising, he was in the saddle all last night."

"That's Lieutenant Franklin, isn't it? Nelson says he's a fine fellow."

"Well—so he is."

"Hollister!" a voice from the doorway hissed. The private glanced at Laura, then got up and went to the soldier who had called him. They exchanged brief words in tones so low Laura couldn't hear, then went into the main room and over to where Lieutenant Marshall lay. Laura watched through the doorway as they gathered up his form, wrapping the blanket over his head, and carried him out of the house. She closed her eyes to whisper a brief prayer. So cruel a death, after having come safely through the battle. When she looked up again Vallé was helping another injured soldier to the empty mattress. She waited by Dutro until his friend returned to resume his vigil.

"I'm so sorry," she said softly.

The young man looked at her, gave a solemn nod of thanks, and took up his friend's hand again. Laura left him and returned to Lieutenant Franklin, checking anxiously that he still breathed, wondering how long he would sleep and praying it would not be forever.

27

I will say this, that Mrs. Canby captured more hearts of Confederate soldiers than the old general ever captured Confederate bodies.

> —Private Harvey Halcomb, 4th Texas Mounted
>   Volunteers

Sleep had evaded Jamie. He had too much to do, and too much he wanted to avoid thinking about. After seeing the wounded provided for, he checked the guard on the train, then rode up to the box canyon where Pyron's horses had spent the day resting and grazing. They whinnied at him, complaining about the snow, though it was lighter here than in the pass. He returned to the valley, passing fires surrounded by huddled men talking of the fight, and quickened his steps so as not to hear their stories. He made coffee, brushed Cocoa down, and one way and another found things to keep him busy until most of the camp was asleep.

It was past three by his watch—Martin's watch—when Jamie heard the sound of a column approaching from the south. He came out of his tent and fetched Cocoa from the small corral by the ranch house, swinging onto her bare back and riding down to the Galisteo road. Here he met Colonel Scurry on horseback at the head of his command, with Lane beside him looking ready to fall from his horse and hit the ground snoring.

Scurry turned to Jamie as the column fell out. "We've outstripped our wagons," he said. "Have you got blankets?"

"A few," said Jamie. "I'll bring them out."

"I'll help you," Lane said, yawning as he dismounted.

"Thanks," said Jamie. "There's plenty of wood around, sir. Have the men build fires. My tent's up by the house, if you'd like to sleep there."

Scurry nodded and urged his weary mount forward. The few houses in the valley had been commandeered by Pyron's battalion, leaving no shelter for Scurry's exhausted men, who began to throw themselves down on the snowy ground. Jamie and Lane hurried toward the train.

"How was the battle?" Lane asked.

"They said the Pike's Peakers fight like demons."

"You weren't in it?"

"No," Jamie said. He waited for criticism, but Lane let it drop, for which Jamie was silently grateful. He saw many familiar faces from the 1st as he and Lane handed out blankets. There weren't enough, but they were gladly accepted by those who had not acquired Union overcoats at Valverde. The men made the meager coverings go farther by spooning beneath them in rows huddled close to fires all down the valley.

Jamie led Lane to his tent and found Scurry drinking the last of his coffee. With him was Captain Owens.

"How many casualties?" the colonel asked.

"Near a hundred," Jamie answered. "Mostly prisoners, the major thinks."

"Where is Pyron, anyway?"

"He has his tent down by the creek. Shall I fetch him?"

Scurry frowned. "It can wait till morning. I'll send another express to the general at first light. We'll dig in here, I think," he said, glancing up at the dark hills guarding the pass. "Let them come to us."

Scurry turned, entered the tent, and without ceremony stretched out on Jamie's bed. Jamie rearranged furniture to make room for Lane and Owens, and brought in an armful of wood for the stove. He sat with his back against a row of boxes and watched the others settle themselves by the flickering firelight.

"Aren't you going to sleep?" Lane asked softly. Jamie shrugged, and Lane turned over, pulling his coat over his ears. Jamie watched him sigh and fidget until he fell asleep, then glanced at Owens. The Georgian's eyes glinted back and Jamie looked away, but he found Owens's presence oddly comforting. He sighed, feeling a little of the tension drain out of him.

Suddenly it was morning. Jamie woke up shivering on his side by the boxes, and got up to rebuild the camp fire outside. Scurry was gone from the tent. Jamie made bacon and coffee, and soon the smells of breakfast woke the others. Scurry returned with Pyron in tow, borrowed paper and pen from Jamie, and asked him to break out shovels for the construction of earthworks.

Pyron's artillerymen hauled a cannon to the hilltop while others tore at the earth topped in fast-melting snow. As Jamie stood watching, a carriage approached from the west and was stopped on the road by the pickets. He rode Cocoa down to see what it might be. Phillips and four of his Brigands had surrounded the carriage, in which sat Mrs. Canby, her maidservant, and numerous baskets and boxes.

"Ma'am!" Jamie exclaimed. "What are you doing here?"

"I've come to help with the wounded," Mrs. Canby said, gesturing at her baggage. Jamie saw that the top basket was filled with rolled bandages.

"You can help with our wounded," said Phillips, his lip curling.

"I will gladly do so," Mrs. Canby said calmly. She turned to Jamie. "Do you need bandages? Lint?"

"Got any whiskey?" Phillips asked.

"Bandages," Jamie said, ignoring him.

"Where is your hospital?"

Jamie led her up to the ranch house crammed with some twenty wounded. Mrs. Canby conferred with the surgeon and gave him half her bandages and several rolls of lint, then went among the wounded soldiers offering fresh, soft bread and dried apples. She spoke to each man who was conscious, smiled and pressed their hands as if they were her own sons, and promised to visit them again. Jamie followed along to carry her basket, marveling at her kindness and at the powerful effect it had on the wounded. They didn't know she was their enemy's wife, nor would they have cared. She was a kind face and a warm pair of hands, and that was a better cure than all the whiskey in the world.

When they returned to her carriage they found Phillips poking through the rest of the boxes under the jealous gaze of the maid. "Leave off," Jamie said. Phillips jumped down with a sour look, and Jamie handed Mrs. Canby into the carriage.

"She can't go through the pass," Phillips said.

"Of course she can," Jamie said.

"She might be a spy."

Jamie laughed in his face. "She can't tell them anything they don't already know."

"Might be carrying secret orders," Phillips retorted.

"My husband would hardly expose me to such a risk," Mrs. Canby said quietly. "And in any case, I have heard nothing from him for three weeks."

"Well, that might be true," Phillips said, "but you're not going into that pass. I can't allow it."

"You will allow it," Jamie said. "That's an order."

Phillips's eyes flashed hate, then narrowed. Jamie pushed his advantage. "Captain, I need a detail for grave duty. Choose six of your men and tell them to report to me in five minutes."

"Major Pyron might not like that idea," Phillips replied.

"Oh? I can ask him to discuss it with Colonel Scurry, but I doubt either of them would enjoy being bothered."

Phillips stood for a minute, jaw working as he fingered the butt of his pistol, then stalked off without a word. Jamie looked at Mrs. Canby, who said with a sigh, "I do not believe military service has had a good effect on that man."

Jamie smiled, for the first time in days, it felt like. "I'll escort you into the canyon, ma'am, if you don't mind waiting."

"Do you believe your detail will report in five minutes?"

"They'd better," Jamie said. He took out his watch and when four minutes had passed he was delighted to see six men on horseback coming toward them. They were the least favored of Phillips's company and did not look at all pleased by the duty they'd drawn. Jamie issued them shovels, then formed them in a small column behind the carriage and rode beside Mrs. Canby as they started down the trail.

They passed through a line of Scurry's men across the canyon where the fight had taken place. All was quiet, and Jamie ordered Phillips's men to start collecting the dead while he continued as far as the picket line with Mrs. Canby.

"Thank you," she said, reaching a hand up to him from the carriage. "I will see you again, I am sure."

Jamie shook her hand and smiled, then bade her farewell and turned to the sad task of burying the dead.

Hard work scraping graves out of frozen ground. O'Brien took off his cap and rubbed a sleeve across his brow, heated though his breath came in icy clouds. He'd volunteered his men for the honor and duty of burying their fallen comrades, and had taken up the shovel himself rather than stand by. It was a way to strike at something legitimately, which eased his feelings, and he didn't much care by now what Slough thought unbecoming.

"Deep enough?" Denning asked between gasps. The second lieutenant had followed his captain's example and wielded a shovel along with the men.

The detail paused while O'Brien glanced at the dismal row of corpses nearby. "Aye. Start laying them in," he said, climbing out of the trench. He watched while a handful of men from F and I companies and one poor fellow from D Company were laid in the grave. Lieutenant Marshall was placed in a separate grave, and the chaplain said a few words. They were about to start filling in the dirt when a private came running down from the ranch telling them to wait, there was one more. O'Brien looked up the road where two men—one of them the fellow who'd sat up all night same as Miss Laura—carried another body. There were tears in the man's eyes, leading O'Brien to conclude it was not Franklin in the blanket they lowered gently to the earth.

He glanced down at the men in the grave, five of them from his company: Peters, Krantz, O'Connor, Breeden, and Duncan. He hadn't realized when he'd agreed to lead them that he would not be bringing them all back to Colorado. He could still see Duncan over a table of cards, pledging to follow him. And Peters, whom he'd saved from killing himself in a fool duel with Denning. How could he have known then that he would feel personally responsible for their deaths?

"Fill it in," he said, turning away and leaning on the shovel as he trudged back up the road to the ranch. He was disgusted with himself for a number of reasons. He'd been cruel to Franklin. He'd been distant from the friends who'd bound themselves to follow him, and reckless with their lives. He'd frightened Miss Laura—no, he shouldn't call her that. What a clod he'd been, thinking only of what he wanted, not even bothering to learn her name. All he needed for a regular Irish wallow of guilt and despair was two or three gill of whiskey.

A long line of men stood waiting to water their horses with buckets hauled up from Pigeon's well. A detail was forming to fetch some corn and flour that had been discovered in a shack up the canyon, good news for rumbling bellies. O'Brien gave up his shovel and went into the ranch house, drawn to his lady like a moth to fire. He looked into the room where Franklin lay awake and talking quietly with her. When the lad saw him in the door he raised a weak hand to beckon O'Brien in, then murmured something to the young lady. She got up and came to the door.

"He wants to speak with you," she told O'Brien, then stepped past him on her way outside. She looked weary and a little cross, making him wish he could somehow ease her, find her a queen's feather bed or a fairy draught that would give sleep and sweet dreams. He watched her go out, then went to Franklin.

The lad lay on a mattress now, pale but no longer heroic. He looked ill. A blanket covered him and he was propped up on a heap of the straw O'Brien had fetched for his bed the night before. He smiled as O'Brien came to sit beside him.

"I wanted to thank you," Franklin said. "It was good of you to bring me here."

"You're welcome, lad. How is it?"

Franklin glanced at the doorway. "The surgeon came to see me this morning," he said, almost whispering. "There is not much he can do for me. I have not told Miss Howland."

O'Brien frowned. Franklin's eyes had that strange, hollow look. "I'm sorry—" Franklin stopped, and to O'Brien's dismay a tear rolled down his cheek. Taking a shaky breath, the lad managed to smile. "I think that we might have been—very good friends." He struggled up on one elbow, grimacing, and reached into his coat. "You'll consider giving my place to Denning, I hope. He's worked hard, he'll do well for you."

"Don't talk nonsense," O'Brien said roughly. "You're strong. Likely you'll mend."

With a soft, sad smile Franklin shook his head. "I don't think so, sir." He brought out his watch and chain, which he offered to O'Brien. "Please take it," he said.

O'Brien held out a hand to receive the golden timepiece. It had hands finely wrought and little glints of gold between the hours. A gentleman's watch.

"Take my saddle, too, if you can find it. I suppose Duke is dead?"

O'Brien nodded, sorry for the loss of the bay. A fine horse. Almost as fine as its master.

Franklin pressed his lips together and swallowed, looking pale. "Is there anything else you need?" he asked. "Money?"

O'Brien shook his head and held up the watch. "I'll hold this for you till you're well again," he said, staring hard at the lad, defying him to die.

Franklin only smiled. "All right. Will you do one more thing for me? You'd do it anyway, but I'll ask."

"What?" O'Brien asked, unwilling to commit to the unknown.

"Watch over Miss Howland. She's alone, far from home—"

"She's with her friends," O'Brien said, gesturing toward Pigeon's main room.

"She needs every friend she can find," Franklin said. "And no one else will watch over her as well as you." His voice had gone sad.

"Maybe it's you who'll watch over her."

The odd smile he'd seen so often came onto Franklin's face. "If it is possible for those in heaven to watch over their loved ones," he said slowly, "I shall do so." He held out a hand, no glove now, only pale cold flesh. O'Brien gripped it lightly, but the slim fingers closed hard on his. "Thank you for having me in your company," Franklin said. "I'm glad I could serve my country, even for a short while."

"You served it well," said O'Brien. "You went brave into the fight." He saw the gratitude in Franklin's eyes and put his other hand over the youth's. "How were you hit, lad?"

Franklin gave a bitter laugh. "Bastard jumped up from behind a rock. I think I killed him." His smile faded.

"Well," O'Brien said, "I think you saved me from getting cut wide open." Strange how hard it was to speak the words. "I think I owe you my life."

"Then I have indeed served my country well," Franklin said. His dark eyes held O'Brien's, pools of calm amidst all the chaos. "You'll go far, as far as you wish. I have complete faith in you, Alastar. I always did."

O'Brien stared back at him, feeling at once that he'd missed a great chance in not knowing the boy better. It was he and not Franklin that had let difference of birth form a boundary between them. Fool to be hindered by such cobwebs. He would not let them stop him in future.

A bugle sounded the officers' call, and O'Brien glanced at the door. "Thank you for coming to see me," Franklin said.

"I'll come again," said O'Brien, but as the words left his mouth a bird's shadow flicked across the window and he sensed it would not be so. He squeezed the lad's hand.

"Don't tell Miss Howland what I've told you," Franklin said. "I'll speak to her myself."

O'Brien nodded, then left him and went outside. A carriage had come and a lady was getting out of it with a large basket. O'Brien stepped forward to help, and she smiled her thanks. Behind her a familiar fair-headed form was reaching into the carriage for another parcel. O'Brien set the basket on the porch and went to her.

"Can I help you, Miss Howard?" he asked.

She turned with a look of surprise. "Howland," she said. "Yes, thank you."

He pulled the parcel out and set it on the porch, unloaded two or three more, and helped a Mexican servant get down from the carriage. "I've got to report," he said, "but I'll come back and carry this in for you."

"We can manage, thank you," Miss Howland said, but she said it kindly. "By the way, Captain . . ." She stopped and glanced down at her hands. "I never thanked you— you've done so much—"

O'Brien shook his head, as embarrassed as she. "Happy to be of service."

"You'll want your coat back, and your burro—"

"Keep them," said O'Brien. "We can settle later if need be." He looked at her, wanting her as always but the feeling was not so desperate now. He'd been charged to watch over her and meant to do it, but she was a free thing and so he had to watch from a distance. Strangely, he no longer found that maddening.

The bugle sounded again and O'Brien glanced to where Chivington's officers were gathering a little way down the road. He touched his hat with a brief smile and left his lady, glad to have won a small measure of her approval, sorry for the heartache she would get when next she spoke with Franklin.

*   *   *

"A pleasant young man," Mrs. Canby said, looking after the captain. She bent to pick up her basket. "You must tell me about him."

Laura lifted a box and followed her into the ranch house. "I have a great deal to tell you," she said. "I am so glad you've come!"

Together they visited the wounded, and since Laura knew most of their names, having spent the night helping to tend them, she introduced them to Mrs. Canby. When they came to Lieutenant Franklin she felt a blush creeping into her cheeks, though she kept her eyes demurely lowered.

"Would you like some apricots, Lieutenant?" Mrs. Canby asked.

"Thank you, but I can't," Mr. Franklin replied.

"He was sick after breakfast," Laura explained.

Mrs. Canby raised her brows. "Where were you wounded?"

"Belly," the lieutenant said, with a sharp glance at Mrs. Canby. Laura looked at her but saw only a slight pursing of her lips followed by a gentle smile.

The lieutenant was keeping something from her. Laura had suspected it and was certain now. It cost her an effort not to frown.

"Are you warm enough?" Mrs. Canby asked him.

"Yes," he said. "Miss Howland has been coddling me most extravagantly."

"Then I'll borrow her if you don't mind," Mrs. Canby said lightly. "It is not good for you to become completely spoiled."

He smiled. "No indeed. Please take her out for some air. She has been trapped inside all the morning."

The ladies went to the little yard out back of the house, where Carmen was using a shed for a kitchen. The fruit Mrs. Canby had brought had been put into Carmen's care, and she and María were sorting it, conversing rapidly in Spanish. The kitchen garden, separated from the corral by a small adobe wall, was bathed in sunshine, and the smell of baking bread seeped from the beehive oven in the yard.

Laura and Mrs. Canby brought chairs outside and sat warming their hands around steaming mugs of coffee while Laura recounted her experiences of the past three weeks. She was astonished to realize how much her circumstances, and indeed she herself, had changed in such a short time.

"You must think me quite brazen," she said.

"Well, braver than myself, perhaps," Mrs. Canby said. "But you seem to have been with good people. Captain O'Brien sounds like an excellent man."

Laura thought of the fight at the river, which she had not mentioned, and the terror of the sleepless night that had followed. Here in the shelter of a winter garden, she was able to admit that the captain had ruled himself to her benefit despite its being strongly against his inclination. She was ashamed to have placed herself in such a dangerous position, and more ashamed for the distress she knew she had caused him.

"I'm afraid," she said slowly, "that I put quite a strain on his patience."

"He seemed anxious to please you," Mrs. Canby said. "I do not think you have anything to fear from him."

"No." Laura turned her empty cup in her hands and thought of a shadow on a tent wall. "Why are men so violent in their passions?"

"I have seen women just as violent," Mrs. Canby said, "and men who were quite timid. I believe we have all the same passions, we merely express them differently."

Laura gave her a rueful smile. "I have been very bad."

"A bit wayward, perhaps."

"My uncle called me a wanton," Laura said, laughing.

"He is hardly entitled to criticize," Mrs. Canby said wryly. "What do you intend to do now?"

"I had meant to come to you, if I still may," Laura said.

"Of course," said Mrs. Canby. "There is plenty of room in the carriage now that we've given over our bandages."

"Actually, ma'am," Laura said, "I would prefer not to leave Lieutenant Franklin while he is ill." Hearing no immediate reply, she glanced up to see Mrs. Canby's eyes gazing at her with an expression she suspected was pity.

"You are very fond of him," the older woman said gently.

"I am more than fond of him," Laura replied. She lifted her chin. "I am aware he does not return my feelings, but I cannot change them."

"Oh, of course not, my dear." Mrs. Canby put her mug down in the snow to take Laura's hands. Her large eyes were full of sympathy, and Laura suddenly found herself weeping. Mrs. Canby enfolded her in comforting arms. "Poor child," she said. "What an uproar you've been through!" She held Laura, murmuring soft words of comfort and stroking her hair until the bout of tears ended and Laura sat up with a watery laugh.

"I've become an adventuress," she said, wiping her eyes.

"Rather a dignified adventuress," Mrs. Canby said. "I think you are too much a lady for the role."

"If I continue at my present rate of deterioration that will not be so for long." They laughed together.

Mrs. Canby picked up her cup. "I must start back," she said, glancing at the sun, which was past midday and starting westward. "María and I will return tomorrow. You're welcome to come with us then, or whenever you wish."

"Thank you, ma'am. You are entirely too good to me."

Laura saw her to the carriage, and as Mrs. Canby and María were arranging a buffalo robe across their laps, bugles began to blow and soldiers to assemble in the road. Laura put a hand on the carriage door. "Perhaps you should wait," she said. "There may be another battle."

Mrs. Canby smiled. "I don't think so," she said. "See, they are going east."

Laura glanced up and saw Major Chivington at the bottom of the road, facing eastward with the flag at his side. She frowned, wondering at the retreat.

"Good-bye," Mrs. Canby said. "I will see you tomorrow."

Laura waved as the carriage drove off toward Santa Fé, shivering at the thought of its driving through the Texan army to get there, but Mrs. Canby seemed to have no fear of them. The carriage disappeared over the western hilltop just as Chivington's column started in motion.

Laura saw a familiar horse approaching. Captain O'Brien reined in his mustang by the portal and doffed his hat.

Laura nodded in response. "You're leaving?"

"Not enough water here for the horses," he said. "We're going back to the river. Don't be afraid. We won't be far off."

"Your coat." Laura ran into the house to fetch it despite his protests. "You may need it," she said, handing it up to him. "Thank you again, Captain O'Brien. I am greatly in your debt." She tried to endow the words with all the gratitude for his forbearance that she could not otherwise express, and offered him her hand.

He took her gloved fingers in his hand and bent his head over them but did not touch them, though she felt the warmth of his breath. The mustang sidled and he let her go. "I hope to see you again, Miss Howland."

"Yes," Laura said. "I hope you shall."

The sudden smile that lit his face almost made her regret the words. How volatile were his feelings! She must be careful of what she said; it would be unkind to cause him further pain by raising a false hope. She stepped back, smiling briefly, and went into the house to check on Lieutenant Franklin.

She found him shivering and, putting a hand to his brow, was frightened at how cold it was. She threw her cloak over him and hastened to build up the fire. When she had a bright roar going she took his hand in hers, striving to send her own warmth into it and praying for his chill to pass. Franklin opened his eyes and managed a piteous smile, then closed them again as another fit of shaking overcame him. Because she could think of nothing else to do, Laura began to sing a lullaby. The melody, wavering at first but growing stronger, soothed her feelings, and when she had finished she began it over again, just for the release it brought her. A silence followed the song's end. Laura realized the hand she held was no longer shaking so badly, and when she looked at the lieutenant she found him gazing up at her with a soft smile.

"My mother used to sing that to me."

"So did mine to me," Laura said.

"She never knew how much it made me mad after horses."

Laura smiled and reached out to touch his forehead. "Better?"

"Yes, thank you. It comes and goes."

"How did you sleep?"

"Well enough. I dreamt I saw my grandmother sitting there, just where you are, waiting for me. She was always very patient, my grandmother."

Laura misliked the sound of this, and tried to make light of it. "That is well," she said, "for I hope she will spare you to us for quite some time."

"Miss Howland—"

Laura looked at his face, deep eyes reflecting firelight.

"I am dying," he said gently.

Laura gulped a breath and held it, trying to keep from crying, but the tears brimmed over and ran down her cheeks.

"Don't grieve," he said. "Please, I'm not worth it."

Laura brushed angrily at the tears and sniffed. "You will have to let me be the judge of that."

"I never wished to cause you pain."

"*You* have not caused me pain," she replied. "If I have pain it is my own concern. Now, how may I make you more comfortable?"

Lieutenant Franklin smiled. "You are so good. May I ask a favor of you?"

"Of course."

"Would you see me buried? Make sure no one messes about with me, when I'm gone?"

Laura had to bite her lip to keep from crying again. After a moment she was able to say "Very well."

"Thank you." His hand squeezed hers, and Laura's heart

filled with an even greater tenderness. How different it might have been had he not been struck, or been struck in some less vital place. The picture of herself nursing him to health and winning his heart was appealing, but she must set such thoughts aside. Ridiculous to torture herself. She had not lost quite all of her breeding. Nor would she permit her foolishness to trouble him. She put on a smile and held her head high.

"May I leave you for a little while? I should help with the others," she said.

"Yes, of course."

"Call if you want anything," Laura said, letting go of his hand and getting up. She went straight to the door, would not allow herself any lingering glances. Dabbing at her cheeks with a much-crumpled handkerchief—the same one the lieutenant had loaned to her—she walked into the main room. Half a dozen faces turned toward her: lonely, frightened, aggrieved. Their need gave her strength. Setting her own woes aside, she went among them with water, clean bandages and smiles, finding healing in the giving of healing.

O'Brien stared moodily into the fire, sucking at a cup of bad coffee. He had got used to the way Franklin made it— Denning was no good at all. He was ever more tempted to visit Kozlowski's tavern, but so far he'd restrained himself. He ought to just go to bed, now that he had his own tent back.

He looked up at the tent, remembering the last time he'd gone near it. Horribly drunk he'd been, but not so drunk he didn't remember the temptation to which he'd nearly yielded. Just the thought set a fire burning low in his gut. He got up and went over to the tent, touched the canvas with his fingertips, then threw back the flap and went in. Her blankets lay by the wall, neatly folded. Taking one in his hands and bringing it to his face, he inhaled deeply, searching for some hint of her in the coarse wool.

"Where's O'Brien?" a voice outside asked.

O'Brien flung the blanket from him and stood up.

"In his tent, sir," Denning said.

Stepping toward the door, O'Brien was startled by a shadow looming on the canvas. He pulled aside the flap and found Lieutenant Shoup, Chivington's aide, about to reach for it.

"Captain," Shoup said, "the major wants you in a staff meeting. Come along."

O'Brien followed him to the ranch house and a room where all the captains of the Colorado Volunteers were sitting around a table and passing a bottle of whiskey. This was put out of sight as the major entered behind Shoup. O'Brien slid into a chair near Sanborn, who'd last had the bottle. The door opened again to admit Wynkoop and Ford.

"That's all of us," Chivington said, taking a seat.

"What, no Regulars?" Wynkoop asked with a sly grin.

"The Regulars are receiving their orders from Colonel Paul," Chivington said. "He has seen fit to come down and annoy us with dispatches, no doubt feeling he should be doing something. For my part, he can take all the Regulars home to Union and be damned with them."

No one replied.

"Now, then. Colonel Slough and I have determined the plan for tomorrow's operations. We will march at four o'clock in two columns. Logan, Wynkoop, Anthony, Sanborn, and Ford—you and your companies will be under my command, the rest will go with Colonel Slough. My column will flank the Texans if we can and fall on them from behind."

"How can we flank them? Don't we have to go through the pass?" Anthony asked.

"We'll go across country," Chivington said. "But that's not to leave the room. Just tell your men we're marching at four o'clock. The Regulars will guard the train. F and I companies will be in reserve under Colonel Slough."

"Sir," O'Brien said, standing, "I company requests the honor of joining the flanking party."

Chivington leaned back from the table and frowned. "Your men are all shot to pieces, O'Brien. Didn't you lose your lieutenant?"

"Isn't that why there are two to a company?" O'Brien asked. A snigger somewhere in the room was swiftly squelched by Chivington's severe glance.

"You've earned a rest," the major said.

"We don't need it, sir," O'Brien said. He thought of spending the next day watching a battle from behind the lines, and couldn't bear it. "With respect, Major, my men have got friends to avenge."

"It'll be a hard march."

"They're up to it, sir."

Chivington looked up at him, frowning and tapping a fingertip on the table. Finally he said, "Very well. I Company will join my column. Tell your men to get to sleep, gentlemen. I'll be closing the tavern shortly. Dismissed."

O'Brien waited while the others filed out, watching Chivington and Shoup shuffle a handful of papers. The major glanced up at him. "Well?"

"Just to thank you, sir," O'Brien said.

"Are you after approval, Captain?"

"No, sir—"

"Because you won't get it by pushing your men beyond their limits," Chivington said, frowning. "I'll have my eye on you tomorrow. Dismissed."

O'Brien left the room slowly. He had not been thinking of his men, true. He'd been thinking of what he himself wanted. Too easy to forget they might not share his enthusiasm. He walked through the camp to I Company's tents, passing men playing cards, singing, talking round campfires. He stopped at a circle where Shaunessy and Morris sat with some others, playing bluff on an upended cracker box with the same old grimy deck Morris had brought all the way from Avery. They looked up at him.

"Make it an early night, boys," he said. "We march at four."

"Four!" Morris protested.

Shaunessy jabbed him in the ribs. "Gaby! That means we're off for a fight. We are, aren't we, sir?"

There was no mistaking the gleam in Shaunessy's eye for one of fear. He was eager, just as O'Brien had told the major.

"Yes," O'Brien said, the weight suddenly gone from his heart. "Get your sleep. You'll want to look your best for the Texans."

28

It was a sad sight to see these young men, so lately in all the strength and vigor of manhood, now lying pale and weak around these fires, suffering.

—Alfred B. Peticolas

In the gray dawn Laura woke, stiff from sleeping against the wall. The fire had burned too low to cast any light. Lieutenant Franklin had made some sound, and she saw he had thrown aside his covers, revealing dark wetness on the bandages over his abdomen. Laura swallowed. She would have liked to change them, but the lieutenant disliked being handled and had asked the surgeon to let the wound alone. No point in changing the dressing, he had said, to which there was no answer. Laura sighed and gently drew a blanket up to his chest, catching his hands when he tried to throw it off again. They were hot with fever. She reached for a bowl of water and a cloth and bathed his brow. The fevers and chills no longer frightened her, but each bout left him weaker, and that was hard, so very hard, to watch.

The fever was building and she had to struggle to keep him covered, he tossed so. Laura spoke soothing words that she doubted he could hear, sang to him now and then, and as far as she was able kept him from hurting himself. At midmorning the fever finally broke and he fell into a quiet sleep. Laura got up to stretch her tired limbs and visit the other wounded, all doing well except for Captain Cook, who was feverish, also, from the wound in his thigh. Out back, Carmen was making tortillas, and had a huge pot of frijoles simmering on the hearth. Laura discovered she was ravenously hungry. Carmen gave her a bowl of the savory beans and a tortilla to sop up the broth.

When Laura returned to the west room she was surprised to find the lieutenant awake and clear-eyed. "Good morning," she said, smiling.

"Morning." Franklin coughed, and Laura tucked up his blankets. He was pale, his cheek a little clammy when she laid a hand against it. "I was dreaming," he said in a worried voice.

"You were feverish."

"Did I talk?"

"Yes," Laura said. "You asked for Captain O'Brien, and said you did not want a woman. Please note my good behavior in taking offense at neither."

He laughed, then coughed again.

"Will you permit me to do something for you?" Laura asked.

"What is that?"

"Write to your family."

Lieutenant Franklin turned his head away, frowning. "My family want no part of me."

"Forgive me," Laura said. "I don't mean to pry into your affairs, but is your mother still living?"

"As far as I know."

"Would she not wish to know what became of you?" He was silent, and Laura added, "Were I she, I would not like to wonder all my life."

"Do you intend to return to the States, Miss Howland?" he asked.

Laura opened her mouth to answer, then shut it again. Certainly she had intended to go back, but in fact she had not thought of it for some time. Odd, for she'd been so very homesick, but now she hesitated at the thought of returning to the orderly, civilized, and somewhat tame environs of Boston. She had felt confined on her arrival in Santa Fé, but somewhere amidst all the turmoil a profound freedom of spirit had risen within her. Inspired by the mountains, perhaps, or the wild skies, the white limbs and flickering leaves of aspen. There was an intensity to this country that made her feel more vitally alive than she had ever done before, and no, she did not wish to leave it.

"It is not possible for me to return at present," she said, compromising.

"Would you if you had the means?"

"I cannot say, and I will not be diverted, sir. Allow me to write to your mother," she pleaded softly. "Make your peace with her."

Mr. Franklin stared intently at her, then sighed. "She wouldn't receive a letter from me. Write to my uncle."

Laura started to rise. "I think Monsieur Vallé will loan me some paper."

"I have a notebook and pencil," he said. "My coat pocket."

Laura reached toward his coat. The top buttons had been unfastened earlier for his comfort, but she had to undo two more to reach his pocket, and blushed a little. She found the notebook and a short pencil, and opened the book to a blank page.

"Mr. Herbert Devon, 1648 Spring Garden Street, Philadelphia," he said. "Tell him. . . ."

Laura glanced up to see him staring at the gray sky outside the window, his face taut with grief.

"That his sister can be proud of her son—"

"No," the lieutenant said sharply. He turned his head to look at her and flashed an apologetic smile. "Write from me, please. Dear Uncle."

Laura wrote.

"On the advice of friends, I wish to inform you that I have been gravely injured and am not expected to survive. Please notify my mother, and tell her I ask her forgiveness for the manner of my departure. If anything of mine remains to be disposed of, let it go to my sister Justine."

Laura finished the sentence and looked up. "Yes?"

"I regret nothing," he said softly. Laura hesitated, and he nodded to her to write it. "I have done what I felt in my heart to be right. May God bless and protect you all."

"Go on."

"That's all," he said. "Let me sign it."

"But you have not mentioned how you were wounded—"

"Please, Miss Howland."

Laura saw from his set face that she would gain nothing by arguing. She placed the pencil in his fingers and held the notebook while he signed. The effort this small action cost him made her heart ache, and he let the pencil drop after only writing 'Char' in a shaky hand.

"Shall I write out your name?" Laura asked.

"No. That will be enough. You will post it yourself?"

"Yes."

"And may I ask you to do one more thing for me?"

"Yes, of course," Laura said.

"Promise you will not attempt to contact my family."

Laura gazed at the lieutenant's anxious face, wondering what rift had caused him to break with his relations, saddened by his determination to keep it from her. "As you wish," she said.

"Thank you, Miss Howland."

"Won't you call me Laura?" she asked, her eyes on the page that she carefully tore from the notebook and folded. When he did not reply she looked up to find him gazing at her with an expression that reminded her strangely of Mrs. Canby.

"Laura," he said, reaching out a hand which she quickly pressed between her own. "Please listen to me. You must not mourn when I am gone. You have had enough of mourning."

"I cannot—"

"It would grieve me very much to think that you wasted a moment over me, when you have all your life before you," he said. "If you would honor me then seek what gives you the most joy. It's what I've always done."

"Your service in the army seems to have brought you little joy," Laura said.

"Oh, no." The lieutenant smiled. "It has been the greatest joy of my life. You cannot imagine . . ."

"What?"

He shook his head and laughed softly. "I only wish you will find as much happiness. A woman alone doesn't have many choices, but don't let that stop you."

"I don't intend to," Laura said.

He smiled, and his eyes were filled with such a light that Laura felt her own heart lifting in response. If only she could sit with him thus forever, she would know no more sadness.

The world, however, continued on, and it was not long before they were disturbed by a sound Laura now knew well, the rumble and clatter of an army on the march. She rose to peek out the door and saw a blue column approaching from the east. Glancing back at the lieutenant, she nodded. "Ours."

"Would you ask Captain O'Brien to step in for a moment?"

"All right." Laura slipped his letter into her pocket and went out.

The air outside was brisk and made her pull her cloak closer around her. The column had halted abreast of the ranch house. Men stacked their rifles and lined up to fill their canteens at the well. The sun was nearing midday, its brightness making Laura blink despite the thin layer of clouds. The valley was frosted in snow, a white powder dusting over the brown earth and green pines. The sunlight shone so brightly back from the white that it hurt Laura's eyes, which were used to the darkness of the house. She searched the faces passing and spotted a friend.

"Captain Chapin!"

She waved to him, and he hastened to the house to shake her hand. "I hear you've become a nurse now," he said.

"Yes, my career with the army has taken a variety of forms," she said lightly.

Chapin laughed. "God bless you, ma'am."

"Can you tell me where to find Captain O'Brien?"

"Not here," Chapin answered. "His company is on another duty."

"Oh," Laura said, disappointed.

"How is Cook?"

"Come and see for yourself." She led him inside, then left him with the captain and returned to the west room, where Lieutenant Franklin looked up anxiously as she entered.

"He is not with the column," she said. "I'm sorry."

The lieutenant looked so disheartened that she sat beside him again and said, "You're very fond of him."

"He's a good man, Miss Howland. He would be a good protector, if you should happen to need one."

"There is only one man whose protection I wish for," she murmured.

Lieutenant Franklin shook his head and softly laughed. "I'm not capable, alas."

A thought occurred to Laura, and ignoring the heat that it brought into her face, she voiced it before she had time to think better of it. "You could give me protection," she said. "The protection of your name." The lieutenant looked startled, and before he could protest Laura pressed her point. "You say a woman alone has few choices. Does not a widow have more?"

"Dear God!" he said, and to Laura's surprise laughed aloud. "Oh, forgive me! You're quite right, of course, but it's out of the question. I'm sorry."

"You are married, then," Laura said. "A match to which your family objected, perhaps?"

Still laughing, the lieutenant shook his head. "Miss Howland, you would have made an excellent spy. You are bold as brass, and determined to ferret out my secrets!"

Laura bit her lip. "I apologize."

He reached for her hand. "No need. I swear to you, I am not married. If I could give you a name that would serve you I would, but I cannot. It would do you more harm than good, great harm, possibly. I cannot risk that."

"The risk is mine," Laura answered.

"No," he said, smiling. "You have not found out my darkest secret. It would shock you, I promise."

"Nothing you could tell me would change my opinion of you."

"No?" Mischief lit the dark eyes.

"No," Laura said firmly. "I shall never feel for another man what I feel for you."

"Don't speak that way," he said, suddenly serious.

"It is the truth."

"You mustn't—"

He stopped, eyes widening. Laura heard it, too: the frantic sound of bugles. With a sense of dread she hurried to the outer door and threw it open. Captain Chapin burst from the next door at the same moment, leapt onto his horse without a backward glance and galloped up the trail in great haste. The soldiers were grabbing their rifles and running west. Two artillery batteries flew past the ranch, scattering the forming column to either side of the trail. Laura watched the smaller gun carriages turn and bump their way up a pine-covered hill on the left, while two larger cannon were planted in the road near the crest of the pass. Before they were settled a horrendous crash sent birds flying up from the trees around the ranch. Laura's pulse quickened as the army deployed into a line in front of the cannon, spreading across the trail and up the hillside, rifles snapping as the battle began.

O'Brien raised his head at the sound of artillery fire. It was not far off, though the hills bounced the echoes back and forth till it was hard to say where it started. Chivington halted the column and called in Chaves and the other guide, a civilian from Santa Fé name of Collins, a newspaper man.

"Are we behind them?" the major asked.

"Not yet," Chaves said. He frowned, looking north. "They are somewhere in the pass."

"Let's cut across," Chivington said, but Chaves shook his head.

"There are hills upon hills here, Major, and box canyons between the mesas. We could find ourselves in a trap. Better to go on until we are certain we are in their rear."

"Well, move on then," Chivington said with no great

grace, and the guides turned their horses westward again, picking their way through the cedars. The major was anxious to be in battle, as were his men. O'Brien glanced at Denning and Shaunessy, their faces straining toward the sound of war. Two days since they had ridden thundering into the face of Rebel cannon, and it was maddening now to be hearing the guns and to have no way to reply. O'Brien wondered where the lines had met, whether they might be struggling over the same treacherous strip of ground he'd charged across. That had been his first battle, he realized, and it hadn't filled him with any particular thrill or terror. It was a fight, and he had been in many fights. This was just larger and crazier, leaving a greater destruction in its wake.

His men, though—that was different. He was immensely proud of them. An invisible mantle of dignity now rested snow-light on their shoulders, making them in quiet moments seem like the noble sons of some ancient warrior king. Not one had quailed. They had ridden into the smoke and din, scattered the enemy before them, and come out in triumph with eyes and guns blazing. All but six.

Those six weighed on him. He wondered if Franklin lived yet or had gone to his last sleep. Not that it mattered. Miss Howland had spoken kindly, to be sure, but she'd shied off as soon as he'd smiled. She was out of his reach, he thought bitterly. A fairy princess was no bride for a troll.

What could he do then? Go back to mining, or find some other occupation and a low-bred wench to bear his brats? O'Brien scowled, rejecting such a life. He had not crawled out of the hills only to flee from the daylight. He was an officer, which was some excuse at least for a gentleman. Moreover, he had vowed to watch over his lady's safety. The thought made him sit straighter in the saddle. Fairytale dreams, he told himself, but it was pleasant to think of himself as a gallant knight, guarding the lady high above him. In the fairy tales such couples were united at the last, but O'Brien could not deceive himself so far as to picture Miss Howland coming to him.

Chivington's voice rang out. "Sanborn!" The captain hastened to his side. "You and your men scout toward Pigeon's," Chivington said. "If you see any Texans, sound the alarm."

O'Brien watched Sanborn detach his company from the column and ride north. He hoped they would find Texans, for he wanted a fight to distract him. Perhaps he'd be wounded in the battle, and then Miss Howland would bathe his brow as she had Franklin's, and sing to him in her sweet voice. He swallowed, remembering how he'd listened to her through the door, drinking in the haunting melody though it only made him ache with need. Now the music of battle called to him instead, and he wanted it just as strongly, yearning for one end or another to his pain.

"You god-damned sons of bitches! Get back to your posts!" Jamie screamed at the guards who were running into the pass. In his anger he jerked too hard at Cocoa's reins, making her flatten her ears.

"We came to get glory by fighting," a German soldier said, "not for guarding provisions and mules!"

Jamie struck at him and his comrades with the flat of his sword, and pelted them with a stream of blue curses that had never before passed his lips. It did no good; they wanted a part of the fight and cared nothing for his authority. By the time he and Rose had regained control, half of the guard had gone down the trail toward the sound of cannon, leaving only a couple hundred to protect the train. Furious, Jamie posted Rose and a dozen of the most trustworthy soldiers smack in the road to prevent further desertions, then rode up and down the train for half an hour, glaring at the guards who were left. The teamsters looked nervous. Jamie gave them sharp orders to get all their harness inspection-ready. It would keep them too busy to think of running, either toward the battle or away from it. It would keep him busy, too, and Jamie wanted to be busy. He didn't want to think about what was happening in the pass. Men he knew and respected had marched willingly into that maelstrom—even the fools of the guard had been eager to join it, while he himself shuddered at the very thought of the smoke and hellfire. He swore to himself in shame and anger, and trotted Cocoa back up to the trail to check on Rose. A familiar carriage rounded the hill from the west, and Jamie rode forward to meet it.

Mrs. Canby greeted him with a worried smile. With her was a lady he remembered from the dinner in Santa Fé, though he'd forgotten her name.

"You can't go in, ma'am," he said, gesturing toward the hills over which floated the roar of battle.

Mrs. Canby glanced at the lady beside her, who looked unhappy, and nodded to Jamie. "We'll help with your wounded, then. How are they faring?"

"Well enough, though crowded."

"We can take some of them to Santa Fé, if that would help."

"It would," Jamie said. "They're packed in like sardines." He accompanied her to the ranch house and helped unload heaps of bandages and food from the carriage. Southworth, the surgeon, chose six men who were well enough to be moved, and Mrs. Canby promised to return for more. As Jamie was helping get the men into the carriage, two privates came panting up the hill to the ranch house bearing a litter. On it was Lane, his head all bloodied down one side. Jamie couldn't help making a sound, and Mrs. Canby's friend—Mrs. Chapin, he suddenly remembered—gave him a piteous glance. He hurried to the porch where the litter-bearers waited to carry Lane inside.

"Ells?" he said, bending over his friend, his voice sounding too high in his ears. "Ells, can you hear me?"

Lane didn't answer. The surgeon directed the men to carry him inside. Jamie followed and stood by while they put him down in a space just vacated. Mrs. Canby brought a bowl of water she'd produced from somewhere and a bandage roll. She started bathing Lane's head while the surgeon knelt over him, prodding and muttering. As

she wiped the dried blood away a nasty gash began to
ooze brighter red. It started at Lane's cheek and got wider
as it ran up the side of his head, disappearing into his hair.
He moaned as Mrs. Canby dabbed at the blood-matted
locks, and Jamie came and knelt by his other side. The
chaplain came over to watch. The surgeon poked at
Lane's head, making him groan harder. Jamie gripped his
hand. "You're going to be all right, Ells," he heard himself saying.

From Lane's tangled hair the surgeon produced a chip of
bone, which he held up in bloodied fingers. "Took a nasty
clip, he did. Another half inch would have killed him."

Jamie glanced up at the man, not daring to ask, but the
surgeon nodded and said, "He'll recover."

"Praise God," the chaplain said.

"Got another one, Southworth," someone called from
the doorway, and the surgeon got up and went out. Mrs.
Canby finished bathing Lane's head and wrapped it in
bandages. A second casualty was carried in, groaning with
pain. Jamie glanced at Mrs. Canby as she stood up. She
smiled sadly at him, then went to help with the new patient.
When Jamie looked back at Lane his eyes were open.

"You're going to be all right," Jamie said again with
greater conviction, and Lane managed a feeble smile.

"Shrop's dead," he said. "Fell leading a charge."

Jamie didn't want to hear, but he nodded.

"Bradford got it, too, pretty bad I think. Did they bring
him here?"

"Not that I know."

"They've shot up the artillery something fierce. It's a
nasty fight." He looked frightened all of a sudden, and
glanced up at Jamie. "Could you bring me some water, old
man?"

"Sure." Jamie went outside, passing the surgeon at work
on the mangled leg of his patient, whose groans were
becoming shrieks. He took his canteen from Cocoa's saddle and turned back, meeting Mrs. Canby at the door.

"We're going," she said, moving toward her carriage.

"Best to get these men into town. We'll come back for more as soon as we have them settled."

Jamie nodded and helped her and Mrs. Chapin into the carriage. "Thank you, ma'am. You're a saint." He watched them away, then steeled himself to return to the darkness and grief of the hospital.

The cannon fire had slackened, making Laura hope the battle was ending, although scattered spitting of rifles could still be heard. Horses were moving around the ranch in great numbers. Standing up to look out of the window, Laura saw it was snowing again, the wind driving gusts of flakes at men climbing the ridge by the ranch with rifles in hand.

Artillery carriages rumbled back down the hill. Two of them stopped in the road by the house, and Laura wondered if the battle was over. She glanced back at the lieutenant. "They've brought the guns back."

"Where?"

"Just outside," Laura said.

"Come away from the window!"

Surprised at his tone, Laura took a step toward him, then a terrible blast seemed to rattle her heart inside her chest. Shards of glass flew past her, tinkling against the walls of the room. One thumped against her cloak but did not pierce it. She was sitting on the floor before she knew what had happened, her limbs having failed to support her.

"Are you all right?" Mr. Franklin said anxiously.

"Yes." To prove it, Laura forced her shaking legs to stand and walked to the door to look out. Artillerymen swarmed around the smoking guns, and the snow was melting beneath them. A smaller explosion and a puff of smoke from the hillside opposite told of more cannon up among the trees. The rifles were increasing their chatter, and Laura heard someone yell "Fire!" She turned away hastily and set her back to the wall as another horrible crash shook the house. Looking up, her eyes met Lieutenant Franklin's.

"Get out my pistol," he said. "It should be in my holster."

"You cannot hold it," Laura told him.

"No, but you can, if need be."

Laura went to him and removed a bit of glass from his blankets, then retrieved his pistol and the cartridge box from his belt. The cannonade continued to shake the house like the pounding of a giant fist. Laura held the gun gingerly while the lieutenant directed her to open it and load the empty chambers. Lieutenant Franklin wore an intent frown that made her strive to work faster. With trembling fingers she set the caps. His voice was calm as he told her how to cock the gun. "If you must fire, hold it straight out and aim at the waist," he said. Laura nodded, though the thought of firing at a living man made her a little sick. She pictured the enemy threatening the lieutenant, which made it easier to imagine shooting. She uncocked the pistol and set it in her lap just as the cannon crashed again. When she looked back at the lieutenant she was surprised to find him smiling at her.

"You're a good soldier, Miss Howland," he said, a gleam of humor in his eye.

"If I ever return to Boston I fear I shall find it very dull," Laura said.

He laughed, then coughed. The house was filling with acrid smoke from the cannon. Laura helped him sit up to clear his lungs, then lowered him gently back to rest. He panted with exhaustion and when she felt his brow it was clammy; another chill coming on. She tucked the blankets up to his neck and put more wood on the fire. There was little else she could do save to hold his hand. The fingers were cold between hers.

"Remember your promise," he said. "See me into the ground."

Laura's throat closed over any words. She nodded. The cannon crashed again and the lieutenant's eyes fluttered shut.

Do not leave me now, Laura thought silently, unable to prevent a tear from sliding down her cheek.

Halted again, O'Brien fidgeted in the saddle while they waited for the scouts to return. The noise of the battle was less clear. Surely they were behind the Texans by now. He moved his horse closer to the major's, intending to ask permission to lead a scout, but Chaves was returning so he held his peace. Chaves and Collins had a man between them, a sullen-looking scoundrel in a plaid wool shirt.

"What's this?" Chivington asked.

"He is not talking, Major, but I believe the emblem on his buckle is a symbol of Texas," Chaves said. He pointed to the star on the man's belt.

"Very well, we're behind them." Chivington echoed O'Brien's thoughts. "It's time we attacked their rear."

"Indulge me a moment, Major, if you will," Chaves said. He left his prisoner in Collins's charge and beckoned Chivington down from his horse. O'Brien dismounted and followed them, as did Captain Lewis, commanding the Regulars in the party. Chaves led the way up sloping ground toward what looked to be the edge of the table mountain they were on. As they neared it they went to hands and knees, cold seeping through gloves and trousers, then crawled on their bellies to the edge of a cliff. Coming up beside Chivington, O'Brien looked down into a valley through which ran a small creek. A house and some horses stood near the top end, but it was the flat bottomland that drew their attention, for on it were parked close to a hundred wagons.

Chivington whistled long and low. A chill of excitement danced across O'Brien's neck.

"You are right on top of them, Major," Chaves said.

29

Major Pyron had his horse shot under him, and my own cheek was twice brushed by a Minie ball, each time just drawing blood, and my clothes torn in two places. I mention this simply to show how hot was the fire of the enemy when all of the field officers upon the ground were either killed or touched.

— Colonel William R. Scurry, 4th Texas Mounted
   Volunteers

"Slough is counting on our support," Chivington said, gnawing his thumb as he frowned down at the valley.

"We can't pass this by!" O'Brien protested. "Sir," he added as Chivington threw him a dark look.

"We ought to be able to take these fellows," Lewis said. "Looks like there are only a couple of companies."

"That can't be all of them," the major said. "It's too small a guard, there must be others." He pointed to where the valley narrowed upstream. "Chaves, go reconnoiter that way."

Lewis volunteered to scout southward and O'Brien went with him, leaving Chivington contemplating the wagon train from the cliff's edge. They backed down the slope far enough to stand without revealing themselves to the men in the valley, then strode south along the hilltop. It was long and level, one of the table mountains that abounded in the country, with the valley below falling away somewhat at the south. Lewis found a place where a tumble of rocks began a few yards below the clifftop, partly screened by pines. He lowered himself over the edge, testing a protrusion with his foot, then setting his weight on it.

"We could come down this way," he said, looking up at O'Brien. "If we're quiet they won't notice us until we're almost on top of them."

"Better hope so," O'Brien said, pointing toward the highest knoll on the far side of the valley. A cannon was perched atop it overlooking the road. Lewis hauled himself back up the cliff and sat on the edge peering out at the gun.

"Don't see any others," he said. "A squad of sharpshooters should be able to take down the batterymen."

"If the major will allow it."

Lewis looked up at him and grinned. "I'm not strong on Volunteers, Captain, but I agree with you. This is too good a chance to pass up."

They scouted a little farther and spied a couple of small houses in the valley but no sign of any men around them. Returning, they found Chivington and Chaves debating.

"We must descend somewhere if we are to follow Colonel Slough's orders," Chaves said. "Let us capture the train and then move into the pass to attack their rear."

"They might have reserves hidden somewhere. They could trap us between two forces," Chivington said. "Even if they don't, these fellows will have a clear shot at us if we try to get down this cliff."

"We found a place that's easier," Lewis stated.

"Show me." All four went back to the spot Lewis had found. The major frowned, indecisive. "We'll be cut off from Slough if we come down here. It's too far from the fighting. And we can't bring those wagons away."

"Burn 'em," O'Brien said.

Chivington glanced up at him under taut brows. "Looking for glory, Captain?"

"No, sir," said O'Brien, though it was half a lie. "If their ammunition is in that train and we destroy it, then they'll have nothing to fight us with."

Chivington chewed his lip thoughtfully and peered at the descent. "We need ropes," he said finally.

"Rifle straps," O'Brien said.

"Sir," Captain Lewis said, "I request the honor of leading the attack."

O'Brien bit back a similar request as the major's sharp
gaze went from Lewis to him.

"Granted," Chivington said, and turned back toward the
waiting column.

Jamie led Cocoa back from the river and sat on the porch
of the ranch house. Leaning against a post, he took out his
tobacco and rolled a cigarrillo. He didn't like to smoke but
he didn't much like anything else about this day, and it
gave him an excuse to stay out of the hospital. Wounded
men had continued to trickle back from the battle, which
sounded less intense now. Maybe it was ending. The afternoon was wearing on. Jamie struck a match to the cigarrillo and inhaled, coughed and inhaled again. It left a bitter
taste in his mouth that got stronger with each pull. He
stopped smoking and merely held it between his fingers,
tapping the ash away now and then and gazing down the
valley at the train. A few flakes of snow drifted fitfully by.
He should check on the guard, he supposed, though there'd
been no more trouble. He leaned his head back against the
post and sighed. How on earth had he ever come to believe
he would enjoy the army?

It seemed a million years since he'd stood in the door of
Webber's, watching the glorious lancers troop by on their
chargers. A lot of those lancers were dead now, buried on
his orders. He felt he would give just about anything to be
back in San Antonio—a merc clerk in a safe, unremarkable
mercantile —with the river twining lazily before him
instead of this creek, rolling hills and live oak instead of
cedar-pecked mesas.

A movement among the cedars caught his eye and at the
same time he heard a distant clattering sound. He watched
a boulder tumble down the cliff half a mile or so down the
valley, then understood all at once what had caused it to
fall: men swarming down from the mesa. Men in blue.

He was up and into the saddle before thought caught up

with action. Cocoa gave a snort and started up the hill before he could ask, sensing his urgency and breaking into a gallop in response. Startled artillerymen jumped up from the small fire they had built as Jamie rode toward them yelling and waving toward the mesa.

"Fire cannon!" he heard himself shrieking. "Fire!"

With gratifying speed the men went to their business, swinging the gun around to bear on the cliffs. The gunner barked out commands to his crew, and Cocoa jumped as the gun sent a shot flying across the valley. It fell short.

"Too far, sir!" the gunner called.

"Keep firing," Jamie cried, turning Cocoa and muttering encouragements she did not need as they scrambled back down the hill toward Rose and his men. Some of the teamsters had grabbed mules and were whipping them up the road to Santa Fé. Jamie made an attempt to stop them as they passed but settled for cursing them instead. Truth to tell, he was much of their mind.

He let up suddenly, hands slackening on the reins as he sat back in the saddle. Cocoa swiveled her ears toward him and huffed at the change as she slowed to a trot.

He could go, he realized. He could ride back to Santa Fé. Fetching supplies for the wounded, he could say, or sending a message to General Sibley. Or perhaps he would say nothing and just ride all the way back to Texas.

He wasn't meant for this, he thought resentfully, watching the enemy collect in a dark-blue clot at the foot of the cliff. The cannon fired again and he winced as the ball whistled high overhead. He was a quartermaster, a noncombatant. He'd been hired for his administrative skills, not for fighting. Valverde smoke rose in his nostrils, and he gave a small grunt of dismay at the unwanted memories: blood spilled by his hand, Martin dead, ranks of terrifying blue warriors.

They were to blame, those men in blue. They had made him become an animal, when all he wanted was to be good and noble and honorable. He tried to shield himself by recalling the blind anger that had filled him on that first battleground, but the piteous voices of ghosts were stronger, ghosts both blue and gray, crying in shadow voices not for vengeance but for all they had lost. They were just men, after all. It was not right for men to be killing each other. It was against God's commandment. Jamie smiled bitterly at this understanding, for he had come to it far too late. He was already a murderer himself.

Well enough, he decided. Murderers ought to die, and he supposed he would rather die fighting than running. Turning his head, he saw Rose sprinting toward him. Hardly a man, Rose, and had not yet stained himself. Jamie could earn some small measure of redemption by keeping him from the coming horror. It would be his final act, a gesture of defiance against the gods of war. Staring at the sergeant's wild eyes, Jamie shook off all other feelings and clung to the shreds of his anger. He swung down from Cocoa and tossed the reins to Rose.

"Ride to Scurry," he said. "Tell him we're under attack!"

"But—"

"Go!" Jamie pushed Rose roughly into Cocoa's side. With a last frightened glance Rose mounted and rode off toward the pass.

"Good-bye, girl," whispered Jamie as the mare passed out of sight. He turned his attention back to the valley, ordered the men guarding the road to move closer to the house and stand ready to support the artillerymen, then stepped into his tent and glanced around, deciding what he'd need. On impulse he opened his kit and pulled out the jacket Momma had made him. Except for the parade on the day they'd left San Antonio, he'd never worn it. A bitter smile curled his lips. If he were to die, he'd die proudly. He shrugged into it, stuffed his few things in its pockets, then reached for his hat and hurried out to organize the train's guard.

White-sheeted wagons stood in neat rows. They had been for him an object of pride and a hated burden, and now he would die in their defense. A mass of blue was forming a battle line while more men poured over the cliff.

Jamie was sure he was greatly outnumbered. Well, he wouldn't make it easy for them. He owed Martin that much.

He gathered his own men into a feeble line and waited, watching the Yankee force assemble below. Rays of late sun poked through the clouds, making the bayonets glint atop their rifles, mirroring the glimmer of the creek. Martin had died by a river, Jamie remembered. It was fitting. He reached up to his hat and touched the star pin—a farewell gesture—and stood at the head of his men, waiting for the attack to begin.

Laura kept her hand on Lieutenant Franklin's wrist to assure herself he still lived. The pulse beneath her fingertips was light and thready. From shaking chills he had sunk into heavy sleep, and she feared he would wake no more.

The voices outside took on a new tone, and she sat up straight trying to hear better. "Limber up," someone shouted hoarsely. "Fall back to the ridge!"

Laura's chest tightened. No more crashes of cannon, but she would have welcomed them in the place of what she now heard: the rumble of the guns moving away eastward. Rifles bickered louder. She risked a peek out of the window and saw the valley strewn with bodies, bloodstained snow. Fighting had erupted atop the ridge north of the ranch, where men in blue were being forced back from the ridgetop, with nowhere to go but down the east side or off the precipitous edge. Wind whipped snow almost horizontally and added its voice to a cacophony of screams and howls. Laura backed away from the window in alarm, returning to sit beside Franklin. A shadow fell across the window curtain and with a little gasp she raised the pistol, but it disappeared again. Bootsteps scraped outside, and Laura heard new voices—strangely accented—Texan voices.

"What's happening?" the lieutenant asked, making her start.

Laura turned and was surprised at how well he looked.

Sleep must have restored him somewhat. Drawing a breath, she answered as calmly as she could. "Our men have fallen back."

His eyes widened a little. "You have the pistol?" he asked, and the urgency in his voice confirmed her fears.

Laura nodded and raised it from her lap to show him. "We are losing," she said bitterly as she put it down again.

"Maybe not," he said. "Sometimes giving ground is the best defense."

"I wish I had your courage."

"Miss Howland, you remind me very much of myself," he said, smiling.

Laura shook her head ruefully. "You give me too much credit, I fear. I am only a woman, after all."

Franklin's dark brows drew closer together. "You of all people should never speak of yourself as 'only a woman.'"

Laura allowed herself a wry smile. "But a woman does not have many choices. You said so yourself."

"Unless she decides to make her own road."

An odd remark; Laura looked at him inquiringly. He returned her gaze, frowning a little, then seemed to reach a decision. "Will you take out my wallet?" he said. "It's in my coat pocket. There's a picture I'd like to show you."

The wallet was slim, containing only a few papers. Laura found a likeness and pulled it out. It was a carte-de-visite of the lieutenant, so handsome and gallant that Laura caught her breath. He was standing with one hand on his sword hilt and an arm resting on a pedestal, smiling the odd smile that she found so fascinating.

"In your uniform," she said. "How smart you look!"

"Not that one," he said. "There's another, tucked behind."

The second image was somewhat worn, its corners softened with handling. It was of another soldier and a woman dressed in a black gown rather like Laura's. Both were clearly related to the lieutenant. "Family?"

"My brother and myself," the lieutenant said in so soft a voice Laura barely heard.

"You mean—"

"I meant what I said, Miss Howland."

Laura held the images side by side to compare them. The young lady was very like Franklin, certainly. She gave a puzzled laugh. "Is it a joke?" she asked.

"No." The lieutenant smiled with a shake of the head. "That is my true self."

"I don't understand."

"Miss Howland," the lieutenant whispered as Laura bent closer to hear, "I make no claim to be a lady, but I am as much a woman as you are."

30

Thus ended the battle of Glorieta Valley, in which we gained a complete victory but at the expense of every comfort.

—Alfred B. Peticolas

"Wynkoop!" Chivington called. O'Brien strolled toward the major in Captain Wynkoop's wake.

"Take thirty of your best shots up the mountainside and pick off those artillerymen." Wynkoop was off on the words, flashing a grin over his shoulder at O'Brien.

"Lewis and his men will take the gun," Chivington said. His eyes traveled over O'Brien's form as if searching for something to disapprove. Finally he folded his arms over his chest. "You're in charge of the second column. Surround the wagons and those houses. You wanted to burn the train, Captain," he added. "Burn it."

"Sir!" O'Brien said, snapping a salute. He turned back to the column. Lewis had already detached his Regulars and was marching them away toward the hill where the cannon lay. It belched smoke and fire at them, the blast rattling back and forth among the hills. In answer a volley went up from Wynkoop's men on the hillside, causing havoc among the gunners. O'Brien turned to the waiting Pike's Peakers. He caught Shaunessy's eye and broke out in a satisfied grin. "Battalion, forward," he shouted, "at the double-quick, march!"

Laura stared at the lieutenant in shocked disbelief.

"See for yourself, if you like," Franklin said with the

familiar odd smile. The crackle of rifles almost hid the words.

Laura looked more closely at the two images, holding them near her face in the window's dim light. It could be the same person, she concluded, but she still couldn't accept what that meant.

"Now you see what a waste it would be to mourn for me," Franklin said.

Laura looked back at the fine face alight with silent laughter. Delicate bones for a man, she admitted, and the hands were so fine, as well. She felt a blush rising at the memory of how tenderly she'd held those hands. "Why?" she asked in a strangled voice.

"I wanted to fight for the Union. To avenge my brother, at first. But once I began I discovered . . ."

"What?" Laura asked in numb fascination.

"Freedom," Franklin whispered. "A freedom I'd never dreamed of! I can go anywhere I please, do what I please, and no one to disapprove or deny me!"

Laura took a sharp breath. The words were so filled with passion that she had no choice but to accept that the lieutenant was a woman, for what man would speak so of rights he had known from his birth? Laura stared hard at the stranger before her, feeling betrayed, struggling to understand.

Franklin nodded. "Disgraceful, I know, but I've done nothing vile, I assure you. Nothing I would be censured for, save the deception. Though I'll admit to having been tempted." The dark eyes glanced away and grew sad for a moment. "You can trust Captain O'Brien, Miss Howland. He's a man of honor, though he may not know it himself."

Laura caught her breath on a sob, and suddenly tears were streaming down her face. She pressed a hand over her mouth, trying to stop.

"You'll forget about me, Miss Howland, after you've hated me for a while."

"I could never hate you," Laura managed to say.

"That's kind. The one thing I regret is having caused you

pain. I would not have done that for the world," Franklin said, and smiled softly. "I have a little money. Will you let me give it to you? To make amends? Then you can return to Boston if you wish."

Laura shook her head. "I couldn't take it," she said. "Your family—"

"It's nothing to them. They're quite wealthy, and would be mortified to know of my . . . escapades." Franklin laughed. "That's why I came west, so as not to involve them. I had planned to enlist in Missouri, but then I heard about Governor Gilpin's regiment and thought that safer. I only just reached Denver City in time." Franklin paused and blinked once or twice. A queer look passed through the shadowed eyes; they seemed to be watching some invisible scene, then they found Laura's face again. "Please take the money. Shame for it to go to waste."

Freedom, Laura thought. Freedom to return home, or to go elsewhere if she wished. Her feelings were all in a tangle, but freedom she could understand. She swallowed, and said humbly, "Very well. Thank you."

"It's in a sock," Franklin whispered. "In my trousers, I'm afraid. I thought it the safest place."

Laura glanced around the room. Some of the wounded men were sleeping, and the others seemed not to be watching. She shifted so that her back was to them and carefully raised Franklin's blankets. The trousers were soaked in blood. Laura glanced at the lieutenant, who smiled and nodded. Cheeks burning, Laura undid the trousers and found the sock in a pocket stitched to the inside. She found nothing else—Lieutenant Franklin was unquestionably a woman. Laura quickly closed the trousers up again, her fingers slipping at the sticky buttons. Another glance over her shoulder reassured her that no one had taken note of her activities. With the heavy sock in her bloodied fingers, Laura turned back to the lieutenant.

"I'm sorry it's such a mess," Franklin said.

Laura glanced around and spotted the bowl of water

she'd used to bathe the lieutenant's face. She drew it closer and put the sock into it, rinsing her hands.

"There's some jewelry in there, as well," Franklin whispered. "Nothing special, just a few trinkets I brought with me. They should bring a fair price. If you don't want my pistol give it to Captain O'Brien, but I think you'd do better to keep it." The lieutenant seemed tired of a sudden and began to breathe shallowly. Laura bit her lip to hold back further tears and shyly took the woman's hand.

"I fought as well as any man," Franklin said. "They never knew the difference. I think that's pretty glorious, don't you?"

Unable to speak, Laura nodded.

"Remember your promise. Bury me yourself, so no one knows."

"Yes," Laura whispered.

"Thank you, Miss Howland. Laura. You've been a good friend."

Laura gazed at the lieutenant's handsome face in grief and confusion, tears spilling down her cheeks once more. She no longer bothered to resist them.

"That's a lovely light," Franklin remarked dreamily, gazing at the ceiling. "Can you see it, Laura?"

Laura's eyes wavered toward the window, where daylight was beginning to fade. "No," she said.

"I wish you could see it," the lieutenant said. "Such a beautiful light." She smiled softly and sighed, and did not breathe again.

"What is your name?" Laura whispered, but the lieutenant made no response. Laura took the cold hands in hers once more. "I never knew your name." Fresh sobs convulsed her; she gave her whole heart to them, weeping freely over the lieutenant's body as the distant cannon resumed its pounding.

The bluecoats came on and Jamie stared at their bayonets. He'd prefer a bullet, he thought fleetingly. As if in answer, the rifles beside him began snapping. He frowned. It was too far, wasn't it? He had drilled so little, but he could see that the shots had done no good. "Cease firing," he shouted, and "Load!" The blue line paused in its advance to deal a volley that tore Jamie's feeble line apart. Half a dozen men dropped to the earth, and shrieks of pain filled the smoke-hazed air. Already the defense was a failure, and the Yankee officer was shouting for them to surrender.

He had failed. Failed even to die honorably. Jamie stared at the Yankee captain in mute despair, then noticed movement among the wagons. The bluecoats had fallen on the train. Jamie glimpsed a man thrusting a firebrand into an ordnance wagon.

"No!" he screamed, starting toward it. A ball sang by him, brushing his sleeve so close Jamie could feel the heat. The instinct that had set him running was futile; with a rolling crescendo of thunder the wagon exploded in blinding light, tossing a Yankee soldier into the air like a toy and setting fire to its neighbors. Before the man landed Jamie had been seized by a dozen hands, and someone yelled, "Shoot the bastard!"

"No!" a harsh voice shouted.

Jamie tore his gaze away from the fire and looked into the fearsome green eyes of the tall man who came up to him. "He's my prisoner," the other said, glaring at the Yankee troops as he fingered the hilt of his sword. None of them answered, and he turned to Jamie. "Best to surrender your men," he said. "I'll see they're well treated."

Irish, Jamie thought inconsequentially, staring at dark stains on the man's coat. He glanced at the remnants of the wagon guard, most of whom had already thrown down their weapons, and nodded miserably. As he handed over his pistol a rumble made him look up toward the hill in time to see the cannon tumbling into the ravine, its carriage smashing to pieces on the rocky hillside. Yankees were everywhere, all over the train, pulling out boxes and invading the ranch house.

"There are wounded up there," he said to the Yankee captain, gesturing toward the house.

"We'll not harm them," the Irishman said. "Denning, take some men and go secure that house. Morris, you and Flannery get a guard together for these prisoners. Who's that fellow was hurt, one of Wynkoop's, isn't he?" He strode off shouting orders, leaving Jamie and his men under guard. They gathered the men who had fallen: three dead and a dozen or more wounded.

"May I send someone to the creek for water?" Jamie asked the sergeant in charge of their guard.

The Yankee sergeant glanced toward the creek. "No. McCraw," he said, handing his canteen to one of the guards, "go fetch them some water."

"And bandages?" Jamie asked. "There are some in the fourth wagon—" His voice trailed off, for as he pointed toward the train he saw chaos. The Yankees were pulling stores out of the wagons, piling them up and setting them on fire. Jamie forgot all else and walked toward the train until a bayonet in his ribs forced him to stop. He stood watching in impotent horror as all the supplies he and Martin had scrounged for—the fruits of his labor for months past—were wantonly strewn on the ground. It hurt like a physical pain to see goods piled atop ammunition crates and then put to the torch. One blast sent bacon and saddles flying in all directions. It would have been comical except that Jamie knew, better perhaps than any man there, that this blow would hurt Sibley's army more than any loss of men. He'd had nightmares aplenty in the last month but had never imagined anything so devastating as this.

More explosions ripped the air. Fire enveloped the wagons, shriveling the sheets into wisps of ash that clung to the burning ribs. Jamie sank to his knees, hiding his face in his hands, unable to watch as his whole train was swallowed in flame.

"It was terrible," one of the privates O'Brien had freed told the major. "They flanked us and we had to fall back to Pigeon's, and then they started charging! They just kept charging, over and over, that's how we were took—"

"Slough's outnumbered without us," Chivington said, frowning at the smoldering supply train. Little remained but a few bits of iron.

O'Brien glanced at the lowering sun. "We could go now. We can still fall on their rear."

"I heard the Texans saying there's a reinforcement coming from Galisteo," the private said, his eyes wide with fear.

Chivington shook his head. "Can't risk it, we'd be caught in a vise. We'd best go back the way we came. What the devil?!"

O'Brien followed his gaze up the canyon. A rider was galloping down the steep valley above the ranch. O'Brien swore; he'd sent men to search upstream, but they'd reported nothing. They seemed to have missed one Texan at least. A few pops of rifles went up, but the rider escaped into the pass.

"I thought you'd secured all the Texans!" Chivington said.

"I'll find where he came from," O'Brien said, and with a hasty salute he got some men together and started up the canyon.

Half a mile above the ranch house they found a steep ravine branching to one side, roped off as a corral. In it were horses and mules—four or five hundred—milling in fright at the smells of battle. No more Texans were found. O'Brien sent a detail to search farther up the canyon and hurried to report the discovery to the major.

"Horses?" Chivington said.

O'Brien nodded. "And draft mules."

"Well, they'd best be destroyed."

"Sir?" said O'Brien.

Chivington turned a glare on him. "You heard me, Captain. Destroy them. We can't take them up that cliff."

O'Brien stared at him in dismay. Killing an enemy in a fair fight was one thing, slaughtering horses another. "Mightn't we just set them loose?" he asked.

"We might," Chivington said harshly, "and then the Texans would round them up again! You have your orders, Captain. Do it quickly."

There was a bad taste in O'Brien's mouth. He gave the major a stiff salute and turned away. Gathering together all the Pike's Peakers who were not guarding prisoners, he led them back up the canyon to the corral. There he stood with his back to a juniper staring at the frightened animals, hating what he had to do, hating the major and the Texans and himself. This was not the glory he had been seeking. This was plain meanness.

"Fix bayonets," he commanded.

Shaunessy looked at him uneasily. O'Brien ignored him, and in bitter indignation gave the order for the slaughter to begin.

The sound was like nothing Jamie had heard, like the shrieks of a thousand banshees or the nightmare howls of angry warriors' phantoms. He stood up, trying to sense where it came from, and though he could see nothing he suddenly recognized what he was hearing. Butchery. Frightened animals squealing in pain, a sound he knew well but had never before heard in such magnitude. He gazed up the canyon toward where the livestock had been corraled, and a new feeling settled in his belly. Hatred. Cold hatred for the men who would do such a thing, who would waste the innocent lives of poor beasts as freely as they had wrecked all the army's provisions. "Yankee bastards," he muttered.

"Captain?"

Jamie turned snarling on the speaker, who stepped back. It was one of the men from the wagon guard, one of the ones who had stayed. Jamie tried to change his face so as not to reflect what he felt. "What is it, Private?"

"I just thought you might like me to bind up your arm, sir."

Now that he thought about it, Jamie realized his right arm was smarting. He glanced down and was surprised to see blood all down his sleeve from a torn place up near the shoulder. He put his fingers to it and hissed for it stung sharp, and he saw a long gash in his upper arm. "Minié ball," he said. "Thought it missed me." He let the private tie up the wound. Aware of it now, he began to ache. He flexed stiffening fingers and sought out the canteen, drained it and demanded more from his captors. Sunlight stabbed in beneath the layer of cloud, gilding the hilltop where the cannon had stood. The scrub trees became bronze and the hills gleamed, magnificent, like El Dorado, but in the shadows beneath where Jamie and his men stood it was already cold. Jamie went up to the Yankee sergeant.

"Let us carry the wounded up to the hospital," he said, his voice a challenge.

"Sorry, sir. Orders are to hold you here."

"I want to speak to your captain," Jamie said.

"Sorry, sir—"

"Don't 'sorry' me, you goddam Yankee scum!" Jamie shouted in his face. "Send someone to your captain and tell him I want to speak to him!"

The sergeant's eyes narrowed but he took a step back. Jamie drew breath to curse him some more but he turned and barked out an order. A soldier went trotting away toward the ranch. The horses and mules had stopped screaming, and now Jamie saw a column descending the valley led by the Irish captain. Jamie paced along the guards until the Irishman came up. There was no new blood on him, but Jamie knew it was he who had ordered the animals to be killed, and the hate in him grew darker.

"It'll be cold soon," Jamie said in a flat voice. "Let my men carry the wounded up to the house."

The Irishman gave a weary nod and ordered the guard to accompany Jamie and his men. Jamie brought the dead along, too, for the shovels had all gone up with the train and they had no way to bury them. When they reached the house they found it overflowing. Several artillerymen had been hit, as had the chaplain, who had been holding a white flag at the time. Jamie stopped to see Lane, who gripped his hand, making him wince.

"Hard luck, old man," Lane said, "but we'll come around."

Jamie just shook his head.

"What, did Scurry surrender?" Lane asked, trying to sit up.

Jamie shrugged. "Don't know. But they've burned the train."

Lane's eyes widened and his mouth fell open. He was adjutant, he understood. "Everything?"

"Everything. Killed the horses and mules."

"Gods! Is that what we heard?"

Jamie nodded. "It's over." Lane lay back, and Jamie gave him a ghostly smile. "See you in Texas or hell."

"Come along," the sergeant said, nudging him. Jamie turned away and could feel Lane's gaze follow him out of the house.

It was indeed over. There would be no seaports in California, no Colorado gold. Unless by some miracle they discovered a source of supply hitherto unknown, the entire army was destitute. Either way, Jamie would have no more part of it. He was a prisoner of war.

The sergeant made him halt on the porch while he gathered the Yankees guarding the hospital. Jamie looked over the charred valley floor. The last rays of sun were splashed across a cliff once more covered with bluecoats, retreating the way they had come. Jamie and his men were marched down the valley and made to climb the mesa behind them. By the time he reached the summit, Jamie's arm was throbbing. He stopped to look back over the valley. To the west the sinking sun had set fire to the underside of the clouds—red and orange streaks seemed to reflect the embers of the ruined supply train. Jamie turned away.

A company of infantry with bayonets fixed herded the prisoners together as they came up the cliff. The Irish captain was there, and with him a giant of a man who was clearly the Yankees' commander. "That the last of them?" the big Yankee asked in a booming voice. "Good." He turned to the guards. "Listen close now. We don't know where the enemy's column is, so if we are attacked, you're to shoot these prisoners, then defend yourselves."

Jamie was incensed. He glanced at the Irishman, who seemed just as angry but only looked away. The Yankee officers got on their horses and formed their troops into a column, then began marching eastward. Surrounded by bayonets, Jamie marched in silent rage into darkness that echoed what lay in his heart.

Laura leaned against the wall and gazed at the lieutenant in the last of the dying light. She had no more tears in her; she was exhausted and numbed by a tumult of conflicting feelings. Outside the sounds of battle had ceased, replaced by the shuffling of many soldiers' feet. The Texans built fires as the Colorado men had done two nights before. They laughed and swapped war stories as had the Pike's Peakers, trampled the portal as they had done. Laura had to remind herself she was surrounded by enemies, for they sounded quite normal to her.

She looked down at the images in her lap, then fumbled in her cloak pocket and took out her father's portrait. She wondered what he would think of the intrepid Lieutenant Franklin. Wiping some dust from the frame, she smiled. He would think her distressingly wild, but then he had not walked in her shoes. Laura sighed. Looking at her father's face, she realized he had trained her to define herself in relation to him. She had lived to assist him, further his career, subjugate herself for his sake. Anger washed through her as she realized he was more like his brother than she had previously understood. Yet he was her father still, and she loved him, though she would no longer feel lost without him. She might not be as bold as the lieutenant had been, but she would never again allow others to control her fate. Perhaps that was the greatest gift Franklin had given her. She opened the frame and slid the lieutenant's two images behind her father's portrait, then closed it up and returned it to her cloak pocket.

A footstep drew her attention. The outer door opened and a man entered. Laura's hand reached the pistol and cocked it as she pointed it at the intruder, who stopped and raised his hands.

"I know you were not much impressed with me, ma'am," a lazy voice said, "but there's no need to put a bullet in me."

Laura frowned and peered through the dimness at the man's face. The mustache looked familiar. The man slowly removed his hat, and she remembered. "Mr. Owens," she said in dull surprise.

"Yes, ma'am. Miss Howland, isn't it?"

Laura nodded.

"Think you might see your way to putting down that pistol, ma'am?"

Laura lowered the gun to her lap but kept it cocked. "What do you want?"

"Looking for a place to bring our wounded," Owens said. "Looks like the house is already full, though."

"Yes."

Owens glanced down at the lieutenant. "Friend of yours?"

"Yes." Laura's eyes wandered to the pale face framed by shadowed curls. She jumped as Owens stepped closer and knelt down. Her hand closed convulsively on the butt of the pistol.

"Quite a surprise to see you here, ma'am," he said. "Didn't think you were the sort to hitch up with a soldier. Married?"

"That is not your concern—"

"Not married."

"I think you should go," Laura said, watching him. He was too far away to reach for the gun, but only just. She saw him glance at it and knew he was thinking the same thing. In the growing darkness she had only glints and shadowy edges to guide her, along with her instinct.

"You don't belong here, Miss Howland," Owens said,

his voice caressing. "Not here in the middle of this trash. You belong in your own home, with lots of fine clothes and pretty things around you. What happened to your uncle?"

Laura was silent, unsure what he wanted or whether to trust him. He had all the marks of a gentleman, but instinct rose a prickle of warning along her forearms.

"You need someone to look after you," he said. "I'd be grateful if you'd give me the honor. I can see you've had some hard days, but you needn't worry anymore. You can have whatever you like—jewels, money—even your own house if you want."

Cold anger flooded the emptiness Laura had felt moments earlier. She raised the pistol again and aimed it below the shadowed edge of Owens's shoulders. "You've made a mistake, sir," she said. "Please go."

"You're a fool if you think you'll get a better offer," he said. His drawl had acquired a nasty edge.

Laura sensed a small movement and said, "Don't!" Owens froze and Laura shifted her grip on the gun. "Back away, sir," she said, trying to sound cold-blooded. "I loaded this pistol myself, and I will shoot."

Owens seemed convinced, for he shuffled back out of reach and then slowly got to his feet. Laura watched his hands, but he apparently thought it unwise to duel with her inside the house.

"Go away now," she said. "Don't come back."

He put his hat on, hiding his face in shadow. "Pleasure to see you again," he said insolently, and went out.

Laura held the gun aimed at the door for a full minute after he'd gone. It became heavy, and she heard no sign of his return so she uncocked it and set it down while she hastily built up the fire. With golden flames chasing the shadows back into the corners, she felt somewhat better.

"Good for you, miss," came a voice from nearby, and Laura gave a violent start. One of the wounded men, she realized. They had all been so quiet she'd almost forgotten them. "I was sorry to hear you so sad, miss," the man said. "Has Lieutenant Franklin gone?"

"Yes," Laura said, wondering whether the soldier had heard her whispered conversation with the lieutenant. There had been gunfire outside at the time, but she was unsure if it had masked their voices.

"He was a good one," the wounded man said. "A real gent, Mr. Franklin. Not like that rat that was just in here." He sounded sincere, and Laura breathed relief. As if coming out of a dream, she remembered the name of the man who was speaking.

"Private Bristol," she said aloud.

"Yes, miss."

"Are you feeling any better?"

"Somewhat, miss. Thank you for asking."

"Would you like some water?"

"No, no. I don't mean to trouble you, miss. You've had trouble enough. Think I'll sleep a spell."

"Sleep well then," Laura said. Sleep was now out of the question for her, and she settled herself against the fireplace once more. A sound made her reach for her pistol, but it was Monsieur Vallé who entered with an armload of firewood. He beckoned to Carmen, who followed him in carrying a broom.

"I thought we should all be together," Vallé said.

"Won't your pantry be raided?" Laura asked.

"It is already empty."

"Oh." Laura watched Carmen begin sweeping up the broken glass from the window. Vallé stacked the wood beside the fireplace.

"Is he any better?" Vallé asked.

"Yes," Laura said, glancing at Franklin. "Much better now."

Vallé took a step toward her. "Ma pauvre—"

Laura shook her head, smiling to keep back the tears, and stood up. She gave him Franklin's blankets and helped him settle Carmen in the corner by the window. When she returned to her place she noticed the lieutenant's holster, and though the belt was bloodied she undid it and sat cleaning the leather with the scrap of cloth from the water bowl. She buckled it round her own waist and slipped the pistol into it, close to hand, then leaned back once more and closed her weary eyes.

31

Except for its political geographical position, the Territory of New Mexico is not worth a quarter of the blood and treasure expended in its conquest.

—H. H. Sibley

The razor needed sharpening, but O'Brien was too tired to bother. It would do well enough. A clean face would only improve his appearance so much when his uniform bore the marks of two battles. He finished shaving and walked up to Kozlowski's house. The sun wasn't up yet. Smells of bacon and coffee floated through the camp, making his stomach growl. He ignored it and went to the house, where he met Major Chivington coming out.

"Good work yesterday, O'Brien," the major said.

O'Brien stared up at him. The men liked Chivington and O'Brien admitted he was a brave leader, but he would never forget being made to slaughter horses, and doubted he would ever forgive it. The major seemed to sense his mood, for he passed by without another word, and O'Brien went into the house.

"Good morning, Captain O'Brien," Slough said in a distant voice as the adjutant led O'Brien through the low doorway. The colonel's eyes had an unhappy look, and O'Brien wondered if the rumor he'd heard—that some of Slough's enemies in the regiment had aimed a volley at him during the fighting—was true.

"I understand you rendered Major Chivington signal assistance yesterday," Slough said.

Assistance was an odd word for it, O'Brien thought, but he merely nodded. "Thank you, sir."

"What may I do for you?"

"I heard there's an armistice, sir. I'd like to volunteer my men to retrieve the wounded."

Colonel Slough was silent for a moment. "That's very generous of you, Captain."

"I left my lieutenant at Pigeon's Ranch."

"Oh, I see. Of course. You may as well bury the dead while you're there. Ask the quartermaster for some shovels, and mind you record all their names."

"Yes, sir," O'Brien said. "Thank you, sir." He went out, pleased not with the duty but with the chance of returning to Pigeon's. It wasn't Franklin he wanted to see but Miss Howland. She was there in that house, in the midst of a whole herd of Texans, and only the Frenchman to shield her. She might not care to see him, but he'd go to make sure she was safe. If the Rebels had harmed her, they'd soon wish themselves in hell.

Laura awoke; some small sound brought her head up, and she saw that Vallé and Carmen were gone. A pale glow of morning seeped in through the shattered window, its torn curtain as still as death. Laura sat up stiffly, her breath hanging frozen in the air, and glanced at the poor corpse of Franklin beside which she had slept peacefully. She rubbed at her eyes. No use crying again. She should get up and see to the living, but there was one thing she must do first.

Glancing at the sleeping wounded, she reached for the little bowl of bloodied water. It was icy cold, and she hastily fished out the sock Franklin had given to her, squeezed out the water, then laid it on a corner of her cloak and undid the knot in its end. Quietly she worked the sock open and took out its contents, counting the money as she spread it in her lap. When she'd finished she was amazed. There were three hundred forty-two dollars in gold, a few bits of silver, and several pieces of jewelry. A fortune. Independence.

Laura stared at the gift, gratitude swelling within her. She picked up a necklace that glinted gold in the dawn-light, a delicate web sprinkled with teardrops of blood-red. Garnet? Or ruby? A trinket, the lieutenant had called it. Laura suspected it was worth twice the amount of the coin.

The door opened, flooding the room with sunlight. Laura jumped, dropped the necklace in her lap, and sought to hide all. As her hand went to her pistol she glimpsed a blue uniform, then the door closed again as the newcomer stepped inside. For a breathless moment Laura stared, hand on holster, momentarily blinded and peering into the darkness for any movement.

"It'll look well on you, miss," a familiar voice softly said, "but best put it away now."

Laura gave a shuddering sigh. "Captain O'Brien."

He came forward and knelt by the fireplace, searching the ashes for a live coal, adding wood. Laura kept a guarded eye on him as she tied her new fortune into Franklin's crumpled handkerchief, but the captain's eyes never strayed toward her. Gratitude filled her heart, and her eyes threatened to spill over again. How good he was! How wrong she had been to mistrust him.

She noticed Franklin's notebook and pencil on the floor. Picking them up, she glanced at the captain, who sensed her gaze and turned his head.

"I think the lieutenant would want you to have these," she said, holding out the paper and pencil. Such insignificant things to most people, but not to him.

He stared at them, and his brows drew together. "Would you still . . ." he began, then faltered.

"Yes," Laura said softly.

The green eyes rose to hers, full of emotion. His gaze was as intense as ever, but it no longer frightened her. He had shaved, Laura noticed inconsequentially; the firelight flickered on his face, casting shadows along its clean lines. She smiled. An answering smile grew slowly, and silent understanding passed between them as he nodded.

"May I ask a favor in return?" Laura said.

"Anything," he said in a rough whisper.

"I promised the lieutenant I would see to the burial."

O'Brien nodded again, glancing at Franklin. "I'm sorry," he said. "He was a good man."

"Yes," Laura said, smiling softly to herself. "He was."

Shreds of daylight were coming in through chinks in the walls. Jamie heaved himself onto an elbow, peering through the dusty light, wondering where he was. Some sort of storeroom, he guessed. He'd been too exhausted to care when the march through the hellish, delirious night had finally ended. His head was still light, he ached everywhere, and his mouth was a desert.

"Hey, he's alive," someone said.

"Russell." A hand patted his shoulder, and Jamie peered up as he realized the voice had been McIntyre's.

"They burned the train," Jamie croaked.

"I know," McIntyre said. "I'm so sorry. I thought about trying to warn you, but—"

"You *what?*" the first voice cried, and a shuffling started as someone got up and came closer. McIntyre stood, and Jamie struggled to sit up.

"Hall, I—"

"You could have warned them and didn't?" Hall said.

"You could have warned them, too," McIntyre replied, his anger matching Hall's. "In the canyon when we were caught. By Colorado men, *your* men! If one of us could have escaped—"

"Bastard," Hall shouted, and Jamie heard a sickening smack of flesh on flesh. Instantly other voices went up from the corners, shouting confusion over the scuffle. Jamie got to his feet and saw McIntyre and Hall grappling, their feet puffing clouds of dust up from the floor.

"Stop it," Jamie said, but his words were trampled in the fray. God damn them, he thought. Hasn't there been enough fighting?

No, there hasn't.

A dam broke inside him. With a cry of inarticulate rage,

Jamie flung himself into the fight, kicking, scratching, hitting at Hall in defense of his friend and in senseless relief of his feelings. Blows fell on him, but he ignored them until the noise and light increased and a sharper blow fell across his shoulders.

"Break it up!" the guard shouted. Jamie fell back gasping, licked at a gash on the back of his hand, then collapsed in the corner and laid his head on his knees, oblivious of the meaning in the guards' angry orders. His panting turned to racking sobs. The door slammed them into darkness again. Jamie couldn't stop crying, even when firm hands gripped his shoulders.

"Russell," McIntyre said. "It's all right."

Jamie shook his head, flooded with grief and despair. McIntyre's arm hugged his shoulders.

"It's all right, Jamie," McIntyre repeated. "You'll get to go home, you know."

Home. Jamie looked up and hiccuped, wiping his torn sleeve across his eyes.

McIntyre's face was shadowed. "You can give your parole and go back to Texas," he said. "Back to your family."

And Emma. Sniffling, Jamie searched the floor nearby and found his hat, battered all out of shape. Emma's star winked at him and he wiped the dust off it with shaky fingers. He would have to tell her. Martin was dead. Tears rolled down his cheeks, but he was too tired to care. He glanced up at McIntyre, thought he saw a sad smile, and leaned gratefully against his friend's shoulder as he sobbed again, finally able to grieve.

O'Brien stuck his shovel into the frozen dirt and wiped the sweat out of his eyes. Bright sunshine was melting the blood in the valley and turning the road into mud, but the spot where he'd dug Franklin's grave was still shadowed. A tall pine stood above it, near the rocky wall east of the house. It was the prettiest place he could find—chosen more for Miss Howland's sake than for Franklin's—but still a poor end for the elegant boy who'd annoyed him so often. O'Brien wondered if there were a family plot somewhere, a blank space on some grand monument that would forever remain empty. Shaking off such useless thoughts, he sent two of his men in for the body, and reached for his coat.

Miss Howland came out with Pigeon and Mrs. Canby, who'd come back to attend to the wounded. A fine lady, the commander's wife. She would look after Miss Howland in Santa Fé. O'Brien winced at the thought, hoping he'd get a chance to see his lady there. Kind of her to promise to teach him, but he knew it was kindness alone. She must stay safe with her friends, and he must return to the regiment.

The chaplain came up, and the men from I Company stopped digging their trench and gathered to watch while he said a short prayer. O'Brien half listened and covertly watched his lady. She didn't cry, but stood pale and quiet in her black dress and cloak, and stayed watching after the chaplain closed his book and the others drifted away.

At a nod from O'Brien the men started filling the grave. She looked up then, straight at him, and walked a few steps away to a small clump of trees, gray branches reaching skyward like long, fairy fingers. He followed, watching her, memorizing every detail of her face, every gesture, in case he never saw her again. She stood in the middle of the dry trees and turned her face to the sun, eyes closed. O'Brien stayed at the grove's edge, gripping two saplings, holding his breath lest his longing escape in any small sound to frighten her.

"This is a magic place," she said, opening her eyes to look at him. "Did you know?"

O'Brien nodded, not trusting his voice.

"Glorieta," she said, turning a small circle and brushing her hand on the tree trunks, the black glove passing like a shadow over the wood. "I always learn something surprising here," she said. "Do you think we'll come through on the way to Santa Fé?"

The question made no sense. "I don't know," he said.

"Of course not. I'm sorry," she said, coming toward him. Her smile lit a fire in his chest, and he took a step back. "I've been meaning to ask you," she went on, "could you put me in the way of purchasing my own tent, so I needn't impose on you?"

Confused, O'Brien blinked. "But you're going to Santa Fé—"

"At some point, I expect, but I think it best to stay with the army until I have collected my pay."

O'Brien was floored. Here was Miss Howland, with Franklin's fine necklace in her pocket, saying she wanted her pay for two days' work as a laundress, all of fifty cents it might be. A smile tugged at the corner of his mouth. "We haven't been paid in six months."

Miss Howland raised her delicate brows. "Then it appears I shall be with you for some time. That is good. We shall have time for lessons, and to become better acquainted."

The hope that sparked inside him was more painful than all his previous torments. She must have seen it, for she raised her proud chin and said, "I can be patient. Can you?"

Could he be patient? Could he bear to have her near and not touch her? Not forever, perhaps, but for now. It was better, far better, than leaving her behind. O'Brien nodded again, and she gave him a shy smile, then began to remove her right glove.

"Do you know, Captain," she said, offering her hand, "after all that has happened, I don't believe we were ever properly introduced. I'm Laura Howland."

"Alastar O'Brien," he said hoarsely, his fingers tightening on hers.

"Alastar," she said, tilting her head. "That's a noble name." She pulled gently at his hand, leading him away from the trees, stopping at Franklin's grave, which the men had finished filling. They stood silently there for a moment. O'Brien reveled in the feel of her hand in his, the faint smell of woodsmoke that clung to her cloak, the sunlight glinting in her hair: small promises of a glorious future. She looked up at him with a silent smile. He returned it, and together they walked down the hill toward the ranch house.

Epilogue

Mr. Herbert Devon
1648 Spring Garden Street
Philadelphia, Pennsylvania, U.S.A.

Dear Sir,

At the request of your relative I send you the enclosed letter, which I wrote out for her, without further explanation. She will, I hope, forgive me for adding that she died bravely, and for saying that in the short time I knew her she was as kind and as generous to me as any lifelong friend.

Very Truly Yours,
Laura Howland

Author's Note

Anyone with an interest in history, however casual, will appreciate that attitudes and usages change over time. This work is intended to bring to life events and circumstances in the American frontier West, and so inevitably depicts some sentiments which, while commonly accepted at the time, would be unforgivable today. It would be a disservice to those who struggled against these inequities to gloss over them. Additionally, terms such as "native" had meanings in Territorial New Mexico different from their modern definitions, which the reader may appreciate the more for having seen them in an older context.

In *Glorieta Pass,* Laura Howland and her uncle, Lacey McIntyre, the Russell family and Captain Martin, Captain Owens, and all of Company I of the First Colorado Volunteers, including O'Brien and Franklin, are fictional, as are several minor characters. The real Company I was an infantry company that fought gallantly in the Battle of Glorieta Pass (not at Apache Canyon or Johnson's Ranch) and suffered considerable losses. Lacey McIntyre and Joseph Hall are based in part on fragmentary information about real people. Ovando J. Hollister (private in Company F and author of *History of the First Regiment of Colorado Volunteers*) wrote that the scouting party caught in Glorieta Pass on the night of March 25, 1862, included a former member of Canby's staff named McIntire and a man named Hall who was well known in Denver. There was also a Lieutenant Joseph C. W. Hall in Dodd's Independent Company (later Company B of the Second Colorado Volunteers), who served loyally throughout the campaign. Inevitable liberties have been taken with historical characters about whom limited data was available, for which the author humbly apologizes.

Every attempt has been made to depict events accurately. Some extrapolations have been made from available facts. For example, the loss of 150 to 200 mules belonging to the 1st Regiment of Sibley's Brigade (4th Texas Mounted Volunteers) may not have been caused by Paddy Graydon's sabotage plan. Contemporary accounts do not connect these events, though they both occurred on the night of February 20, 1862. Most histories indicate the mules wandered away seeking water.

Some temporal shifting of minor events was necessary for narrative continuity. An example is the removal of the Confederate flag from Wallingford & Murphy's in Denver City, which actually took place on April 24, 1861, not in May. No major events were altered.

Suggested Readings

This short bibliography represents a selection of references useful to readers wishing to learn more about the New Mexico Campaign.

Alberts, Don E. (ed.). *Rebels on the Rio Grande, the Civil War Journal of A. B. Peticolas*. Albuquerque: University of New Mexico Press, 1984.

Colton, Ray C. *The Civil War in the Western Territories*. Norman: University of Oklahoma Press, 1959.

Hall, Martin Hardwick. *Sibley's New Mexico Campaign*. Austin: University of Texas Press, 1960.

Hollister, Ovando J. *Colorado Volunteers in New Mexico* (orig. published in 1862 as *History of the First Regiment of Colorado Volunteers*). Chicago: The Lakeside Press, R. R. Donnelly & Sons Co., 1962.

Josephy, Alvin M., Jr. *The Civil War in the American West*. New York: Alfred A. Knopf, 1991.

Mumey, Nolie (ed.). *Bloody Trails Along the Rio Grande, A Day-by-Day Diary of Alonzo Ferdinand Ickis*. Denver, CO: The Old West Publishing Company, 1958.

Simmons, Marc (ed.). *The Battle at Valley's Ranch, First Account of the Gettysburg of the West, 1862*. Sandia Park, NM: San Pedro Press, 1987.

Simmons, Marc. *The Little Lion of the Southwest*. Chicago: The Swallow Press, 1973.

Thompson, Jerry D. (ed.). *Westward the Texans: The Civil War Journal of William Randolph Howell*. El Paso: Texas Western Press, 1990.

Whitford, William C. *The Battle of Glorieta Pass: Colorado Volunteers in the Civil War* (orig. published in 1906 as *The Colorado Volunteers in the Civil War*). Glorieta, NM: The Rio Grande Press, 1991.

About the Author

P. G. Nagle was born and raised within fifty miles of Glorieta Pass. An avid student of music, history and computer science, Nagle currently resides in Albuquerque, and is at work on *The Guns of Valverde,* the sequel to *Glorieta Pass.*

Excerpt from

The Guns of Valverde
(coming soon from Forge Books)

The Volunteers' camp was all in an uproar. Marching tonight—no, tomorrow—no, wait for new orders. O'Brien sat on a cracker box outside his tent watching Logan's company pull down the camp they had just pitched the night before. He kept his small pleasure at being proved right to himself. When the orders first came to prepare for a march, Ramsey had gone to the post wearing a foul expression, and had not yet come back.

Captain Chapin approached from the fort with a fistful of papers. Before he got close, O'Brien asked "Are we marching tonight, then?"

"Not your company," Chapin said, handing him a page. "Yours and F Company will escort Clafin's battery tomorrow."

O'Brien glanced at the paper, then looked up at the adjutant. "Word from Canby?"

Chapin nodded. "He's left Fort Craig."

A cold chill poured down O'Brien's arms, making them heavy. If the commander had left his snug fort at long last, then likely they'd see some real action. Good, he decided. The lads were more cheerful on the march, and they wanted a chance to finish the job they'd begun.

"I want to ask you something," Chapin said.

O'Brien glanced up, raising his brows. The adjutant looked to be in a foul mood. "Are Slough and Paul still squabbling, then?" he said, grinning. "Pull up a seat."

"Never mind them." Chapin folded his arms. "What are your intentions toward Miss Howland?"

O'Brien was so caught off his guard that he gaped. Then he felt his face beginning to burn, and looked away.

"She may have no family," Chapin said in a low, stern

492 ♦ P. G. Nagle

voice, "but she has plenty of friends to watch over her. Some believe you have compromised her reputation."

"I never touched her!" O'Brien looked up, angry at the accusation, the more so for how hard it had been to leave her alone. "I promised to take her to Mrs. Canby and I did!"

"She stayed in your camp, unchaperoned." Chapin took two paces toward him, and dropped his voice lower. "A gentleman would offer her his name."

"I did," O'Brien said, his throat tightening on the words. The heartache was returning, that he'd kept at bay for so long. He stared at the toes of Chapin's boots. "She'll have none of me."

"She told you that?" Chapin sounded surprised.

"She didn't have to say it." O'Brien saw again the shock in her face, before she had turned away. He squeezed his eyes shut, but the vision remained. Captain Chapin could not know how much he had wanted to marry her.

"Well," Chapin said in a gentler voice.

Go away, thought O'Brien. If you wanted to punish me, you've done it.

"Well, you'd best mind your step, Captain."

O'Brien looked up at him, frowning.

"You're being watched." Chapin touched his hat before passing on in the direction of Wynkoop's tent.

What the devil does that mean? wondered O'Brien.

"Forty days, at best," Jamie said.

"That's nearly two months." General Sibley picked up an open champagne bottle from his desk. "We can make a go with that!" He emptied the remainder of the bottle into his glass and raised it to the east, where the sun was still climbing outside the palace windows. It was cold in the big room. No one had lit a fire.

Jamie glanced at Lane, who was staring between his thumbs at the floor. Colonel Scurry lounged in his chair, one arm draped over its back, and was also silent. Colonel Green would have had something to say, but he had just arrived from Albuquerque and was off meeting with his captains, getting their reports on the 2nd's condition.

"General," Jamie said, searching for words that would not offend, "we've got food for that long, but we still don't have much ammunition."

"Wasn't there any in that cache you found?"

Jamie shook his head. "No, sir. Just blankets and food and some clothes. It was meant for the Indian Agency."

"Well, Green's fellows can share."

"Sir, even if we redistribute what's in their boxes, and pass out the rounds I just purchased, we won't have enough for a fight. Not half enough for a seige."

The general was slumped in his chair, his smile dampened by the furrow that seemed branded onto his brow. He sipped his champagne and stared dully at Jamie.

Jamie glanced at the unhelpful audience again, then met Sibley's gaze. "We can get to Mesilla on forty days' rations," he said slowly. "Captain Coopwood came up a trail through the mountains to avoid Fort Craig—"

"Never mind Fort Craig, dammit," Sibley said, sitting up and flashing his eyes. "We're bound for Fort Union!"

"Sir, we can't take Union. We don't have the resources—"

"Balderdash!" Sibley rose to his feet. "We took their battery away from them at Valverde! Chased them off the field! We can do the same at Union!"

"We had a supply train at the time," Jamie said bitterly, but he knew he had lost the general's attention.

"I've sent to Governor Lubbock for reinforcements," Sibley said. "Where's that map?"

"Behind you, sir," Lane said, nodding toward a heap of papers on a table. Sibley strode to it, extracted a large map of the territory, and frowned over it.

"We'll move the army . . . here. Manzano. We can keep an eye on Craig, and watch the roads to Union and Stanton. When our reinforcements arrive, we'll march on Union."

Jamie was silent, trying to calculate how long it would take an express to reach Austin, and how long for a regiment—if there happened to be one ready—to march from there to Manzano. Too long, he knew that much.

Sibley returned to the desk and picked up his glass, favoring his staff with a confident smile. "We'll win this yet, gentlemen!" he said, raising the glass toward the northwest. "On to San Francisco!" He downed it in one pull, turned, and threw it toward the fireplace. It missed, smashing against the wall and leaving a pale stain on the whitewash. Lane winced at the sound. Sibley strode out of the room, leaving silence in his wake.

Jamie gazed at the two empty champagne bottles on the desk. With a sigh, he stood up. "Thanks for your support, gentlemen," he said, picking up his hat.

Lane looked up at him. "He won't listen to any of us, Jamie."

"He might've listened to all of us."

At least Manzano is closer to home, Jamie thought as he followed Sibley out.

Get caught reading.

Jake Lloyd reading ENDER'S GAME.

A Message from the
Association of American Publishers